THE GIRL FROM KYIV

Also by Sue Stern

Rafi Brown and the Candy Floss Kid
'Easy graceful effortless writing… making you want to know what happens next.'

JACQUELINE WILSON

The Child Who Spoke With Her Eyes
'An unforgettable portrait of a mother who awakens to her spiritual identity and purpose while caring for her special needs child. A poignant powerful, inspirational read.'

MARY SHARRATT, award winning author of Revelations

How I Broke Mama's Commandments, chapter one of this novel published as a short story in Migration Stories, Crocus

THE GIRL FROM KYIV

SUE STERN

Publisher name: Red Bank Books

Address, 80 Fog Lane, Didsbury Manchester, M20 6AG UK

A CIP catalogue record of this book is available from the British Library.

ISBN: 978-0-9574948-3-1

For Sid, Anthony and Richard

CHAPTER 1

AT LAST, WITH A jolt, the ship's engines ceased. The sudden brief silence was followed by an eruption of noise – everyone praying, talking, calling to others. Then a great sloshing sound of water hitting the ships' sides, hammers slamming into wood, burnished metal being beaten, the whistles and shouts of workers on the quay, and the swish and boom of punts and boats and liners. Beyond all this, Sophia heard the hum of a great city and drew in a breath of delight.

'We're in London,' she cried. 'London! It's wonderful.' She felt a hand on her shoulder. Turning, she found Dov standing behind her.

'They call it the *Smoke*.' He gave her his usual mocking grin.

'Maybe, but I am so happy to be here. To arrive at last.'

'And I'm not,' he said, an expression of disappointment shading his eyes. Or was he joking again?

'Why? Why aren't you happy?'

'Because I couldn't persuade you to join the comrades in England, to fight the glorious battle.' Her face dropped. He shook his head. 'Just a little joke. But Sophia, my dear, in case you ever need me, here's my address and the address of the meeting house behind Tottenham Court Road.' From his pocket, he drew a sheet of paper, the addresses written in English script, which he read aloud to her: 'The Grafton Hall Club. Remember? The anarchist meeting house.'

'And this one?'

'Dunston Buildings, where I live in Stepney Green. A great commune,' he said joyfully. 'You'll find me in one or the other.' Bending, he kissed her on both cheeks. 'Much luck to you, Sophia Krichevska. Always remember, we need intelligent girls like you.'

'Dov, you've almost persuaded me to stay, but can't I join the Socialist movement when I reach New York?'

His gaze full of amusement, he smiled down at her. 'Of course. Besides, you'll be with your brother. *Do svidanya,* Sophia.'

Surprised at how sad she felt, she answered, '*Do pobachennya*, Dov.'

She watched him wind his way towards the gangplank. He turned, waved once, then disappeared amongst the first-and second-class passengers. She wondered if they'd ever meet again, thinking sadly of the fascinating week she'd spent with him as they'd crossed the Baltic Sea, this fiery revolutionary who'd talked nonstop of the new world they'd create – a world of justice, freedom of speech and equality which would emerge after the Revolution. After they'd destroyed the Tsar and his loathsome Black Hundreds.

She straightened her shoulders and lifting her heavy travelling bag, joined the crowd pushing towards the exit when, all of a sudden, porters came running towards them, grabbing at their trunks and bags. Unable to grasp what they were saying, the passengers fought to prevent them from stealing their precious belongings. But at once, two English men appeared, holding up their hands.

'Do not be afraid. These porters are with us. We are from the Poor Immigrants' Temporary Shelter,' one of the men said, addressing them in both German and Yiddish. Sophia sighed with relief. With his twinkling blue eyes, he reminded her of her father.

'We check all arrivals, make sure you have somewhere to stay in London. You won't be fleeced by agents or porters since we have a list of all the travellers, on every ship.'

'The shelter is open to all,' continued his companion, 'and it has facilities for the most observant of you.'

They went from person to person, checking lists, asking for details, and writing them in little notebooks. When Sophia told them she was to meet her brother, Sasha, already in London, the man with blue eyes and greying hair jotted her name down in his notebook with its watermarked cover.

'Just in case,' he said.

Finally, following the crowd, Sophia walked down the ramp, her legs unsteady and wobbling after so many days at sea. Reaching the quay, and dragging her case behind her, she began to search for her brother. She noticed a small group standing close to the disembarkation point but she couldn't see him amongst them. She frowned. *He must be further back, or maybe I've missed him.*

Skirting families and single passengers, she made her way behind the tall boxes of goods waiting to be transported.

Dozens of port workers and ship hands marched back and forth, calling, shouting to each other, trundling boxes and oddly shaped packages to and from the berthed ships, but still, there was no sign of Sasha. Her heart beginning to race, she took panicky breaths as she searched. She clutched her hands together. Feeling close to tears, she looked around for the men from the shelter, for they would surely help her, but even they had gone.

Sasha, where are you?

Her search took her behind bales, then to the edge of the dock where stevedores were chaining boxes and cartons to be swung up into waiting ships. She ran along the quay, wanting to ask where she could find Sasha but fearful of speaking to strange men, knowing her English was inadequate and forgetting all she knew in her terror. She saw the dockworkers glance up at her, odd expressions on their faces. Forcing herself to take deep breaths, she held herself together and attempted to quieten her fears. *Stop*, she told herself. *You're being a fool! No wonder those men are watching. Sasha will be here soon. Breathe slowly and your heart will stop pounding.*

But now a man was approaching. Something in his manner, the way he bent forward, the shabby clothes he wore, made her heart race again, and she bumped into a pillar in her confusion. She shot a glance over her shoulder; he was closer now, a leering smile splitting his face. She couldn't make out what he was saying, and as he stumbled along, she saw him jerk his head from side to side as though on the lookout for something or someone. Then she noticed two women marching behind him. The man must have heard their determined tread, for he looked furtively over his shoulder and, making a sudden dash towards a pile of boxes, he disappeared.

The women walked swiftly towards her. They were well dressed in sober blues and grey. The one in the grey dress, wearing a matching hat with a tiny veil over her eyes, spoke to her in Yiddish.

'You speak English? German? Yiddish?'

'Russian, German, also Yiddish, and I'm learning English.'

'Are you all right?' the woman responded in German, peering closely at Sophia who nodded in confusion. 'Good. Did he say something to you?' She exchanged a glance with the other woman. 'We're from the Ladies' Protection Society. I'm Mrs Hendon and my friend is Mrs Lucas. We've arrived in the nick of time, I see.'

'My name is Sophia Krichevska,' Sophia said, wondering who they were, why they were talking about the man in such suspicious tones.

'Are you alone?' asked Mrs Lucas.

When Sophia explained her predicament, the women turned and looked about.

'It's rather late for anyone to arrive now.' Mrs Hendon said. 'And that man…'

'Not a good place for a young woman to wait unaccompanied,' interrupted Mrs Lucas. 'You see what happened? But be assured, we're here to help you.'

'Thank you,' Sophia said. 'But why?' Her voice drifted off. Now she was completely confused. Searching in her handbag, she took out a folded sheet of paper with her brother's address. 'He sent this to me.'

Mrs Lucas looked at it briefly. 'I think, my dear, that it would be wise if we took you to the shelter.'

'The shelter? What if Sasha comes and I've gone? How would he know where I was? No, I must stay.'

The women looked at each other.

'Listen, Miss Krichevska, we'll wait for twenty minutes in case your brother's detained. But if he doesn't come, we must make sure you're safe.'

'Surely that's what he would want?' said the other lady, with such an air of authority, Sophia recognised she was used to giving orders. 'Your trunk will follow you.'

'But how shall I find Sasha?' Sophia whispered.

'They'll help you at the shelter. Someone will go to this address or take you there,' said Mrs Lucas, in a rather more gentle tone.

They stood guard over Sophia until Mrs Hendon lifted a watch from her bag and consulted it. 'It's time. We shall go.'

They led Sophia to a waiting automobile, where the driver touched his cap before opening the car doors. She climbed in after the ladies, so consumed by trepidation she barely noticed the journey.

At the shelter, Mrs Hendon spoke to a woman seated behind a heavy walnut desk. Then, shaking Sophia's hand, the two English women wished her well and left.

'Well, Miss Krichevska, we'll soon sort you out. My name's Mrs Haber.' Despite her misery, Sophia became aware of a warm cheerful lady, with thick red hair and the lovely white skin that went with it. She didn't wear a scarf or a *sheitel*, a wig. 'Born here,' Mrs Haber continued. 'I'm a cockney. My family come here in 1850 and I went to school just down the road. Best country in the world, I always say. Anyway, until we find your brother, and we will, I promise you, you'll need a bed for the night.'

'But he might come here today,' Sophia said anxiously.

'He might and he might not. Don't worry, I promise if he don't come today, we'll find him tomorrow.'

'I have an address where he's been staying. Maybe I could go to look for him?'

'That's good. But we can't do it today with all the new arrivals. One of us will go with you first thing in the morning, I promise.'

Sophia let out a sigh, relieved to abandon her urgent need to find Sasha. Reassured by Mrs Haber's cheerful demeanour, her motherly concern, she became aware of her intense fatigue and was happy to give in.

'Thank you, Mrs Haber. You're very kind.'

Mrs Haber patted her on the shoulder and led her up to the women's dormitory, where curtains for privacy could be drawn around each bed.

'This one's yours. I can see you're dropping.'

Sophia sank down on the bed while Mrs Haber nodded her approval. 'You've met some of them rich ladies today, almost aristocracy,' she remarked. 'Saved you from a fate worse than death, they did.' Sophia's eyes widened. 'The white slave trade – prostitution.'

'Really? In England?'

'Everywhere. It's when young women come alone and don't speak the language. And them ladies, very upper-class but kindly, who you wouldn't expect to go down the docks whenever a ship arrives, but they do. You're not the first girl they've brought to me, no you aren't.'

So, she wasn't the first, which reassured her somehow. Sophia lay back with a sigh. 'What a comfortable bed this is, Mrs Haber. I could almost sleep.'

'Then let's do the necessary.'

Downstairs, Mrs Haber gave her tickets for meals and – the most wonderful thing – told her when she could take a bath, her first in weeks. Once more, she reassured Sophia she'd have no problem finding her brother. 'It happens again and again,' she said. 'Tomorrow, I'll draw you a little map; I'll send someone with you, and you'll find him, sure as eggs is eggs.'

And the bath. At last, soothed by the beautiful hot water, the vista of white porcelain, the shiny taps, the cleanliness, Sophia began to feel more like herself.

She slept soundly, her first night in England.

CHAPTER 2

THE FOLLOWING MORNING, SHE showed Mrs Haber the note with Sasha's address.

'They're called Rifkin. My brother stayed with them. Here, in Goulston Street.'

She pronounced the street name with care.

'Goulston Street? Just by Petticoat Lane, runs parallel. Only a few minutes walk from here. But Sophia, I'm sorry, I've nobody to go with you.'

'I speak some English,' Sophia said, 'I'm sure I'll find it.'

Nothing could dissuade her. With Mrs Haber's careful directions: walk up Leman Street, turn left onto Whitechapel High St, pass the tube station—

'Tube?'

'You know, the Underground, the Metro station.'

'Oh yes, Metro.' Sophia breathed out her relief.

'Walk a little, cross over and that's Goulston Street on the right.'

With a card for the shelter in case she got lost, though Mrs Haber assured her that everyone knew it, she walked through the front door, descended the steps, and gazed around. People, people everywhere, walking, pushing carts, on horse-drawn trams, talking and calling to each other. Her head buzzed with the noise and, on reaching Whitechapel High Street, passing shops whose names and goods were written in Hebrew script, where people sold cucumbers, bagels and vorsht from barrows, and men with long beards and women wearing scarves hurried by, her eyes widened – she could have been back in Kyiv.

Within a few minutes, she'd found the street where gaunt grey blocks of flats towered above her. When she asked a woman how to find number thirty-six, the woman told her to go through the central archway of the middle block. The numbers would be on a plaque on the wall, outside the entry. She would soon see it. Sophia followed her instructions and found the entrance to the ground floor, climbing a few steps to find herself in a narrow corridor. Number thirty-six was three doors along. After a moment's hesitation, she knocked, and a young woman with beautiful straight features and blonde hair drawn back from her face opened it.

'Hello, can I help you?'

'I am Sophia Krichevska. My brother was staying with you—'

Before she could finish, Mrs Rifkin's expression changed. 'Please come in.'

Sophia stepped inside the crowded living room. Something in the woman's demeanour, the tone of her voice, made Sophia's heart begin to pound against her chest. 'Is there something wrong? Where's my brother? Is he ill?'

'No, but I'm afraid you're too late.'

'How do you mean, too late?'

Reaching over a fireguard strewn with drying baby clothes, Mrs Rifkin took a letter from behind the clock and handed it to Sophia. 'I'm very sorry to tell you this, Miss Krichevska – your brother left last week for America. This is the letter he asked me to give you.'

Sophia went white. Swaying, she clung to the table. Mrs Rifkin rushed forward and gripped her arms, pushing her into a shabby, lumpy armchair.

'Tea,' she cried. 'Take a glass – tea.' Lifting the kettle from the hob, she poured water into a teapot. Within seconds Sophia was holding a glass of hot, golden tea.

'Sugar, sugar,' the woman urged, and lifting lumps with sugar tongs, she dropped them into Sophia's hand. Once the tea had done its work, Sophia took courage and, sitting up, read the letter.

> My Dearest Sophia,
>
> Forgive me, but I've had to go without you. The agent swindled us. Only one ticket was valid for America, even though I paid for two. It was for a Cunard liner, leaving earlier than we'd planned.
>
> Of course, I didn't know. I had to take the ship or we'd have lost all the money. I'll send you a ticket from New York when I can. Mr Rifkin helped me when I was looking for a room. They are very kind people and I know they'll help you.
>
> Your heart-broken brother,
> Sasha

She gasped. Bending her head, she steeled herself not to cry; her eyes averted, she handed the letter to Mrs Rifkin, asking if she should translate it from the Russian.

'It's not necessary. When I was a teacher back home, we taught everything in their language.' Mrs Rifkin read the letter, nodding and frowning. '*Ganufs!* Thieves, the lot of them. But surely we can help you in some way. I'll call my husband.'

Shock gave way to anger, and Sophia straightened her shoulders.

'How can people do such a thing? We trusted them. How can they be so wicked?'

'They can and they do,' said Mr Rifkin, coming through the door. 'What a horrible surprise for you, Miss Krichevska.'

'Sophia,' she muttered, 'please call me Sophia.'

He gazed at Sophia with such sadness she might have been one of his family.

'Moshe, I'm sure we can help,' said Mrs Rifkin. Taking a straight-backed chair and sitting down beside Sophia, she added, 'You must call us Moshe and Hannah Leah. Enough of the formality.'

But already thoughts were buzzing around Sophia's mind: *I can't tell Mama; I'll have to find work until I have money for a ticket. What about Dov?* Clasping her hands tight in her lap and lifting her gaze, she said, 'I am all right now, thank you, Hannah Leah.'

'That's good. I'm sorry we haven't room for you here, but this is all we have – two rooms on this level, two in the basement. The baby sleeps in our room, the boys on settees in here. My father is in the basement room where we keep the stuff I sell on my stall in the market. That's where your brother slept, but there are rats... Mother sleeps in the downstairs kitchen.'

'Rats?'

Hannah Leah laughed. 'He said it was only for a week or two, and he didn't mind.'

'That's just like him.' Sophia smiled. 'Anyway, please don't apologise. I'll look for work. I'll surely earn enough to pay for my ticket to America. You've been so kind. I don't want to trouble you anymore.'

Hannah Leah stood up.

'I have a better idea. Lots of people use their back room to take in a lodger. I'll ask around. And Moshe, you could see if Mrs Lazarus needs anyone.'

'I work in Batty Street for a couple called Lazarus. She's a bit of a battle-axe, a difficult woman, but he's all right. By the way, I take it you can sew?'

'Of course. Since I was nine, I've used Mama's sewing machine.' A spark of hope flared in her heart and her lips curved once more into a smile.

'Where are you staying now?' asked Hannah Leah.

'At the Poor Immigrants' Temporary Shelter.'

'That's good. Well, as soon as we know anything, one of us will call by.'

'Thank you.' Tears welled up at their kindness, but determined to be strong, she wiped them away. 'Can I ask you something? Do you know a man called Dov Feldman? He told me to look for him at the Grafton Hall Club. Do you know where that is?'

Hannah Leah and Moshe exchanged amused glances.

'Of course, we know him. A true revolutionary if ever there was one. He's a close friend of our cousin Aaron Littenberg, who lives in Soho, near the club. Where did you meet Dov?'

'On the ship. He offered to help me.'

'Dov and his comrades are doing valuable work politically, and we're all grateful.' She stopped, about to say
more but thought better of it. 'You're allowed to stay at
the shelter for two weeks. They have a list of rooms for
rent. Between us, we'll find something, and if not, well,
you must come here.'

Sophia wanted to fling her arms around them both but
restrained herself.

'Now I know why Sasha told me to come to you if I
needed help. Thank you.'

Walking back, a hundred questions racing around her mind,
Sophia became aware of the brouhaha, the racket of vehi-
cles of every size thrusting their way along Whitechapel
High Street. How different from Archangelsk and, especially, from Kyiv, where they'd lived until she was sixteen
and had their own house in the Jewish area. People would
drop by or visit, especially for the Sabbath or the holidays and, since there were hardly more than two hundred
Jewish people altogether in Archangelsk, they knew them
all, coming together, especially during the long winter
months, to read, to discuss philosophy and religion, to
talk about the future.

And here she was in this strange corner of London, with
its lowering clouds, its grey and yellow stone buildings,
where the mingled odours of horse dung, cooked cabbage,
and something worse filled the air. Turning into Leman
Street, a wave of sadness made her pause. Giving herself

a little shake, she climbed the steps to the shelter entrance and pushed open the door.

'So, Sophia,' called Mrs Haber, lifting her gaze from a drawer she was searching. 'Did you find him?'

Sophia sank onto a chair and told her story. When she mentioned that Mr Rifkin worked at a workshop owned by a family called Lazarus, Mrs Haber gave her a quizzical look. 'Oh yes, they are on our books and if I'm not mistaken, they said they wanted a beginner.' Bending again, she drew out a foolscap folder, tracing down the page with her finger.

'Yes, there it is. I'll go with you on Sunday and see how the land lies.'

Up in the shadowy dormitory, Sophia lay down. However clean they were within, the windows outside were dark with grime, casting a dull light on the empty beds and the faded floorboards. I am so alone, she thought. What can I do? *What Is to Be Done?* The words of the socialist novel her brother had given her before she left Archangelsk sprang into her mind. Dov had been excited when she'd shown it to him on the ship.

Dov — he was the answer.

She would ask Mrs Haber at once. With a lighter heart, she ran down to the desk. But when she showed Dov's addresses to Mrs Haber and Mr Fuchs, the gentleman who supervised the kitchens and handled problems Mrs Haber couldn't deal with, they weren't so happy.

'We will tell you where it is, of course,' said Mrs Haber reluctantly, 'but do you need to go there?'

'The Rifkin family is very kind but I don't know them, and now my brother has gone, I am quite alone, except for Mr Feldman.'

'It's not such a good thing for a young girl to get involved with those people,' said Mr Fuchs, 'Not that I don't agree with their politics. I do. Our lives are improving, thanks to people like them.'

'Then why not?' Sophia demanded.

'It's… it's their morals, see,' said Mrs Haber doubtfully. 'Look, you can go, but promise me you'll come straight back. I'll be waiting for you. Don't let me down. We don't want no more trouble, do we?'

CHAPTER 3

AND SO, ON HER second or maybe her third day in London, Sophia found herself on top of a horse-drawn omnibus, travelling down Tottenham Court Road. She had almost recovered from the shock of not finding Sasha, the sun was shining, the sky was a hazy blue, and everyone walked through London with a smile on their face, it seemed to her. She was enchanted.

If only Papa could see me now.

Yet, she would not blame him for how he'd altered since they had fled Kyiv. After the *Okhrana*, the Tsar's secret police, had battered at their door and demanded they leave or be deported to Siberia, Papa had never regained his self-respect. That night, from the room she shared with Alexei her little brother, she'd heard her father's fury and slipped out of bed, creeping to the living room door to learn why he was so angry. She was sixteen at the time; she remembered clearly how her parents were sitting by candlelight, their dark shadows looming and swooping on the wall.

'Someone has betrayed me,' he was shouting.

Dropping his head in his hands, he sobbed. Someone who owed Papa money for the medicine he'd dispensed in his pharmacy had accused him of stealing. It was lies. All lies. And her mother shushing him, putting her hand on his arm. Amazed, embarrassed, she watched her father weep like a girl. Before they could decide what to do, there'd been the Kishinev pogrom. It had cruelly affected her family and she couldn't bear to remember it. Only then had her father made up his mind and they'd finally fled Kyiv, making the long, tedious journey to Archangelsk, from where they would take a ship to Europe or America. It was the cheapest crossing, Papa had told them. But, to add to his despair, he was forbidden by the authorities from setting up a pharmacy. Forced to open a dairy, he'd become morose over the months and the idea of emigration had faded away, like dry leaves on an unlit path.

Not so Sophia. In Kyiv, she'd attended a girl's school and loved learning. When she was seven or eight, her favourite game was to play doctors and patients with her brothers, always insisting on being the doctor. Papa used to chuckle: 'That's my clever daughter, Doctor Krichevska.' But in Archangelsk, he would remind her of what a feather pillow she had for a brain. Full of outlandish ideas, too much reading, and one day, he said, her learning would ruin her. As for her obsession with becoming a doctor… Last year, when her application to the Medical Faculty in Moscow University had been rejected, he had raised his eyebrows and shrugged: 'You know there's a quota. Only so many boys are allowed into medical school. It's not for women, especially Jewish women. You can be a schoolteacher or nurse, that's it.'

When I reach America, thought Sophia, *I shall study medicine and nothing will stop me.*

The Grafton Hall Club wasn't hard to find. Pushing open a door, she entered a small vestibule; to her right was a flight of stone stairs, while immediately to her left was a heavy oak door. A hubbub of noise issued from the room behind it: loud conversations, vehement shouts, groans, bursts of laughter, silences.

Thinking she might be interrupting an important meeting, she turned the handle as quietly as she could and slipped in. Shutting it behind her, she looked around. The room was much larger than she had expected. So many people sitting at tables, standing in groups, all talking animatedly. She caught words and phrases in German, Russian, French and Italian being sprinkled through the conversations without anyone pausing to question their meaning. The air was hazy with smoke and she screwed up her eyes in her search for Dov.

But it wasn't necessary. He was there, laughing his familiar laugh, in the centre of everything. He was addressing half a dozen people sitting at a table. A young woman with golden hair and wearing a bright red dress sat leaning against his shoulder. At that moment, the woman stood up and clapping her hands, called, 'Comrades, Dov has something important to tell us about his latest trip.'

Sophia saw Dov blow the woman a kiss.

Taken aback, she opened the door quickly; she would slip out, run to Tottenham Court Road, and jump on the omnibus. In the safety of the shelter, she would hide herself away and cry her heart out into the pillow.

But he saw her.

'Sophia, you've changed your mind!' he shouted.

In a second, he was by her side, kissing her six times just as Sasha would have done. Interrupted in their discussions and conversations by the announcement and then by Dov's excitement, everyone in the room turned to stare at her. Before she could explain why she'd come, Dov shouted: 'Meet our latest recruit to the cause, the girl from Kyiv, Sophia Krichevska!'

Colour rose in her cheeks and she pulled herself away, but he held her firmly. 'Comrades,' he repeated, 'our new recruit – intelligent, bright, eager – make her welcome!'

She found herself in the centre of the room with Dov's arm around her shoulder. People shouted, 'Welcome, Sophia Krichevska. Join our happy band. Dov's friend is our friend.'

But then she heard a voice, low and mocking. 'How do you know this?'

It was the girl in the red dress. When Dov answered, speaking slowly, with authority, Sophia noted how the others listened.

'I know,' he affirmed, 'because we travelled the entire journey together from Petersburg to the London docks, an education—'

'Not *une éducation sentimentale*, I hope,' drawled the girl, eyebrows raised.

Despite the blush spreading to her hairline, Sophia clenched her teeth. She stepped forward. 'No. It was socialism. I'd already discussed this with my brother, but I learned much more from Dov.'

'You see?' Dov looked down at her with pride. 'Spirited as well.'

'Come, come,' called a woman sitting near the fireplace. No fire, just a few cinders in the grate, but in the hearth stood a gas ring with a huge black kettle perched upon it, steaming gently. 'What kind of greeting is this? Welcome to England, Sophia Krichevska. Though we have no samovar, a glass of tea will surely help you feel at home, in this strange land.'

There was a rumble of agreement; people smiled and nodded as though greeting her again. Taking a deep breath, still conscious of the girl's unfriendly gaze, Sophia murmured, 'Thank you.'

'Quite right, Blema from Borodetz,' shouted Dov. 'What a barbarian I am.'

'A barbarian you certainly are,' called Blema, pouring tea into a glass, and bustling round the tables. 'You haven't even found your friend a chair.' Shaking her head in mock exasperation, she pushed the sugar bowl into Dov's hands, while indicating his chair with an imperious nod of the head. 'Sit there, my dear. He can find another, or stand, since he's so fond of doing so.'

Sophia perched on the edge of the chair. A young man with dark brown hair and blue eyes, dressed as smartly as Dov, was already sitting at the table. He smiled, about to speak when Dov interrupted. 'What a peasant I am. Let me introduce you to my dear friends and comrades and we'll talk in a civilised manner.'

'Rubbish,' exclaimed the girl. 'Don't believe him, Miss Krichevska.'

Dov gave her a warning look.

'To your left, we have my good friend, Aaron Littenberg.' A smile of recognition lit Sophia's eyes but she waited for

Dov to finish speaking. 'Coming from a *shtetl* near Brest-Litovsk, Aaron never knows if he's Polish or Russian, which results occasionally in a state of mental confusion.'

'Frequently true, Miss Krichevska.' Aaron laughed.

'Whereas to my left, Rosa…' Dov straddled a chair to face Sophia, something hard in his eyes. 'Rosa from Petersburg: *Piter* through and through and doubting nothing.'

Rosa gave him a scornful look.

Leaning in, Aaron offered Sophia his hand. 'Welcome indeed, Sophia Krichevska. When did you arrive?'

'On Tuesday.'

'A greener.' Seeing her surprise, his eyes crinkled up. 'You know, like a new young shoot, rising from the ground. We're all called that in the beginning.'

'I'm a greener? I love that thought.' Sophia grinned.

Dov turned to Rosa.

'Now Rosa, you're no greener, how about saying hello to Sophia?'

'Glad to meet you, Sophia Krichevska.' Smiling, she took Sophia's hand for a second before letting it fall. 'So he found you on the ship?' Sophia nodded. 'Well, you've arrived just in time for a furious argument.'

'Nothing of the kind.' exclaimed Dov. 'A political discussion.'

'*The* political discussion,' pursued Rosa. 'The only one, Miss Krichevska. Propaganda by the deed or education for the masses. Which is it to be? And what is your opinion on the matter?' She sat back in her chair, one eyebrow raised, a little smile playing around her mouth, her eyes watchful.

Sophia had never heard the expression *propaganda by the deed*. She felt discomforted, as though their conversations on the ship had taught her nothing. Was she so stupid? Then she noticed Dov's face had flushed darkly, just as when she'd told him how her family had been forced out of Kyiv by the Tsar's secret police.

'Not a matter for laughter, Rosa. But first I shall inform the comrades of my latest visit to the land of the Tsars.' He said this scornfully, and for a moment, his eyes rested on Sophia. 'Then we shall discuss this rationally.'

He rose and began to speak. Everyone fell silent.

As he talked of events in Russia, her mind flew back to those fascinating hours she'd spent with him on the voyage, talking about socialism. About the new Russia that could evolve once they had rid themselves of the Tsar and his corrupt regime.

She had met him the day after they set sail. They were crossing the Baltic Sea, making for Riga, where more passengers would come on board with their feather bedspreads, their trunks, and their children. She was standing at the bow of the ship, glad of the wind lifting the stench of steerage and the putrid smell of logs, like rotten vegetables, on the cargo deck above theirs, when she heard:

'Enjoying the view?'

She turned. A young man was making his way towards her. Fair hair, brown eyes, a good jacket, and older than her. Yesterday, she'd glimpsed him watching her descend the staircase to steerage, and for a brief second had wondered who he was; with this new life on board ship – the hubbub of adults shouting and calling, children crying, the bodily odours, the overflowing latrines – she'd forgotten him entirely.

He joined her at the railing, his gaze on the expanse of the blue-grey waves. She took a step away from him. Being a girl with three brothers gave her a certain ease with young men, but she recognised the subtlety of boundaries.

'I am enjoying it, especially the fresh air,' she said.

'Where are you going? England or America?'

'Both. I'm meeting my brother in London. Then we travel to New York.'

'Quite some journey.' He turned to look at her. Bending his head slightly, he held out his hand. 'Dov Feldman.'

'Sophia Krichevska.'

His hand was warm.

She glanced down to see if he was wearing a ring, but he had shoved his hands back in the pockets of his very elegant brown jacket. Besides, it meant nothing. Usually, only married women wore a ring; they were the ones who were bound, she thought. Looking up, she saw he was smiling a wide smile; he had a dimple in one cheek which added to his very handsome appearance. She knew at once that she liked him.

They were silent for some moments, then he said, 'Did I see you praying with the others as we set sail?' He turned to look at her.

'Praying?' She frowned at this unexpected question then recalled she'd been whispering a message to Mama. 'I wasn't praying. Should I have been?'

'Of course not. I wouldn't dream of imposing my ideas on anyone, one way or the other. Perhaps you're an atheist.'

'A New Woman.' Sophia lifted her gaze to his.

'Then a woman after my own heart.' She gave him a questioning look but clearly he was following his own line of thought and didn't respond. Instead, he said, 'I shall take a walk around the deck since the sun is so hot. Very nice to talk to you, Miss Krichevska. I hope we meet again.'

She was in 'her place' at the bow of the ship the next afternoon when Dov Feldman walked over to her. He was wearing a different coat: dark blue, with burnished buttons, and was smoking a small cigar.

'How are you today, Miss Krichevska?'

'Sophia,' she said. 'Please call me Sophia.'

'Krichevska. You must come from Ukraine.' Dov turned towards her, his cigar alight.

She hesitated as memories clouded her mind. 'From Archangelsk.'

He raised his eyebrows. 'A woman full of surprises. So you live in one of those wooden houses by the sea?'

'A wooden house, yes – but not by the sea. From Kyiv, originally,' she continued. 'We were forced to leave two years ago. The Okhrana ... the Kishinev pogrom ... my aunt...' She fell silent.

'Kishinev? Pogroms?' She glanced up and nodded. 'Killed, wounded, homes destroyed, businesses pillaged. Violence is all Russia understands. We can't let them treat us like vermin, Sophia. That's why we need revolution.' He flung out his arm.

Yet hearing him talk of the dead, the terrible image of what happened to her aunt leapt into her mind. Her beautiful Aunt Rachel with the bright brown eyes, raped and dying on the kitchen floor. Mutilated. She could not speak, but heard him saying in a tone full of concern, 'I'm sorry, Sophia. I've upset you. It was thoughtless of me.'

'It's all right,' she said, her voice barely a whisper. Giving herself a little shake, she resolved to be strong and banish the dreadful memories from her mind.

'Are you from Petersburg?' She had a hazy idea there'd been no pogroms in the capital.

'Of course. All the best people come from there.' He grinned at her.

There was such a change in his manner, something roguish, engaging in his smile, she stepped back, but found herself laughing and blushing at the same time.

'Why are you leaving the country?' Hopefully, this question would hide her embarrassment.

'I travel to and fro between Petersburg and London, several times a year.' He glanced down at the book she was carrying and raised an eyebrow.

Despite her passion for scientific knowledge, Sophia loved romantic novels. It was something of an anomaly in her character, she believed, something she kept to herself, she could not say why. Chastising herself for feeling awkward, for what was so dreadful in reading *Anna Karenina,* she passed the book to him.

'Have you read it?'

He examined the cover, flicked through a few pages, and handed it back to her.

'I'm a great admirer of Tolstoy, a follower of the French anarchist Proudhon. He rejects the power of the state and believes in education for all, but I must admit I haven't read this book. I've heard it's a great novel, an ill-fated love story, isn't it? No Romeo and Juliet, I understand.'

Conscious of a certain aloofness in his expression and

surprised by an uncharacteristic desire to please him, she said, 'My brother Sasha gave me the novel *What Is to be Done,* to read on my journey. About socialism.'

Dov's eyes lit up. 'Chernychevsky. Excellent. And have you read Peter Kropotkin, the early Socialists?'

'No.' She furrowed her brow. 'But discussing socialist ideology filled our dark, snow-bound days of winter.'

'Then let's continue into the Spring!'

She blinked now and inhaled deeply, forcing herself back into the present. Clasping her glass of tea, she listened and watched his animated expression. He talked about the successful transportation of leaflets and magazines. Referring to *propaganda by the deed*, he described an attack on an army general.

Here it was again. She furrowed her brow. What could this be?

'Propaganda by the deed is the *only* way to spread revolution,' shrilled a woman.

'I completely agree.' Dov drew himself up; all humour had left his face. Almost in alarm, Sophia registered his grim expression.

'You forget where you are.' Aaron called to the woman. 'This isn't back there…'

'Odessa, Timbuktu – it's all the same,' Dov shouted.

'You fail to distinguish between the governments of the East and the West.' Aaron said tersely. 'Remember what Rudolf Rocker said only last week? Anarchism is a state to be attained, not a political theory.'

'Weakness! Cowardice! Action is not sitting on your arse, hiding your eyes from the world, Aaron. You of all people know that. You know what the world can do to us. Everyone in this room knows.'

He went on to describe the progress of the revolution, how textile workers were setting up combat units, defending themselves against the Tsar's police; how workers in Baku had burned down two costly oil installations. His listeners roared their response. Sophia stared around, not daring to speak. She heard *expropriation, anarchy, Social-Democrats, Zionist-socialism, the way forward, traitors, the ruling classes, the banks.* Listening intently, she gathered there was more than one kind of socialism, but why had Dov attacked Aaron when he spoke of Rudolf Rocker? Hadn't Dov himself talked glowingly of this man on the ship? But though people appeared to hate the person they were arguing with, she knew it was simply political difference. She was determined to understand.

'We need expropriation here,' a woman cried.

'Absolutely,' roared Dov. 'Are you all so rich you don't need their money? Let the bankers eat dirt.'

Sophia could barely breathe, hearing his passionate voice, their laughter. They agreed, disagreed but he stood unmoving. There was a scraping sound: Rosa had drawn her chair closer to hers and was whispering in her ear. 'Don't listen to Aaron. Dov's a great force in the movement. Goes back and forth proclaiming revolution.' Sophia drew away but Rosa moved even closer. 'Encourages comrades to do the same. All underground work, you understand.'

'I don't…'

'Propaganda. Pamphlets and leaflets we print here and take over there. He sets up secret groups, teaches the masses. He's everywhere. Fearless!'

Sophia followed her gaze to Dov, pride blooming in Rosa's eyes. He'd crossed the room and was arguing with a man by the fireplace. She could hear his mocking laugh, his shouts of pleasure on winning a point. She took a shuddery breath and dipped her head. *He's forgotten me, and why should he remember? I'm nothing to him or to the work he does. And clearly, Rosa wishes I'd never appeared.*

She stood up. She would leave, return to the safety of the London shelter.

'What a welcome to this great country.' Aaron Littenberg touched her arm. 'You must think it's a mad house. If you like, I could explain things.'

She liked his kind, warm manner. 'I do want to understand. Maybe another time.'

'We'll be leaving soon, then you can speak to Dov. He'd be very upset if you disappeared before talking to him.'

She sat again, aware that Rosa had drawn her chair away, her gaze fixed on Dov.

'It is confusing,' she said, 'Dov didn't use this expression *propaganda by the deed*, we spoke always of the effects of the revolution, nothing more. And that word, *expropriation*, what does it mean?'

'Look, you know how it is with us Jews.' He spread out his hands as though to encompass the whole room, 'It's in our very souls to argue, to see every possibility, and then to take the reverse. From all those generations of study and *pilpul* – that crazy, detailed discussion about each word, phrase, even a point of punctuation, in our religious teachings, the *Torah*.'

Because she knew the *Torah*, the five books of Moses, with their ample commentaries, she sat back with a sigh of relief.

'Yes, I do know about that.'

'The Russian Orthodox Church teaches Jew-hatred to every child. Hence the pogroms. You know from your own life how the Tsar sees us. But it's not only about us. Intransigent, deaf to all demands for modernisation, for representation, the Tsar has one response. *Violence*. Look at Bloody Sunday, earlier this year. The people marched peacefully to present a petition to the Tsar, carrying his picture, and waving crucifixes.

'How did he respond? With the bayonet and the sword. Hundreds of poor people slain. After this, the workers themselves saw that in their cursed country, violence would be the only route, and I certainly played my part.' He rubbed his shoulder automatically. 'So now we can understand *propaganda by the deed*. It means violent action in order to spread the concept of revolution. Assassination is an example of that, while on the other hand, robbing a bank is *expropriation* of the bank's funds. The money goes to finance the revolution. One way or another, violence is all the Tsars have ever understood. Now it has worked: that great country is in turmoil, the masses rising up, claiming their rights.' He paused. 'Here is where I disagree with Dov; I don't believe it's suitable for England.'

'My brother and I discussed this for hours. But I thought revolution must happen in every place at the same time. Not here?'

'Of course, it must happen here. But there are ways and ways. You've heard of Rudolf Rocker? The Messiah to the Jews they call him.' He laughed. 'A German Catholic who learned Yiddish – an extraordinary man. His way is different. You should meet him.'

Sophia became aware of Rosa listening and then heard the harsh scrape of a chair on the wooden floor. She glanced up as Rosa shouted: 'Dov, I'm leaving.'

Dov looked around. As though he'd come to himself, his gaze fell upon Sophia and he smiled.

'I'm not leaving until I've spoken to our new comrade.'

Sophia glimpsed a look of uncertainty in Rosa's green eyes, as she glanced towards her.

'Please yourself,' Rosa muttered, placing a white straw hat bound with a purple ribbon on her head.

People were collecting books and pamphlets, and putting them into bags. Having consulted a watch he'd drawn from his waistcoat pocket, Aaron took Sophia's hand, saying, 'I'm sorry we have to leave. It's been a pleasure talking to you. I'm a tailor,' he added, 'trained in the shtetl, the stupid one in the family according to my very religious father, but it's allowed me to find work in the West End.'

'Lucky man,' said Dov, who'd come over and was resting his hands on the back of Sophia's chair.

But Rosa, biting her lip, was still waiting. 'You're not coming?'

'I want to talk to Sophia.' Dov frowned 'Maybe tonight, Rosa. It depends on my work.'

CHAPTER 4

'Come, Dov,' Aaron said, 'I have to lock up.' Producing a key, he led them through the vestibule and out of the street door, which he locked, then checked to be sure.

The sun was still shining. Sophia felt its warmth on her face and her heart lifted. Errand boys flew by on bicycles ringing their bells and weaving their way around horse-drawn drays, much to the disgust of the drivers. Cracking their whips on the backs of the poor horses, the men shouted at the boys, who shouted something cheeky she couldn't understand and laughed. An occasional motor car, its horns and metal attachments glinting in the sun, passed them by. Sophia caught a scent of lilacs, reminding her suddenly of home, of her family. She took a deep breath, trying to capture the perfume.

Dov swept out his arm, that familiar gesture. 'Soho, this is what this area's called. As I said just now, our esteemed comrade is lucky to work here.'

'Why lucky?'

'Because,' continued Aaron, as they walked, 'besides the less salubrious occupations of certain residents...'

'You'll find the world over,' said Dov.

'In addition to that (or maybe as a result, I don't know), Soho is the entertainment district. Actors, dancers and singers all frequent the establishments along the road – the public houses, the grocers, even occasionally, the tailors.'

Dov gave Aaron a great clap on the back. 'I must tell you this man knows everything about opera. A *maven*.'

Aaron laughed. 'That's certainly true – when I can afford it. But what can I say to you, Sophia? Be a little wary. This man,' he poked Dov in the chest, 'can be something of a hot-head.'

'I'm soft as a kitten,' shouted Dov. 'Nothing for her to fear. Nothing at all.'

'Well, comrades, I must leave you.' Aaron paused. 'Two waistcoats await me. Shall we see you again, Miss Krichevska?'

'My brother stayed with Hannah Leah and Moshe Rifkin. They've offered to look for a room for me. I believe they're your cousins.'

Aaron stopped in his tracks.

'They are. Moshe is my second cousin; Hannah Leah comes from Visokaye like me. They will do everything to help you.' He lifted his hat. 'Dov, are you coming on Sunday? I'll make sure everyone is present. Send me a postcard if you can't make it.' He looked at Sophia. 'Goodbye, Sophia Krichevska, we'll meet again soon, I hope.'

Dov folded her arm under his and she had a moment's uncertainty. Would people think she was connected with him in some emotional way? Engaged? But no one here would know her, she would not be judged.

'Now, Sophia, you didn't search for me because you'd changed your mind, did you?'

'No,' she smiled up at him.

'Your brother wasn't there?'

'How did you know?'

'Happens again and again. I suppose the tickets weren't valid?'

She shook her head. Suddenly she was crying. Dropping her head, she reached for a handkerchief in her bag and turning away, wiped her eyes.

'You need some food.'

Sophia told him she was fine.

'No. it's lunchtime. I'll go back with you to the shelter but first, you must eat.'

Even though she told him the people at the shelter would be concerned, that she'd promised, he swept away her protestations.

'It will add twenty minutes to your journey. They wouldn't want you collapsing in the streets, would they? Come, Sophia, I'm taking you to a teashop and you can taste good English food for the first time. I promise it won't be the last.'

He led her down the road to a cafe that had large letters inscribed above the bay window. She spelt out: A B C. Peering through the window, she saw people sitting at tables, waitresses wearing frilly white caps, a black velvet band around the rim, and carrying trays of food. Dov swung open the heavy glass door, ushering her inside. It was busy, there was a quiet babble of conversation, and the appetising smells of toast and coffee made her mouth water. They followed a young waitress to a small table beside the wall, where Dov sat with his back to the door so Sophia could see both inside and out.

She draped her jacket over the chair and sat down. Women were sitting together in twos and threes, chatting, eating, laughing. At home, no respectable lady would think of going alone to a public place, even for a glass of tea.

'You see, English women are already gaining independence. Truly, they are the New Women.' Dov laughed.

Of course, that's how she'd introduced herself on the ship. But now she was in the company of English people and when the waitress handed her a daintily edged menu, she stared at the words in a flutter of uncertainty and slowly spelled out: *ham sandwiches, egg sandwiches, cheese sandwiches…*

Dov took over. 'You can have iced buns, fruit cake, Bath cake, Chelsea buns.'

At the adjoining table, Sophia noticed a woman eating a boiled egg; it sat in a gold-rimmed eggcup, another egg lay beside it in the saucer. The woman selected a slice of finely cut white toast gleaming with soft yellow butter from the plate and cut it into narrow slices. It smelled delicious.

'Do you think I could have that?' she asked Dov.

'Why not? And after, you must try some English cake. It's very good.'

'What will you have?'

'An iced bun, large and sticky.'

'Then I'll have one too.'

'And how do you like the eggs? Soft, medium, hard?'

Sophia laughed. 'Soft to medium, please.'

The waitress was hardly more than a child. Dov gave her the order with such ease, Sophia was overcome with admiration. She picked up the menu again. Milk, tea and sugar were so like the words in Yiddish. When their order arrived, Dov took a great bite of his sandwich while Sophia carefully removed the top of the egg, scooping out the white then dipping her spoon in the yolk. With the crunchy white toast, the sweet butter trickling over the edge like golden sauce, it tasted glorious. Compared with the rye bread they ate at home, this was fine as cake; she was hungry and barely noticed what Dov had ordered. Once she'd started on the second egg – her hunger a little satiated – she looked up. Dov was taking his time, gazing around the room, everything being registered for some future occasion, Sophia was sure, but then she noticed something pink and delicate in his sandwich.

'What did you choose?' she asked him.

'Ham.'

'But it's not kosher,' she gasped.

'Sophia, my darling, you'll have to forget those ancient tribal prejudices if you're to be free as you say. What is so awful about ham – or pork, for that matter? How is it different from lamb or beef?'

She bit her lip and turned her gaze away from him to ponder this.

'Are all socialists like you, abandoning everything we've been taught to respect?'

'No, I respect the right of all human beings to be free; to progress, to discover their true selves. I deplore all those who enchain others as a right – the Church, the aristocracy, the State. Eating ham, or crabs, or what you will, has no bearing on these great things, but neither the Church nor even our esteemed rabbis, most of them, can see beyond their sacred texts. There are certain progressive rabbis, even some of the most orthodox, the Chasidim, who have a better vision of humanity than many of the *dayanim*, the judges in our courts.' Taking a deep breath, he bit into the iced bun. 'Wonderful!'

Troubled, she shook her head. How could she reply to his denunciation of traditional Judaism? They fell silent.

'Sophia,' Dov paused, 'you don't know how delighted I was to see you again. Why don't you accept my offer? Come and live with me at Dunstan Houses, be part of the commune. It's a great family.'

How she wanted to do that. Already, in these first days of being in England, she'd experienced loneliness, a feeling she didn't belong. Something she'd never imagined would happen to her, for she found people fascinating, was always keen to learn and understand. This offer was so appealing, for now, she longed to be with others, with a family, but Mama's voice was clear: *Do not let yourself be carried away.*

'Maybe sometime, but right now I need to return to the London shelter.'

Thinking about her mother filled her with such disquiet, she half stood up. 'Oh Dov, I haven't sent my parents a telegram to say I've arrived. That I'm safe.'

Further difficulties crowded into her mind: her parents wouldn't have known that they'd been fooled by the ticket agent, that Sasha had gone without her, that she was here alone. It would greatly disturb them.

'Wait until you get back to the shelter. There could be a message from your brother. If there isn't, wait. Send a telegram when you know something definite.'

She sank back into the chair, relief filling her heart.

They finished the meal with a cup of tea; Sophia tried hers with a little milk and rather liked it. Dov paid, and they went out onto Tottenham Court Road.

Returning to the shelter, they sat on top of the omnibus and Dov told her the names of famous buildings; of the landmarks they'd passed earlier – Poultry, Cheapside, St Paul's Cathedral, Newgate, explaining how they were all from mediaeval times when London was a tiny city, beside the great river Thames.

He exclaimed with anger when he caught sight of barefoot boys wandering along the pavements begging, and Sophia asked if there was as much poverty here as back home. They arrived in Aldgate in the East End, with its noise, dirt, and tiny shops, Yiddish scrawled in white letters across the grimy windows. Dov said he would come in with her to face Mrs Haber. She averred it wasn't necessary, but he took no notice, carrying on along Leman Street until they reached the shelter.

'I'm busy over the next couple of days,' he said. 'Supposing we meet again one evening next week? Say, Friday.'

'Here?' Sophia asked.

'No, I'll come in for you. No young lady stands alone on street corners, even in tolerant London. I'll take you to the Sugar Loaf pub where you'll meet the East End comrades. Would you like that?'

'I'd love to.'

'Right, let's confront this lady dragon.'

Together they entered the shelter, where Mrs Haber gave a little cry when she saw them.

'At last, Sophia Krichevska, I was getting worried about you.'

Dov winked at Sophia. He swept off his hat and bowed. 'Forgive me, Madam. It's entirely my fault. 'I am Dov Feldman. I understand you're looking after my friend, Miss Krichevska, and I want to thank you for it.'

'Oh, Mr Feldman, that's what we're here for. A young lady on her own. Who knows what might occur when she doesn't speak the language? Did she tell you what happened to her in the docks?'

'She did, but you had nothing to worry about today because she's with me, safe and sound.' Dov smiled, and Mrs Haber melted like the snow in spring. 'She needed to eat. I took her to a tearoom so she could sustain herself, have her first taste of English life and food. That's why she's later than she promised.'

'Ah, well you done a good thing, though there was food here if she'd been on time. Never mind, I hope you enjoyed it, Miss Krichevska?'

'Oh, I did.'

They both laughed, the barriers were down, and Dov was fast becoming Mrs Haber's friend.

'Ladies, I've much to do. Sophia, you're in good hands, so if that's all right with you, I shall go.'

'Of course, you must. Thank you for coming with me.'

Bowing lightly to Sophia and Mrs Haber, he lifted his hat and disappeared into the East End sunshine.

'Well,' said Mrs Haber. 'Nice young man there. Still, I waited until he'd gone because you never can tell, can you?' Sophia frowned. What did she mean? 'A lady come whilst you was out.'

'To see me?'

'Yes. A good-looking woman with fair hair. Said she was Mrs Rifkin. Strange I don't know her, but then she said they come here from Deptford only a few weeks back.'

'Mrs Haber, what did she say?'

She pulled an envelope from a drawer and presented it to her. 'Said it was something you'd be pleased with. And she invites you for shabbes lunch.'

Sophia barely registered this as she feverishly tore open the blue envelope with its American post office stamp. A telegram from Sasha:

> Arrived.
> Address. 37 Hesther Street. New York.
> Send yours in telegram.
> I'll contact Mama.
> Letter following.

Sophia cried great tears of relief and joy. At last, encouraged by murmuring from Mrs Haber, who was well used to such emotion, she dried her eyes.

'It's from my brother. He's reached America. I have his address. Mrs Haber, please, please could you help me send two telegrams, one to my mother and father, one to Sasha.'

Later, wondering when her parents would receive the telegram, she made her way to the communal dining room.

And though happy to see the lighted candles, one set for each table, she felt no desire to talk. Mr Fuchs made *Kiddush*, the blessing over the wine, and they chanted *amen*. He passed round thimble-sized cups of wine, one for each person, and plum juice for the children. They washed their hands, waiting in silence until Mr Fuchs had made the blessing over the bread, tearing it into small pieces just as they did at home. Piling the bread onto a plate, people passed it down the tables until everyone had taken a small portion.

Then the meal: chicken soup with noodles followed by plainly boiled chicken from the soup, potatoes, carrots and new beans. Finally, a woman carried in a large enamel container of *lokshen-kugel*, noodle pudding, bright with raisins and sultanas. A glass of tea with lemon, and they'd finished. Small prayer books were passed to the men; Sophia smiled – she knew the words of the blessings, but many here were observant and didn't allow women to sing – their voices might entice the men to evil thoughts, God forbid. So she listened as the men sang the grace after meals.

Little conversation followed; children slept, their heads resting on the white cloth while babies slept in their mothers' arms. So glad to have made this long journey, and to be in a place of safety, the adults quietly wished each other good night and went to bed. Once she had folded her clothes, Sophia crawled under the blankets. Though exhausted, she couldn't sleep at first, her mind occupied with thoughts of her brother, of her parents so far away, but eventually, her eyes closed and she slept.

CHAPTER 5

S HE AWOKE THINKING OF Dov.

'Stop it,' she told herself. 'That first afternoon, he asked you if you were praying when you'd simply been whispering a message to Mama, you told him you were a New Woman. Then *be* one.'

On the way to the Rifkins, walking the rowdy dusty streets where the rich odorous tang of *cholent*, that stew of bones and beans, was issuing from every house she passed, she saw herself back home, with Mama preparing the food, Papa sitting by the stove, reading perhaps as he smoked a pipe, and her brother Alexis, spending all his time making animals from pieces of wood. She could hear Mama's voice, 'This boy is a veritable genius with his hands.'

Tears welled up in her eyes, but she blinked them away, vowing they would all join Sasha in New York, the very moment they had the money. She reached the Rifkins' home and knocked at the door. It was opened by Hannah Leah. With her blonde hair swept above her head, her straight, beautiful features and her upright stance, she looked like a queen, and this should have been a fine house, Sophia thought, rather than two rooms in a tenement building.

'Sophia, it's good to see you.'

They descended a flight of stone steps into a basement flat, where an identical green door led into a proper kitchen. A large table filled the room; a black-leaded cooking range stood against the far wall, with a coal fire burning, even though it was May. A tiny, bent lady appeared from the corridor. Her lined white face and pale grey eyes contrasted oddly with her black wig.

'My mother, Mrs Levi, who looks after us all,' said Hannah Leah. 'Mother, our guest is here.'

The old lady whispered a few words of greeting but Sophia saw she was concentrating on the dinner; bending over, she wrenched back the bar across the oven door, and with a tea towel in both hands, lifted an enormous covered dish, the Sabbath cholent. Sophia wondered that she had the strength for her arms were so thin they resembled the legs of a frail bird. An older man stood near her, swaying backwards and forwards over the prayer book, singing softly to himself.

'Father, meet our guest, Miss Krichevska,' said Hannah Leah.

He bowed his head, a brief smile on his face, but continued to pray. With his huge grey beard and strong, straight features, he might have been one of the prophets, Sophia thought. Moshe sat at the head of the table; three children, two boys and a girl, sat on one side while a baby girl propped up against a cushion sat close to him.

'Welcome, Sophia,' called Moshe. 'Good shabbes! Our children,' he continued, pointing to the boys. 'Ralphie, born in Visokaye, our muddy *shtetl,* and nearly ten. Jack, the first English one, who's eight and Lily, sitting beside him, is seven.'

'Good shabbes, everyone.' Sophia beamed, delighted.

Wearing a blue apron to protect her dress, Lily ducked her face behind her father's arm as it rested on the table.

'Our baby, Annie, just a year old,' said Hannah Leah, taking the smallest one into her arms.

Lily peeped up from her father's arm and again hid her face when she saw Sophia smiling at them. The boys' hair was brown like their father's, but the girls would be beauties when they grew up, Sophia thought, with blonde curls and blue eyes like their mother.

She took her place next to Hannah Leah while Mr Levi made the blessing, holding up a silver wine cup intricately moulded. He took a large sip of wine from the cup, passing it down to his son-in-law, then it crisscrossed the table until they'd all taken a sip, even the grandmother, who stood waiting to serve them. Silent, they followed him to a grey porcelain sink in the corridor, washed their hands in the ritual way, and returned to the table. Making the blessing over the bread, Mr Levi tore off small pieces, which he passed around the table.

Now they could speak.

'Mama,' said Hannah Leah to her mother, 'don't stand there. Sit with us.'

But the little lady refused until all were served: first the children and then the adults. At last, drawing up a rickety wooden stool, Mrs Levi perched herself at the corner of the table. The stew, cooked gently overnight, filled the room with its meaty smell.

'This is so delicious,' Sophia said to Mrs Levi. 'The dumpling melts in your mouth. It's just as we cooked it at home, in Kyiv.'

'Sophia, I have good news for you.' Hannah Leah leaned across the table to touch her arm. 'I don't know if you've noticed the signs in windows as you came here, *beck room and loshings?*'

'I did, but I thought it was something English. Mine is not as good as I would like. I couldn't make sense of those words.'

'It's a sort of English.' Hannah Leah exchanged a smile with Moshe. 'It should be back room and lodging. But if you say it with a Jewish accent, it comes out like that.'

'*Beck room and loshings,*' repeated Moshe, and everyone, including the children, laughed.

'It's not easy to find somewhere to live, especially if you're a single woman,' continued Hannah Leah. 'They can rent a room to three men and get the money, three times over if you understand me. *Beck room* means you rent a back room you pay for weekly whereas *loshings* or lodgings means you get breakfast and an evening meal. But I couldn't vouch for what the food would be. What do you think would suit you, Sophia?'

'Somewhere I can do a little cooking.'

Hannah Leah rested one hand on the table, still holding the baby on her knee. 'Then we might have exactly what you want. Not with us, but in Wentworth Buildings, just down the road. A woman I met in the corridor told me her sister, who lives in Wentworth, is looking for someone. We don't know them well because we've only recently come here. But the woman I spoke to seems nice enough.'

'Do you know anything about the room?' Sophia said.

'If she wants to let the living room, it will be identical to this,' Moshe said. 'Or it could be the back room, overlooking the inner yard. This woman is a widow and her daughter's just had a baby. She goes there most days after work.'

'Would you like to see it?' Hannah Leah raised her eyebrows encouragingly.

Sophia thought quickly. The buildings were tall and ugly, there were five storeys including the basement flats, dirt, and litter everywhere, but everyone she'd spoken to was kind and welcoming. *What choice do I have?*

'Yes, please. When can we go?'

'After lunch, or if she's out, we can leave a note.'

Mr Levi had been deep in the prayer book, now he rose. 'Grace after meals.'

Singing this cheerful song of thanks completed the meal, and when Mr Levi announced he was returning to *shul*, to the synagogue, Sophia thanked him for this wonderful afternoon. He pointed to Mrs Levi. 'Thank my wife and daughter. I had nothing to do with it.'

Entering Wentworth Buildings by the inner courtyard, they climbed to the first floor, making for the end flat. Hannah Leah knocked on the door and an elderly woman wearing a black skirt and coat, her thin sallow face marked by sadness, opened it immediately.

'Good shabbes, Mrs Vine. I'm Mrs Riskin and your sister lives on the floor above us. She said you might be looking for a lodger. Our friend Miss Krichevska who has just arrived needs somewhere to live. But I see you're going out and I don't want to...' Hannah Leah's voice took on a questioning tone.

'My sister told me about the lady looking for a room, and I do want to let mine, so now's as good a time as any. Come in.'

She held open the door and they walked in. Sophia was confronted by a dark heavy sofa, a few faded cushions arranged along the back, pushed against the wall. With its small square table covered by faded oilcloth, its kitchen cupboard and the black leaded stove, the room was identical in size and shape to the one they had just left. But the walls were painted brown, matching the wooden floor. It felt dingy and drear, and she drew back.

Hannah Leah touched her arm as though to say *just take a look*.

'I've slept in here since my husband died.' Mrs Vine indicated the sofa. 'It's warmer, so the back room I want to let. Come.'

They followed her through – a high, metal bed stood alongside the window. Sophia saw what resembled a low cupboard covered with a white cloth, while a battered wardrobe leant against the wall adjoining the living room. A tarnished mirror hung above the mantelpiece. Yellowing net curtains covered the window.

Returning to the living room, Mrs Vine stated, 'I can't do food. By the time I'm back from my daughter's, I go to bed and that's it.'

'Mrs Vine, if you're happy for me to use the stove, I can look after myself.' Sophia gave her another smile; the woman seems so reluctant, so downcast, she wondered if she meant to let the room at all.

'Are you working?' Mrs Vine glanced up.

'I have a little money with me until I find work, which I'm sure I will in the next few days.'

'All right. When do you want to come?'

'Whenever it's convenient for you. I can stay another week at the London shelter.'

'It's five shillings a week and I want you to pay me every Sunday.' She lifted her worn, faded eyes to Sophia, who shot a questioning look at Hannah Leah. She nodded as though to say that was a usual amount for renting a room.

'That's fine, and of course, you'll have the money every Sunday.' Sophia gave Mrs Vine another smile.

'I work at home on Tuesday. You can come then.'

Where is this? How do I go there? How much? Such a jumble of anxious queries Sophia heard as she approached the desk next morning. Mrs Haber and Mr Fuchs patiently explained how to reach certain streets, whose addresses had been written on torn and folded scraps of paper; they drew little maps and even filled out simple forms for people who could neither read nor write.

It was her turn.

'We've talked this over,' said Mr Fuchs. 'Mrs Haber will go with you this afternoon. You've found somewhere to live, so now you can look for work. Better that way – the authorities need you to have an address.'

'See, Sophia, we have a list of workplaces, usually in tailoring for a beginner...' said Mrs Haber, brandishing a sheet of paper.

'I was a teacher in Archangelsk in the little school Mama set up with a friend. I taught there for two years while I was studying.'

'Miss Krichevska,' Mr Fuchs said carefully, 'those ladies who brought you here told us you were educated, even spoke several languages, but English?'

'Are the children's lessons in English?'

'They have to become little English men or women. They even change their names. It's Jane, not Hannah. And Morris, not Moshe. That's what the government wants.'

The idea disturbed Sophia. 'I thought this was a tolerant land.'

'It is,' said Mr Fuchs, 'but the established Jewish people, who in the eighteen fifties came from Germany and Austria, have anglicised themselves. They want all new immigrants to do the same.'

Sophia frowned. It seemed authoritarian to her. Still, she recognised what she should do to improve her chances here. 'I'll have to take English lessons as soon as I can.'

'Some ladies set up shops in their houses – when they're married, of course. Or if you don't like the idea of a workshop, you could take a stall in the market. Could you do that?'

English money would be a problem, Sophia knew, although she had certainly helped Mama in the little dairy they kept in the back room. Her mother had maintained the general Jewish policy of charging low fees for the school, and Papa earned a little in addition, letting out small boats.

'Tell me about the workshops, please.'

Mrs Haber pointed to the list, where several workshops were seeking to employ a hand. 'What they mean is unpicking, basting, that kind of thing. Heavens, your mother did learn you to sew?'

Drawing herself up, Sophia said, 'I've used a machine since I was nine years old.'

They searched up and down Ellen Street, Golding Street, Christian Street, where the workshops were on the fourth floor of those tall old houses, visiting more than a dozen, all with ten or twelve workers packed into small, overheated workrooms. Finally, they tried Mrs Lazarus. Sophia asked why they hadn't gone to her first, but Mrs Haber shrugged saying she was an awkward customer. In Batty Street, they climbed the four flights of stairs to the workroom, where a stout little woman with a grubby apron covering her broad bosom, and grey hair straggling from under a stained scarf, opened the door to them.

'Yes?'

'I'm from the London shelter,' announced Mrs Haber, almost grandly. 'Mrs Lazarus?' The woman nodded. 'We understand you might be looking for a worker?'

'Might be.'

'You're on this list.' Mrs Haber raised her eyebrows and tapped the sheet of paper she'd taken from her bag. 'Miss Krichevska has just arrived and is eager to find work.'

The woman stared at Sophia, then narrowed her eyes.

'I was looking for someone,' she said, 'but I'm full now.' She began to close the door.

'I'll take your name off, then?' Mrs Haber turned as though to leave.

'What's all this?' A large man, his skin pockmarked, hairs bristling from his nose, appeared behind the woman. Mrs Lazarus spoke to the man, evidently her husband, and made to close the door again, but he flung it open.

'I've got more piece work. Sleeves. You can sew, unpick, do hemming?' he asked Sophia.

'Yes.'

'Take her for a couple of weeks, and we'll see.'

He disappeared into the workroom, leaving his wife at the door.

She shrugged.

'You'd better come in.'

As the woman turned, Sophia wondered if she was pregnant. But Mrs Haber whispered: 'Have a quick look round then you'll know what you're in for.'

It was hot, and the stink of sweat made Sophia feel she was back on the ship again.

Two men were treadling fiercely, their eyes focused on the cloth beneath the needle. A presser, his back to her, was at the far side, lifting huge steam irons which hissed as he flattened the cloth. He turned, caught her eye, and winked – it was Moshe. She lifted her hand briefly to acknowledge him.

Mr Lazarus was leaning over a bench, a tape measure looped around his neck, his large hairy hands delicately smoothing out parts of a garment. Beside him on the bench, lay several pairs of black-handled tailor's shears, while a thin pale woman sitting on a stool was unpicking the bastings from a pile of sleeves. All the men worked with their sleeves rolled to the elbow. In workshops they'd already visited, small dirty windows were placed too high to let in any light; here large windows stretched across one wall, but were clamped tight shut and were almost black. The rhythmic clatter of the sewing machines made her recall the train to Petersburg, but together with the hissing of the flat iron, the noise was discordant, harsh, making her head spin. A frown pierced her forehead.

'Try,' Mrs Haber muttered. 'Not much else you can do.'

Sophia's attention was caught by the young woman now winding cotton threads around her hand before dropping them into a cardboard box, for she lifted her gaze to give Sophia an encouraging smile. That moment of warmth decided it for her.

'Yes,' Sophia nodded to Mrs Haber.

'Mrs Lazarus,' announced Mrs Haber, 'it seems Miss Krichevska is happy to accept your offer of work. You know we always vouch for the people we bring here.'

Back at her sewing machine and without raising her eyes from the intricate business of buttonholes, Mrs Lazarus shook her head as though indifferent to this fact.

'Ask her what they pay.' Mrs Haber nudged Sophia's arm.

'What are the wages, Mrs Lazarus?'

Mrs Lazarus manoeuvred a piece of material before replying. 'The usual, four shillings a day, though being a greener, you'll get three shillings and sixpence.'

Sophia had prepared herself. Removing a notebook and pencil from her bag, she worked out its equivalent in roubles. It was so little, she raised her gaze to Mrs Haber, surprise in her eyes.

'It's the same everywhere, I'm afraid.' Mrs Haber turned to Mrs Lazarus. 'What about the hours?'

'Eight to eight, or nine, depending.'

Sophia gave a tiny gasp. 'All right,' she muttered, 'when can I start?

'Wednesday.'

'I need you to sign this.' Mrs Haber placed the agreement on the sewing machine flap, and the woman signed with large, childlike letters falling down the page.

Back at the shelter, Mrs Haber gave Sophia a brief hug, taking her by surprise. 'So now you're set up with a room and work. I do likes a girl with gumption, I do. Reminds me of myself when I was young.'

'Mrs Haber...' A little embarrassed, Sophia hesitated, 'Mrs Haber, do you think you might give my new address to Mr Feldman? He said he would come by on Friday.'

'I shouldn't but I will.' Mrs Haber chuckled. 'But take care, Sophia. He's a heartbreaker if ever I saw one.'

Sophia flushed pink.

'Thank you and thank you for all you've done for me.'

Sophia wrote her first letter home that night, full of details about the ship, the journey, the people she'd met. She avoided mentioning Dov, fearing her mother might read between the lines. She finished the letter by saying:

> *My darlings, there's nothing to worry about now, even though Sasha had to leave without me. I'll soon have earned enough for the ticket to New York and then we can send for you.*
>
> *With all my love,*
> *Sophia*

CHAPTER 6

FEARFUL OF ARRIVING LATE on Wednesday, she left the flat at half-past seven, saying a brief word to Mrs Vine, before joining others hurrying through the streets. Her first beautiful day in London, with the sun already high above the chimney pots, the sky a hazy blue, and shadows dancing up and down the pavement as she walked. She smiled, despite feeling her heart pound against her chest.

Reaching forty-four Batty Street, she ran up the stairs and knocked at the door, which was opened by Mr Lazarus, broad and bristly.

'On time,' he boomed. 'Sit next to Hymie Myerson over there. The machinist,' he added. 'You'll see a pile of sleeves. Take out the bastings and put the sleeves on the pressing table. There's a stool next to Betsy. Watch her.'

'Yes, Mr Lazarus.' Sophia gazed around, puzzled. It was only a quarter to eight, the workshop seemed even more crowded, and everyone had their heads bent over their work. *I won't ask if I'm late.* 'Where do I leave my things, Mr Lazarus?'

'Pegs behind the door.'

She hung her jacket next to the others; a low shelf above the pegs held containers for pins and needles, and in one corner, a wooden cigar box, with words written in green ink around the lid: *Arbeter Fraint, Worker's Friend*.

What could it mean?

Betsy tried to smile when Sophia joined her, but her face glistened with fatigue and she seemed barely able to lift the material that morning. Still, the work was simple and sleeves piled up, ready for the presser. Sophia made her way between sewing machines to the pressing bench at the rear, beneath the wide dusty windows.

'Hello, Moshe. How are you?'

'Don't say anything. Act as if you don't know me.' He threw a serious glance at Mrs Lazarus, who continued to sew buttonholes on various garments. 'That woman … you never know what she might do.'

Sophia lifted her finger to her lips to acknowledge their secret. All morning she unpicked white cotton bastings until she thought she might topple off the stool. At least, she could move, stand up, walk a few paces over to Moshe. By twelve, when they stopped to eat, the men were wiping their faces and necks with wrinkled handkerchiefs and the reek of sweat was so strong, she tried not to breathe. The pounding of treadles and swish of pressing irons had become so insistent, she felt as though someone was hitting her over the head.

Mrs Lazarus had left her sewing machine some minutes before; she stood at the door shouting: 'Dinner.'

The men stopped. Two women, seated at the back, who had not said a word or acknowledged Sophia, now followed Betsy, who'd run down the stairs. As though oblivious, Mrs Lazarus barked: 'You can come too,' giving Sophia an angry look. 'You have food?'

'Some bread,' Sophia replied. 'I would have brought herring but it might have seeped into my bag.'

There was no response from Mrs Lazarus. Sophia decided to ignore her and made plans to buy cheese and a couple of eggs on her way home. Hard-boiled would be safe.

They sat crowded together around the table, where a pot of tea and chipped cups were placed on a faded blue-squared oilcloth.

'Help yourself,' Mrs Lazarus barked.

A machinist called Harry Brown joined Sophia, saying he'd worked there on and off for five years. When she asked him where Betsy had gone, he said there were three little ones at home, two more at school and the husband had the consumption. Betsy had gone to feed them. 'That's how it is,' he added, shaking his head.

After the meal, Sophia followed the men outside, where they leaned against a wall to smoke while she stood a little apart, glad to breathe air that was free of cotton shreds. They were talking about the working conditions.

'At least we have half an hour for dinner,' said Mr Myerson, an earnest, stooping man, whose black-rimmed glasses made Sophia think of an owl. 'When I came over fifteen years ago, I only saw my wife on Saturdays; we worked all the hours God gave us.'

'And the Devil,' someone added.

'The Devil has plenty to answer for.'

'Do you ever sleep in the workroom?' Sophia asked him.

'We do when there's a big job on. This isn't such a job, but Lazarus wants to go places. He says if he finishes this lot quickly, the West End masters might give him a batch of jackets to make up.'

'That would keep us in work for some time,' Moshe said.

'Don't believe it. His wife ruins everything he touches…' someone said, but the others averted their gaze and stayed silent.

'Back to *Gehenna,*' Mr Myerson groaned. 'Though what we've done to deserve a bit of Hell, I don't know.'

It grew hotter and hotter; now she regretted the beautiful day, grey clouds and rain would have been more comfortable in an attic workroom such as this. Her neck ached, her arms and fingers were sore. Massaging her elbow, she caught sight of Mrs Lazarus' eyes on her and stopped, fearful of the woman's reaction. At four, they had a glass of tea and could avail themselves of the latrine, as Mrs Lazarus called it, a foul place in the yard behind the building.

Betsy was missing the following day. However thick the walls, they could hear Mrs Lazarus in the kitchen, screaming at her husband, and his deep voice telling her it wasn't his fault if a hand didn't come in.

'You know her husband is very ill. The child told you this morning.'

He was trying to pacify her, probably embarrassed by her outbreak.

'I don't care,' she yelled. 'I don't care. It's our work, our money. She's finished here. I won't have her back.'

The other workers bent their heads as soon as Mrs Lazarus marched through the door over to Sophia.

'You'd better baste these. If Mr Myerson is satisfied, you can do the rest.'

Sophia thanked her, feeling uneasy at taking work from a woman who desperately needed it. As she sewed, she wondered if something awful had happened to Betsy, and imagined how broken she'd be when she learned Mrs Lazarus wouldn't take her back. She sighed. Seeing her face, Mr Myerson whispered, 'Don't worry too much about Betsy. There's always the Friendly Society. You know?'

'No,' she whispered, careful to keep her eyes down.

'Every week, you put a penny or two in a fund and if someone in the family's ill, they pay the doctor's fees.'

'Or when a lady is confined,' added Mr Brown, his gaze on Mrs Lazarus. 'We were glad of it last week, I can tell you – my wife had twins. The midwife was there night and day, but all went well, thank God. And now we have two more mouths to feed,' he added cheerfully.

They'd finished by eight o'clock; Mr Lazarus paid the men, while his wife paid Sophia. 'You get less because you're a greener. Come in on Monday and see if we've any work for you.'

'I thought he said two weeks?' Sophia was unwilling to confront her but needed to be sure.

'If there's work.'

'What about tomorrow?'

'Nothing tomorrow. The order's finished.' Her face, pock-marked and unyielding, told Sophia to keep silent or she'd make sure there'd be no work ever.

Moshe was waiting outside. As they walked slowly along Batty Street, he said, 'It's never a full week. You just take what you can.'

'I didn't know,' Sophia said wearily. Her legs felt heavy and her back ached from the hours of unpicking the bastings.

'He likes you, Mr Lazarus, I can tell, but be careful with his wife.' Again, he called her a tartar.

'Yesterday, I saw a box on the shelf with the words *Arbeter Fraint* written in black ink across the side. What is it?'

'*The Worker's Friend*. The anarchist newspaper.'

'Anarchists?'

'The ones who follow Rudolf Rocker.'

'Dov told me about him.' She didn't continue. 'Where can you buy the paper?'

'They sell it on street corners. You'll see.'

'He said they meet in a place called the Sugar Loaf pub. Is it nearby?'

He paused to look at her directly.

'Your brother and I discussed various socialist theories, but the Sugar Loaf pub – well, it's not a place for a young lady.'

Smiling to herself, choosing to ignore this, she asked, 'Why is the box in the workshop?'

'We put in a copper or two when we can, to support them; we go to all the big meetings they organise but their regular meeting in Hanbury Street is on Friday evening.'

'I suppose most people don't go because it's the beginning of shabbes.' They turned into Wentworth Street. 'What exactly is a pub, Moshe?'

They stopped outside the archway into Wentworth Buildings.

'Like a tavern back home. You know, where the peasants drink vodka until they can't stand up. Here, men drink beer and spirits. Women also drink. I've seen them emerging drunk, shouting obscenities.' He shook his head.

Why had Dov told her to look for him there? Surely it couldn't be such a dreadful place? They shook hands, and Sophia climbed the stairs to her room, smiling at the thought of seeing Dov the following evening.

CHAPTER 7

FRIDAY. ALL DAY SHE thought about Dov, and strangely too, of the Sugar Loaf pub. Such a beautiful name, reminding her of a folk tale, one that a babushka would tell her grandchildren: Once upon a time, there was a tavern made of sugar in the shape of a loaf. One day, two children went to buy vodka for their father, but when they walked inside, a witch kept them prisoner, until a powerful fairy broke the spell, killed the witch, and freed the children. Would the Sugar Loaf pub enchant her too, or was it the thought of Dov being there?

She stared at herself in the mottled mirror above the fireplace and drew her eyebrows together: *You'd better Read Mama's Commandments again*. Going to her trunk, now her table, she took out a list of 'commandments' her mother had written before she left.

> *Do not let yourself be carried away.*
> *Beware the power of words.*
> *Be restrained in what you do.*
> *Do not give your trust too easily.*
> *Be wary of those with extreme views.*
> *Show compassion.*

Do not judge others.
When life is burdensome, help another person.
Remember our love.

I haven't given my heart too quickly, she thought, but I am letting myself be carried away. I must stop this at once. *Keep busy.* Sitting on her bed, she wrote another long, reassuring letter home, telling them about her new life in England. She ended by saying that once she'd earned enough money, she would certainly join Sasha in America. Then her parents and brother would come and they'd be together again. She folded the letter, slipped it into an envelope, and wrote the address, wondering how long it would take to reach Archangelsk.

In the front room, Mrs Vine was cooking for her daughter and seemed more cheerful. She asked Sophia how she was settling in, then her face lit up when she talked about the new grandchild. 'Beautiful already, bless her.'

'Who does she look like?' Sophia smiled at Mrs Vine.

'Like me.' She lifted her thin face to Sophia and shook her head, as though to suggest how impossible that was.

'That's wonderful. Actually, there's something I'd like to ask you. About washing. I know you can wash clothes in the basement, in the sink, or use the boiler. But I haven't had a bath since staying at the shelter. What do you do about that?'

Mrs Vine rested her arms on the table. 'You've got Schewzik's, the Russian Vapour Baths on Brick Lane. Schewzik, he owns it. Ladies go on Wednesdays. Or you have the public baths along Goulston Street.'

'Which do you recommend?'

'Oh, Schewzik's, everyone goes there. You pay a few pence for soap and a towel. Or you can bring your own. There's plenty on the market down Goulston Street.'

She tasted the cholent and added salt.

'Thank you very much.' Sophia nodded. 'I'll post this letter to my family, then have a look round. Get to know the area better. Good shabbes, Mrs Vine.'

Having passed her letter under the grille to the postmaster, she asked how she could reach Brick Lane, and a dozen people in the queue gave her directions. Something struck her as she listened – if Dov didn't come that evening, could she, would she, go to the Sugar Loaf *alone*? She would.

'Can you tell me how to reach the Sugar Loaf pub?'

There was a pause, but then a young woman in the queue called, 'You going to the meeting?'

'Maybe,' Sophia said.

'Perhaps I'll see you there.' She proceeded to explain the route, which turned out to be only five minutes' walk away.

Friday again, chicken soup and cholent, Sophia thought, making her way through the busy streets. Tonight she'd be eating alone, but instead, she would see Dov. She smiled at the thought. The Vapour Baths were halfway along Brick Lane, and she stopped to admire the oriental-looking porch and curlicued ironwork around the windows. Halfway up the road, she found the turning for Hanbury Street. The Sugar Loaf pub stood dark and squat on a corner. She sighed. Dirty and forbidding, all closed up, it had no resemblance to a fairy tale. She peered through a window blackened with dirt and could just make out tables and chairs. But then a poster in Yiddish fixed to a lamppost caught her eye: *Capitalism. The Error of Marxism. Anarcho-Federalism.* At the bottom in tiny print, she read *Concert on the Fifteenth of June. All performers welcome.* And finally: *All Friday meetings at eight o'clock prompt.*

She had come to the right place.

At a quarter to eight, she peered through her window to the area between the buildings and with a jolt of disappointment, knew that Dov wasn't coming. She folded her lips. She'd wait five more minutes, then she would leave. She so hated to be late, Mama used to say she would meet herself coming back. She frowned, took her watch from her bag once again, and waited. Five minutes later, she drew on her hat, put on her jacket, and straightened her shoulders. Leaving her room, she said: *You will go to the ball, my dear.*

Her heart beat faster as she walked, feeling both scared and emboldened by her daring. *I would never walk alone at night in Kyiv or Archangelsk but here I feel freer, almost a different person, and all the restrictions we had there have disappeared. Is that what being a New Woman feels like?*

People were already entering the Sugar Loaf pub and she wondered if they were anarchists or simply customers going for a drink. By the time she reached the door, she was alone. She hesitated, then taking a deep breath, followed them in.

It was dark and noisy; men in peaked caps, drinking and smoking. crowded the table. Someone was singing, perhaps a woman, she thought. On seeing Sophia, a young man at a nearby table whistled, reaching out to touch her sleeve but she shied away, relieved when a woman pulling pints behind the bar, called, 'Anarchists? There.'

Recognising the word, Sophia walked swiftly to a door at the back.

She found herself in a long room, with people already sitting on benches talking loudly in every language. She let out a sigh of relief.

Finding a space at the end of a bench halfway down, she gazed around. Young men and women, often as thin and white-faced as Betsy, but talking, gesticulating, lively and excited. At the other end of the room, a woman with lustrous black hair was handing out newspapers from a table. People stopped to chat, as they paid her.

A tall heavily built man with thick fair hair, and wearing black-rimmed glasses, which glinted occasionally when light pierced the dusty window, rose from a chair.

He must be the famous Rudolf Rocker. Sophia leaned forward, keen to hear every word.

'Comrades,' he began. People fell silent. 'Comrades, we have important things to discuss this evening and I need your full attention. You all know that the accursed Aliens Act is going through Parliament as we speak.' People groaned and Sophia frowned, wondering what this could be, but the answer came at once.

'It will restrict the number of immigrants coming from Eastern Europe and elsewhere, but what is worse, it plays into the rising hostility of local working people, fanned by the extreme right-wing movement of the British Brothers. In fact, it was instigated by their leader. What can we do to counteract this despicable thing?' People called out various answers. Nodding, he carried on. 'The answer as ever is to ally ourselves with our gentile brethren in the Trade Unions.'

'But, Rudolf, they hate us. Either we're rich, evil Jews dominating the world or we're dirty, poor Jews contaminating the country,' someone shouted.

Rocker shook his head. 'We'll continue to approach local trade unions and endeavour to communicate, tell them our plans to destroy the sweating system to enable all workers to have decent conditions and pay. This has always been our aim, as we have discussed many times before, even though the political system is against us. Courage, my friends. We will win through!'

'The British Brothers stand at street corners, terrifying the children,' a woman called out.

'They think they're winning, but they use hatred to fight their cause. On the other hand, look how we've succeeded in educating the Jewish people. We fight these dreadful conditions as a united force, whereas they try to rouse the local people by blaming foreigners for their poverty. But the real root of local hatred is economic. *Economic,* I repeat. While the sweating system is in place, I'm sorry to say, English workers will struggle to find employment, and so long as our Eastern European brethren accept a pittance as pay, we're caught up in this vicious cycle. But we shall change this.'

'One of our own people in Parliament, may he be cursed, supports the Aliens Act,' called another voice.

'Don't be side-tracked by anger. We must, I insist, must prepare for a strike of every single sweatshop worker. This means you and your fellow workers. The long hours and dreadful conditions will cease; these are men and women, human beings treated worse than the machines over which they slave. So, proper pay. Shorter hours.'

There were cries of agreement; people banged the floor with their feet.

'But how do we encourage sweatshop workers? What will move them when they're submerged in their poverty? It is not propaganda, rhetoric, empty slogans, and it's certainly not violence.'

Sophia's heart beat faster, her breath came more quickly. *How would Dov respond to this?*

'People's lives are not determined by their membership of a certain class,' Rudolf Rocker said, 'but by their daily experience of the society in which they live. What brings people into the anarchist movement is not the material effect of modern economic life, terrible as it is, but it is their sense of outrage. *Outrage*. Not only hunger of the body, but hunger of the spirit, of the soul, which demands its rights. Remember this when we encourage people to join us. Their hunger for justice. Justice, justice, this is what we are pursuing.'

He spoke so nobly, tears filled her eyes. Despite herself, she cried, 'Yes, justice is what we need.' She hid her face in her hands to hide the rising heat in her cheeks.

'Well said, young lady.' She lifted her flushed face. 'Welcome...?' His smile lit his eyes.

'Sophia Krichevska,' she whispered.

'Sophia Krichevska, you're most welcome here.'

He continued to talk, moving on to what he called the 'Great Revolution' taking place despite the Tsar, his savage Black Hundreds, the Cossacks, the effete noblemen. People asked questions, reporting what they'd heard from families or had read in newspapers. Sophia sat back, relieved everyone's attention had turned from her, listening and watching the eager faces of the audience while, from the main room, she heard coarse laughter and slurred shouts. Here was warmth and kindness.

My anxieties are like thistle-down when I consider the great work they're doing. Surely this is another way to heal people, and I belong with them? Surely Mama would approve?

Rudolf Rocker sat down. People converged again around the woman selling the newspaper. Could this be Rudolf Rocker's companion, who had refused to marry because she thought marriage was imprisonment? A brave woman. Sophia watched Rudolf walk down the aisle, surprised when he stopped beside her.

'Miss Krichevska, have you found work?'

'Oh yes,' she said, her voice shy, 'in a tailoring workshop in Batty Street.'

'Do they have our newspaper?' He handed her a copy of the *Arbeter Fraint. The Worker's Friend*.

'I'm not sure, but there's a cigar box on a shelf with those words written on the lid. So perhaps they do.'

'They will certainly read it. Please take this copy.' He shook his head when she bent to search her bag for money. 'See what you think.'

'Thank you.'

Smiling, he returned to the front of the room, while she turned her gaze to the newspaper.

Someone placed a hand on her shoulder, and she turned. 'Dov!'

He smiled down at her. 'I'm very sorry I didn't come for you, but I see you've made your way here on your own.'

She beamed up at him. He was about to say more when several voices called: 'Dov, Dov, you're back. Tell us what happened.'

She saw Rudolf beckon him to the front of the room.

'I have to report on my trip. I won't be long.'

Once again, he told them about the metalworkers' strikes in Petersburg, the uprisings all over the country, emphasising the great revolutionary spirit that had entered the minds and hearts of the people. As he finished, the woman with lustrous black hair walked towards Sophia.

'Milly Witcop. Glad to meet you, Miss Krichevska.'

'Sophia,' she said quickly.

'Sophia. Well, Sophia, did you work at all back home?'

Sophia told her story and Milly smiled. 'So, you've been a teacher. Do you read much? Do you write?'

'Both,' she answered.

'When you've settled, and attended a few more meetings, you might like to come to a newspaper planning meeting. On Thursdays.'

Sophia shot her a look of amazement. She had barely arrived and already they were asking her to be involved.

'Thank you. Thank you so much, I'd love to.'

'How's your English?' Another woman joined them. 'I'm Nellie Duncan.' They shook hands.

'Not very good, Nellie, but I intend to learn it as soon as possible.' Speaking good English was paramount if she were to become a doctor.

'Come to the class I run on Sunday evenings. Dov can bring you.'

Sophia shook her head in disbelief at their warmth and generous offers.

'How kind of you. Could you give me your address? I'll write it in my pocketbook.'

'Come at seven o'clock.'

Thanking her, Sophia turned to the newspaper and read:

Five thousand copies sold weekly. Do you know someone who doesn't read The Worker's Friend?

Show them this! Get them to buy their own copy and our cause will spread through the whole of London, not just the East End.

'And of course,' said a young man, who'd come to sit beside her, 'many more than five thousand are reading it now. It's passed around the workshops. Sam Dreen at your service, Miss Krichevska.'

About her age, she saw, he was slim with fine features and wavy chestnut coloured hair. He pretended to sweep off his hat as Dov strolled back.

'Greetings, Sam,' Dov said. 'How goes it?'

'All good here, but I'd rather be in your pocket while you're toing and froing to the Tsars' domain, however evil they are.'

Dov clapped him on the shoulder but then they heard the landlady in the other room calling something Sophia could not make out.

'We shall close the meeting,' said Rudolf.

They rose slowly. As they left, Milly called: '*Germinal* is out next week. Articles about philosophy and literature, that kind of thing. It might interest you, Sophia. Are you coming next Friday?'

'Of course, I am,' Sophia answered.

'We're planning the concert then. You'll be very welcome.'

A five-minute walk to Wentworth Buildings, with Dov striding beside her, her heart beating uncomfortably fast. She told him about the workshop and the room she'd found. Through the archway, she pointed to her window, saying how lucky she was to find lodgings with a widow who was often away.

'The East Enders at the Sugar Loaf, did you like them?' He was twisting the signet ring around his finger as he spoke, and she glanced down, wondering why.

'I did,' she said soberly. 'So inspirational, and I'm interested in the political material in the newspapers they bring out.'

'I'm away for a while now, Sophia.' His face took on a serious look. She turned her gaze to him, eyes wide. 'But go to the Sugar Loaf when you can. They've taken to you.'

'I shall. But you've only just come back. When will you return?'

'I'm not permitted to say. Soon, I promise you.'

CHAPTER 8

TINGLING WITH WARMTH AND cleanliness, Sophia sat in the anteroom of the Brick Lane Vapour Baths, drying her hair with a towel. Yiddish. A flurry of women chatting and calling to friends, then a sudden familiar voice.

'Sophia. It is Sophia?'

She lifted her gaze.

'Yes? Oh, Mrs Gutenberg.' She beamed.

'So why aren't you in New York, becoming a doctor?'

'A long story, but how marvellous to see you. Are you coming or going, Mrs Gutenberg?'

'Going.'

'Me too, back to Wentworth Buildings.'

'Just round the corner from me. Are you ready?'

Sophia tied a scarf around her damp hair.

'You look like an orthodox girl, with your head covered modestly. It suits you.'

They laughed, Sophia felt a burst of joy that she was with someone she knew, almost – no, definitely – an old friend, whom she had met on the ship coming over. In the street, she exclaimed: 'So good to see you, Mrs Gutenberg. Are you settled with your son and his family?'

'We all have to adapt, Sophia. *Nu,* so tell me.'

About Sasha leaving for America without her, then renting a room and working in a sweatshop — that was easy. Sophia hesitated when it came to the anarchists but burst out: 'I didn't expect such poverty. Do you think it's better in New York?'

Mrs Gutenberg shook her head.

'Depends where you land, I suppose but I've had *mazal,* good luck. The midwife round here has the rheumatism — stairs, you know, and she's happy for me to take over. So, already I've brought three babies into the world.'

'In two weeks?'

'Human nature, Sophia. And that woman who gave birth as we set sail from St Petersburg, I bumped into her in the market.'

'The woman I helped you with? How she even managed to embark on the ship when the Russian Emigration Officers are so severe with their examinations and restrictions, I can't imagine.'

'She was hidden by her black shawl and skirts. To them, we look the same.'

The memory of those first moments sailing away from Russia flashed into Sophia's mind. They had barely left St Petersburg when Sophia had whispered her last goodbye to her mother and followed the rest of the passengers down the steps to the lowest level, where it was so dark, she needed to press her hand to the wall to guide her. She had almost reached the entrance when she heard a crescendo of screams, making her draw a sharp breath. A woman was giving birth, she recognised this at once.

Should she continue? Her compulsion to help was overwhelming. Moving as fast as her skirts would allow, she entered the hold that ran the full length of the ship and stopped. At the farthest end of this tomb-like place, the men stood huddled together, their faces turned away. But a few feet from the entrance, a group of women had made a kind of protective circle to hide the labouring woman. It was from here the turmoil came.

Sophia found herself praying: *This time, this time, please let them survive.*

As she hovered, a sturdy-looking orthodox woman pushed past her. The woman's blonde hair was almost hidden by a scarf looped beneath her ears and tied at the neck.

'Take this to them,' she commanded, thrusting a bucket of hot water into Sophia's hands. 'One of the sailors took pity. The water's hot. Be careful not to spill it. I'm going for more.'

Sophia took the bucket of steaming water, carrying it with both hands, anxious not to slop any over the sides when she reached the circle of women who made way for her. Nearing the labouring woman, Sophia saw that a blanket covered most of her body but an older lady kneeling on the planks beside her had drawn it back and Sophia found herself gazing on the woman's nakedness – and the head of the child crowning.

She inhaled and let down the bucket, which almost tipped over. She retrieved it swiftly, blood draining from her cheeks at the thought of what might happen. Another woman kneeling on the planks, her right arm tight beneath the woman's shoulders, her left beneath the woman's arm, shouted, 'Push. Now. We can see the head.'

'I can't,' whispered the woman in labour. 'I have no strength. It's finished. Pray for me.' Her voice disappeared into the terrible groaning. But the other women kept urging her on, entreating her, doing what Sophia's mother would call 'talking her in', which meant, in Yiddish, believing she could do it.

'Dip the rags in the water,' commanded the first woman, who had returned. She had the palest of blue eyes, while wisps of blonde hair emerged from under the scarf.

Sophia dipped the rags in the water.

'Hand them to me.'

So she worked with the two midwives, if that's what they were, desperate to see the baby born alive and breathing. The woman gave a grunt and a scream. The others prayed and cried and encouraged. Covered in blood, the child slipped onto the sheet. The pale-eyed woman lifted him up and gave him a smack. He began to cry. Someone took him from her and wiped the blood away with wet rags.

All the women called: 'A boy. You have a boy!'

Sophia smiled with relief.

'Quiet. She hasn't finished yet. We must wait for another contraction.'

After some minutes the blonde woman sighed. She pulled back the woman's skirt and pressed her hand low on the belly and the afterbirth, a pulsing mass of blood and veins and skin, emerged. She bent and bit the cord in two with her own mouth, then knotted it close to the baby's tiny red belly. The afterbirth stopped pulsating.

She gave the women a dry look.

'Now you can shout. I was afraid she wouldn't do it,' she added, as though to herself.

'Could you have found a doctor ... if ... one were needed?' Sophia dared to ask.

'What, a ship's doctor, even if there were one?' The woman shook her head. 'Butchers, all of them. They'd have killed her or the little one. Or both.'

A woman dipped more rags into the second bucket and washed the baby briefly. 'The water's getting cold. Enough already. Let him have a warm beginning.'

Another woman ran to the father within the cluster of men, and he shouted, 'It's a boy. A boy, thank God.'

The men returned to their places. Sophia sat down on her folded feather quilt, on the low bunk which marked out her place on the deck. The woman with pale eyes came over. 'Thank you,' she said. 'For a young girl, you did well.'

'Not so young,' Sophia said. 'I think you may have been married at my age.'

'How old are you?'

'Nineteen.'

'Still young, but yes, already I had two children. So how did you manage to stay without fainting away? You saw your mother give birth?'

Sophia shook her head. 'No, but I've helped her at confinements. There are so few of us in Archangelsk where I come from, it was essential. I have brothers, two older, one younger, but I must have been at school when Alexis was born.'

'Still, you did well.' The woman's gaze was serious.

Without a second thought, Sophia told her of her ambition to become a doctor.

The woman stared as though she'd said something immoral. 'What about marriage? Your parents haven't arranged your wedding?' Had she been foolish to tell her this? Her parents were educated, modern people, and she assumed this woman was unlettered, even ignorant. But she had misjudged her, she wasn't so easily shocked. 'I'm Ettie Gutenberg,' the woman continued. 'If you're travelling alone and need anything – any help – come to me. My place is there.'

Mrs Gutenberg went back to her family and Sophia lay down on her *perrona,* her feather-filled eiderdown. Across the deck, the woman who'd given birth sat nursing the baby, peaceful but tired, while the rest of the family were gathered around her.

Thoughts had spun around Sophia's mind, then. What Mrs Gutenberg would have called the Evil Inclination, the *yetzer ha ra* was certainly clamped upon her shoulder. Everyone had one, it was believed, together with the Good Inclination, the *yetzer ha tov,* perched on the other. Always a choice. Well, her Evil Inclination was whispering in her ear, asking her why women must suffer, why they should be punished when they brought a child into the world. Didn't Adam and Eve both eat the apple? So why did men go free? The literature her brother had given her before he left reinforced these burgeoning, rebellious thoughts.

She had other motives for leaving Russia, of course. Not simply to become a doctor, but because of the violence and injustice she loathed, and her yearning to improve things. After a while, when she'd eaten some of the bread and cold meat Papa's friends had given her for the journey, for she didn't know what kind of food would be provided, she made a little tea. There was a samovar at the end of the deck, which they could use. She'd brought lemons, cutting a couple of slices to float in the cup that she'd kept wrapped in paper in her bag. Holding a cube of white sugar between her teeth, she drank the tea, and the sweetness and bitterness combined cheered her, making her feel strong again.

They had met often after this, on the ship.

Mrs Gutenberg touched Sophia's arm, bringing her back to the present. They were reaching the corner.

'Well, this is my turning,' said Mrs Gutenberg.' I'm up there on the third floor. You want my address?' Sophia wrote it on her little pad and gave hers to the midwife. To Sophia's surprise, she gave her a brief kiss on the cheek. 'Don't forget, call by one day when you're not at work.'

Next morning, at the workshop, Mrs Lazarus announced: 'Betsy's husband is dead. Last night. The funeral's this afternoon. Mr Lazarus will go.' Glaring at Sophia, she said, 'You can do her work.'

Sophia sank down onto the stool.

After a few minutes, she pretended to take a few sleeves to Moshe to be pressed. Leaning close, she whispered, 'How will Betsy manage with no money coming in?'

'There's the Board of Guardians, sometimes they help. Not usually the workhouse. Thank God, Jews don't go there.' Softly he described its horrors: separating parents from children, the grinding unpaid work, the hunger, the illness, death. 'I'd rather take my own life than that.'

At the silent dinner table, Sophia asked where Betsy lived. Somewhere near the docks, they told her. Mr Lazarus had the address. She'd already decided to visit Betsy and see what she could do to help.

She found the tiny street close to Millwall Docks. Then, down a narrow dark passageway to a dead end; three small houses built around a courtyard, upper rooms projecting over adjoining buildings. Night seemed to have fallen, it was so shadowy. Going from door to door, with no response, she descended crumbling steps to the basement, trying not to inhale a putrid smell, far worse than that of Batty Street. Now, which one? Holding her breath, she knocked. A little girl appeared, her face dirty and tear-stained, unwashed hair falling over her eyes.

'Is Mama there?' Sophia said.

The child nodded.

'Please say Sophia has come to see her.'

Then it was Betsy, eyes red and swollen. Sophia's heart beat faster to see the ritual tear in Betsy's dress made by the rabbi, a flapping gash of material, exposing her white skin.

'Miss Krichevska, Sophia...' Grabbing Sophia's arm, she dragged her into the room and swayed. '*Oy vey ist mir*,' she cried, her head turning from side to side. 'What will become of me? Of the children?' Flinging her arms around Sophia's neck, she sobbed terribly.

'No, no, Betsy, don't cry like that. It's not good for you. It's not good for the children to see you like this.' Gently, Sophia unlatched her hands. 'Sit here, Betsy. 'She helped her onto an old rush-backed chair and took a sharp breath.

Everywhere she saw clothes, shoes, babies' underwear – on the floor, the bed, the two visible chairs. Wearing only a vest, a boy crouched before the fireplace, digging a stick into the cinders that spilled from the grate to the hearth. Wide-eyed, skinny, white-faced children watched her. Betsy stood up, lifted a sleeping baby from an orange box and cradling him, sat down to weep and rock again. Only the girl who answered the door was dressed.

'Betsy, Betsy,' Sophia put her arm around Betsy's bony shoulders, 'this is the worst time. Things will get better. Look, I brought you milk and bread and some cheese and oranges. For the children. Tell me where to find cups.' Betsy continued to sob. 'Betsy,' Sophia said, grit in her voice. 'Please stop crying. Your children need food. Show me the cups and where I can find water to wash them.'

The little girl found several grimy cups under boxes and on a small table.

'Courtyard, there's a tap on the wall,' Betsy muttered.

Thanking the girl, Sophia found the dripping tap in the littered courtyard. She rinsed the cups until they were cleaner, then returned. 'Come on children, here's a cup of delicious milk for you and Mama too.'

Little by little, she found clothes, dressed the children, tidied the room.

Finally, calmer, Betsy told Sophia her story: they'd come from a shtetl in the Pale of Settlement to make a better life. Her husband had caught tuberculosis. That was it.

'I haven't enough money to live. Better we should be dead.'

'No, no, something will be done,' Sophia reassured her but worried about what that could be. No water, no food, too many children, filth, and bad air — no wonder they looked so underfed, so peaky. Anyone of them could fall ill or worse. It was unbearable.

There was a loud knock on the door, and Mr Lazarus peered in.

'How is she?'

'Bad,' Sophia whispered.

He pushed past Sophia while Betsy hid her face.

'Listen, Betsy,' he said, 'you mustn't worry. The Friendly Society—'

'*Nisht gut*. I couldn't keep up the payments,' she whispered.

He faltered. 'Then we'll see what we can do. The funeral would have been paid for, as for a stone...' he shrugged. To Sophia's astonishment, he muttered, 'See how we live! Just like beggars.' Turning again to Betsy, his voice under control, he said, 'I'll go to the Board of Guardians, make enquiries ... and thank you, Sophia.'

Going home, she passed the Socialist People's Restaurant on Princelet Street. Not wishing to eat alone in her room, she went in. People sat on either side of tables on long benches, the smell of their food enticing. She could barely wait in the queue, she was so desperate to fill her stomach with something, anything. She took her plate of meat and potatoes to the first vacant seat near the counter and people made room for her. Ravenous, she remembered she hadn't eaten a proper meal for two days.

That Friday she arrived late at the Sugar Loaf pub, eager to talk about Betsy, ask what she could do, but Milly called, 'Here's a seat, Sophia. Tell me, have you ever done any fundraising? We always need new ideas.'

'Sorry, I know nothing about that. I shall learn from you.'

'We're discussing the concert in two weeks, and if we have time, the Masked Ball later in the year. You know, *a poiren?*'

'Oh, a peasant ball.' Normally, she would have been thrilled but not this evening, her thoughts still preoccupied with Betsy.

People greeted Sophia and chatted, and the noise rose.

'Now, now, let's discuss this together.' Milly frowned. 'For the concert, I need volunteers to sell tickets, others to sell programmes on the night; then people to control the crowds, and one or two at the literature stall.' Turning to Sam Dreen, whom Sophia had briefly met the week before, she said, 'In the main hall, or the foyer?'

'The literature table will be in the hall. No room at the front.'

'So, everyone, what will you do?' She leaned forward and scanned their faces.

Someone asked if there was a need for people to direct the crowds.

'Absolutely, already tickets are going,' Rudolf said.

'We must sell them all,' Milly added.

People volunteered for this and that, but Sophia hung back, uncertain.

'How about you, Sophia?' Milly's head was down as she noted the replies.

'The English money... I couldn't tell between a farthing and a halfpenny.' She flushed red. 'Can I help with the crowds?'

They laughed, though not in an unkindly way.

'You can help me at the literature stall. Is that all right?'

While Milly was filling her list, Rudolf passed copies of the magazine *Germinal* around the table.

Maybe I will find answers here. Sophia glanced at the pages, noting an article where Rudolf refuted Marxist philosophy, which surprised her. She would certainly read it when she got home. She folded the journal and concentrated on the discussion around the table, and then Milly lifted her head.

'Sophia, would you like to come to the planning meeting for the *Arbeter Fraint* next Thursday?'

'I would love to but there's so much I don't understand.'

'You will learn by being there,' Rudolf said, with a laugh.

'It's this, really.' Opening the journal on the page about Marxism, she held it out. Rudolf leaned over. 'My refutation of Marxism?'

'I discussed this with my brother and with Dov Feldman. Marxism, I mean.'

'Those early articles you wrote, do we have them still?' Milly turned to Rudolf.

'We do,' he asserted. 'I've kept a couple of each edition.'

'The vanity of the man.'

'I am never vain.' He stroked his enormous blonde moustache. Milly raised her eyebrows. 'It's very simple.' He paused, coughed, pushed up his spectacles. 'I reject centralised control – it concentrates power in the hands of a small group of people or even with a single man. Far more dangerous than what preceded it.'

'How do you know?' Sophia said.

'Human nature,' he replied, unexpectedly bitter. 'I saw this in Germany, especially in the rigidity of the Social Democrats, the movement I joined when I first became passionate about change. But their inflexibility and narrowness of thought betray them. What I want to encourage is federations of people who are free, who will work with others in harmony.'

'It sounds beautiful,' Sophia said. 'Can it succeed?'

'Education, understanding, and generosity, above all – that's what is needed. Not hatred, but the opening of hearts and minds to the other. Indeed, I want to encourage the Jewish workers to form unions, to communicate with the English in theirs. We're all workers.'

She lifted her gaze. How brave and inspiring he was. No wonder the others leaned forward, nodding and smiling.

'Come to our place in Dunstan Houses if you're free tomorrow or Sunday. You can read some of the early editions he's kept.' Milly's eyes twinkled.

'I'd love to.'

'Comrades,' Rudolf's voice dropped, 'to return to the concert. My bodyguards will be with me.'

From light to dark, the mood altered.

Milly must have seen the look of surprise on Sophia's face, for she proceeded to explain the reason. 'There's an organisation which loathes immigrants. It stirs up hatred amongst ordinary people. Called the British Brothers League, Sophia, it started about five years ago.

Rudolf continued the story. 'It's gaining adherents amongst the local population, saying immigrants take their jobs, ignore or reject English ways. A local Conservative MP, Captain William Stanley Shaw, is one of the leaders. This makes our work even more difficult.'

'Antisemites,' someone called.

'I didn't know there was antisemitism in England.' Sophia stared around at the other members, a look of horror in her eyes. One or two nodded, their expression grim.

'But Mr William Morris, an important English writer and socialist, thinks as we do, and has written about it in his newspaper *Commonweal*,' Milly hastened to add, seeing her discomfort. But Sophia, there could be violence that night. It's happened several times before. You don't have to be at the forefront immediately.'

'I'm not afraid,' Sophia said. 'Better I should know the facts.'

'Bravo,' they cheered.

With all this, the arrangements for the concert, and the possibility of protest, there'd been no opportunity to raise her anxieties about Betsy, but gripped by their high ideals, with fire in her heart, she felt already that this was where she belonged.

The meeting ended. When they broke up, she asked Mrs Duncan about English lessons and discovered she would be her only pupil for the time being. Would she mind?

'Wonderful. I'll learn even faster. How often can I come?'

'Let's arrange that on Sunday. Probably twice a week, and I'll give you homework,' Mrs Duncan laughed.

'I can't wait.'

CHAPTER 9

THE FOLLOWING AFTERNOON, SHE set off early to find Dunstan Houses in Stepney Green. Dark clouds billowed over the rooftops and drops of rain spattered her face. Maybe the rain, heavier now, confused her, or maybe it was her trepidation at going to the great man's home, but she seemed to be walking miles down Whitechapel Road, unable to see where it became Mile End. Milly had told her to look out for ancient alms houses close to the turning but she couldn't find them. Every kind of stall, from food to knick-knacks, ornaments to pots and pans, edged the pavement. She was forced to step off the kerb into the road itself, holding up her skirts so they wouldn't trail in the orange peel, apple cores, papers, even clots of horse dung, in the gutter.

She passed a formidable grey building: the London Hospital. Then, at last, the alms houses and, crossing the street, she saw a sign for Dunstan Houses. Her heart began to beat quickly. She stopped, staring up at a magnificent building four storeys high. Turrets shaped like the roof of a dacha at each corner, iron balconies with fluted trellises at the centre of each wing where the stairs turned, and girdling the building was an iron fence. It resembled a castle or a church. Stretching away before her were the trees, shrubs and flower beds of Stepney Green. Breathing in the sweet smell of newly mown grass, she heard birds singing. Even the rain falling heavily on her shoulders didn't spoil her delight.

But now to find the Rockers. Milly had told her to look for the Cressy Place Building, along one side. Spurred on by the thought of seeing them, though not a little anxious at the same time, she found the right block and walked steadily up to the fourth floor. Passing identical brown wooden doors, she reached theirs and knocked.

Milly opened it. 'How wet you are. Take off your jacket. I'll hang it over a chair and find a shawl for you.'

Milly and Rudolf lived in one room. A bed against the wall, ancient bookcases crammed with books with many more piled neatly on the floor, and papers stacked high on the bed. Looking across the room, Sophia saw that Rudolf was working at a table beneath a window, his back to them.

'Here's the shawl and some early copies of the *Arbeter Fraint*, 'Milly said, handing Sophia some newspapers. 'You look for Rudolf's articles about Karl Marx, while I make tea.'

She went through another door, returning shortly with two glasses of tea. She passed one to Sophia. 'I don't believe in God, but if I did, this is what I'd thank him for.'

Sitting beside her, Sophia saw the strength of her features, her skin brown as a Gypsy's, the beautiful shining hair plaited and rolled into a bun. They talked for a while, exchanging information about themselves: how working as a seamstress, Milly had managed to bring her family from Zlatopol, in Ukraine, to London, ten years before;

how she'd met Rudolf at an Arbeter meeting; her orthodox parents' horror at their daughter living unmarried with a Catholic. Sophia told her why her family had been forced to flee Kyiv.

'And if I hadn't met Dov on the ship, I wouldn't be sitting here now.'

'What a character. A true revolutionary. Argues fiercely with Rudolf – but we love him.'

A true revolutionary. That description again.

'His room's on the ground floor, overlooking Stanley Green.'

I must have passed it as I came in. Maybe they'll know when he's returning.

As though divining her thoughts, Milly said, 'You never know his movements. I worry always he'll be picked up by the secret police. It's dangerous work.' She folded her lips as though she'd said too much. Sophia inhaled quickly, noting the closed look on Milly's face. *There's so much I want to know about him*, Sophia thought, but at least Milly can answer my questions about Betsy.

'So many in this dreadful situation,' said Milly, when she'd heard the story. 'We try to maintain a fund but with what? Everyone gives their last penny to support the movement. You'll see girls like yourself, thin and hollow-eyed, but still, they come. That's why we must work to break the sweating system.'

Sophia frowned, she wanted something specific that would help.

'At home even the serfs are free, selling their vegetables in the marketplace, but here we're slaves again. I've been here a month, I've seen what's happened to Betsy, I've experienced it, but why? How has this awful thing happened?'

'The sweating system? I was a seamstress before I came. Others were tailors, cobblers, cabinet makers, but for the majority, the religious men who'd only studied in religious academies, the tailoring trade was their only option. Friends and family or people from their village gave them work. How then could they join a union? Even Lazarus, where you work, a so-called master, depends on getting piecework from the big tailors in the West End. He's just as poor as his workers. And the English trade union movement refuses to let us join – they *hate* the Jews. That's how the sweating system came about.'

'I was at school in Kyiv where Papa was a pharmacist. After we were forced to leave and go to the North, he could only rent out boats. I don't recall seeing factories or workplaces of any kind there. Ships, of course. Nor did I know about trade unions. I've so much to learn.'

Milly poured more tea and passed Sophia the sugar.

'Oh, Sophia, you've no idea what a weight was lifted from my mind, from my soul even – although I was very pious when I was young – when I let go of all the ancient restrictions, and dedicated myself to this powerful movement, that people should work and live!'

'Hear, hear,' said Rudolf, emerging from the paper he was writing. 'How about a glass of tea for me? Good to see you, Sophia. Come any time. Ask any questions, we'll welcome them.'

Before she left, Millie asked her if she'd like to help with the leaflets advertising the concert, which would be printed the next morning. Most of the group would be involved, taking the material back to their own flats and collating them there, at about six o'clock, Sunday evening.

'Many live around here: my sister Polly and her husband, Ernst, just down the corridor; the Linders and the Kerkelivitches on the floors below. and Milly and Lazar Sabelisky, he looks something like Rudolf—'

'Like Rembrandt?' Sophia interrupted.

'He does…' She laughed. 'They live in Jamaica Street round the corner.'

'Was Mrs Linder the pretty one?' Sophia tried to match the names and faces of people she'd met at the Sugar Loaf.

'Yes, fair hair, blue eyes. She sits next to Tanya and Alexander Schapiro in the corner. Alexander's a friend and follower of Prince Kropotkin, like Rudolf.'

'So many names to remember,' Sophia said.

'It won't take you long.'

Sophia had a moment of recollection. Ever since Dov had mentioned the word 'commune' on the ship, she'd wondered what it was. 'That's why they call this a commune because you live so closely together.'

'Exactly. Then the young ones, like you, live in various streets in the East End. That's the beauty of it here, like one great family.'

The London Hospital. On the way home, uplifted, Sophia knew she couldn't walk past without going in. Mounting wide steps in the company of others, visitors perhaps, and reaching a grand doorway, she saw smaller entrances on either side of the great doors and took the one to the left.

She found herself in a roomy vestibule opening onto corridors and, she imagined, waiting rooms. Everything gleamed – the floor covered by a light brown shiny material she'd never seen, tall windows letting in the light. Nurses in lilac or blue dresses passed by chatting, their high white hats stiff and starched. She marvelled at their collars, wondering if they were uncomfortable. She inhaled the familiar odours of bleach, and carbolic soap, and was that sulphur? A little spurt of joyful recognition, as she recalled Papa in the pharmacy saying it was used for fumigation. Cleanliness, which delighted her.

An elderly man with a large black beard and wearing a top hat and morning dress, stopped to speak to her. 'May I help you, madam?'

She hastened to find the words in English.

'Thank you. I have come to look.'

'Are you visiting someone? A little late now. Most of the visitors should have left.'

'No, I just see hospital. Is all right?' She hesitated. *My English is dreadful I must study at once.* But he smiled approvingly. She ventured another sentence. 'Is beautiful. Clean.'

He straightened his back.

'Indeed. We're very proud of it.' He paused. 'Though I say it myself, I've had something of a hand in this. Rowland Plumbe, madam.' Seeing that his name meant nothing to her, he added, 'Architect.'

She recognised the word. 'You architect of new building?' For clearly this was brand new. Before he could give a smile of assent, she said, 'Sophia Krichevska.'

They shook hands.

He began to point out innovations, but she could barely follow.

'The floor, you see, is a new substance, linoleum. Easy to clean. Strong.'

'Linoleum. I never see it. And warm?'

'Exactly. We have sanitary towers with baths, water closets and sinks. An X-ray department. And here is the new Maternity department.'

A nurse carrying a tiny baby swaddled in a white shawl, emerged from the door, as he pointed to it.

'Maternity? For new mothers?' This she understood. She took a breath, her heartbeat quickened. *This is where I want to be.* The feeling was so intense, heat rose in her cheeks, and she stopped walking for a moment. Happily, Mr Plumbe didn't notice.

'May I ask where you are from?' He turned to her.

'I am from Ukraine.' Encouraged by his interest, his warmth, and why not? She added, 'One day I want be doctor.'

'Ah.' He raised his eyebrows. 'Why not there?'

'Not many women allowed.'

He nodded, clearly interested.

'Miss Krichevska, did you know we have an excellent school for lady doctors in this very city?' Seeing her frown, unable to grasp what he'd said, he sounded out the words.

'We have the London School of Medicine for Women.'

'A school here for women to be doctor? Where it is?'

'Not too far.' He smiled at her eagerness. 'A little north of Soho, in Hampstead. You have heard of Hampstead?'

She shook her head. 'But I've been once to Soho, to see friends. So, this school in place called Hampstead? How I go there?'

'I usually get my driver to take me,' he reflected. 'I think you get the horse-drawn tram to Soho, but then perhaps you take the Underground. Would you like me to enquire?'

'Oh yes, please.'

A woman in a black dress, wearing a tiny rose-shaped cap with frills, marched down the corridor and stopped beside them. The imperious look in her gaze made Sophia step back.

'Excuse me,' she said, her voice sharp; giving Sophia a cursory look, she briefly closed her eyes as though shutting her from her sight. Opening them, she rasped: 'I need to speak to Mr Plumbe. Urgently.'

'Matron, how do you do?'

Ignoring his formality, she said, 'What I want to tell you is…'

'When Matron wants something, you have no choice but to attend. A moment, Matron.' Clasping Sophia's hand, he said, 'Delighted to meet you, Miss Krichevska. I hope your friends can tell you how to find the school, and one day I'll see you here, in a white coat, a stethoscope around your neck.'

The Matron stared. He lifted his hat, then followed the woman along the corridor.

At the flat, she found Mrs Vine asleep on the settee. Opening the door must have wakened her for she stirred and said, 'Sophia? Everything all right?'

'Yes, Mrs Vine. Actually, wonderful.'

'So, tell me.'

Sophia sat beside her. Excitement about the medical school spilled over. 'Did you know…?'

Mrs Vine listened, saying little. Finally, she said, 'Would be very good to have a lady doctor. Some women dislike a man touching them other than their husband. They won't go to the hospital. Especially the older ones.'

In her room, Sophia thought, God or fate has led me to this place, to the London School of Medicine for Women, but what about joining Sasha in New York? What about seeing Mama and Papa again? She gazed out of her window. And Dov, what would he think?

CHAPTER 10

No, THEY WERE TOO kind. She couldn't possibly come again for lunch at Hannah Leah's, but maybe she would drop by in the afternoon. It was good not to be alone on the Sabbath. But what did she hear when she approached the basement door? *Singing.* A rich tenor voice, fluting children's voices. Opera with a Yiddish accent? She knocked softly, Hannah Leah, a finger to her lips, a smile in her eyes, opened the door and beckoned her in.

Aaron, the boys, and even little Annie, continued to sing until they'd finished the aria. Before the adults could begin to applaud, the boys grabbed at Aaron's waistcoat and sleeve, shouting, 'What did you bring us, Uncle Aaron? What is it today?'

'I promised if you sang the entire aria, you boys would have gobstoppers and there'd be barley sugar for the little one. Here you are.'

The boys shoved the gobstoppers into their mouths until their cheeks bulged. Hannah Leah broke off a piece of the barley sugar stick for Annie.

'That was marvellous.' Sophia grinned at Aaron. 'How did they learn it?'

'He just sang it over and over and we learned it quickly,' said Ralphie, the older one.

'What's the name of the music?'

'*Mi chiamano Mimi*, from *La Bohème*,' said Aaron. 'You know it?'

'A little. My mother always said it would be wonderful to attend the opera in Petersburg, but it never happened.'

Taking a chair, he asked Sophia how she was getting on. 'Moshe told me you found work with Lazarus.'

'I was lucky,' she hesitated. 'Long hours, but you know already.'

'You've also discovered the Sugar Loaf pub?'

'I was there the other night for the concert planning evening. I'm helping with the literature stall.' She paused. 'Tell me, if the concert's on Saturday evening, how do people buy tickets when it's forbidden to spend money on the Sabbath? I forgot to ask.'

'They sell them during the week. People don't feel they're breaking the rules that way.' Aaron laughed.

'We're all going to the concert next week,' Ralphie piped up, and the boys exchanged excited grins.

'Are you singing?'

'I want to, but Mama says we're too young.'

'You have wonderful voices. I hope you will become opera singers when you're older.'

'We shall.'

To Hannah Leah: 'I didn't know you supported the movement.' She threw her a questioning look.

'We aren't members, it's impossible with young children, but like everyone around here, we go to the concerts or whatever fundraisers we can afford.'

Aaron was turning his glass of tea in his hand.

'I've been thinking, Sophia, that it's always very crowded and hard to get a seat. Would you like to go with me?'

He didn't finish, but a touch of anxiety in his gaze reminded her of talk at the Sugar Loaf last week when Dov mentioned the British Brothers who hated foreigners. Perhaps he was thinking of them. She wasn't frightened of going alone but it was new, he was kind and she should accept. For a brief second, she wondered what Hannah Leah might think, perhaps it was improper? But Hannah Leah was beaming as though she approved.

'Thank you, it would be good to go together.'

They left at around four o'clock, walking slowly up the street and she found herself saying, 'I never expected there would be such antisemitism in England. Supposed to be so tolerant. What's happened? That's one of my myriad questions…' She gave him a rueful smile.

'Antisemitism? My father would say that antisemitism will never die, that there's no escape. I don't think that way. Like Rudolf, I believe that we can change things.' At the corner, he said, 'By the way, I'll be singing at the concert. But that's not why I suggested we went together. Not at all.'

Was there a look in his eye that made her take a breath? No, she was imagining it and at once she thought of Dov. Quickly she said, 'See you next week. I'm looking forward to it, especially to hearing you sing.'

She'd never seen or heard anything like this. A hundred and fifty, maybe two hundred Jewish people all together in one place, talking, shouting across Crown Hall, kissing friends, leaning over seats to ask a question, and in the aisles, two or three debating something political she thought – on the one hand, on the other – as though they were still in religious academies. Like one enormous family. The noise, the laughter, the warmth encircled her and joy flowered in her heart. The savoury sweet smell of fish balls, the tang of oranges blended with the homely smell of sweat in the warm evening. Women were unpacking paper bags, passing food to their children.

'What are they doing, Milly?'

Looking up from counting the change, Milly laughed. 'So they shouldn't be hungry while waiting.'

'It's always food...' Sophia returned the grin, then admired the literature table. 'You've done everything, already.'

The Workers Friend newspaper, the magazine Germinal, pamphlets, and even classics translated into Yiddish. She took up Anna Karenina. The very edition she'd brought with her, still in her trunk together with La Dame aux Camélias, now in translation. She opened the book and sat down. Reluctantly, she closed the book and returned it to its corner on the table. Milly went backstage, leaving her alone when an older man came over. After a moment he bought a copy of Germinal.

'I'm so sorry, I don't know how to do the change yet,' she told him.

'How long have you been here?'

'About a month now.'

'It will come very quickly. I'll show you.' He counted out the change, and she watched and thanked him. Lifting her eyes, she gave a little start, took a shocked breath. Two people walked down the aisle towards the front row: Dov and Rosa.

Dov and Rosa. He didn't tell me he was back.

Her heart lurched when she saw Dov remove Rosa's shawl with such a familiar touch, Rosa placing her fingers on his mouth. Sophia averted her gaze as the joy, the excitement, the wonder of being here fell away. She glanced over to them, wanting and not wanting to see what they did. Dov was talking to everyone, clapping people on the back, laughing, while Rosa sat, eyebrows raised, an amused look in her eyes. Sophia pressed her hands to her heart as though to protect it, then took a shuddering breath.

'Leave the literature table, Sophia. Come and join the others in your seat. It is between mine and Aaron's.' Milly's busy voice dragged Sophia from her thoughts, and she took her seat on the front row with the Arbeter Frainters.

I mustn't let it upset me. I'm here with these wonderful people. I want to be with them.

Sam Dreen ran up the stairs and walked to the front of the stage, a row of chairs behind him, a piano to one side. Rolling paper into a cornet, he bellowed through it: 'Ladies and gentlemen, friends, *chaverim,* we're ready to begin our wonderful concert, so *please* take your seats.'

The hubbub continued. He banged the coiled paper on the piano keys, a cacophony of noise and at last, they fell quiet.

'Comrades, we're delighted you're with us tonight. The concert will be superb and we'll enjoy it tremendously, but first, I want to introduce someone who needs no introduction, our comrade and leader, Rudolf Rocker—.'

A great roar of approval. Rudolf walked to the front of the stage. They shouted his name again and again. Their whistles, their clapping, their stamping, and the higher voices of the women all blended into a deafening tumult of welcome. Three heavily built men stood behind him, eyes scanning the hall. Bodyguards. Surprise jolted Sophia from her reverie. *Would something happen?*

Rudolf lifted his hands.

'Thank you, my friends, thank you. By coming here, you are supporting our cause. You know we work together to free everyone from the scourge of the sweatshop system. Together, we will build and strengthen the Jewish trade unions – some indeed are effective already. The cabinet makers, stick makers, and bakers, you've already achieved better conditions for your members. We want this for everyone, especially those of you in the tailoring trade.'

More cheers and whistles.

'Please buy the literature. Buy *Germinal*, collated and printed by younger members. I write the editorial and oversee the articles, so they don't offend the sensibilities of our elders and betters…'

'Who does he mean?' Sophia asked Milly.

'The rabbis, the big established families.'

'Offend them. Let them know how we live.' A woman cried.

'We will. But now let the concert begin!'

It seemed that every household in the East End had a fiddler. Then, jugglers, an accordionist, comedians whose somewhat crude Yiddish jokes made the crowd roar, and finally, it was Aaron.

Sophia clutched her hands tight in her lap.

'Comrades,' he said, 'I shall sing you arias from the great Italian opera, *La Bohème*. It's the story of Mimi, a poor seamstress living in poverty in Paris. She meets Rodolfo, a student. They fall in love but cannot marry because she is dying from consumption.'

Such a sigh from the audience who knew only too well the dreadful outcome of tuberculosis.

Aaron sang, and they listened, his voice very fine and moving. Sophia didn't know Italian and guessed the others didn't either, but its poignancy brought tears to her eyes. Women wept quietly, men blew their noses. Aaron reached the end of the song and they shouted for more.

'Thank you. Here's something more cheerful from *Cavalleria Rusticana*.'

When he finished, they applauded, whistled, and stamped their feet, and he bowed.

'Wonderful,' Sophia whispered when he joined them. 'You have a marvellous voice.'

'You're very kind,' Aaron smiled. Taking the seat at the end of the row beside the literature stall, he smoked a cigarette with an air of relief.

During the interval, Sophia pretended to tidy the pamphlets as her thoughts continued to swirl. *He didn't tell me when he was coming back, and he's with her. But he promised nothing. Why am I so upset?* She straightened her shoulders when she saw Dov approaching the table, Rosa trailing behind him.

'Good evening, Milly and Sophia. Sold any good books lately?'

'We've done very well with the newspaper, Dov. Good to see you again. And how are you, Rosa?'

There was a touch of sharpness in Milly's tone that made Sophia glance towards her, but Rosa only said, 'Well, thank you, Milly.'

'They've caught you in their honey pot, Sophia. A worker already.' Dov grinned.

Why was he was talking this way? Hadn't he told her to go back to the Sugar Loaf pub, that they'd taken to her? She looked down at the literature, searching for some kind of response.

'All your fault, Dov Feldman,' she said, lifting her head. 'If we hadn't met on the ship, I wouldn't be here, would I?'

'We'll never know,' he answered. 'Another radical thinker might have brought you along. Who knows what's in our destiny?' He leaned over the table, smiling at Milly. 'I hear Prince Kropotkin, that great radical, is here tonight.'

'Rudolf will bring him after the interval.'

'I must see him.' Dov gripped one hand with the other.

'Why do you want to see him?' Rosa frowned. 'A member of the aristocracy?' She pulled at his arm as though to restrain him and gave him a disparaging look.

'He's renounced his princely line. He's a great man, imprisoned in Petersburg and then Siberia for the socialist cause. I revere him, Rosa.' He nudged up his shoulder to loosen it from her grasp. 'You can do what you like.'

'I shall speak to Rudolf over there.' Rosa tossed her head. 'Who are those men he's talking to, Milly?'

'The young one is a journalist with the *Jewish Chronicle*. The older one is from the Yiddish newspaper. Rudolf believes he can get them on our side, but they think we cause sedition and mayhem. I keep telling him he's wasting his time. He won't listen.'

Rosa walked away.

Sophia had listened to Milly's angry exchange with surprise; she watched Rosa greet Rudolf, smiling when he introduced her to the journalists. Sophia returned her gaze to Dov who was watching Rosa, a hard look in his eyes.

'She always seeks the limelight,' he muttered.

Milly looked from one to the other, cleared her throat and in a brighter tone, said, 'And how are you, rabble-rouser? When did you get back?'

'Two days ago.' *Only two days.* It was odd, but Sophia felt better. 'Rudolf has his bodyguards tonight, I see,' in an undertone.

Taking a copy of the *Arbeter Fraint,* Milly came closer, and in the same tone: 'We didn't know whether it would be the Brothers or the Bessarabian Tigers.'

'Who are they?' Sophia said.

'A gang. Bad Jews. Extortionists, always ready to do anything illegal for money. The police can't touch them because the people are afraid. We're not all angels...'

Dov turned to Aaron, still sitting down, and clapped him on the shoulder.

'So how goes it, my old comrade? You sang most movingly.' He pretended to wipe his eyes.

'Barbarian! Cossack!' Aaron pulled his shoulder away. 'A black bear, that's what you are. But I'll allow you to sit with us if only for news of the old country.'

'Still fighting. Uprisings everywhere.' Dov took a chair and, leaning in, Sophia caught him saying, 'On the ships, crews are challenging the ships' masters, the Tsar's regime…' He whispered something, then stood up. 'I must find Peter Kropotkin.'

'He's ill, Dov. His doctor told him not to come. Don't tire him out.'

Then it was the second half.

The stage door opened. An older man with an immense white beard, a round shining bald head, and wearing a white shirt with loose sleeves and tall peasant boots, his whole face alight with pleasure, slowly climbed the steps, accompanied by Rudolf. The audience cheered and cheered, then fell silent. Refusing a chair, he advanced to the front. One of the Arbeter Frainters leapt onto the stage to translate his words into Yiddish.

'Comrades, comrades, thank you for this great welcome. Thank you for supporting this great movement. We have marched together. We have fought together. So many here, I recognise. And many more would be here if they could.'

'Twenty-five thousand of us marched with you to Hyde Park Corner!' someone shouted.

'A blessed multitude. We marched to protest about the pogroms in Kishinev. We met together to set up the Anarchist Federation. But today, I tell you of the culmination of our efforts,' he paused, beaming round at the audience. '*The Workers' Friend Club*, where Jew and Gentile will come together for education, entertainment, and to further our political objectives. Our friend Rudolf and the Workers' Friend Group have been planning this for months. It will soon be a reality.'

Delirious applause, but then Prince Kropotkin swayed a little. Rudolf caught his arm and supported him. They spoke together. With a heavy sigh, the Prince took the chair.

'Peter has asked me to continue,' Rudolf said. 'I'll be brief: the club will open next year in Jubilee Street, but it can't happen without you. We don't need money – well, of course we do.' Laughter from the audience. 'But today, I ask for volunteers to sign a list Milly has at the literature desk.'

She jumped to her feet, waving a sheet of paper like a flag.

'Carpenters, cabinet makers, upholsterers, can you help? We need your skills to build chairs and tables, desks and bookcases. We need painters and decorators. We shall provide the materials.'

'When do you want us?' another voice called.

'After the Jewish festivals, September, October, but it would be good to have names now, provisionally. Thank you, comrades.'

He helped Kropotkin to stand; he waved, and the audience responded. Sophia felt her heart expand and rejoice. A word from the psalms, she thought, but that's how he inspires us. Leaning on Rudolf's arm, Kropotkin made his slow way through the stage door, followed by the bodyguards.

'A holy man.' Sophia turned to Aaron. 'I hadn't expected anyone like that here, I don't know why.'

'He is like Tolstoy. Both great men.' Aaron nodded soberly.

Sophia pondered the sacrifices made by people who dedicated themselves to a great cause. Would she ever be capable of such single-mindedness? A little voice within her said: *You want to be a doctor? Then you will.*

On the stage, fiddles were tuning up, a clarinet player joined them; they began to play wedding music full of joy and melancholy, Gypsy music, Hungarian and Ukrainian folk music, Yiddish music all in one. Like everyone in the room, Sophia's heart overflowed with longing for her family, her homeland. She forgot Dov, she forgot Rosa. The people clapped their hands and sang together. Then came *The Marseillaise*, the anthem of revolution. The entire audience stood and sang whether they knew the words or not.

Leaving Crown Hall with Aaron, Sophia noticed two or three local men in caps, standing across the way and holding up placards, the words 'Immigrants Go Home. Scum. Layabouts' scrawled upon them. With a shock, she observed their scowling expressions, their hostility. Sophia stared but Aaron spoke to her in an undertone, 'The British Brothers. Don't even give them the benefit of our interest. Best to ignore them.'

This rather diminished the joy she'd felt during the concert.

But I will face everything to be a New Woman.

CHAPTER 11

SOPHIA HAD COME TO like Mr Lazarus, to admire him for his patience with his wife. Two weeks ago he had beamed round at the workers and announced that he had obtained an order from a West End master tailor for five dozen waistcoats, and everyone had shouted, *Mazal Tov!*

'They are for Rosh Hashanah but it's late this year, almost the end of September. If we do well, please God, there'll be more work for us all.'

Sophia had been promoted to a treadle machine along with the men. But with an irony of fate, while Mr Lazarus had finally achieved his ambition, his good luck seemed short-lived because his wife was definitely and hugely pregnant. Sophia recalled how she'd wondered if Mrs Lazarus might have been pregnant the day she'd come looking for work. Now, in early September, Mrs Lazarus had grown large, she waddled with splayed legs, sometimes gasping as she held onto her chair, her hand on her stomach or at her back, and while she usually worked with fierce intent, she kept stopping the machine, her face crinkled into an expression of pain, fear and even anger.

Sophia asked Moshe about this when they went out, for the men to smoke and for her to inhale some fresh air, he reminded her that he and his family had come here only a few months back and he didn't have an answer. Overhearing their conversation, Mr Mendelsohn said that when Lazarus and his wife lived in Poland, probably twenty years ago, he understood she had lost three children at birth, so today when she must be well over forty, it wasn't surprising she was both horrified and afraid. Even refusing to have a midwife or doctor to assist her when it was her time, so his wife had told him.

Sophia's eyes widened.

'That's absolutely when she needs someone.'

'She's, what can I say, a very stubborn woman. Don't waste your breath.'

Yesterday Mrs Lazarus had not been in the workshop. Today Mr Lazarus was waiting at the door, his hair standing out like a star, pulling at his beard, his face stricken with anxiety. It seemed he was waiting for Sophia to arrive.

'Mrs Lazarus is not well,' he told her, 'and there's still work to do on the waistcoats. Have you ever sewn buttonholes, Sophia?'

His expression was so anguished, Sophia wanted to reach out and touch his arm, but she placed her wicker basket under the pegs and hung up her hat and coat. She had talked to Ettie about this impossible situation with Mrs Lazarus, and Ettie said she would come to assist, but only if the woman agreed. By her grim expression, Sophia knew that without a midwife or doctor, the outcome might be disastrous. She'd decided she would tell Mrs Lazarus about Ettie, though not yet. On a practical level for their livelihoods, it was essential they finish the consignment in time.

'I'll do my very best. I have sewed buttonholes by hand but not by machine. I'm sure I can do this.'

'There are some scraps of material you'll find in the cupboard beside my wife's chair. Use them to practice on.'

'What an excellent idea.'

He let out a sigh of relief, almost a groan.

'How is she?'

He stiffened, his face took on a look of alarm.

'She needs rest, that's all.'

Once Mr Lazarus had left the workroom, presumably to see to his wife, Sophia heard the men talking quietly together. Moshe turned from the pressing table and shook his head, then held up his hand as though to discourage her from jumping in too soon.

Settled at her sewing machine, she felt the weight of Mr Lazarus's expectation on her. She knew the finish of every garment mattered especially to the West End master tailors. If her work was poor, there would be no more orders; so much depended on her skill to take over what Mrs Lazarus evidently could not complete.

She straightened her shoulders and leaning forward, with the uttermost concentration, practised the fine movement necessary, the foot control the treadle required, the deft turn of material so that she didn't sew too far, too fast. After half an hour, holding up her various attempts to the light, she'd finally got the knack and had sufficient mastery of the machine to make satisfactory attempts. *I'd better show them to him.* But raising her eyes, she saw Mr Lazarus' shears lying abandoned on the bench. He had not returned.

Without consulting the men, Sophia slipped into the kitchen, closing the door behind her. At once she heard soft moans and strangled cries coming from the bedroom through a doorway to her left. She frowned.

So her time had come, Mrs Lazarus' labour had started. The clatter of sewing machines, the hiss of flat irons and the thick walls must have blanketed the sounds until now. Sophia hesitated but recalling how she'd become Ettie's handmaid over the past few weeks, assisting at several births when she could, thrilled to be learning about a woman's body, how it worked, when it did, to bear and produce new life, she crossed the kitchen and knocked softly on the bedroom door. Perhaps this was the time to tell them. Mr Lazarus opened it, his gaze ever more harried and fearful.

'Who's that?' Mrs Lazarus' voice was hoarse, angry.

He closed the door behind him.

'I don't want her to know you're doing the buttonholes. She'll get more agitated but I promised I would complete the order by the end of this week.' He pulled at his hair.

Sophia took a breath, resisted what was the end of her tongue and decided it was too soon to say anything about Ettie, only when the time was right. *I'll know when it is.* Instead, she showed him the rows of neatly sewn buttonholes on the scraps of blue and gold material.

'What do you think, Mr Lazarus?'

'Yes, they'll do.' He glanced back, a guilty expression in his eyes as though he'd betrayed his wife by allowing a hand to do her special work.

'*Oy vey ist mir,*' Sophia heard, followed by another desperate groan and a series of stifled cries.

I'll say something now.

'Do you know about Ettie Gutenberg, the midwife who has taken over in these streets? I met her on the ship, I help her when I can. She's—.'

'No. No. No midwife, no doctor.'

She heard the desperation behind this assertion for his voice cracked and he furrowed his brow. It wasn't a normal response, but it was clear he couldn't gainsay his wife in this most intimate of circumstances.

'Shall I carry on with the buttonholes?' She stepped back.

He nodded. Sophia thought she saw tears in his eyes, as though dreading what was about to happen.

In the workshop, she found the remaining waistcoats piled on a far bench, beside Moshe's station. She whispered what had happened and he shook his head.

'Never get between a husband and wife, my mother used to say, and it's the best advice you can have.'

At first, Sophia was nervous about her task, but she soon got into the rhythm. She loved to sew for it helped her to think, freeing up her imagination, and now was no exception. With her head down, hands moving the material deftly, while her feet controlled the treadle, she thought about the three months since she'd arrived in England and how her life had been transformed.

There was never a moment to spare: there were the newspaper and magazine planning sessions on Thursday evenings, which she attended whenever she could. Then Friday nights at the Sugar Loaf pub, where she learned so much from Rudolf and the other Arbeter Frainters. There were English lessons and homework from *The Progressive English Grammar, with Exercises*, which she loved and was racing through, eager to start the second book, even though it was forty years old, but as her teacher said: English grammar is English grammar, so what's the difference?

She'd earned money, and been fortunate most weeks to get work with Mr Lazarus. *Although I'm not earning enough to buy a ticket for myself, let alone for Mama and Papa*. She felt a pang of guilt, yet this didn't seem to matter so much. So long as they were safe in Archangelsk, hundreds of *versts* away from the pogroms, she didn't need to worry about them. And finally, she was helping Ettie, whenever she could.

I'm so busy, I've almost forgotten about going to America. Why didn't this matter? It's essential to my plan for becoming a doctor, she thought, but it's gone underground. Then she remembered the London Hospital, her conversation with the architect, and vowed she would seek out the college for women doctors when she next had free time. Go there, make enquiries.

There was one sadness, although she couldn't honestly call it that – she'd hardly seen Dov, and when she had, he was with Rosa, coming occasionally to the Sugar Loaf pub on Friday, always ready to argue with Rudolf, to lighten the discourse with his quips and jokes. Every time, she'd felt her heart beat faster, her face flush, and she'd averted her eyes so that he didn't suspect her feelings. It was good, she decided, that he was mainly with the West End revolutionaries. This didn't prevent her from sighing.

In the workshop, they began to hear hoarse sounds coming from the bedroom, the groans becoming louder.

Then Mr Lazarus' voice, speaking in a reassuring tone although what he said was muffled.

Sophia determined to ignore all events in Mrs Lazarus' bedroom and turn her attention to the article Milly had asked her to write for *Germinal*. This way, she would control her compulsion to tell Mrs Lazarus about Ettie. The article's title: *A Greener's First Impressions of the Sweating Industry*. She had felt so honoured to be asked for a contribution and had accepted eagerly. But now words and phrases filled her mind and they weren't about being a greener, but about the women she'd met with Ettie, the dreadful conditions they endured giving birth. The squalor, the dirt under the beds, the grimy sheets, because it was so difficult to wash them in the public wash house, the myriad little children whom Ettie would shoo away, so they wouldn't watch their mother writhe. It was a wonder to Sophia that any of them survived, mothers or babies.

Mr Lazarus came back into the workshop. They continued to work. The groans became louder and louder, piercing the walls. The men glanced up, then shrinking into themselves, bent over their work. Sophia folded her lips, resolved to concentrate, for her stomach was twisting with the desire to run into Mrs Lazarus. At lunchtime, Lazarus asked them not to go into the kitchen. They could eat their lunch sitting beside their machines, provided they were careful not to drop any crumbs or morsels of cheese or meat on their work.

Afterwards, when they went down for a breath of air, the men smoked in silence, probably wishing they were miles away.

Around five o'clock, the screaming began.

Mr Lazarus dropped the shears. He covered his eyes with his hands and Sophia saw tears trickling between his fingers.

This is dreadful. A midwife, any midwife, should be with Mrs Lazarus at this moment, assessing her, giving her something to dull the pain, making sure the baby is all right.

Without saying a word, Sophia grabbed her jacket and hat and slipped out of the door. She ran until she reached Ettie's building. Up the stairs, along the corridor to the end, she knocked frantically on the door. When Ettie opened it, she said, 'She's in labour. Screaming, but still she won't see anyone. She's in a bad way.'

In the workshop, the men sat frozen, embarrassed and shocked to be party to this private anguish, unsure whether to leave or wait for Lazarus to tell them to go. Seeing Sophia, followed by Ettie Gutenberg, they uttered a communal sigh of relief.

'Mrs Gutenberg, we hope she'll let you in,' Moshe said.

'Oh, she will,' said Mrs Gutenberg. 'Through there?'

They went into the kitchen, and without knocking, Ettie marched into the bedroom, with Sophia close behind. Such a sight of disarray met their eyes. It was dark, the curtains drawn as though to hide something evil. Bed sheets and cover were strewn on the floor while Mrs Lazarus lay bathed in sweat, her face glistening in the light from the open door, her nightdress ruffled up, her exposed rotund body barely covered by the sheet. Arms stretched up behind her, she clung to the bed head with both hands and as she writhed, the bed clanked and shook. A chamber pot revealed beneath the bed needed to be emptied. A stink of sweat mingled with urine filled the air, and Sophia guessed the window had been shut, to hide any sound. Mr Lazarus paced up and down, his eyes wide with terror.

Ettie gazed around then walked over to the bed. Leaning close to Mrs Lazarus, she spoke softly to her in Yiddish. There was no response. She repeated whatever it was. Eventually, Mrs Lazarus opened her eyes and seemed to be trying to focus. For some minutes, she lay almost still, then letting go of the bed head, she clung to the sheets that swirled around her. Ettie's words, whatever they were, had penetrated her anguish, and Sophia longed to know what she'd said, for slowly, the woman nodded, then closing her eyes, began to groan once more.

'Mr Lazarus, your wife has agreed for me to stay. Please open the curtains and the window. We need light and fresh air.'

With a stunned look on his face, he followed her instructions.

'Thank you. We need to see what we're doing. Go to the workroom, Mr Lazarus,' Ettie said, lifting her gaze. 'Tell the men to leave. Even if they haven't finished, they'll come back another day. Then find newspapers and towels for Sophia.' Turning to her, she said, 'Boil the kettle and heat up the shabbes urn. And Mr Lazarus, it will be better if you stayed in the kitchen or went for a walk. This is women's work. Oh, perhaps you can empty this chamber pot?'

Such a look of relief and gratitude filled his eyes as he stumbled with it towards the door. 'I can't thank you enough,' he muttered.

'Thank me when it's all over. Now, go!'

Straightening the sheets, Ettie bent to examine Mrs Lazarus, while Sophia hurried Mr Lazarus out of the room.

Then together, moving Mrs Lazarus to one side and the other, Sophia and Ettie covered the mattress with newspapers, spreading upon them the roller towel Sophia had unhooked from the kitchen door. Mr Lazarus had given her two or three threadbare towels he'd found beneath the sink but this was sturdy. The movement, the reassurance in Ettie's hands and voice had its effect already. The screaming stopped but the groaning carried on.

From then until nine o'clock, Ettie worked with her patient, asking Sophia to make infusions of chamomile or rosemary tea, gently massaging Mrs Lazarus' back and stomach with a mixture of oils she always carried. It was a long harsh struggle and it seemed they were not getting anywhere.

Ettie looked up. 'You must go home, eat something, Sophia. I guess you haven't had anything since one o'clock. I don't want you fainting away in front of me.'

'I'm all right.'

'No, you're pale. Maybe there's something in the kitchen here. Besides, Mr Lazarus needs food.'

He was sitting slumped over the table. On the stove, Sophia discovered a large saucepan of cold barley soup. She heated it up.

'We both need to eat. Please try a bowl of your wife's soup.'

'I can't eat while she's suffering.'

'You must. Don't give way. Even though I don't feel like it, I'll join you.'

'What about the midwife?'

'I've taken her some tea. She never eats while she's with a woman in labour, not until the baby is born. It's as though she's in harmony with them. I think that's why she's such a marvellous midwife.'

Around midnight, when Sophia wondered if Mrs Lazarus could take any more, she reached the critical stage.

'Now,' shouted Ettie, '*push*.'

It was awful to watch. Mrs Lazarus contorted her face into a terrible grimace, she grunted and shouted, but then suddenly, the baby emerged. A soft white silent body. Ettie lifted the baby –a girl – with a look of despair. There was no response. The head lolled on the baby's thin neck. Sophia, so close to the bed, could see her white limbs, soft and floppy. No breath, no heartbeat. Sophia stared, her mouth open, her heart pounding. She noticed that Ettie glanced at Mrs Lazarus with a frown, for now, she too lay still, motionless as her child.

'Sophia, tell Mr Lazarus to get Doctor Feldstein at once. His wife needs an injection which only a doctor can give.' She lifted the baby from the bed. Folding her lips, she said, 'This baby must live. Bring me the two washing-up bowls, fill one with warm water, not too hot, the other with cold water from the tap. You've heated the urn? Bring it in also. We need towels or anything you can find.'

Sophia ran into the kitchen. Mr Lazarus was asleep by the fire, and she shook his shoulder.

'Mr Lazarus, wake up. You must get the doctor. Right away. Mr Lazarus, stir yourself.'

She didn't tell him about the baby.

Slowly he came to, his face contorting into a look of fear when he recalled where he was and what was happening. 'The doctor?'

'Yes,' she shouted. 'Go now.'

He slung on his jacket, and she heard him walking slowly downstairs, picking up speed as he reached the outer door. More towels, but where could they be? She found a thin one with ragged edges, in the bottom drawer. Running into the workroom, she remembered there was some sheeting where she'd found the scraps of material for buttonhole practice. Back to the kitchen, the urn was bubbling on the kitchen worktop. As quickly as she could, she filled the *fleishik* bowl with hot water, the *milkich* bowl with cold, then carried them into Ettie, running back for the urn, the towels and the sheets.

What Ettie did would remain with her forever.

Ettie lifted the baby from the bed and thrust her into the bowl of cold water, then into the hot. Next, urging Sophia to spread out a towel at the end of the bed, she laid the tiny limp figure on the towel and began to massage her chest, both hands encircling her body, on and on, for what seemed hours.

Shocked beyond speech, Sophia could barely whisper, 'Ettie, what are you doing? The baby is stillborn.'

'I must try.'

Like some crazy juggler, she hurried the child between the two bowls, now plunging her into cold water, now into the steaming one. Sweat ran down Ettie's face and her sleeves were sodden. Once, when the baby almost slipped out of her hands, Sophia saw her lips moving, as though in prayer. Yet she marvelled at how Ettie persevered, rubbing the child with a rough towel, crushing and releasing the little chest with both hands, trying to get breath into the body.

The door opened.

Doctor Feldstein arrived, raised his eyebrows at what he saw, but saying nothing, took off his hat and coat, and approached Mrs Lazarus, motionless on the bed. Behind him, Mr Lazarus slumped against the doorpost.

'She needs pituitrin, Doctor,' Ettie said, breathing heavily as she pressed the little chest.

And then, as she spoke, like a tiny miracle, the baby gave a short, sharp heave. Then another, and another. A bubble of mucus came from one minute nostril and the baby gasped, deeper and deeper.

Then, a cry.

A smile of relief, even of triumph, flickered across Ettie's face.

'You've saved her. Ettie, you have *saved* her.' Overwhelmed by joy and amazement, tears streamed down Sophia's cheeks.

'Thank God. Now we need something warm to cover her.'

'I saw a shawl hanging on the door. I'll get it.' Sophia ran past Mr Lazarus staring in shock at the baby and dragged the shawl from the hook. Ettie had dried the baby with the remaining towel and now took the shawl from Sophia, winding it carefully around the tiny body. Holding her close to her chest, Ettie turned her attention to the doctor, her gaze anxious.

He glanced up, then having broken the ampoule, with a hypodermic syringe he injected some kind of liquid into Mrs Lazarus's arm. He massaged her chest at first, gently, then ever more firmly. She too stirred, beginning to take deeper and deeper breaths, until she opened her eyes just as the baby gave another tiny cry. The doctor nodded towards the baby, a look of admiration in his eyes.

'Is that my baby?' Raising herself from the bed with the help of her elbows, Mrs Lazarus stared with vague eyes, as though in a wonderful dream.

Mr Lazarus dropped to his knees and wept.

'Mazal tov, Mr and Mrs Lazarus. You have a beautiful daughter,' said the doctor putting away his instruments. He circled the bed to speak to Ettie. 'So you're the midwife I've been hearing about. Where, may I ask, did you learn to do this?'

'In Brest-Litovsk, where I began. It was a young courageous doctor who showed me what to do. I'm very glad it worked tonight. I must admit, I had my doubts.' Ettie inhaled deeply, straightened her scarf which had become dislodged by her efforts, and said, 'I think a cup of tea would be in order. Although we haven't finished yet, have we, Doctor Feldstein?'

'I'll stay a few more minutes, Mrs...?'

'Mrs Gutenberg. Perhaps it would be wise, for we need to make sure everything has come away. Well, Mrs Lazarus, would you like to hold your baby for a moment? Then your husband can take her, for we have more work to do.' She turned to Sophia. 'You've done well, but go home now and sleep.'

Sophia was reluctant to leave, but a sudden weariness weighed down her limbs and she found herself leaning against the wall to stay upright.

'I'll go if you don't need me. But I'll come by very soon. You're truly a miracle woman, Ettie.'

Everyone nodded while Mrs Lazarus cradled her baby in her arms, a blissful smile on her pockmarked face smoothing out the frowns and crevices until she was almost beautiful.

Trudging through the empty streets lit by a pale moon, Sophia couldn't stop thinking how the baby was dead, then alive. How wonderful that must be, to save a life. And if Ettie hadn't been there… She shook her head at what would have happened. Reaching her door in the corridor, a great certainty fired her thoughts and all weariness faded away: there had to be women doctors, a combination of Ettie and Doctor Feldstein, for all women, not just for older terrified women like Mrs Lazarus. That must be the conclusion of her article for the magazine. Sophia's heart thudded in her chest; what was more, she would certainly seek out the *London School of Medicine for Women,* as soon as she could.

CHAPTER 12

'WHAT A STORY. So the baby survived and is she still all right?' Milly turned to Sophia sitting beside her on the settee.

'Oh yes, yes. I saw her for a few moments on Friday morning. She's so lovely, and I can't describe the change in Mrs Lazarus. It amazed me – softer, smiling, even, you might say, younger.' Sophia shook her head, but then her expression changed, and a tiny frown played over her forehead.

When Milly asked, 'Did you finish the waistcoats?' Sophia took some moments to answer, forcing herself to come back to the present.

'We did, thank goodness. We worked all Thursday and Friday morning. That afternoon a couple of the men went with Mr Lazarus to take them to the master tailor in Soho.'

'All's well that ends well.'

'I'm not sure.' Sophia hesitated, a frown flickering across her forehead again.

'What is it?' Milly turned.

'Milly, I'm afraid you'll think I've been wilful ... headstrong.' Sophia burst out, then averted her gaze. 'That's what Papa used to say when I was young. That I always wanted to do things my way.'

'I don't understand.'

'You asked me to write an article for the *Arbeter Fraint*. I was so surprised and even honoured. My very first article. You suggested I should write about my impressions of the sweating industry.'

She could hardly carry on speaking, but Milly patted her arm.

'It doesn't matter if you couldn't do it, or if you were too busy. Is that why you're so upset? There's always another time.'

'No, I wrote about something else.' Sophia took a deep breath. 'About women.'

'But that's excellent. Is it the papers I see peeking out of your handbag? Or is that something private?'

Confused by how emotional she had become, Sophia closed her eyes for a moment.

'I was so fired up about what happened with Mrs Lazarus, and what I've seen helping my friend Mrs Gutenberg, it simply poured out of me.' Seeing Milly was not angry, she handed the article to her. '*Why Women Need a Woman Doctor*. That's the title. Would you ... like to read it?'

Milly shook her head. 'Oh, Sophia, you've forgotten the essence of our beliefs. Of our work. We encourage people to be free, to discover their potential, to learn and grow. That's why we hate the servitude of the sweating system.' She shook her head and smiled. 'That feeling you just expressed, that you've done something wrong, that's the little girl talking, not the young woman I'm getting to know. Of course, I'd like to read it.'

Sophia passed the article to Milly and, leaning back, let out a long sigh of relief, then began to fiddle with her skirt. Noting this childish movement, she clasped her hands together resting them on her knee. But then, another thought: Milly would find it poorly written, unsuitable for the magazine. She held her breath.

Milly turned to the last page, and after a couple of minutes, lifted her gaze.

'It is marvellous. I don't know what you've been worrying about. You've spotted something we haven't covered because I spend my days as a seamstress, and so far, have no children. That's why it hasn't come to my attention. Of course, the sweating system controls women's lives as much as it does men's, for all the reasons I won't go into now. I'm sure Rudolf will like this very much.'

Sophia wondered if she should ask Milly about the School of Medicine for Women. Had she heard of it? Did she know where it was? But hearing the sound of familiar voices and bursts of loud laughter, followed by the heavy tread of men's feet, she bit her lip.

With a turn of the handle, Rudolf entered the room, with Dov close behind him. She blushed, and bending her head to hide her face, pulled a handkerchief from her handbag and blew her nose, surprised at how even the sound of his voice made her heart flutter. In a flash, she knew she couldn't reveal her curiosity about the medical school to Dov. He would view this as evidence she would stay in England. A triumph for him, for hadn't he asked her to stay on the ship even before she'd arrived? She was confused and uncertain. It must stay her secret.

Deeper still lay something she could tell no one: her promise to her parents to take them to America and the fear she'd betrayed their trust by seeking information about a medical school in London, and not New York.

'I'll put the kettle on. I know you'll both want a cup of tea after that long meeting.' Milly stood up.

The men hung their jackets and hats on pegs behind the door. Rudolf went to fill his pipe from a tobacco pouch on the mantelpiece, while Dov walked around the settee and stopped.

'Sophia, how wonderful to see you. I've been thinking about you lately.'

He took an upright chair facing her. Rudolf sat in a large kitchen chair with wooden arms. A chair of many colours, Sophia saw, predominantly painted bright green but here and there were patches of former colours – red, yellow, blue – revealed of its former incarnations.

'Good things, I hope.' She couldn't help smiling at him.

'Of course!' he grinned and taking a cigarette from his gold-tooled case, offered one to her.

'No thank you, Dov. Smoking is not a prerequisite for being an anarchist.'

'Quite right,' called Milly, pouring large cups of tea.

'Why've you been thinking about me, Dov?' Sophia made sure there was a little glint in her eye to hide the fast beat of her heart.

'Rudolf and I have been discussing a particular issue. But knowing Milly, I think we have to drink the tea first, for it might get cold, and Milly will never invite me again.'

'What nonsense you spout, Dov.' Milly resumed her place beside Sophia.

'There's been a problem and I want to ask Sophia if she can help solve it,' said Rudolf smiling at her.

Sophia raised her eyebrows, curious to know what it was.

'Just a minute, Rudolf, here's the article she's written for us. About her experiences with the new midwife, Mrs Gutenberg, although she wisely doesn't mention her by name.'

'That woman you met on the ship who disapproved of me?' said Dov.

'How did you know?'

'Her expression, whenever she saw me talking to you,' he said. 'But where did you meet her?'

'At the Vapour Baths on Brick Lane, and she lives two minutes' walk from me.'

'It's a *shtetl*, the East End,' Dov muttered.

Seeing Rudolf frown, Milly said, 'What do you want to ask Sophia?'

Rudolf explained they'd been discussing the propaganda material they sent to comrades abroad. An entirely secret endeavour. Those in the East End knew about it generally, but not the details.

'I remember now,' Sophia said, 'Rosa told me you sent propaganda to the Tsar's domain. Isn't that what you call it, Dov?' She laughed self-consciously, unsure if he'd like what she'd said. 'It was when I first went to the anarchist meeting house in Soho.'

The others exchanged glances.

'Well, Sophia, we'd like you to be involved with this. The article you brought today is another example of your dedication to the cause.' Rudolf nodded gravely.

Sophia drew a breath, her gaze travelled to each one and she noted the seriousness of their expressions. Why were they so grave? Was it something Rosa had done?

Dov leaned towards her.

'It was Rudolf's suggestion, but I echo it absolutely: we'd like you to come with me to the printer on the days I carry the material to my room and sort it into appropriate amounts before it's transported. Rosa has been doing this, but she says she doesn't care to continue.'

They were watching her.

She knew this was a kind of initiation, a deeper, particular involvement with the anarchist movement; she felt proud to be invited but needed to know more.

'This is dangerous, I think. Illegal? What would happen if we were discovered?'

'Dangerous because it's illegal. You can imagine the reaction of the British authorities, and of course, over there, you'd be imprisoned or sent to Siberia, if they discovered who the organisers were. But it's fundamental to our work to support the Great Revolution.'

Rudolf was watching her reaction. He'd always described the upheaval and strikes in this way and Sophia knew how he cherished their contribution.

'What exactly would you like me to do?'

Dov reached out and touched her arm. 'Very little. About every six weeks. Usually, on a Sunday, I go to the printer, whose workshop is at the other end of Dunstan Gardens, formerly an ancient stable – it's entirely hidden and the few horses grazing there would persuade any passerby that it's simply a stable, nothing more. I collect the material and carry it to my room here. All I need is a pair of willing arms to carry the boxes with me. That's the first step.'

It wasn't too onerous, and her heart leapt — *I'd spend time with Dov, but I mustn't let this influence me,* she told herself sternly. 'The first step?'

'Best to begin slowly,' said Milly. 'See how you feel about it.'

Sophia usually wrote home on Sunday, together with a letter to her brother in New York; then there was English homework, going to her teacher's house for the next lesson, more studying. But every six weeks? She could work around it on those days, surely? And Mr Lazarus had said there would be less work after Christmas, although that was unpredictable. She'd still have time during the evenings to practise her English. She looked up. They were such good people, with such high ideals, her heart was fired with admiration and warmth for them.

'Yes, I'd love to do this, dangerous or not.'

'Excellent,' said Rudolf, his eyes lighting up behind his glasses. 'Dov will explain it all to you.'

'When you're ready to leave, I'll come back with you on the tram, Sophia. Then we can talk.' Seeing her look of surprise, he added, 'I'm going to the Grafton Hall Club in Soho, I have people to see and you're, as it were, on the way.'

Sitting beside him on the tram, she was deeply conscious of Dov's warm body so close to hers. He'd chosen the back seat, where they could talk quietly, without arousing suspicion. Sensing there was something deeper in their decision to ask her, something connected with Rosa that she felt she should know, she asked him what it was.

'Are you allowed to tell me?' It was wise to ask since she was beginning to recognise the complexity, the secrecy of the Arbeter Frainters' work.

Dov leaned back against the seat; Sophia noticed he was deep in thought, his gaze fixed in the distance. His silence suggested he was recalling something he could never tell her, perhaps intimate moments with Rosa. She drew away from him at this idea, and conscious of her movement, Dov glanced down at her.

'Naturally, I can tell you.'

Rosa had come with him in the past to collect the material, but she hated walking across the muddy field, having to avoid the horse dung to reach the printer's. Rosa had many great qualities – fearless, ready to take risks, and passionate about the revolution. He told Sophia that Rosa wanted him to move to the West End, and couldn't understand why he would live at the other end of town close to the Anarcho-Federalists, when Dov himself favoured revolutionary activity.

'Why don't you live there? Rosa's right.'

'However well we know each other, there are things I won't reveal to her. I live at Dunstan Houses for many reasons: I like peace; I can think and plan there and am less likely to be discovered. Though I disagree with much of Rudolf's philosophy, I love him and all the comrades who live so close together, in little houses nearby, in other rooms at Dunstan Houses. Many of the people you meet at meetings live around there. That's why when we met on the ship, I called it a commune.' His voice was low, but full of gladness. Glancing up, she saw he was smiling.

'I know,' she said. Passing the London Hospital, Sophia's heart gave a little jolt but she kept her mind focused on Dov, on what he was saying. 'You haven't answered my question about Rosa.'

'She's changing. She told me she'd like to have a house, where revolutionaries coming here would stay, instead of in some flea-filled room in the East End. Yet owning property is against our principles. I suppose that's some kind of dream. She likes the limelight and is becoming too easy with her words. I was relieved she'd had enough of the printer's.' He laughed. 'Thanks to the horse dung.'

They were nearing her stop.

'How will we work this?' Sophia prepared to stand up.

'Give me your address.' Hurriedly, she scribbled it on a scrap of paper. 'A week today, I'll collect the material. I'll call for you around two o'clock.'

There was something soft in his gaze making her rise quickly. Over her shoulder, she said, 'Till next week, Dov.'

CHAPTER 13

SOPHIA HADN'T SEEN HANNAH Leah for several weeks but when she caught sight of her on Sunday morning, she waved and Hannah Leah beckoned her over. A crowd of women pressed against her stall laden with bric-a-brac, chipped coronation mugs, tattered aprons, anything that could be resold. A woman had just passed Hannah Leah a letter, which she was reading to her. The woman threw her arms in the air and cried out. Another woman comforted her, leading her away wailing and sobbing,

'Many can't read so I read their letters to them. Good news, bad news, there's always something from the old country. Of course, their children can read to them. Though sometimes it's personal and they don't want their children to know. Anyway, Sophia, I've heard all about you and the miracle-working midwife, Ettie Gutenberg!'

'I don't think she'd like to be called that,' Sophia smiled. 'But I should have realised how quickly the news got round.'

'Well, you never know, I might have to avail myself of her services sometime in the future.'

Sophia reached over the collection of stuff and picked up a blue umbrella, rather frayed but still usable.

'I'll buy this, Hannah Leah. How much?' Seeing her face, Sophia insisted.

Hannah Leah sold some items from her stall and read two letters carrying good news, where the recipients went away smiling. Leaning against the wall, she said, 'What are you doing for the New Year? It's only a couple of weeks. Please come to us if you're on your own.'

Sophia hesitated. She'd already learned that most of the anarchists were atheists, some extremely intolerant of religion and its practices, but her longing to celebrate as she might have done at home was so poignant she thanked Hannah Leah for the invitation.

'Let me bring something, cook something as a contribution.'

'My mother would be offended if you did. Perhaps some fruit, or sweetmeats for the children.'

'The first day is the end of the month isn't it?'

'Yes, it's a shabbes. We'll be expecting you then.'

Sophia was about to leave when she recalled hearing Moshe coughing as he worked; she'd asked him if he was ill, but he shook his head. 'It's the threads from the material, I breathe them in sometimes, but I am very well.' He looked haggard when he coughed but, with the noise in the workroom, no one noticed. Sophia made to turn away but felt she had to ask.

'Hannah Leah, I've heard Moshe coughing at times. Is he all right?'

Hannah Leah drew herself up, glanced around to see if any customers were approaching, and said, 'No, but he insists he's fine.'

Nothing more was said, though they exchanged a glance.

Sophia returned to her room where she sat on the bed, thinking about the following Sunday when she would meet Dov again. She smiled to herself.

It seems like an age, she thought, and I can't wait, yet also I'm apprehensive. How can you be both at the same time? What are you scared of? Is it the secret work – no, I'm committed to that. I'm not afraid of Dov, I know him, and yet... She stopped.

Woman, you're being silly, ridiculous. Then another thought: *I'm beginning to understand how the heart can change a person's personality. I've always been so single-minded but now I don't know what to think or feel. Stop it! Settle down at your 'trunk table' and write to Sasha in New York.* Sitting cross-legged on the floor, she would write to her brother. It was weeks since she'd heard from him.

Sunday, at last. Mrs Vine had gone to her daughter's, thank goodness. Sophia knew the arrival of a young man coming to see a woman on her own might shock Mrs Vine. It would travel around the community within a day, and everyone would think ... whatever they usually thought.

When the knock came, she drew herself up, straightened her skirts and vowed to be restrained and business-like. She passed through Mrs Vine's room to open the door.

'Come in, Dov. My room's at the back.'

He followed her in and glanced around. 'What a splendid view over the central court, the opposite blocks of flats and people's washing.'

'I live as everyone does,' she said, surprised at his mocking tone, a note of defiance in her voice.

'I'm joking. It's good, Sophia. It helps you truly experience why we need the Revolution. So, are you ready?'

'I am.' Taking up her bag, she said, 'Shall we go?'

They took the tram down the Mile End Road to Dunstan Houses.

With its parallel paths on either side, the gardens of Stepney Green with their shrubs, trees and flowers stretched out before them.

'I love the feeling of being in the countryside. There were beautiful parks in Kyiv and dense pine forests around Archangelsk.' Pointing to the trees, Sophia said, 'Now they're golden and yellow and rust coloured with the start of the English autumn. It's beautiful.'

He grinned. 'There's always a place for you in Dunstan Houses, if you wish. Anyway, this is what happens: we walk to the far end, in a small field beyond there's a row of stables. Well-hidden, insignificant amongst the others, that's where you'll find our printing press. That's where we're heading.'

They walked the length of Stepney Green until she saw horses grazing in the further field, and a stony path winding its way, almost overgrown by grass and spattered with yellow or brownish clumps. She peered, wrinkled her nose. 'Horse dung?'

'Absolutely. Be careful where you tread. It's also wet and mushy alongside the stones.'

No wonder Rosa had decided to forego this particular contribution to the revolutionary cause. Dov opened the gate and was already hopping along the path or walking in the wet grass to avoid the dung. At times, she saw his boots sink deep into the clay holes, high with water. Lifting her skirts over her left arm, her legs bare, Sophia made her uncertain way, almost losing her balance in her efforts to avoid the steaming, stinking horse manure, and avoiding the verge when she could.

'This is an initiation in itself,' she called to Dov, marching a few steps ahead.

He didn't reply, intent on reaching the stables. Then turning, he took her hand and led her to the door, where he gave three knocks and waited. Sophia could hear horses whinnying and moving around in the stables nearby, but then became aware of the clanging and banging of a machine working rhythmically.

A man with black hair appeared, opened the half-door, and leaned over.

'Greetings, comrade, I was expecting you.'

'Comrade,' Dov returned, but when the man saw Sophia, he raised a questioning eyebrow.

'An Arbeter Frainter,' Dov said. 'Sophia Krichevska.'

'Greetings, Miss Krichevska.'

'Sophia, meet Nathan Narodiczky, our illustrious printer. Without whom all would be lost.'

'Don't exaggerate, Dov. You'd find someone else, but welcome, Miss Krichevska, to my fly-infested domain.'

Leaving the half-door open, they entered a totally dark area and Sophia wondered how the printer could possibly do his work. She peered around but could make out only a velvety gloom. As her eyes adjusted, a grey light seeping through a high window sketched in a large printing machine, where the printer now stood, leaning forward, his arms stretched out as he adjusted something which rattled. Straining her eyes again, in the other direction Sophia discovered two cardboard boxes standing on a low table.

'Is the order ready?' Dov said.

'Over there.' The printer indicated the table, with a turn of his head.

'And the other things I ordered?' Dov lit a cigarette.

'Finishing them now.'

The great mechanical roar of the machine resumed; Sophia covered her ears with her hands as it cast out sheet after sheet of printed paper, which fell haphazardly on a broad bar at the front.

'Forty copies?' asked Dov, intent.

'As agreed,' said Nathan.

She shuddered. Flies were landing on her hair, her eyes, her mouth. She swept them away but crowds took their place – a plague, ever-present. They were thick on Nathan's head too, his shoulders, even his hands, but he seemed oblivious.

'You'll have the money on Friday,' said Dov, who shook his head from side to side to throw off the flies.

'How long this time?'

Nathan stacked the sheets and handed them to Dov.

'Not sure.'

'You're going away again?' Sophia said quietly.

'Like a yo-yo,' Nathan observed. 'And where do you come from, Miss Krichevska?' He made the usual response when she told him. 'Jews in the Arctic Circle? Amazing.'

'But from Kyiv originally.'

For the first time, he looked directly at her.

'Ah. I know Kyiv. Was a student at one of the yeshivas there: my father wanted me to be a great rabbi. Seeing what was happening to our people, I knew there was one answer. We must return to our land. Three times a day, for two thousand years, we've prayed to return, and now some of us have. The bravest, in my opinion.'

'I've heard of them. They've gone to Palestine to work in the swamps, dying of fever, of malaria. Living, I believe, in even worse conditions than we do here. And you want to go there?' Sophia shook her head.

'Certainly, when I've built up my own printing business and have something to offer, I will.'

'Are you leaving us?' Dov frowned.

'For the time being, I stay here, supporting the cause, but maybe soon…'

Dov nodded, something in his gaze told Sophia he wasn't surprised. People had to move on, do what they needed to do. He lifted the smaller box and placed it in Sophia's arms. 'All right?'

'Yes,' she said.

He lifted the larger box from the table, saluted Narodiczky, and they went out into the light to make their hazardous way back to Dunstan Houses. It had been overcast when they'd made their way to the stables but now the sun shone low in the sky, directly into their eyes.

Carrying the boxes was not without event, and although Sophia carried hers like a strangely shaped baby, on her hip, she struggled to keep her balance. Reaching the gate, she slipped and cried out.

'Put the box down,' Dov called. 'I'll come for it.'

She would have fallen, but he caught her by the shoulders. Their gaze met, her heartbeat raced to feel him so close, and she saw that strange look in his eyes. Gathering herself together, she pulled away. 'I just need practice. I'm definitely going to carry the box. You go ahead, Dov.'

He told her she was obstinate but collected his box and they carried on along Dunstan Gardens; as they walked, he pointed out the beautiful 18th-century houses on the far side and even, he said, 'A school for Jewish children.' When she asked him about it, he said she would have to ask Milly, for he knew nothing more.

His room on the ground floor was at the end of the corridor. Unlocking the door, Dov motioned her in and asked her to put her box beside a low table on the right. This is where they would count out the leaflets and pamphlets, sorted according to whether they were going to Moscow, Petersburg or Warsaw. The distribution, once they'd reached their destination, would be carried out by the bookshop in Vilna.

He closed the door and she gazed around.

A monk's cell, bare but for the essentials: a cupboard, a bed, two chairs and a table. A few books on a stool at the bedside. No pictures on the walls, no photographs. She marvelled at the austerity of it, thinking of Rudolf and Milly's apartment three floors above, the walls covered with books, pictures in the kitchen, and everywhere papers, newspapers, and articles in the course of being written. It felt she thought with a shiver, as though no one lived here, and she was puzzled. Was such a flamboyant character, a magnet for other people, a charmer and she guessed, a man of secrets, a nobody?

Dov, meanwhile, placed the boxes on either side of the table and asked her to count them out in twenties, which he would bind together with string, loosely tied. They worked side-by-side in silence. The smaller box contained hundreds of leaflets, which meant more counting. These would be transported to Brest-Litovsk and redistributed within the Pale of Settlement. Such focus in his eyes, such stillness in his body spoke of his absolute dedication and Sophia hardly dared disturb him, but in the end, she said, 'How do they reach their destination?'

Dov put his finger to his lips. An hour passed. Finally, he loosened his shoulders, lifting his arms to the ceiling and stretching out his hands. 'Done! Now let's sit down.'

They sat together on the bed. 'So, Miss Krichevska, what are your thoughts? How do you feel about continuing with this?'

'The only danger is the horse dung. Of course, I'll continue.'

'Wonderful, but there's another danger we haven't mentioned and Rudolf insisted I inform you: Spies. Are you aware of that?'

'*Spies?*'

She looked about. Through the window she glimpsed a woman taking a dog for a walk, some boys with their hoops, an old man sitting on a bench in Dunstan Gardens.

'But who could be spying? That woman with her dog? The old man?'

'Probably not here. I do this on Sunday mornings when most are at church. But Sophia, there are indeed spies. Often on the ship, I think I'm being watched by some odd person. So far, I've been lucky, but there are immigrants, supporters of the Tsar, ready to betray us to George the Fifth's henchmen. Think of that, and the outcome. Will you carry on? Do only what you want to do.'

Sophia closed her eyes for a moment. The thought of spies was terrifying, and her mind moved over the possibilities – being returned to the country, tortured and imprisoned in one of the notorious prisons, *exiled*. She opened her eyes, determined to be realistic. Surely a young woman like herself would arouse no suspicions?

When she said this to Dov, he grinned. 'Excellent. So you want to learn the next step?'

'I do, Dov. I do, absolutely.'

There was such passion, such conviction in her voice, he turned to her. An unexpected softness in his gaze, the warmth in his face surprised her. Taking her gently by the shoulders, he bent and kissed her mouth.

'*Dov.*' Her heart beat so loudly in her chest, he must have heard it. She blushed, drew herself away, and found herself saying, 'You can't do that if we're to work as comrades...'

'Why can't I?'

A series of painful memories passed through her mind: Rosa's reaction to her in the anarchist meeting house in Soho, when she arrived, Rosa at the concert putting her fingers on Dov's lips and, later that day, the way he guided her through the crowds, one hand at the base of her neck, in such a gesture of intimacy. Sophia didn't want to show these feelings, ugly ones, perhaps, and she bent her head. But the words slipped out despite herself, 'What about Rosa? Aren't you with her?'

'What about freedom, Sophia?' Dov took her hands.

She drew her eyebrows together in an expression of concern and uncertainty. The entire ideology of the anarchist movement came down to this – freedom. She was sure she believed in this until reality challenged her. I'm naive, she thought, pretending to be a believer, but beset by atavistic beliefs. Sadly, for she didn't want him to think she held such an antiquated attitude, she raised her troubled gaze to him.

As though guessing her thoughts, Dov said softly, 'It takes time to abandon beliefs or creeds with which we've been indoctrinated. Yes, indoctrinated, though we don't believe we are. But something you must know, Sophia, you will never come to any harm through me. That is my promise.' At that moment she felt closer to him than in all the time she'd known him. 'So, you want to know the second step?' She nodded. 'If you're free tomorrow, we'll go to Ruderman's bookshop.'

CHAPTER 14

RUDDY OF VISAGE LIKE his name, and with his jet black hair and high cheekbones giving him something of a Slavic look, Ruderman took the box from her, with a little bow of greeting. While Dov and Ruderman talked, Sophia explored his glorious bookshop, drawn to the medical books which didn't quite defeat her, for now she could read some of the descriptions beneath the diagrams. She roamed the shelves, finding translations of Tolstoy, Chekhov, and Gorky into English, often by Rudolf. She knew his mission was to educate the East Enders, who'd had little education apart from religious learning, and that was often minimal, and promised herself she would buy some of these books when she had the money.

Conversation over, Dov called her to the table. He'd been discussing the latest batch of pamphlets to be transported; now he explained the system to her. Ruderman had established a connection with Kletzkin, the famous Yiddish publishing house in Vilna, Lithuania. Yiddish papers and books published by Kletzkin came to Ruderman, who in turn sent their literature and books back there, filling the base of larger boxes with the contraband and covering them with the usual, 'respectable' translations. Someone over there was pocketing a generous bribe – it had gone on for years.

They left and stood outside. Dov was making for the West End, Sophia planned to see Ettie, and they were about to part when Dov said, 'There's a 'love-in' at Rudolf and Milly's on Rosh Hashanah next week. Come with me?'

She thought of her promise to go to Hannah Leah's for lunch, that to go to Stepney Green she'd need to take the tram – although she could walk of course. But more was the unaccustomed idea of taking part in something so alien to the holy day and this flawed her. Biting her lip, a little frown wrinkling her forehead, she hesitated.

'It's the evening of the first day,' he continued, seeing her uncertainty (so he still used the accustomed language, for there were two days to the New Year Festival, the first and the second), and Sophia, it's a joyous occasion, a reward for the Arbeters for their hard work. You know how Rudolf loves to enjoy life.'

'The evening? Will there be many people there?'

Relieved she wouldn't have to explain anything or miss the celebratory lunch with the Rifkins, she saw, with a start, that desiring to join the family at Goulston Street was a link with her own, so far away. A connection with home.

'I'll be there. There's nothing licentious or immoral about what happens. Can you imagine such a thing with either of them? No, it's one of the treats they arrange for the innermost circle of workers. It's a joyful, happy evening.'

She was almost convinced.

'I'd think I'd like to go.'

'Wonderful. So, come around seven o'clock on Saturday evening and we'll go together to their room.'

In the week leading to the New Year, as predicted, there was only a day and a half of work in the sweatshop, and they were back on the sleeves again. The much-anticipated reorder of waistcoats hadn't materialised but Lazarus was so besotted with his baby, the workers hadn't the heart to complain, comforting themselves with the knowledge the waistcoats had allowed them to put something away for the holiday.

Walking home on Tuesday afternoon, Sophia paused, as an unexpected feeling overtook her. Was this melancholia? She'd read about it in books but never experienced this dark sensation of heaviness girding her head, an immense sadness in her heart, and wondered what it could be. It was as though someone very dear to her had died, and picking up her skirts she ran, pushing her way through the ever-increasing crowds on Wentworth Street. Supposing something *had* happened at home? Would there be a letter, a telegram? But when she swung open the door and found her landlady calmly kneading dough for bread, and neither letter nor telegram awaiting her, she sank down on the bed and stared through the window, seeing nothing.

Reflecting on the weeks and months since her arrival – the sweatshop, the Arbeter Frainters, and she even let her thoughts dwell briefly on Dov – nothing sprang out to explain this feeling. She stood up and leaned out of her window. She watched clusters of women carrying bags and boxes, chatting briefly as they passed, then hurrying to climb the stairs to their flats, little children trailing after them. A puzzled frown creased her forehead. And then, as the heavenly aroma of baking bread filled the room, it came to her.

Bread. Baking bread. Baking *challah* with Mama every *Yom Tov*, every festival. Since the age of nine she'd baked, soon learning the art of moulding the tiny ladder, the ladder to heaven, and adding it to the special round challah they ate on this holiday. The sadness, the sense of loss she was feeling, was the longing to be with her family and to share all the steps of their own particular ritual, not so different from others, but theirs, in Kyiv.

Homesickness.

She breathed back tears, but images filled her mind. First, it was honey: the amazing discovery that you could buy honey in the Arctic Circle. Leaving Kyiv, her mother had taken several pots with her, for how could there be honey in such white wastes? But when Sophia had gone to the market for vegetables and found a beekeeper selling honey, she ran home to tell Mama. Together they returned, learning that the Arctic queen bee had developed a tiny fur coat to protect herself from the icy atmosphere and that she gained strength before flying by helping herself to nectar from Arctic roses and bog blueberries. She and Mama had been amazed at the power of nature to adapt.

Why can't you adapt to these new circumstances? But logic was not as powerful as emotion, and she went on to recall baking a dozen loaves of challah, chopping the fish by hand for gefilte fish, and making fish soup with fish heads and bones. Eating it with the *lokshen* noodles as they might have with chicken soup – their own version of the special meals for Rosh Hashanah, according to what they could buy in the markets in the far north.

And dipping bread in the honey as they passed it around the table, to ensure a sweet year. She closed her eyes, wishing she could fly through the air, back across that wild expanse of countries, mountains, forests and rivers, to sit at the table with her mother and father, with Alexei. She straightened her shoulders. Despite the tears in her eyes, she had to do something. She recalled her mother saying, 'When you're sad, help someone else, and your sadness will pass.'

She looked in her purse: enough to buy a small pot of honey for Ettie, for Betsy and for Hannah Leah. Out again, on Wentworth Street, she observed the growing sense of anticipation. Women shouted at the stallholders in the crowded markets of Wentworth and Goulston Streets, exclaiming at the cost of potatoes or carrots, arguing and bartering the price; stalls were selling raisins in twists of brown paper for noodle pudding and others sold silvery fish to be chopped and boiled for gefilte fish. The women pushing and shoving around the stalls demanded the heads of the fish – 'to be the head and not the tail' in the coming year, as it was customary to believe, and fishmongers in their blue and white striped aprons raised their hands in frustration, for how many fish heads could one fish have?

She bought a little food, together with flour and yeast, to make bread for Betsy.

Later, she found Betsy looking bright and tidy. Betsy kissed her for the honey, saying they would go to the Poor Jews' soup kitchen, where a Rosh Hashanah meal would be provided for them all, and how she was so looking forward to it. Together, throughout Wednesday afternoon, they kneaded and moulded the bread and chatted, and by the time it was ready for the oven, Sophia felt considerably happier. It was good to cook with somebody else, and she smiled as she walked home.

On Thursday, Ettie greeted her warmly, thanked her for the pot of honey and asked her what she was doing for the festival. When Sophia said she was going to friends, Ettie nodded approvingly. She and her husband would celebrate with their son, who lived a few streets away. The last pot of honey Sophia would take to Hannah Leah on Friday afternoon, before the holiday. Gazing through the window on Friday morning, she saw older children struggling to carry squawking hens, whose necks would soon be wrung, ready for the soup and the meal. And she laughed, not because of killing the poultry, but because it was comical to see the boys' faces – usually boys – and felt glad she could laugh again.

She made a small meal for herself for Friday evening, and lighting the candles, said the blessing and thought of them at home, with only a note of sadness in her heart. And suddenly, as though from another world, she recalled Dov's invitation to go to Rudolf and Milly's on Saturday evening. And was glad.

The women of the East End didn't normally go to the synagogue, Sophia knew, but as she walked down the street to the Rifkins the following day, the first day of Rosh Hashanah, she passed men returning, young men in groups chatting, and a few women walking with their husbands, perhaps to the grandparents for lunch.

The children greeted Sophia warmly, running to see if she had sweetmeats in her bag.

'You must eat them after lunch,' Sophia said, and their faces fell.

All were in their usual place but there was an extra person. Aaron stood beside Hannah Leah's father, Mr Levi, at the top of the table. He came to shake hands and they greeted each other: *Good Yom Tov*, in the traditional way. Sophia was puzzled, for wasn't he an anarchist who had rejected religion and religious practice? She kept this thought to herself. Blessings were said, they passed round slices of apple to dip into the honey, then pieces of the challah bread which they also dipped, to ensure a sweet year.

Then came the meal: chicken soup, an immense piece of brisket cooked overnight, *tzimmes*, that delicious dish of carrots and prunes accompanied by an equally large potato kugel, a savoury potato pudding of eggs, onions, matzo flour and grated potatoes. All dutifully served by Mrs Levi, who looked even older and tinier and more bent. For dessert, Hannah Leah passed round slices of honey cake and fruit, and they sat back, barely able to move, glad of the lemon tea as digestive. Occasionally, Sophia noted with some anxiety Moshe getting up to disappear into the corridor, from where they could hear him coughing. But on returning, he would hide with a laugh and a joke about how deeply shaken he must have been. The meal finished, they sang the grace after meals, Aaron's mellow tenor rolling around the room.

'Can I help you clear up?' Sophia said as they rose from the table.

'My father won't let us do anything till after shabbes, but thank you for asking. No, we'll do it later, as we'll need the crockery for the Second Day.'

'Then if you're sure,' Sophia said, 'I'll go home and have a little nap.'

'We all need that,' said Moshe.

As Aaron walked with her, and as though he'd guessed what she'd been wondering, he answered her question about his attending the festive meal, saying he could no longer believe in God but loved the old traditions.

'What it is to be a Jew… On the one hand, an Orthodox believer—'

'On the other, an atheist who believes in seeking the good of all mankind,' broke in Sophia.

His face lit up with admiration. 'So you know…?'

'My mother is an educated woman and she wanted me to have the same education as my brothers. We learned Torah together at the kitchen table. I know how one discusses all the possibilities of a principle, of a quotation in the Talmud and then the alternative. On the one hand, a scholar says, on the other, says another. Because there are always alternatives, although at the end you follow the wisest rabbi.'

'Hannah Leah is educated in *Yiddishkeit*, in Judaism, and in secular knowledge, but there are not many women here like you two. Don't you find it difficult?'

'I must admit today I was uneasy about celebrating Rosh Hashanah and yet I wanted to, as I think you did.'

'You're right. I love the old traditions, the singing. Hannah Leah knows my doubts and uncertainties, but she never comments. What I do know for sure is that I can never again believe in God.' His words exploded with such vehemence, Sophia turned to look at him, wondering what this was about.

'You say it with such anger,' she murmured.

'Have you time to listen to my story? It's brief.'

They had reached the doorway to her buildings. Sophia took a few steps into the stairway, which was secluded. 'Of course.'

From an inside pocket, Aaron drew out a much-fingered photograph and showed it to her. 'My brother.'

She gasped, reached out. 'May I?'

He handed it to her.

'He's in chains. That's horrible.' She'd heard of this, but the horror of it became a reality at this moment. 'He's a revolutionary?'

'Yes. The terrible thing is that when he took his leave of our family and went to shake our father's hand, my father refused. My father, the esteemed Dayan, learned rabbi and judge, but a man lacking all compassion.' The kind of rabbi Dov hated, Sophia thought, and with good reason. 'The only time he smiles is on Simchas Torah.' Seeing the distress on her face, he apologised. 'Truly, forgive me, I don't want to spoil such a beautiful day.'

'You haven't spoilt it. I'm very moved that you told me this. Is your brother married?'

'Yes, and his wife followed him to Siberia. Not something I tell everyone, but meeting you at Hannah Leah's today, and knowing you're committed to the anarchist movement, I felt somehow I should – could – explain myself, even discuss it with you.'

'Of course.' She gazed up at him, noting the sadness in his eyes, 'I feel touched that you told me and I'm feeling a little confused too. I so admire Rudolf Rocker and his teachings, but I was relieved and delighted to share the festival with the Rifkins. But Aaron, what about freedom?' With surprise, Sophia heard herself repeating Dov's words.

'You're right. Freedom, as Rudolf says. Freedom to be.'

She wanted to find a happy conclusion to their conversation.

'Aaron, you have a beautiful voice and Hannah Leah told me you own many records of opera singers, who bring you joy and relief.'

'I do.' He took his watch from his waistcoat pocket. 'Quarter past four already. There's a meeting I want to attend later, so I must get the omnibus back to Soho. Sophia, thanks for being so understanding. I do hope to see you soon at the Sugar Loaf pub. *Shana Tovah u Metuchah.*'

'A happy and sweet year to you too, Aaron.'

What powerful feelings these Jewish holidays evoke in those far from home, she thought, as she climbed the stone steps to her room. She wondered if Aaron would be at Rudolf and Milly's later. Mrs Vine had not returned and Sophia was glad to fill her bowl with lukewarm water from the kettle, and go through to her room. With careful movements, she undressed but for her chemise and underskirt, hanging her white blouse and dark brown skirt on hangers in the narrow wardrobe. Sliding under the covers, she lay for a while thinking of Aaron, guessing there must be more to his life that he hadn't revealed, for clearly, he was in his thirties, older than Dov, and certainly older than herself. Turning her thoughts to the family in Archangelsk, she drifted into sleep.

She is standing outside a little wooden house by the sea, it is her home yet not her home. Snowdrifts almost cover the windows and she can barely make out the door. On her hip, she balances a large box. Putting it down in the snow, she takes a deep breath and batters on the door with all her might.

'Mama, Papa, Alexei, are you there?' No one comes. She knocks again but her hands are freezing in her mittens, she can no longer feel her fingers. Colder and colder. Snow falls in enormous swirling flakes, covering her mouth.

'Mama,' she beseeches, ' please open the door, I'm so cold.'

It opens. Her mother appears, dressed like a peasant woman in a dark blue scarf and black skirt and blouse. Behind her stands her father, yet not a father, a man with wild grey hair, a rugged red face, a peasant, too. But her mother approaches, arms outstretched, 'Sophia, my darling, you're here, we've been worried about you but now you're home.'

The father who isn't her father elbows her mother out of the way and steps forward.

'What's this large box on the doorstep?' He peers. 'We don't want that filth here.'

He makes to close the door.

Revolutionary Material. The words seem to appear in thick black script across the top of the box.

'No!' she cries. 'There's nothing revolutionary here. It's a present for you.'

'Of course, you must come in.' Her mother shoots her father an angry look.

Suddenly she's in a tiny room, where candles flicker on the table, shadows dance dark on the walls. Alexei is there, staring at the box.

'Let me open it.'

Before anyone can move, he has torn off the lid, and the sides fall open of their own accord. A gigantic square honey cake dotted with glace cherries gleams in the candlelight.

'See, I baked it in Mrs Vine's oven.' She lets out a sigh, almost a moan.

The low-ceiling cottage is transformed. She's in the sitting room of her real home in Kyiv, with her true mother and father, both wearing their usual clothes. They throw their arms around, kiss and hug her. Alexei breaks off a large corner of the cake and eats it. They smile and laugh.

'It's scrumptious, Sophia. I could eat it all!'

The room fills with warmth and love and laughter.

As Sophia stirred, her heart brimming with the rich comfort of home, she smiled and opened her eyes. White clouds were turning grey over the chimney pots, and the sky darkening. Reaching for her watch, she saw with a start that it was after six. For some moments the dream was in her head and she wondered about it, but she shook herself. Time to get ready.

She was splashing her face with cold water when she heard voices. With a towel, she dried her hands and face. A man's low voice and Mrs Vine's, cheerful, lively, questioning. It must be Mrs Vine's son-in-law coming to fetch her.

Now, what should she wear this evening? Surely it required something light-hearted rather than the sober brown skirt she'd chosen to wear at the Rifkins, more appropriate for the day. Some weeks ago, she'd bought a length of material, dark blue with light blue flowers around the edge, from a stall in the market. She had been sewing a skirt with buttons down the front, in the style worn by the anarchist women, by hand, in her spare moments, and had finished it the day before. The white blouse with a lacy insert at the neck she'd worn earlier would go well with it. She was just buttoning the skirt when she heard a tap at the door.

'Sophia, are you awake?'

'Yes, Mrs Vine. What is it?'

'You have a visitor.' Mrs Vine's voice was unusually upbeat and cheerful.

A visitor? Forgetting she'd unpinned and loosened her hair before she slept, Sophia opened the door and peered around. Her heart flipped.

Dov. He was sitting on the settee, flicking cigarette ash into a saucer, while in the armchair by the fire, clearly, under his spell, Mrs Vine smiled like a young girl.

'Oh Dov, Dov!' Sophia couldn't hide her delight. 'I thought we were meeting at your place. I didn't expect you.'

'Mr Feldman was telling me he couldn't allow you to travel alone in the evening.' Mrs Vine leaned forward, an approving look in her eyes. 'Quite right too.'

Dov rose and took Sophia's hand. 'We did agree to that, but as Mrs Vine said, it's not right for young women to travel alone around London at twilight.'

How unpredictable he is, Sophia thought, such a charmer. 'I'm glad you've come.' She put her hand up to her hair, loose down her shoulders, feeling suddenly undressed. 'I won't be a minute.'

Again, Dov gazed with that soft look in his eyes she was getting to know, and she backed into her room.

She was ready; as they left, Mrs Vine wished them *Good Yom Tov* and they returned the greeting. Descending the gloomy staircase, now deep in shadow, Dov took Sophia's arm until they reached the outer door.

'Shall we walk or take the tram?'

'I'd like to walk. It will freshen me up.'

Along the Mile End Road, the streets were unexpectedly crowded: men running to synagogues, families returning home, young couples going to friends or family, and everyone they passed wishing them *Good Yom Tov* and *Shavuah Tov*, a good week.

In the apartment windows above the shops, candles bloomed, lit for the second day, as Dov said. He knew all about the New Year Festival of course, but she hadn't expected him to acknowledge it. On passing the great London Hospital on the other side of the road, a different light lingered at the large windows, dimmer along the corridors. Electric light. She mentioned to him she'd heard they had a generator since it was a newly renovated hospital.

'How do you know?' He turned his gaze to her.

'Oh, I heard it somewhere.' A little flustered that she'd revealed anything about her findings, she lifted her chin and walked faster.

CHAPTER 15

CLIMBING TO THE TOP floor of Dunstan Houses, they heard voices, laughter, and a strange twanging musical instrument.

'A tamburitza!' Dov said when she raised her eyebrows. 'You'll see.'

He pushed open the door, and she stepped in. What a transformation. Here, only two weeks ago, the four of them had sat around the fire, and now more than twenty young workers were squashed in, sitting on the floor or the table, standing by the wall. Towering over them, his back to the fireplace, Rudolf plucked at the tamburitza, a curious instrument with a long arm and mandolin-shaped body, and singing loudly with gusto, his eyes alight behind his glasses.

'Come here by me,' Milly called. Making her careful way through those sitting cross-legged on the floor, she saw some were in close discussion while others had joined in with the singing. Sophia found a lone chair and Dov squeezed in behind her.

'You've come to a different land, Sophia my darling. A transformation is it not?'

'Transformation, you can say that again. But what is Rudolf singing?'

'A German drinking song!'

'He learned these songs when he was young.' Milly laughed. 'Would you believe it, this one is in Latin.' In a strong Yiddish accent, she said: *Gaudeamus Igitur.* 'It means let us be joyful. One of Rudolf's mottos. I tend to be more of a pessimist,' she said as an afterthought.

Since waking up earlier, Sophia had experienced such a rollercoaster of feelings, including doubting whether she was right to come to the 'love-in', but now she leaned back in the chair and allowed the joyous ambiance to settle her heart.

'Now Yiddish songs,' Dov shouted.

They sang in Yiddish, Russian and German and while Milly and Sam Dreen passed round glasses of tea, several of the men drank beer. Occasionally, Rudolf stopped playing, reached for his tankard on the mantelpiece and swigged some down.

Drawn in by the atmosphere, Sophia relaxed. *They've forgotten their miserable lives in the Tsar's domains, in the Pale of Settlement, and the dreary exhaustion of the workshops. This is their new family.*

Milly touched Sophia's arm. 'Do you sing?'

'Not very well.' Sophia drew back.

But someone had heard and called, 'Sophia's going to sing for us.' It was taken up by the others, who chanted and clapped, until she blushed, shrinking into the chair. Dov took her hands, pulled her up and led her to stand before the table.

'You sing, and afterwards we'll sing together.'

Fragments of the dream she'd had that afternoon floated in her mind; she recalled a lullaby Mama used to sing when they were small.

'I'll sing the *Song of the Little Fox*.'

Somewhat plaintive, but with a good refrain, *Bayu-bay-ushki-bayu, Ne lozhisya na krayu…* One by one they joined in, but the mood darkened, for it took people back to their childhood, to the families they might never see again. What should she do? Furrowing her brow, she threw a quick, 'help me' glance at Dov.

'Come everyone,' he shouted.' Let's have something loud and cheerful.'

He began a tune she'd heard the peasants sing in the Archangelsk market while waiting for customers. She joined in, they sang together, his hands on her shoulders, swaying from side to side. The song ended to immense applause.

'*More, more.*'

He turned her to face him and bending, kissed her with passion. Everyone shouted and cheered.

Rudolf came forward. 'Time for more dancing. What will it be?'

'The Squat Dance. Let's do it, Dov.' Sam Dreen jumped up.

'What's that?'

'The *Kazatski*.'

She shook her head.

'We'll show you.'

Dov stood opposite Sam in the tiny space beside Rudolf, who began to play. Crouching down on their haunches, folding their arms, they kicked out their legs. Faster and faster they danced, while everybody clapped and whistled and shouted. They collapsed, falling back against the crowd, panting and laughing. Dov stood up, groaning loudly. Grabbing Sophia's shoulder, he fell against her, pretending to be exhausted.

'We all need a drink,' called Milly. 'Someone pour lemonade while I make more tea.'

'Drink this.' Sophia poured Dov a glass. 'Then tell me how you know this dance.'

He gulped it down with a satisfied 'Aah... All right. A little about my family.'

Something significant was about to happen. Never had he mentioned family, nor, she thought, how he could dress so well, be so worldly-wise. Her gaze intent on his face, she waited.

'My grandfather taught me. He's a Chasid, a very religious Jew who believes in the power of dance and song as a spiritual path to God. When I was six or seven, he told me the story of Mendel, a poor villager, who begged a great rabbi for a blessing to cure his bed-ridden little daughter. Mendel's only riches were his skill in dancing the *Kazatski*. Seeing him dance, the great Chasid joined Mendel in the dance. Cured, his little girl leaped from her bed and danced with them. The great Chasid said: 'All you need is the heart!'

How could suave, sophisticated Dov come from a line of Chasidic Jews, describing the kind of fable the ultra-religious would tell their followers. Apart from Ettie Gutenberg, she had seen few Chasidim in the East End; one or two, perhaps, walking swiftly to the synagogue, talking in quiet voices near the market. Even their Yiddish was strange to her.

She bent her head. Perhaps dancing completed this day, not traditionally, but spiritually? From celebrating Rosh Hashanah as she'd always done, she'd moved into the world of the anarchists, but in the end, 'the true revolutionary', as they called him, had shared this esoteric spiritual understanding of the divine that she would ponder later, because Rudolf was now playing gentle, reflective tunes, and they took it in turns to dance in the minute, central space. Despite Sophia's pleading, Dov wouldn't yield their place to anyone else.

'I must be close to you,' he whispered. 'This is the only way, unless we go to my room.'

It was dark, people paired up in corners, kissing, fondling. Dov took Sophia by the hand. They made their way to the ground floor, humming the tunes, walking dreamily along the corridor until they were at his door. He drew her into his room.

Looking thin,' Ettie said, when she met her later that week. 'Are you eating enough?' With a sudden realisation, she took some money from her purse. 'A little something to repay your help over the months.'

'I couldn't, you'll need it. I'm really all right, Ettie.' Sophia hesitated. 'I can eat in the Socialist People's restaurant for very little.'

'You've almost completed your apprenticeship, so here's your pay. I insist.'

She pressed the money into Sophia's hand.

'All right, just this once. I'm sure there'll be work next week after Yom Kippur. Till then, I can manage.'

Ettie seemed to be on the point of asking Sophia something, but thought better of it.

'Fast well!' She hugged Sophia, then winding her way through the crowds on Wentworth Street, she turned once to wave.

Back in her room, Sophia sat on the bed and sighed.

I'm in turmoil. This is not like me at all and I feel so strange. Dov, love, religion – all flying round my head as though I'm on a whirligig, a roundabout, and I don't know how to stop it. How to get off.

Only a few kisses, these words had circled her mind all week. *Only a few kisses,* she said out loud and laughed. But what was happening to her? She went to the window, as though seeing others could clarify her thoughts, but this added to her confusion since everyone was in another kind of turmoil, preparing for Yom Kippur, the Day of the Shofar, the Day of Atonement.

She took deep breaths, telling herself to be calm.

Only a few kisses, that's all it was. True, he had continued to kiss her on the tram coming home. In between, Dov had recalled the uprising on the Battleship Potemkin in July. The strikes spreading to other ships in the port of Odessa. The people's support. The death of officers.

"Matushenko, a peasant, was their leader, and rightly so. And why, my darling Sophia, did this happen?'

It was as though he was checking her knowledge of the Great Revolution taking place at this very moment, but because of his joy, his exuberance, she cried: 'Maggots!'

'Maggots in the borsht!' He flung out his hands. 'They thought so little of these men, they could feed them on vermin. Maggots,' he shouted again.

She was almost relieved to reach her buildings and descend from the tram.

'Will I see you tomorrow? It's the second day, and...' She hesitated, then decided to be confident. 'I'll be here. Perhaps we can go for a walk?'

'My darling, I will surely be with you some time tomorrow. But there are meetings and things I must arrange. Otherwise, I'll see you during the week.'

He kissed her and strode away.

But on Monday, Mr Lazarus shook his heavy head mournfully when she sought work.

'Sorry, Sophia. Please God, there'll be some after Yom Kippur.'

Without work, she had ample time to question her own adherence to religious practice. On the one hand... (she laughed hearing herself say this), she cherished her memory of their years in Kyiv when they had attended the beautiful Brodsky synagogue. She loved the prayers, the formality, the order, and when a particularly wonderful chazan had been employed, she would listen to his voice and feel uplifted to another realm. Happy, too, to sit on the balcony with the women while her mother read from the women's prayer book in Yiddish, translating some of the psalms and prayers for women who couldn't read. At fourteen, when Mama had been ill, she'd taken over this task for her mother.

Since there were too few of them to have a synagogue in Archangelsk, they would meet in each other's houses and celebrate the festivals together. Sophia recalled the upset of the previous year when Sasha had refused to accompany them.

'I'd be a hypocrite,' he shouted. 'I don't believe in all that rubbish any more. It's the opium of the people.'

In her quiet, persuasive voice, their mother said, 'Please come. Do it for the sake of the community if nothing else. You know there are fewer than a hundred of us here and everyone counts. We must support each other.'

'Do as your mother says.' Their father stood there glowering.

But Sasha had dug in his heels and stayed at home.

And now, in the East End of London, she had only to walk down the steps, turning left or right, and she would pass dozens of synagogues or *shtibles*, small rooms above the shops where people from a particular location or village would pray. In these Days of Awe, there was a certain atmosphere she'd never experienced before – yes, a feeling of turmoil, of so much to do, but also a sense of expectation, a thoughtfulness, even an anxiety, as though every single person was truly preparing for the Day of Judgment.

On the other hand ... there had been the pogroms, especially Kishinev.

She dropped her face into her hands as though to banish the image of her little aunt, always called little because she had been petite and quick-moving, who'd had a weak heart. When the Russians raped her she'd died, and they'd cut off her breasts. *Animals*. Sophia shook her head, anger rising like a molten flow from her heart to her brain. 'God, where were you then?' she cried out loud, rising from her chair by the window. 'Where *were* you?'

Her mother had said that it was men, not God, who'd done this horrifying deed, but still... They had talked.

It had stimulated much reflection on the terrible fate of generations of Jewish people: expulsions, inquisitions, attacks by Cossacks, the Orthodox church, the Tsar. How could they continue to believe in a God who clearly didn't protect them? Then, helping her mother with confinements in Archangelsk, she had been heartbroken at the death of a mother and her baby.

Now she felt like a chameleon forced to shake off one skin in order to reveal another. But the old skin clung to her still. She wanted to talk this over with someone. Dov? She questioned the wisdom of that. He'd already told her to abandon the old traditions, expressing his hatred of the rabbinate, or most of it. Were there rabbis he respected? A passing thought. What about Aaron, but then there was his stern, unbending father.

She must solve this problem alone.

And still Dov hadn't come.

CHAPTER 16

ON FRIDAY, AT THE Sugar Loaf meeting, she listened to the others deep in an endless discussion about the revolutionary uprisings everywhere, many determined to return, to be part of it. All had been religious, she thought; now they observed nothing.

She told herself to abandon her musings, for Milly had finally turned the conversation to the Yom Kippur Ball, which would take place in three days' time. Rudolf fell unusually silent, taking out his pipe, patting down tobacco, lighting up. Listening to the discussion about the arrangements, and agreeing to take the money at the door – her contribution – Sophia still wondered about the very fact of a masked ball on the holiest day of the year.

She lifted her hand. 'Rudolf, what should we really be doing on Yom Kippur?'

He reflected, then addressing the entire group rather than directing his answer to her, he replied. 'The place of the believers is in the house of worship, the place of non-believers is in the radical meeting.'

'But this is the only holiday we have.' Sam Dreen's face turned red. 'We work hard for the movement. Everyone needs something to lighten their hearts.'

'What about the 'three-days-a-year' Jews? The ones who only go to the synagogue the two days of New Year and the Day of Atonement?' called Polly, Milly's sister. 'There are dozens, maybe hundreds who don't believe. Last year, so many people came to the ball, we could hardly move.'

'It's true our movement is about freedom of thought and belief,' said Rudolf, but in the slowness of his response, Sophia guessed he wasn't in favour of the ball. Nevertheless, she knew that, for him, the freedom of the individual was paramount. Sophia let her thoughts drift while the discussion continued. Her religious dilemma faded as she thought about Dov and those kisses in his room; she dwelled on how she'd felt that night, how extraordinary it was. She blushed, feeling her heartbeat quicken. She longed to see him, to be with him. Why hadn't he come as he'd promised? She took a deep breath, so deep in thought she hadn't noticed they were closing the meeting.

Milly shouted, 'Please be at the hall around three o'clock. We need everything in order before people arrive. Sophia, you know what you're going to do?'

'So sorry, Milly, I was miles away. You'd better tell me again. And how to get to Rhondda Grove.' Sophia made a rueful grimace.

Sunday, the day before Yom Kippur. She had settled down for lunch – black bread, a few slices of cheese, a large pat of butter, pickled herring and a hard-boiled egg, when Mrs Vine called, 'Sophia, your gentleman friend is here.'

Dov.

She blushed as she opened the door, heart pounding in her chest. To cover her emotion, she said, 'Come in. Just having lunch. Would you like some?'

'I'm always hungry!'

He sat on the bed, while she took the chair by the window, facing him.

'Delicious,' he said. 'I adore this food.' He loosened his shoulders and beamed at her.

'Tea?'

'Of course. Can I smoke?'

'Of course. Here's a saucer.'

He walked to the window, staring out or deep in thought, she couldn't tell, but she almost ran into the kitchen to hide the effect that even his smile was having on her. Mrs Vine, at the stove, gave her a pat on the shoulder, as though to approve, but saying nothing. Sophia barely noticed, her thoughts of the past week swirling.

The kettle's whistling crescendo acted as a kind of spur to her thoughts:

I want to know everything about him, his family, how he became a revolutionary, how he let go of his Jewishness. Maybe something awful occurred to him, as it did with Aaron. Fired up, she carried the teapot back and poured cups of tea.

'Dov, I've been in such a state of confusion since Sunday.' With a deep breath, she continued, 'I need to talk to you.'

'There's something I want to tell you too, but you begin.'

While he stood with his back to the window, his face in shadow, she perched on the bed and couldn't make out his response. She began to describe her painful feelings, how surrounded by all these traditional Jewish people she felt like a traitor, how she worried about abandoning something she loved, but on the other hand was absolutely committed to political activism.

'I'm sure your life in Petersburg was not dissimilar to mine,' she said, 'yet you've sloughed of any vestige of religious upbringing. How did you do that?' Her face scrunched up in worry, on the edge of tears. Raising her gaze to his, she hoped he wouldn't think her a fool, but to her surprise, he took her hands.

'Sophia, my darling, let's go out. I like to be in the open and this feels a little...' He indicated the room. 'Have you seen the Tower of London or London Bridge? I love that place.'

Bewildered by this answer, his unexpected attachment to a bridge, of all things, she took a deep breath. 'All right.'

They followed Whitechapel High Street to Aldgate High Street, but whenever she tried to talk, he placed a finger on her lips. 'Wait until we get there.'

Fifteen minutes later, he said, 'What do you think?'

Before them rose the Tower of London, its battlements and huge towers speaking of solidity and strength.

'Is it a fortress? A castle?' She gazed at the massive white tower, with its stone turrets and rounded narrow windows, which seemed impermeable.

'The Crown Jewels are there, just as in Peterhof.'

'Royalty. All the wealth in so few hands. How can you admire that?' She gave him a quizzical look.

'Now you know one of my faults. Despite my implicit belief that the rich should be swept away, there's something about the unbending strength of these buildings that fascinates me!'

To their left lay St Katharine's docks. Ships, tenders, tugs, military vessels filled the Thames River, which gleamed in a brief flash of sunshine. To their right, the City of London.

Then, Tower Bridge. Drawing her to him, he guided her up the steps. Even so, traffic roared back and forth crossing the river.

'I love the water.' Dov leaned over the parapet. 'When I was young, I used to escape to the river Neva and watch ships and boats travelling to the North Sea, to Europe, to America, and I vowed I would see all these places.'

'In Archangelsk, I would think the same. Ships coming from Europe all the way to Archangelsk. The Tsar's Navy. But I also loved to wander the woods.'

Leaving the bridge, they walked until they'd found a bench beside the Thames.

Sophia took a breath. 'Can we talk now?'

With a flourish, he said. 'Of course.'

'Generally, I know exactly what to do or what I want,' she said, 'but I've never felt so confused. I don't recognise myself.' She turned her worried gaze to him. 'You've let go of the practising side of Jewish religion, how did you do that?'

'You remember I told you my grandfather was a very orthodox man, a Chasid?' He took her hand.

'I couldn't believe it.'

'My father was brought up in his court—'

'Court, what do you mean?'

He paused. 'You probably knew that from the eight-eenth century, a new movement developed in Judaism, *Chasidim*. It means pious or pure. Chasidic Jews rejected the rigidity of the majority of rabbis, called *Misnagdim*. Leaders emerged, with many followers. These leaders, or *rebbes*, encouraged ordinary people to experience a mystical connection with God. The Chasidim believed every soul was precious. They welcomed the masses, whereas the *Misnagdim* extolled learning and ignored or even despised the poor, unlettered Jews. My father grew up expecting to be a Chasidic leader like my grandfather. But longing to study medicine, Papa persuaded him to let him study at Moscow Medical School.'

'And became a doctor?'

'Yes, and one day he attended a musical recital, where my mother was giving a concert. She is a gifted pianist. Studied at the Conservatory in Petersburg, her family was allowed to leave the Pale of Settlement because of her. My father fell instantly in love with my mother and never returned to his father's court.'

'That's beautiful.'

'Maybe. Anyway, over the years we would visit my grandfather, who would have long conversations with my father, probably encouraging him to return. After a child-hood illness when I was twelve, I developed pneumonia. My parents sent me to recuperate with him, in the coun-tryside. During those months, I became fascinated by the stories, the singing, even the prayers. I made up my mind to be a rabbi like Grandfather, whom I adored. I was always a wild, somewhat tempestuous child, but I seemed to fit in. But came the time to study for my bar mitzvah, and I changed. Maybe it was the boring, critical teacher my parents had employed, maybe my age. Whatever, I rejected the meaningless words I was saying, telling my parents I would do this for their sakes, but after that, I refused to study anymore.'

Sophia sighed. 'My brothers were the same. Did your parents tell your grandfather?'

'I don't know. I rejected everything and I guess my father, who'd been relieved I would take his place in the dynasty was ashamed, full of guilt.'

Dov gazed out over the Thames, his eyes dark.

'Was that all?'

He smiled at her. 'That's my clever Sophia. While I was learning my portion, a bookbinder came to renovate books in my father's study. He opened my eyes to the real world, something I craved, although I didn't know it at the time. Talked about revolution, about poverty, about … all the things you know. Even gave me a little book he'd written.' Drawing from his pocket a small square booklet with a yellow cover, he handed it to her. She flicked through pages, recognising words: *society, privilege, poverty, degradation.*

'What did you do?'

'He told me to see for myself the life in the poor suburbs of Petersburg where the new factories were rising up, and I did. I saw dereliction, men beating women in the street, barefoot ragged children, common enough in our blessed country. Remember, Sophia?'

'That day, returning from the meeting house in Soho. Of course I remember.'

'I'd been so sheltered.'

'So had I.'

'Naturally. Who wants to expose children to such misery, to the ugly side of humanity? And, you know, these people can't help it. They are sunk in it. But I became despondent, the misery of the world began to oppress me, and naturally my parents couldn't understand. For two years, I withdrew from my family; I am one of five: I have an older sister who is married, two younger brothers and my little sister.'

His eyes lit up, when he said her name, but his expression becoming sombre, as he fell silent and stared out over the river.

Sophia glanced at his face. Why did he look so wretched? She took a deep breath, deciding this wasn't the time to ask.

Dov straightened his shoulders. 'I wanted to become an engineer. I enjoy doing things with my hands, love mathematics, it all fitted in. On my way back from school, I would pass a cafe where students sat arguing, discussing politics in loud excited voices. One day, I slipped in and took a seat nearby, listened to their discussions. They got to know me, told me what to read, lent me books. My socialist education had begun. By the time I reached university, I knew that my destiny was to become a revolutionary.'

'What about your grandfather?'

'During one vacation, I travelled over to see him and told him my plans.' He paused, frowned. 'You know about Kabbalah?'

'What is it?'

'An esoteric understanding of how the world was created, which you're not allowed to study until you're forty. When I finished talking to Grandfather, he said, 'Our task is to heal the world. If this is your path, so be it. You will discover if you're right. Then come back to see me.'

His use of the word *healing* made her turn to him. 'And I want to heal people,' she said softly. He caught her to him as they sat there, but said nothing. 'So he accepted it?' she continued. 'Even though it's a rejection of religion?'

'I learned a little more about Kabbalah. The Chasidim believe that after the world was created, sparks of the divine were hidden in the world, and it is our task, with devotion, *mitzvot*, singing and dancing, to return the sparks to God. The broken world will be healed. That's the essence of it. I'm doing something similar, parallel.'

Sophia stared out over the river.

'I've nothing like this to guide me.'

'Something will show you the way. For the time being, follow your heart.'

'Yes,' she said, a sudden spark of joy brightening her eyes. 'That's good advice.'

'Come. It's getting chilly. Let's walk back.'

Turning her face to him, he kissed her. A woman was passing with a young boy rolling a hoop.

'Mama, those people are kissing,' he shouted.

'I hope one day,' called Dov, 'you'll be kissing someone as pretty as my friend here.'

CHAPTER 17

AKING ON YOM KIPPUR, she listened. For once in these crowded tenements, there was something like silence. Not completely so, for how could there be with so many people living above and below, or on either side? She could hear footsteps, men walking to shul already, but there was a quietness that took her breath away. Sitting up, she shivered, thinking of what she had promised to do today. Go to the masked ball. And fasting? She wondered if she could actually eat. She had barely eaten the previous evening, and in theory, should be fasting until after sunset today. Twenty-five hours.

What shall I do?

She eventually heard Mrs Vine close the outer door. Still in her night clothes, Sophia went to the stove. She poured boiling water onto a spoonful of tea leaves into a pot bought from Hannah Leah, and hands trembling, stirred it, then taking a cube of sugar from the sugar bowl, put it between her teeth. Impossible. She couldn't drink tea with or without sugar. What a waste.

Leaving the teapot in the hearth, she climbed into bed. Thinking of her mother, she said aloud: *I do believe absolutely and completely in the work that we are doing here in the*

East End. We're helping people have better, healthier lives. Surely, that's enough?

In letters to her mother, she'd described the grinding poverty, filth, children with bare feet, women who aged, thin, haggard, old at thirty, as they sat at sewing machines twelve or fourteen hours a day, the men who died in their thirties from lung disease. Reflecting on these letters, she made up her mind. Her comrades, the Arbeter Frainters, worked for the greater good, they were her inspiration. She would certainly, absolutely, go to the ball.

Still, I can't eat.

She fell asleep; it was nearly two o'clock, when she awoke. Quickly, without looking in the tarnished mirror above the mantelpiece, she washed her face. Her room felt alien – bed unmade, nightclothes bundled under the pillow, the pot of cold tea in the grate.

A couple had recently moved into the room above hers, and she could hear them talking in subdued tones, a man to his wife, and the higher wail of a child, a young baby, waiting to be fed. She heard a door close, heavy footsteps running down the stairs. No doubt the man was going to the synagogue, leaving his wife behind, for you couldn't take so young a child to prayers.

It was time to get ready for the ball. There would be masks, fancy dress. She took up the red mask she'd made, the brightly coloured skirt from Rosh Hashanah, and a dark shawl her mother had sent for the winter months, transforming her into a passable Ukrainian peasant. Casting a quick glance around a now tidy room, she went out. Hundreds were emerging from synagogues, and she paused, marvelling at the crowds talking quietly in ones and twos, filling the pavements, spilling over into the road, for it was the break before the afternoon and evening service.

She made her way down Brick Lane, with the intention of taking the tram to Bow. Only ten minutes' journey, Milly had told her, but at the corner of Fournier Street, she heard a muffled, repeated beat. Others were frowning, muttering, listening. Standing by the Spitalfields Great Synagogue, the *Machzikei Hadath*, where men in their white prayer shawls were pouring out, she saw two lines of people marching towards her. Was it the British Brothers League? When the columns of men and women passed, she covered her mouth with her hand, her heartbeat racing.

Rosa.

Rosa leading, a *bogatyrka,* a peaked army hat with a red star pin, ironically atop her flame-coloured hair which was streaming loose down her shoulders. Behind her, twenty or thirty people marched in unison, handing out sandwiches to passers by, smoking abundantly, shouting and singing revolutionary songs. All forbidden on this holiest of days. Some waved the red flag as they sang the *Marseillaise*. She recognised a few fiery newcomers to the East End group, recently arrived from Poland, still attached to violence, to propaganda by the deed, and a problem for Rudolf. The rest must surely be members of the Soho revolutionaries.

A wave of horror filled Sophia. She watched Rosa approach a man emerging from the synagogue and wave her half-eaten sandwich beneath his nose.

'Hungry?' Rosa shouted, grinning.

'*Haserai!* Pig! Blasphemers! Evil doers! May you rot in hell!' He recoiled, his face contorted in disgust, then he pushed her so violently, she staggered backwards and almost fell. Other men following down the steps and seeing what was happening began to scream curses in Yiddish. In their white prayer shawls, they bent and picked up stones, pieces of wood, anything they could use as weapons, and began to beat the marchers around the shoulders and face.

One fought back, shouting, 'Blasphemer yourself! You know it's forbidden to carry anything and you're holding a weapon!'

More and more, they emerged, disturbed by the racket.

Sophia's heart beat wildly. Heat rose in her neck and face, while shock, shame and fear flooded through her. How could they mock people for their religious practice like this?

She heard someone shout: 'Die in *Gehenna*. Die in Hell!'

'Where is it?' answered one of the marchers.

Surrounded by furious men and women, Sophia was hemmed in, fearful, but she wanted to stop the whole thing, for she understood how blatant, how outrageous this was. About to run over to Rosa, to tell her to cease, she heard the sound of heavy footsteps approaching. People on the pavements suddenly pulled back. Sophia caught the words *Bessarabian Tigers* repeated here and there. A group of men in workmen's clothes, holding sticks and batons raced in and out of the marchers, beating them on the head and shoulders, fighting with anyone they could. The Bessarabian Tigers, the gang which played cards at the Romanian restaurant on Settle Street, who used extortion and violence to get money from the people. Bad men, Milly had said. Then Sophia overheard the words *British Brothers* – that English far-right group who hated Jews.

Which were they? Surely it was the British Brothers.

She heard a scream. One of them was pummelling and kicking Rosa. Sophia stood frozen. A marcher near the end of the line shouted, 'I'm getting help from Rhondda Grove!'

He disappeared in the direction of the tram stop.

She had to reach Rosa; hands shielding her eyes, she wound her way through the fighting men and, with difficulty, dragged a barely conscious Rosa to the pavement. Blood poured from a deep cut in Rosa's forehead onto her clothes. As Sophia bent to examine the cut, one of the attackers punched Sophia's shoulder and the back of her head but she was so intent on sliding her folded shawl beneath Rosa's head, she barely noticed. There was so much blood, Rosa so white, Sophia feared she might be dead. People looked on in horror; a woman in holiday clothes skirted around them. Others crowded near, silent.

'*Pikuas nefesh*,' Sophia looked up at the women, her voice urgent, commanding. 'Save life! Even on Yom Kippur, especially on Yom Kippur, you are commanded to save life. I need bandages or pieces of material to stop the bleeding. *Quickly*.'

The women muttered together, then one said, 'I'll get something.'

Going into her house only a step away, the woman reappeared with strips of white material torn from a sheet. Two or three women crouched down to lift Rosa's head, while

Sophia wound pieces of material around her forehead, but still the blood seeped through turning the material the colour of rust.

The fighting continued all around with cries and grunts and groans.

There were shouts from the end of the street. Dov and Aaron appeared and began to fight with the gang members. Within moments, Sam Dreen and others from the Sugar Loaf pub group arrived and joined them.

Police whistles. Exchanging anxious glances, the women who'd formed a protective circle around Rosa pulled away. Young policeman with dome-shaped helmets and brilliant buttons down their jackets charged up with truncheons, beating those fighting to separate them. As they fell back, the police were taking down details, Sophia noted with alarm. She sat on the curb, cradling Rosa in her arms, when a police officer marched over and demanded their names too, then ordered her to take Rosa to the London Hospital. Her heart racing, terrified of being implicated as an 'enemy alien', Sophia lifted her gaze in search of Aaron or Dov. They were further down the road being questioned. She called to them, her voice frantic. Finally, they ran back to her.

'Take her to the London Hospital.'

Between them, they lifted Rosa. Accompanied by Dov, Aaron carried her down the road towards the tram stop. Only now did Sophia become aware of pain in her shoulder, the throbbing headache. She managed to stand, but felt unexpectedly weak; swaying against a wall, she prayed she would not pass out.

Dov turned and raced back.

'My God, Sophia, are you fasting?'

She nodded. 'I'll be all right.'

'Take a few sips of this. Not too much.' From his pocket, he took out a small flask. 'When we get to the London, I'll make sure they give you food.'

'Miss Krichevska, wake up. Doctor is here to see you.'

Her eyes were sealed like a letter home. As she dragged open her eyelids, a dull pain surged through her head and behind her eyes. Turning to escape, a knife probed her shoulder. She groaned, focused her attention on the white ceiling, then moving with care, found she was in a long, blurred room with rows of beds and tall windows that seemed to shimmer and fade. She blinked several times to clear her vision but now the beds, windows and chairs appeared double. Sophia's heart pounded in her chest. *Am I dreaming? What is happening?*

A woman loomed up, her face too close. Sophia took in the lilac hue of her dress, the white of her apron, the frilled head covering, and closed her eyes. She felt someone helping her to sit, a pillow being pushed behind her head.

'Miss Krichevska, how are you feeling this morning?' Another, deeper voice.

It came to her then, that she was in the London Hospital. She took a shuddering breath. 'I don't see clearly. Everything's double.'

A hazy shape of a woman wearing a white coat appeared in her vision.

'You have concussion. That's why we're keeping you here.'

'In the hospital?'

'Yes, the London. How's the pain?'

Sophia exhaled, relieved. She touched her head, letting her arm fall onto the counterpane.

'It's bearable.' Sitting up felt better. 'How long have I been here?'

'Since yesterday afternoon. Your friends brought you.'

She remembered the attack on Rosa, the bleeding, the battle in the streets and the police coming to arrest them. A sudden awareness made her heart race: Yom Kippur. But how she got here, she couldn't recall.

'Will this go?' She pointed to her head, not daring to touch it again.

'Rest and sleep are the cure. I'll ask Sister to put screens alongside the bed to divert the light, which will also help.' The doctor paused. 'Miss Krichevska, your friend—'

'Is she all right? Where is she?'

'At the end of the ward, by the nurses' station. We inserted a few stitches, she's fine now. But you did well to staunch the bleeding. Where did you learn to do this?'

Grasping the mattress with both hands, to keep her head steady, Sophia attempted a reply. 'I've worked with a midwife. I ... I applied to study medicine in Moscow.' *Why have I blurted that out like a child?*

'Indeed. Well, Miss Krichevska, I'll see how you are this evening.'

As the doctor continued her round, Sophia stared; beneath her white coat, the doctor wore a long, coloured robe, a sari, and her black hair was coiled at the nape of her neck. She must come from India, the Far East, yet how could that be? Lying back, Sophia wondered at herself for not registering something even more significant: *the doctor is a woman*. Clearly, her brain was still fuzzy, and sleep drew her down. *I'll be back to normal, I hope, when I wake again.*

But Rosa? Sophia opened her eyes; there seemed to be hundreds of patients huddled or sleeping or sitting up in the rows of beds, on either side of the ward, which stretched away like the steppes. She couldn't see Rosa. As she drifted deeper, Sophia wondered what Rosa had told the doctors; what would the police do, and would Rosa know?

She had to speak to her.

It was lunchtime when she woke again. A woman was trundling a container on wheels, handing out plates of greyish meat swimming in thin, lumpy mashed potato. For dessert, came a bowl of white unrecognisable slops.

'What is it?' Sophia pointed to bubbles resembling white frogspawn.

'Tapioca,' said the woman.

Thank goodness, sleep had restored Sophia and the outline of objects was no longer in double, though her head still ached. But this food? She tasted the meat and her face crinkled up in disgust. Impossible. Anyway, she wasn't hungry. The woman returned and silently removed both plates, but handed Sophia a cup of sweetened tea poured from an urn with a spigot, so brown it was indistinguishable from coffee. Sophia drank it gratefully.

Then she noticed patients sitting up, combing their hair, tidying bed covers, and she glanced at her watch: two o'clock. A nurse unlocked the doors at the far end and visitors streamed in. A woman walked in her direction.

'Ettie, how lovely to see you!'

'As soon as I heard, I went to your room and collected a few things. Nightdress, brush and comb, handkerchiefs, cardigan.' Ettie unpacked a small bag and glanced round. 'Here's a bowl of barley soup, not so hot, but it'll do you good.' From her own bag she lifted a bowl covered with cheese cloth, then a spoon, and a bagel wrapped in brown paper. 'Butter on the bagel. And a small piece of honey cake. They don't have kosher food here and by the look of you, you need some nourishment.'

'Ettie, I can't tell you how happy I am to see you. Thank you!' As she drank the soup and munched at the bagel, Sophia told Ettie about the inedible lunch and they laughed. Handing the spoon back to Ettie, Sophia said, 'How did you know where I was?'

'By seven o'clock last night I should think the whole of the East End knew exactly what happened and where you'd gone. The *Yidden*, at least.' Ettie folded her hands in her lap. 'You weren't marching, were you Sophia?'

Conscious she'd been going to the Ball, reprehensible in Ettie's eyes, Sophia threw an embarrassed look at her.

'No, I wasn't marching. When I saw they'd attacked Rosa, a woman I know, and she was bleeding, I had to run over and do what I could.'

Ettie folded her lips. 'A bad business. Jews should never draw attention to themselves, that's how pogroms begin. These revolutionaries don't realise how dangerous they are for ordinary people, especially foreigners like us.'

A widespread view. Another dilemma to solve, but not now.

The nurse came down the ward shaking the bell. 'Visiting time ended.'

Ettie kissed Sophia, saying she would visit her tomorrow, if Mrs Finkelstein didn't produce her baby. 'But I'm sure someone will bring food this evening. Everyone knows what's happened.'

'They might discharge me tomorrow.'

'Don't be in a hurry. A rest will bring roses to your cheeks.'

Sophia's attempt to see Rosa was thwarted by the Sister, who told her sharply to return to bed, it was too soon to be on her feet, and indeed, the ground felt as though it was moving up and down, as if she were back on the boat. Even the lumpy, thin mattress felt like a kind of haven, and she lay back again and dozed.

More visitors at seven o'clock. Milly and her sister Polly bringing bread, cheese, fish balls, an orange, a small knife and a table napkin to wipe her fingers. They peered at her anxiously.

'How are you?'

'Better than this morning. It was terrifying. Everything was doubled and blurred but, thank goodness, not anymore.'

'That's a relief. We were so worried and upset, Sophia. You know Rudolf dislikes these marches and demonstrations, which always turns the population against us, when we need to be most united. We did have an inkling about it.

We heard some of the newcomers talking at the Sugar Loaf pub, those who'd recently arrived from Poland. They still think they're fighting the Tsar, can't abandon their belief in violence and protest. It's a real problem. Then we heard it was Rosa.' Bright red points of anger flared on Milly's sallow cheeks. 'When we heard you were both in hospital, I must tell you, Rudolf was very angry.' She inhaled. 'But knowing that won't help you recover.'

Sophia dipped her head. 'Did you see Rosa, as you came in? Near the door?'

They shook their heads.

'I would have given her a piece of my mind,' said Milly.

'My sister is always the gloomy one,' said Polly, attempting to lighten the conversation. 'What's worse, you missed your first Yom Kippur Ball. Were you going to wear fancy dress?'

Sophia pointed to her skirt, folded at the bottom of her bed, and the bright shawl she would have worn. 'I was going to be a Ukrainian peasant girl.'

'Instead you became Florence Nightingale.' Milly shook her head.

They chatted about the club to be opened after Christmas, but Sophia couldn't help returning to the question that had been circling her mind all afternoon.

'Milly, Polly, do you know how the Bessarabian Tigers got involved?'

They exchanged glances.

'Rumours are it could have been Rothschild, who paid them. He hates us.' Milly folded her lips. 'Some say it was local shopkeepers. They resent the Socialist People's

Restaurant taking business from them because it's so cheap. And it was open yesterday. Even the established Yiddish newspapers dislike us. You know how they try to make children into little English gentlemen and ladies, forcing them to speak English at school. Always the same thing, don't draw attention to yourself. Be invisible. What could be more visible than what happened?'

'It could have been the British Brothers League,' said Polly. 'Worse still.'

'I can't believe Jewish people would attack other Jewish people. To think it might have been instigated by a man like Rothschild.' Sophia drew a breath. 'Whoever it was, I'm shocked such a thing could happen in London.'

When she asked them if there'd be a court procedure, Milly told her not to worry, they would vouch for her. Drawing a letter from her handbag, she passed it to Sophia.

'This is for you. From Dov.'

Sophia's heartbeat quickened; taking the letter, she read her name on the envelope, written in Dov's regular, etched writing.

'He's leaving today.' Milly continued, throwing a cautious glance round the room though clearly, nobody was listening. 'He doesn't know how long he'll be away.'

'I'll read it after you've gone.'

Visitors were stirring, nurses drawing down the blinds, and they heard the bell ringing for the end of visiting time.

'Thank you so much for coming. The doctor said she'd be here this evening; I might go home tomorrow.'

'Someone will pop by to let us know. We'll look out for you.'

They kissed. Sophia watched them walk to the doors, stopping to exchange a few words with Rosa, clearly returned from wherever she'd been. For a brief second, Sophia longed to know what they'd said – but now, now, she would read Dov's letter. Her heart pounding, she turned onto her side, drew the counterpane over her head, and opened it.

> *My Darling,*
> *I can't describe my feelings of devastation and anger when I saw what happened to you yesterday. All because of Rosa. I stayed by your side until the night sister – a termagant! – threw me out. They told me they had given you a sedative to help you sleep, that it was mild concussion and you'd be better in a couple of days. Thank God, but I needed to see that myself. To think this has happened again.*

Sophia raised her eyebrows. What did he mean: *this has happened again?* She searched for some clue, something he'd said before, but nothing came. She inhaled deeply, shook her head and continued:

> *Sophia, my darling, if anything happens to me, if I never come back, I want you to know that I love you. I always have. Ever since that moment we met on the ship, even before we'd left Petersburg. Because of the life I lead, I couldn't tell you. But I'll be with you soon, my beautiful girl, and we can live together, if that's what you want.*
> *I love you, Dov*

She gasped, read it again and again. Tears spilling from her eyes, she marvelled at the final paragraph. He loved her with passion, that was clear. She'd hidden her feelings for him, yet now she was sure. But in the next breath, he was warning her he might not return.

What must I think? Pushing back the counterpane, she sat up. Folding the letter, she reached for her handbag that Ettie had looped over the chair, and pushed the letter into an inner pocket. Lifting her head, she was taken aback to see Rosa walking with slow, careful pace down the ward, stopping occasionally to clutch at a bed end, as though for support. Sophia's face grew hot with anger, the anger she'd felt in the street seeing Rosa taunt the worshippers leaving the synagogue. But Sophia's anger gave way to surprise: as Rosa got nearer, Sophia saw that her face was drawn, chalky white, her beautiful gold hair straggly, matted with blood, the hospital bandage binding her forehead almost covering her eyebrows. The proud, defiant Rosa had become a thin, hunched little woman.

Reaching Sophia's bedside, Rosa gave a nervous smile.

'May I sit down?' She indicated the chair.

'Of course. You look very tired. Why did you come?'

Rosa sat and took a deep breath to restore herself.

'If it wasn't for you, I don't know what would have happened.' Her voice was halting. 'I'd certainly have lost a lot of blood. Maybe my life.'

'Surely not.'

'They seem to think so.' She stretched out her arm, touching Sophia's hand with her own. 'Thank you, Sophia.' Puckering up her mouth, head bent, she averted her gaze, then, with a touch of the old Rosa: 'Why on earth did you get involved? I saw the look of disapproval on your face as we marched.'

'*Rosa.*'

'Sorry, I shouldn't have said that. Especially now you're here. What happened to you? When Aaron carried me in, I was barely conscious, and this morning, the nurse refused to tell me.'

'One of the Bessarabian Tigers, or whoever it was, attacked me, while you were lying on the ground. Given me a headache, a painful shoulder. It's mild concussion, they say.'

'What a pair we are.' Rosa grinned and Sophia couldn't help but smile.

Eyes flashing, Rosa said, 'I don't regret the march. I want people to think for themselves, not follow the old traditions like sheep. Look where it's got them: the Tsar, domination by the rabbis, poverty, losing their children to the Tsar's army. It needs to change.' Sophia leaned in to argue, but Rosa continued, 'I am deeply sorry you were injured. If I can do anything to help you, anything at all, just tell me. Come and see me in Soho whenever you need something. Come and talk.' She hesitated. 'Actually, Sophia, there's something I want to tell you about D—'

'Miss Minz! What are you doing out of bed?' The night sister charged down the ward, her heavy tread resounding on the wooden floor, small eyes glittering, tramlines across her forehead. 'Go back to bed immediately. Doctor wishes to see you.'

'*Mamzer*,' Rosa whispered, in Yiddish. Ignoring the sister's injunction, she stood up slowly. 'Be well, Sophia! Don't forget, come and see me and we'll talk.'

'Get better quickly, Rosa. I'll come when I can.'

Sophia watched her return to her bed. A different Rosa. *There's more to her than I'd realised,* Sophia thought, playing over the conversation in her mind. Was Rosa going to tell her something about Dov? Sophia chided herself: *You're obsessed with him, it could be a thousand other things but still, still... I have to know.*

CHAPTER 18

Back at Wentworth Buildings, a pale grey light through the window cast a thin beam on the letter, as Sophia lay on her bed for three days, reading it over and over again. *I love him*, she thought, folding it against her heart, as though to keep her love secure. She longed for him to walk through the door, so she could tell him. On Friday, however, something leapt out at her, causing her to sit up, a frown teasing her forehead.

Dov hadn't asked *her* if *she* loved him. He'd assumed it. Supposing she already had a fiancé in Ukraine, a sweetheart in Archangelsk, who wanted to marry her? Dov had not enquired. Wondering whether this was indicative of Dov's character or typical of all men, she wished she were more experienced. A smile smoothed her forehead. He knew, without asking – by the way they had kissed, after the love-in, by the way they had sat so close together on the tram. And he'd opened his heart to her at Tower Gardens, trusting her. He'd seen it in her eyes. Yet questions lurked beneath her joy, and she laid the letter beside her, as they chased through her mind, demanding an answer.

Last week I was frantic about my betrayal of Judaism, this week it's about me and a man. I'm so troubled. I hate the feeling of anxiety. I like to be certain, clear in my direction. This has rarely happened but when it has, I've had one solution: to write it down logically, read it as though it applies to somebody else, and then I have clarity again.

Of course, she thought sadly, *I could also discuss things with Mama.*

Well, she isn't here, so find a way yourself, Sophia Krichevska!

Taking a notebook from her bag, she listed *questions* on one side of the page, *answers* on the other.

Question one: What does Dov really do over there? Is it dangerous? Who would know? Answer: Rudolf and Milly and probably Rosa.

Question two: Why would he 'never come back'? She shivered on writing those words, but it had to be done. Who would know? Answer: Rudolf. Maybe Rosa.

Question three: What does Rosa want to tell me, is it about Dov? Answer: Go and see her.

Her head throbbing, she let the notebook fall onto the brown coverlet and closing her eyes, she shivered. The room was so icy. Thank goodness she'd lugged her *perronet* from the Arctic to London. Taking two shawls from the end of the bed, she wrapped them around herself and crawled under the covers, dragging the *perronet* up to her nose.

In Archangelsk there would be deep, freezing snow. Her mother would venture out to the market shrouded in fur coat and hat, fur-lined gloves on her hands. In October now, there would be an hour or so of daylight followed by the dark of night, even in daytime. Her mind roved over the gatherings they would have, the parties to brighten their lives in that place of darkness.

But now, as Ettie and Hannah Leah brought her a little food or a bowl of soup, they would say that it was exceptionally cold for English weather. And the warmth and weight of the covers made her relax and she marvelled at the kindness of these women. Even Mrs Vine, pursing her lips, had agreed to wait for the rent till the following week.

Sliding up against the bedhead, Sophia reached for her bag and searched her purse. Four shillings. She turned her gaze to the empty fireplace and wondered if she had enough for kindling. That would warm the bedroom a little. No, it would have to be food; she wouldn't accept any more from her friends, they needed it for themselves.

The doctor had told her to rest for two weeks, stay away from work, but that was impossible. She needed money. Later today, she would take herself out and buy a few vegetables, some bread and eggs from the stalls on Wentworth Street. Surely that would do no harm? On Sunday she would see if Mr Lazarus had work for her. Otherwise ... otherwise, she envisioned herself standing in line at the Waste. That empty ground, strewn with rubble, where thistles sprang up between stray bricks, and unemployed men stood waiting for some small workshop owner to offer them a few hours' work. Selected like slaves. She had never seen a woman there, but if she had to go, she would. Her head throbbed now, and she rubbed her aching shoulder.

Her mind retraced its steps to Rosa. What was it Rosa wanted to say? Some secret about Dov? She let out a sigh, almost a groan. If anybody knew his secrets it would be her, for they'd been together for ages, probably lovers. She frowned at a sudden risky thought. Supposing Rosa was lying? Supposing she was enticing her to Soho with some nefarious plot or deception in mind?

She sat up. *You're really in a bad way to think such twisted thoughts. Where's that confident person who set off on a journey of adventure, leaving Petersburg five months ago? What about your promises to the family?*

Tears spilled from her eyes, but she swiped them away. Folding her lips, she told herself to 'talk herself in'.

I'll wait till Dov returns and ask him myself. Although I must be naive to think that because he loves me, he would answer.

She had to stop. The dull ache in her head was becoming sharper.

She got up, wrote to Sasha in New York asking him if he'd put away money for tickets for their parents, and then a letter home, telling them more about London, such a great city. She described the Tower, sitting in Tower Gardens, tourists gazing in admiration at the ancient monument where the Crown Jewels were kept. After a moment's indecision, she added she had met a very nice young man in the socialist movement. Just a mention, to give her mother something to think about, nothing more. This was the briefest communication with Mama, while recognising that she really wanted to unburden her heart, seek Mama's advice. She omitted the march on the Day of Atonement and her accident, for what good would that do?

Rubbing her shoulder, she put on her coat and hat, and went down to Wentworth Street, bought the provisions she needed for soup, and with care, walked to the post office to send away her precious letters. With relief, she also discovered there was work and, the following week, she was back at the sewing machine, delighted to see Mrs Lazarus working too, the baby fast asleep in her Moses basket despite the workshop racket.

'By the time she grows up,' Mr Lazarus said proudly, 'we'll have a place big enough for thirty workers, and she can do whatever she wants. She won't have to sweat it out here.'

'Please God,' said Mrs Lazarus, who even smiled.

Sophia wrote several postcards to Rosa, enquiring when she could see her, but Rosa did not reply. Sophia's longing to see Dov, to throw her arms around him, to ask him these aching questions, kept her awake at night. The fear that he wouldn't come back grew like a black bear stalking its prey. She could not throw it off.

One Sunday, she made a decision: I shall go to Poland Street and speak to Rosa in her flat.

The journey from the East End to Soho was like a return to the start of her life in England but in reverse. Her English vastly improved, she could ask questions, understand answers, engage in conversation; she recognised English people by their mode of dressing, whether they were working class, the women wearing shawls or shabby jackets, the men in peaked caps; the middle classes by their hats and coats and somewhat self-satisfied expression; the upper classes with their glittery motor cars, their goggles and driving hats, honking their horns through the plebeian horse-drawn buses and trams. Oh yes, she thought, I've learned about the class system in this country, just as I knew it in Kyiv.

Stairs everywhere, thought Sophia, as she climbed to Rosa's first-floor flat, admiring the elegant banisters probably dating from the last century. She found the door, and with an intake of breath, knocked, hoping Rosa would be there, planning what she would say. Moments later, Rosa swung open the door, apparently unfazed by Sophia's arrival.

'I've been waiting for you to come.' Her tone unfriendly, her green eyes hard.

Sophia frowned. 'Did you receive the postcards I sent you?'

'Of course.' A gleam of anger appeared in Rosa's eyes and Sophia stepped back.

'Then why…?'

Rosa folded her arms. 'Why? Because I changed my mind.' She gave Sophia a challenging look.

Uncertain whether this referred to what Rosa wanted to say in the hospital, or something entirely different, Sophia took a breath.

'What do you mean?' Since Rosa stayed silent, Sophia shrugged. 'It's clear you don't want to see me.' I was right after all, Sophia thought, she's not to be trusted. Turning on her heel, she made for the top of the stairs but felt a hand on her shoulder. She flinched from a residue of pain, and was forced to look back at Rosa.

'Sophia, I'm so sorry. Is it still painful?' Rosa's expression took on a look of remorse.

'Sometimes.' This softening in Rosa's voice might perhaps be an opening. 'How is your head?' But at once, feeling foolish and before Rosa could answer, Sophia carried on: 'If you really don't want to see me, though I don't know why, I'll go. Goodbye, Rosa.'

'No, I do want to see you. I was rude and I'm sorry. Come in, do you want to share my lunch?'

Startled by this sudden change of mood, Sophia said stiffly, 'I have already had something, but if you're sure, I'll come in.'

Beaming, her eyes agleam with pleasure, Rosa drew Sophia into the room.

Sophia's first impression was of a high-ceilinged narrow room, with an alcove at the far end revealing a set of shelves, a two-ring burner on the top. Below, a tray with a small, coloured enamel box, the teapot and carefully stacked crockery, on the bottom, a tea canister, sugar bowl and an angular cheese dish together with various containers. The smell of cooking was overlaid by the sweet scent that Sophia guessed Rosa wore, for it lay, a fine covering in the air. Pale pink and lilac cushions were arranged against the bedhead. A very feminine room.

'Come and sit here with me at the table. I'll make some tea.'

While Rosa was doing this, Sophia's attention was caught by a card propped up on the mantelpiece. She read the words: *Rosa's Retreat*, written in fine Italic script, and was intrigued.

'Have some tea,' Rosa said, pushing over the sugar. Finishing her meal, Rosa sprang up to put the dishes in a bowl on the alcove floor then rejoined Sophia, who had taken a lump of sugar, secretly amazed at the swift transformation in Rosa's mood.

'Why have you changed your mind about seeing me?' Sophia asked.

'Can I be frank?' Rosa sat back, her eyes hooded.

'I'm not afraid of the truth. Be as frank as you wish.'

Sophia hoped for the truth, but noting Rosa's mobile features, one moment shining with smiles, another tensed in an angry frown, knew she was an actress, playing many parts, and thought it wise to take whatever Rosa said with a pinch of salt.

Rosa settled herself in the chair, the cup of tea nestled in her hands.

'When we were in the hospital, I was immensely grateful to you. You saved me.'

'I wouldn't say that.'

Rosa leaned in. 'Those women coming back from shul or going to their families, would they have lifted a finger to staunch the bleeding? Not a hint of it. They stood and stared, probably thought I was a woman of easy virtue.'

'But they did help.'

'Only because you reminded them about saving a life. I wanted to do something to thank you, to repay you but...' Her eyes became hard, angry. 'You're with Dov now, aren't you?'

Her hatred felt like a spume of filthy water flung across Sophia's face.

'I suppose you could call it that.' Sophia sighed. 'I don't see how we can talk properly if you feel like this.' She half rose from her chair. 'Clearly, my presence is upsetting you.'

'No. You must listen to me. Please sit down.'

From anger to pleading, Rosa's gaze could not be avoided. Sophia sat again.

Rosa began to talk, her words spinning from her without pause. 'I met Dov at the revolutionaries' cafe in Petersburg when I was sixteen. I had just slammed out of the house after a row with my horrible stepmother. She married my father only for his money. By then he'd grown fat and stupid and I'd told him so. We have a factory, a printworks, and my father's a very successful man.' She raised her eyebrows. 'He wanted me to go to finishing school in Switzerland, I refused. If it wasn't for my little brother, still living there, I would have cut myself off completely. That woman hates me, conspires against me, inventing terrible things I'm supposed to have done. That day I had had enough. I packed a small bag and left. Then in the cafe, I saw Dov with the revolutionaries. You know only too well how easy it is fall in love with him, which I did.'

She stopped and picked at the tablecloth.

'After a few years, I became deeply involved with the revolutionary movement – I believe in it, Sophia. I do. Around that time, I must have been twenty, Dov and I agreed to be free to go with someone else, if we chose. Free love. I had to agree or I'd have lost him completely. I believe in this too, though it was Dov's idea.'

'Did he go with others often?' Sophia furrowed her brow.

'A couple of times. Didn't last.'

Sophia licked her lips as though suddenly dry. 'How did you know about me?'

'He was spending more time in the East End. Never came here. Anyway, people told me.'

Sophia drew a quick breath; she hadn't realised she had become common knowledge. It irked her, somehow.

Rosa carried on, 'It had to be you. I saw how he looked at you, the day you came to the Grafton Hall Club. I challenged him that evening and you know what he said? *Of course, I seek the young ones as recruits to the cause.* Recruits!'

Sophia took a sip of cold tea.

'He always comes back to me.' Rosa's gaze was triumphant, then it fell. 'Except this time, he didn't. Now you see why I've changed my mind about you.'

'But he's been away for weeks,' Sophia said with a frown. Rosa scrunched up her mouth and stayed silent. Sophia let out a breath, her gaze turned to the floorboards. Finally, looking up, she muttered, 'I so hoped we could be friends. There's no one here my age to talk to, to share my thoughts with. But I understand how angry you feel. I'd probably be the same. I'll go back to the East End.'

Rosa's eyes widened. Her gaze softened.

'Friends? I've not had a friend since I was twelve.' She clapped her hands and laughed as though Sophia had offered her a bag of the fruit pastilles or lemon sherbets she'd buy for Hannah Leah's children. 'Don't go, Sophia. If it wasn't for Dov, we could really be friends.' She pounded the table with her fist. 'Why should a man come between us? Women stand up for women. Stay, Sophia. You must stay and we'll talk.'

Reaching across the table she grasped Sophia's hand.

'What about?' Astonished but pleased by this sudden *volte-face*, Sophia grinned.

'Us. The world. The revolutionary movement, everything!'

'In the Bible,' Sophia said, 'men had many wives, but women had no choice. We have. Yes, I shall stay.' If this was another of Rosa's ploys, she thought, a game of charades, pretence, she would play her part and see what transpired.

They talked, finding similarities in their educational achievements; while Sophia excelled in science, Rosa's gifts were in languages and art, which allowed her to find steady work at a nearby milliner's. When Sophia pointed to the card on the mantelpiece, Rosa chuckled.

'My secret deviation from the path of socialism. Others have their 'sins', I know. Mine is to have a house with bedrooms, sitting room, kitchen and scullery, where the comrades will meet, *chez moi*. Space to walk and move.' She smiled saying the words in French. 'All of them: Lenin, Trotsky, even Kropotkin if he wanted. Whoever needs a bed would come to me, and stay as long as they wished, not in some rat-filled doss house in the East End. Rosa's Retreat – I love the sound of that!'

'How will you buy it?'

'Saving up.' Rosa grinned. She pointed to the tiny box that Sophia had noticed on the tray.

There came a sharp rap at the door and Rosa jumped up. 'That will be Florence come for the hat I promised her.'

A young woman, pretty in a ravaged sort of way, kohl around her eyes, her coat open to reveal an unseasonably low corsage, appeared.

'Florence, this is my new friend, Sophia. Sophia, meet Florence who's helped me enormously.'

'Is that hat ready?' said Florence. 'The hat what you made for Liza, with the pink and white roses?' Turning to Sophia she said, 'Liza's had no end of gentlemen since she bought it, so I've asked Rosa to make one for me.'

'Here it is.' Rosa took a felt hat from the cupboard, handing it to Florence, who tried it on and observing herself in the mirror, gave a little squeal. 'It's gorgeous, Rosa. I love it.'

Handing some money to Rosa, she gave a little wave to Sophia, and left.

'Who is she?' asked Sophia, with a quizzical look.

'Florence, one of the prostitutes I've got to know since I've lived here. Come to the window, you might see them now, before it gets quite dark. They walk up and down, around and about. And many come for a new hat when they have the money.'

Sophia followed Rosa to the window; looking down, she saw one or two women walking up and down, leaning towards a motor car that had stopped, chatting together as they waited.

'I'm in a different world,' Sophia said, with a wry laugh.

'The real world. Once I asked Dov what prostitutes would do after the Revolution. He said they'd be paid like any other worker, and I agree with that.'

As they sat down, Rosa jumped up again and rummaged in a drawer. 'You may need this, one of these days.' She waved a circular rubber object in the air.

'What is it?'

'A contraceptive device. Called the Dutch cap. Florence introduced it to me.' Rosa handed it to Sophia, who frowned as she examined it.

'Does it work?'

'A Dutch doctor, Aletta Jacobs, clearly Jewish like us, she devised it. She's a firm believer in birth control for women.' Rosa sat back. 'As I said,' she gave Sophia a roguish look, 'you might need it one day. Are you sleeping with Dov?'

Sophia's head jerked back and she blushed.

'I'm thinking about those poor women in the East End. The babies who die, the mothers too. Wouldn't this be a liberation for them?'

Rosa raised her eyebrows, a look of admiration in her eyes. 'That never entered my mind. I guess women everywhere would welcome this. There's another type of contraceptive, Florence says, called the *capote anglaise*, that men use. According to Florence, it's easier and quicker but I doubt you'd get those men to use one.'

Rosa gave a little chuckle which Sophia, already intent on this discovery, barely heard.

'Do you think Florence could obtain some for me?'

'Some? How many are you thinking of?'

'Three, four, six. I don't know, but as I go around helping Ettie with confinements, I'm sure I could recommend this. Afterwards, perhaps, especially if she's had seven, eight, nine children and she's worn out.'

'I'll ask her.'

Before Sophia left, for it was growing dark and cold, with fog curling around the roof tops, Rosa explained how the contraceptive should be inserted, how it must be used. Sophia stared in surprise, then she kissed her.

'I want to be a doctor. This would be one of my armaments to protect the women I'll look after. Thank you, Rosa.'

Going back, Sophia replayed the afternoon in her mind, wondering if Rosa truly wanted a friend or if was this another ploy. An actress, no wonder she had such a mobile, expressive face.

But still I didn't find out what she wanted to tell me in the hospital.

CHAPTER 19

'THERE'S A PARCEL FOR you on the bed,' said Mrs Vine, when Sophia came back from work.

In her room she recognised Rosa's writing and unwrapped the brown paper with care. Six Dutch caps, two more than she'd expected. She gave a tremulous smile at this new, delightful feeling of defying ancient rabbinic rules in order to protect women.

Rewrapping them in the paper, she tucked them into a deep pocket in her trunk. Now she could plan how to introduce them to those exhausted women she'd met working with Ettie. Only a few days ago, they had assisted at the birth of a woman's fourteenth child, a puny, skinny little thing, who barely cried when Ettie slapped her. As for the mother, hollow eyed, gaunt and worn, Sophia thought she could have been sixty, not forty. The mother took the tiny thing in her arms with weak resignation, thin tears straying from her eyes.

'I don't know how I'm going to feed this one. I had no milk for the one before. He died at six weeks.'

Riven by anger and pity to hear these words, Sophia decided to call in later and show her the Dutch cap, hoping she wouldn't reject it. None of this must reach Ettie, of course, horrified by any talk of contraception.

Now to read Rosa's letter.

Sophia settled in her chair by the window to catch some gleams of light from the buildings opposite. It was dim and gloomy in her room since the cost of gas in the meter was rising and Mrs Vine was reluctant to 'feed it'. Opening the envelope Sophia drew out a single sheet of paper and peered at Rosa's elegant script.

> *Ma Chère Sophia,*
>
> *Here are the Dutch caps as promised. Don't worry about paying for them until you have the money. Good luck with persuading the women to use them. It'll be hard. They'll be afraid of their husbands, or of the rabbis.*
>
> *As you are my friend, I feel I must tell you something. It's what I was going to say when that gorgon of a night sister interrupted. It will be a shock for you, so prepare yourself.*

Sophia's eyes widened; holding the paper closer to her eyes, she read the next sentence, and gasped.

> *Dov is married.*
>
> *It was a shidduch, an arranged marriage, organised by his grandfather, I believe, when he was young. That's all I know, as he's very cagey about it. It's of no significance to me, because I believe in free love. But it might matter to you. Come and see me next Saturday afternoon if you wish and we can talk.*
>
> *À bientôt, ma chère amie,*
> *Rosa*

Married? The word leapt into her mind like a scream. How could that be? She's deceiving me, it's another of her games. Sophia's gaze stayed glued to the word as if it could offer up a clue. She was falling into a deep trench, a morass of black water, mulch, creeping insects, and Rosa's disconnected face grinning up at her.

'No!' Sophia cried. 'He can't be!'

She said this with such force, Mrs Vine put her head round the door. 'All right, Sophia?'

'Yes, I'm all right, thank you.' Sophia's voice was hoarse, clutching at a moment of relief until Mrs Vine returned to the kitchen.

Her heart shuddering in her chest, she turned to the window. The buildings loomed up in the dark, the yard bleak. If only she could talk to her mother. She would know how to advise her. What would she say? *You must think rationally.*

Sophia inhaled deeply and straightened her shoulders. *I am a new woman*, she said, hearing the words as if someone else were mouthing them. Repeating them, she felt stronger. *I'm an anarchist, we believe in free love.* I should not care that he's married. I believe absolutely in helping the poor, in improving their lives, in education ... but this... She clutched her hands together under her chin.

It has shocked me. And I do care.

After some moments, she thought: maybe I should have expected it ... a charismatic man like Dov... She saw his face as they'd sat by the Thames, illuminated with joy as he talked about his grandfather. *Was he trying to tell me something then?*

Her mind flitted to his letter. He says he loves me. Does he also love this woman who was chosen for him? But he's so resolute, how could he have agreed to such a thing? Her heart contracting, weighed down with this knowledge, she gave a hollow laugh. *Dov, I'm actually jealous of this woman whoever she is, and I'm furious with you. Come back, tell me the truth.*

But what if he doesn't return, the Evil Inclination on her shoulder muttered with its hot, bitter breath, what then? She pulled her face away from its wily tones, her cheeks bright with anger.

You will never, never say that again, she whispered to it. *Never. He will come back.*

Over the next few weeks she whirled though the East End Streets, resolved to keep mind and body so busy she could not obsess over Dov. Driven by guilt about not saving for tickets for her parents, she paid Mrs Haber at the shelter a visit to ask if she knew an English newsagent where she might work at the weekend, earn a little money and practise her English. The following week, on entering Alf Green's shop in Poplar, Sophia hesitated. Surely this man with his handlebar moustache and huge belly was one of those who'd attacked them on Yom Kippur?

Before she could speak, he bellowed, 'If Mrs Haber sent you, tell her she can take a funny run. And you, go back to Palestine or Poland or wherever. You come here taking our jobs, living in our houses. You're vermin. Filth, get out!'

She fled, stopping at a street corner, legs like jelly, heart racing in her chest, bruised by his hatred. Thankfully, she still had work at the workshop, where head down, she'd treadle furiously, producing beautifully seamed sleeves or waistcoats or whatever Mr Lazarus could obtain from the West End. Whenever she had a moment to spare, she'd stand at street corners to sell the anarchist newspaper.

Then there was work with Ettie, but two deaths made her despair and deepened her scepticism about a beneficial God. There was the baby Ettie could not save despite her skill, the mother who haemorrhaged in the London Hospital after Ettie had sent for Doctor Feldstein and even he could not stop the bleeding. Attempts to convert mothers to the use of the Dutch cap were greeted with astonishment and recoil. Rosa had been right, the women told her all was *beshert*, written above, and nothing could change divine will, even if it was cruel and inhumane to Sophia's eyes.

Despite all this busyness, Dov was ever in her mind. Resolved to have clarity about Free Love, she asked Milly to bring over one or two copies of *Germinal* in which Rudolf had written articles elucidating the views of Anarcho-syndicalism. If she could read and analyse the issues, and goodness knows, this was an issue for her, she could let go of her anxiety. One evening, sitting on her bed, magazines splayed around her legs, her cheeks began to burn. *What has happened to me? I'm losing myself in this passion for Dov. I can't think or breathe or act. It has to stop.*

She was hurrying along Brick Lane, where a crowd of excited people had surrounded a man reading aloud from a Yiddish newspaper. They were in a dense circle outside Lily King's newsagent shop, barring Sophia's way. It was Sam Dreen reading, and seeing her, he called, 'Sophia, listen to this!'

She hesitated. Several people in the crowd urged him to continue.

'The Moscow printers have come out on strike,' he shouted. 'And for why?'

'Because their bosses refused to pay for quotation masks!' A man shouted.

People roared with laughter, knowing this was the trigger for more.

'Listen everyone,' Sam continued, 'We're having an important meeting tonight about the Revolution. It's spreading across the whole country. Even to Siberia. The meeting's at the People's Palace. Eight o'clock,' Sam passed the paper over to Sophia, as he spoke. 'Come early or you won't get a seat.'

'I can't believe it,' she said, her eyes on the article.

'It's true, so be there at half past seven, if you can,' Sam said, taking her arm. 'There'll be hundreds and we'll need people at the door and in the hall.'

The Jewish East End was on fire. Every evening, to acclaim each new development, there were huge meetings. Five thousand people would squeeze into the People's Palace. Scores more stood outside arguing, gesticulating, discussing. Some even considered returning home, but others were more cautious, reminding them of those Black Hundreds, the Tsar's evil men launching pogroms or mowing down protesters in the street.

Sitting with the other anarchists, Sophia listened to the speakers and her heart filled with pride at the progress of the Revolution. Through October and November there were also demonstrations and meetings. Different speakers reported on the strikes by the oil men, the printers and the metalworkers. The university teachers, train drivers and telegraph workers, even peasants and schoolteachers. The audience would rise to its feet, cheering for ages, on hearing that the whole of the 'Tsar's Domain' was striking for representation, free speech and press, proper wages, an eight-hour day. The end of the Tsar, of autocracy and political repression, of violence and false imprisonment.

It was unbelievable.

One night at the end of November, Sam Dreen told her that Dov was now active with the reformed Petersburg Soviet. He'd been a founder member in January, until it was banned later in the year. This Soviet was leading and coordinating the General Strike in Russia. That was why he'd gone so swiftly to Petersburg; these were the fruits of his work, his daring, his passion. Sam was fervent with praise, but Sophia's heart sank. Now she knew Dov would never return to her.

CHAPTER 20

ITTING ON THE TRAM, articles about free love tucked in by her side, Sophia wondered at the thick yellow-ish fog curling against the windows, and hoped the driver could see the route. The tram, an obstinate beast, continued along the rails, stopping for passengers to mount or descend. Peering through, she recognised the London Hospital, a ghostly building, and as they trundled on, she imagined they could bump along until, suddenly, the fog would clear and they'd find themselves on a glowing island, sun beating down, the sea calm and blue. Luscious plants would move softly in the breeze and Dov would be waiting for her.

She smiled, and recognising the cottages near to Dunstan Houses, rang the bell to alert the tram driver. Alighting, she saw with relief that it was clearer. She crossed the road, climbed the low flight of steps to the side entrance, and went in.

She was aware of someone leaving a room further down the corridor, for a door banged shut and, for the briefest of moments, thought of Dov, but her mind told her he was in Petersburg. She made to climb the stairs when she heard her name.

She turned. Her face flushed. She stopped, a look of amazement and disbelief in her eyes. 'Dov. You're back?' It was more a query than an affirmation. 'I... I didn't...'

He strode down the corridor towards her. 'I promised,' he said grinning. 'You doubted me?'

Tears pricking her eyes, she cried, 'Yes, no...' Forgetting the magazines, which fell to the floor, she flung her arms around his neck.' Dov, Dov, after all this time, I was positive you'd never come back.'

'I need you more than ever now. Did you get my letter?'

'Of course, I did.' She lifted her face and he kissed her.

'Where were you going with those old copies of *Germinal*?'

'Returning them to Milly.' Embarrassed by her reason for borrowing them, she hastened to gather them up.

'They can wait.'

He led her to his room and shut the door.

'My darling Sophia, all these weeks I haven't stopped thinking about you.'

She shook her head. 'Me neither, I mean I filled every moment because your letter thrilled and terrified me. In the end, the only way to stay sane was to keep doing things. And I have so many questions...'

'No questions.'

Kissing her hair, he unpinned it, until it rippled around her shoulders and down her back.

'My beautiful girl.'

He lifted her onto the bed.

Soft and caressing at first, Dov's kisses became more demanding. Her eyes closed, Sophia responded with fervour. A filament of thought passed through her mind: *I don't care anymore about his wife or his mistresses, or Rosa. Now he's mine.*

Hours later, she sat up. It was dark but for the dim lights coming from the opposite buildings. Thinking Dov was asleep, she slipped from the bed and gathering her clothes, started to dress.

'Where are you going?' He was propped up on one elbow, rolling a cigarette.

'Home.'

'Stay here with me,' he begged.

Warm with love, she hesitated. Astonished and moved by what she'd experienced, her thoughts floated like slivers of thread to the workshop floor. Years ago, it seemed now, she had planned to ask him about the *shidduch*, yet the moment she'd seen him in the corridor this afternoon, every reasonable question had fled her mind.

'It would be better if I went home, but Dov, I want to see you tomorrow.'

'Tomorrow we can spend the whole day here.'

'I can ask my questions?'

'One of the things I love about you, Sophia.' He laughed. 'The English call it a 'bee in your bonnet'. You never give up, when you want to understand something, when you want clarity. It's rare for a woman.'

'What do you mean?' She gave him a puzzled look.

'Clear thinking.'

'*Dov.* How can you possibly say that? Women can think and do exactly the same as men.' Strength was returning to her. 'What about the women in the movement? And Emma Goldman, whose writings I have just studied?'

He shook his head. 'I'm sorry. Of course, you are right.'

She took a deep breath. 'Will you come on the tram with me?'

'I'll go anywhere in the world with you, Sophia Krichevska.'

Tears filled her eyes and she wiped them away.

'Come,' she said, 'it's already eight o'clock.'

They took the back seat of the tram, but how different this journey was from the previous occasions. Sophia sat with her head resting on Dov's shoulder, he with his arm around her. They spoke little but for commonplaces about how the fog had unexpectedly lifted, or that smoke spiralled up from a thousand chimneys as they passed. Dov would kiss Sophia's hair, hastily bundled up with hair pins, and she would lift her gaze to his, marvelling at the look in his eyes which spoke of the knowledge they shared of each other: she trusting that her smile echoed his.

At Mrs Vine's door, she whispered, 'Don't come in. She might be in bed or in her night things.'

'Till tomorrow,' he said, bending to kiss her.

Sophia turned the key as softly as she could; she looked back and saw Dov still leaning against the wall, at the top of the staircase, watching. She blew him a kiss and shut the door. A small gas lamp flickered on the table where Mrs Vine still sat in her dressing gown, knitting a blue garment, a cardigan perhaps for her grandchild. Sophia caught Mrs

Vine staring at her hair, some of which had tumbled to her shoulders. She peered at Sophia's face. She blushed, wondering if the landlady guessed or even *knew* what had happened. Mama would certainly have known so was this obvious to every woman? Sophia's shadow on the wall leapt as she prepared to go to her room, then became still.

'It's late, Sophia. Did your young man bring you home?'

'Yes, Mrs Vine. He's just left.'

'You could have invited him in.'

'Another time, I'm quite tired this evening.'

Mrs Vine gave her a sideways look.

'It is rather late. I'm going to bed myself when I've finished this row.' She knitted for a few seconds, pierced the ball of wool with both needles, and wrapped the tiny cardigan in a piece of scrap material. 'I always do that, it's so dirty here, especially with the fog. I don't know how it gets inside the building but it does. Well, good night, Sophia.'

'Good night, Mrs Vine.'

In her room, Sophia sat heavily on the bed and closed her eyes. With an effort, for she was curiously tired, she stood, removed her coat and hung it on the hook they'd fixed to the door, since there was little room in the wardrobe she shared with her landlady. As in a dream, Sophia undressed, taking her washing bowl from where she kept it in her trunk, pouring cold water in it, to soak her undergarments ready for tomorrow, when she'd wash them thoroughly in the basement washroom.

Blood, she thought idly, when I was thirteen and 'became a woman' and now, when I truly am. And pain... the word seemed to come unbidden. She exhaled, thinking about the miraculous body which so fascinated her. Once in bed, she lifted her eyes and with her hands clasped together, said, 'Thank you!'

Eventually, she slept.

CHAPTER 21

'COME IN, COME IN!' Milly said, a rare smile brightening her face. 'Almost ready.'

'Beetroot borscht,' exclaimed Sophia. 'You've made borscht?'

'No, it's my sister's offering. Polly doesn't work so she has time to fiddle around with dishes like this.'

'Can I help?' Sophia hung her hat and coat on a peg behind the door.

Milly shook her head. 'Make yourself at home.'

'We always do!' Dov laughed, going to greet Rudolf, who was deeply intent on something he was writing, his head bent.

An hour before, Sophia had arrived at Dov's room.

'I have only fifty minutes to kiss you,' he said, eyes drooping in mock disappointment. He lifted her up and twirled her around, and laughing, Sophia cried, 'Stop it. Stop it, Dov. What on earth…?'

'Milly and Rudolf have invited us to have dinner with them. They always eat at one o'clock.' He pointed to a travelling clock on his desk. 'Only forty-five minutes left.'

'We can't go empty-handed. I must take them something.' Sophia smoothed down her rumpled skirts.

'How bourgeois!' He grinned, eyes mocking.

'True, but in this case, I don't care. Where can we buy, perhaps, bread and cheese or maybe some chocolate?'

They went to a tiny house nearby, where a woman kept a shop in her front room, selling a little of everything. They came away carrying a large round black loaf, some homemade cream cheese in a brown paper bag and two bars of Cadbury's chocolate. Sophia took these into the tiny kitchen where Milly was heaving an immense blackened saucepan off the stove.

'A small contribution from me and Dov.' Sophia put the offering on the low paint-peeling cupboard that took up half the room.

'Thank you.' Flushed from the heat of the stove, Milly said, 'We'd almost run out of bread. We can finish the meal with the cheese and I'll divide one bar of chocolate between us, the other I'll put away or Rudolf will devour it in its entirety. He has such a sweet tooth.'

When they kissed, Sophia felt an unexpected closeness with this determined little woman, whose thick black hair was plaited around her head and, with her Gypsy-like brown skin, reminded Sophia of the Indian doctor at the London Hospital.

Walking the two steps into the living room, she saw Dov stood with his back to the fire, smoking and deep in thought.

'Aren't you tempted to explore their library?' Sophia asked him. 'Who'd have thought that anyone could have so many fascinating books? Karl Marx, Bakunin, George Bernard Shaw, Oscar Wilde, the French Revolution. I could stay here forever.'

'I'm very happy to stand and do nothing.' Dov grinned.

Milly carried in the steaming saucepan. 'Dinner's ready. Please sit down. Rudolf, leave that speech you're writing.'

Four large broad-rimmed soup bowls, and a variety of unmatched knives, forks and spoons were already on the oilcloth covered table. A sweetish pungent odour filled the room, as Milly ladled the glistening rich red soup into the plates, and Sophia said, with a little crack in her voice, 'I could be at home.'

They ate in silence, at first, but conversation soon spilled out when Rudolf reminded them of what an extraordinary year this had been.

'The Great Revolution rolling out before our eyes. Month after month there have been strikes, uprisings, marches affecting the whole of that vast country, even as far as Siberia and the Urals. Then the October Manifesto.'

'Whenever we discussed this at the Sugar Loaf pub, I've been surprised by how many people expressed the desire to return.' Sophia gave Rudolf a questioning look.

'I agree with you. Despite the terrible conditions, the antisemitism and the Tsar's violent edicts, it's still home in their eyes.'

'Russia will never alter,' said Milly, putting down her spoon. 'Only socialism will do it. I hope they remember that. Anyway, to change the subject, would anybody like more soup?' She lifted the lid of the saucepan and peered in. 'There's some left. No? I'll bring in the stew.'

They wiped their plates clean with chunks of rye bread and Milly carried in the stew, thick with barley, groats and tiny slivers of meat.

'Truly magnificent,' said Dov, sniffing appreciatively.

'Sometimes she allows me German food,' said Rudolf, 'but I'm adaptable!'

'At the very beginning, at Bloody Sunday in Petersburg, you were there, Dov, weren't you?' Milly was ladling large portions to each plate, as she spoke.

'Do you know about Bloody Sunday?' Pushing up his glasses that slipped frequently down his nose, Rudolf smiled at Sophia.

'Dov mentioned it on the ship. A strange story.' Dov laughed and she wrinkled her brow. What was funny about that? The others had given Sophia a surprised look when she said 'a strange story' but let her continue. 'Weeks after the event, in January, we read a short piece in the Archangelsk newspaper, a few lines only.'

'Dov, how did you get involved with a man like Father Gapon, a Russian Orthodox priest?' Turning to Sophia, Milly added, 'Gapon was the man who wrote the petition for the Tsar, a begging list to improve the awful conditions of the workers. They were marching that Sunday to the Winter Palace, thousands upon thousands of them with Gapon and Dov leading the way, when those terrible events happened.'

'I understand the people thought him a saint,' added Rudolf. 'A poor naive fool really, though I respect his wish to communicate with the Tsar in a peaceful way, but politically, simply a stooge for the authorities.'

'Why was that?' Sophia looked to each one.

His head bowed, Dov didn't reply, and Sophia wondered at the strange mixture of anger and guilt in his eyes. He finally took a deep breath.

'We'd been working with the Putilov metalworkers, long before the priest came on the scene, handing out leaflets, holding meetings, discussing political action. When he appeared and we learned he was setting up the *Assembly of Factory and Mill Workers,* at the behest of the Tsar's ministers, we were suspicious.

Our group, the Petersburg Soviet, decided to monitor him. Of course he didn't know. I was elected to meet him, then lead the march with him.'

'Sophia,' Milly leaned forward, her deep dark eyes serious, 'when four metalworkers lost their jobs, I believe the priest was furious and called out the men. A hundred and twenty thousand joined the strike. Imagine what the Minister of Interior thought of that.' Milly gave a disparaging smile. 'They'd warned the priest against industrial action, so he changed his tune, wrote a petition directly to the Tsar, which they were to present on this particular Sunday.' She sat back, resting her cheek on her hand.

'You're right, Milly. He was a government agent, set up by the authorities to control the new union, and suddenly he believed in the workers' cause. Without realising it, the man had changed sides and become an impassioned advocate of socialism. The government grew suspicious of his socialist leanings,' said Dov. 'We were suspicious of his connection with the *Okhrana*, the secret police.

It was imperative we became involved; I and my comrades had met the previous evening, each one of us had a factory or a mill to bring out.' Dov stopped speaking and dipped his head. 'The turnout that morning was amazing. Mothers with babies tied within their shawls, children, old men carrying icons, workers from every place, all in their Sunday best, all marching behind us, singing hymns. 'He gave a brief smile. 'Even the sun shone on the snow. We'd made a simple raised stand from a couple of planks, a dais, where Georgi Gapon could address the people, and I stood beside him keeping my eye out for whatever might happen. He had just finished speaking, the people roaring their approval, when suddenly, shots rang out.

Sophia could not take her eyes from his face.

'The palace guard galloped through the crowds, shooting anyone in their way. Forty people killed in a flash. An old man carrying a religious banner dropped before my eyes, another one took it up.'

Dov's eyes were bleak.

'Did you know the Cossacks were stationed at the Troitsky Bridge?' said Rudolf.

Dov shook his head. 'We saw guards all around but were astonished when they began to shoot. The Cossacks...' His voice broke.

'Slashing with their sabres at anyone.' Rudolf removed his glasses and wiped his eyes with a large handkerchief.

'Two hundred people were killed,' said Milly, hitting the table with her fists. 'About eight hundred more wounded.'

'How did the priest react?' asked Sophia, unsure whether she should speak.

'I heard him saying *There is no God anymore, there is no Tsar*. I knew that already.' Dov's voice deepened, and to Sophia's amazement, he passed a hand over his eyes, then inhaled deeply.

'How is Katya now?' Leaning forward, Milly placed her hand on Dov's arm.

'She is fairly well.' Dov gave a thin smile.

'Such a dreadful thing. I don't how you bear it. I would want to kill somebody.'

'You wouldn't really, Milly, I know you.' Rudolf made a clicking noise with his tongue.

Sophia's heart seemed to leap into her mouth. She shot a glance at each of them, bound by a knowledge she didn't share. Who were they talking about? Was this Dov's wife? She experienced a shrivelling of the heart, a touch of surprise that a name could affect her so deeply. Her hands tightly coiled together in her lap, she waited for Dov's reply.

'At the beginning, I felt like that, but naturally, it's worse for my mother.'

'Who is Katya?' she burst out, unable to contain herself any longer, her voice rising with emotion. 'Is she your wife?'

'Why would you say that?' Dov jerked his head to face Sophia, a deepening flush in his cheeks. 'Katya's my *sister*.'

Sophia gasped and sank back, shocked by his sudden anger, by the revelation.

'I didn't know.'

'Some things are so painful, we hide them even from ourselves.' Dov took her hand.

'You should tell her, Dov,' Milly said quietly,.

He inhaled deeply and began to speak.

'From my place on the platform, at the height of the massacre, I caught sight of a young girl wearing a blue hat forcing her way through the people. I knew at once it was my sister and I was terrified. I called out to her but with the noise of the horses, the pandemonium of screams, groans, cries, sounds of people fleeing, she couldn't possibly have heard me. She had defied Papa and come to the march. I leapt off the platform and reached her, just as she was felled by a palace guard with the edge of his gun.' Sophia saw tears in his eyes. 'One good thing. I was there in time to prevent her being trampled by people screaming and falling all around her. She was unconscious. I carried her home.'

'How come she was there?' Sophia swallowed.

'Because of me. *Me.* All my fault.' Dov dropped his head, guilt and despair in his eyes. He groaned.

'No.' Milly murmured. 'The Tsar... *Russia.*'

Inhaling deeply, Dov carried on. 'The night before, at the dinner table, I'd told my parents what I was doing the next day. Katya, the sister who is closest to me, announced she was coming. My father forbade it; I begged her not to, saying she could join the socialist movement when she was eighteen.'

'How old is she?'

'Sixteen. That morning she was asleep when I crept out and I was relieved. Ironically, I almost tripped on our little cat as I walked down the corridor, but the house was still.'

Another deep breath.

'Good thing your father is a doctor.' Milly nodded slowly, her mouth in a grim line.

'When we got back, Papa examined her, said it was a head blow, concussion, and she could be unconscious for several days. Mama nursed her, together with Maria, who has helped us for years. I was horrified, horrified.' Turning his gaze to Sophia, he said, 'You remind me so much of her.'

'That's why you wrote in your letter that it had happened again.' Sophia wanted to take him in her arms to comfort him, but she blinked away tears, knowing he would shun her pity.

'Yes. So obsessed with my own plans, I bring danger to everyone I love.'

Sophia gazed at him, wondering how this carefree, outrageous man had become so broken, so full of remorse.

'You mustn't blame yourself.'

'I do. I *do*.' Eyes closed, he pounded his head with his fist.

'You asked her not to come. And, Dov, you say she's a little better.'

'She's frail.' He shook his head. Opening his eyes, he turned to her. 'Can't walk without help. Papa sought a neurologist, but he found nothing.'

'She was much better in the summer,' Rudolf said, his kind eyes smiling through his glasses.

'When we met in May, 'Dov grasped Sophia's wrist, 'I saw in you the woman she might have become.'

'She will, with time, I am certain,' breathed Sophia.

'I shall hold that in my heart.'

He gave her a brief kiss.

For some moments they sat in silence. Eventually, Sophia took a deep breath. 'Dov, I think we should go. We've enjoyed this beautiful dinner and I'm sure Rudolf and Milly have lots to do.' Turning to Milly, she said, 'Can I help clear up?'

'Not at all.' Milly smiled. 'Why don't you take a walk down Stepney Green? The trees are beautiful now, holding their bare arms up to the sky.'

Leaving the building, Sophia saw that the sky was dark blue and a wind was blowing, sending up tiny stones from the path, some catching her face as they walked, and she wiped her eyes. As they swayed and creaked, branches of the trees seemed to beseech the heavens; she thought they were almost more beautiful now they were spare and black, than when rich with green in the spring. It was cold; she pulled her coat collar closer to her neck, but welcomed the damp fresh air, breathing it in deeply.

'*Lecha dodi.* Come my beloved...' Dov began to sing the song for welcoming the Sabbath on a Friday evening.

'What a man of contradictions you are.' Sophia said, as she joined in. Singing, they reached a bend in the path where with his arm around Sophia's shoulder, Dov stopped walking.

'London reminds me a little of Petersburg, with its fog and damp and cold. But let's go back to my room. A glass of vodka won't come amiss.'

'In Archangelsk it will be twenty degrees below and everyone wearing their fur-lined boots and coats and hoods. Yes, let's go back to your room and maybe we can talk?'

Dov frowned at this, and she wondered at his sharp change of mood, wishing she could see directly into his brain. She thought of Sigmund Freud, with his belief in the existence of the subconscious, regretful that she hadn't read any of his work.

Dov's room was identical to Rudolf and Milly's, with a small kitchen by the entrance. From a low cupboard opposite the gas stove, Sophia saw him take out a bottle of vodka, hold it up to her as she stood by the window and when she shook her head, pour himself a large glass. His head tilted, his expression was sombre as he came into the room, and she wondered if he was thinking about her ill-advised question at dinner. She folded into herself uncertain, although she saw that his gaze was not fierce, rather puzzled and uneasy.

Had Rosa invented the whole marriage thing to challenge her?

That Dov would return to England at the very moment the revolutionaries were successful made her pause. Whatever Rosa might think or say, Sophia knew Dov loved her. But what about now? She felt a pulse in her throat as her heart beat faster. She sat at the little table where Dov was standing and raised her gaze to his. He downed the glass of vodka, silent. Rolling a cigarette, he lit it. His voice low, intent, he said, 'What makes you think I am married?'

'Someone told me.'

He leaned in, eyes fixed on her face. 'Rosa?'

'Yes, it was Rosa.' She drew herself up and folded her lips, determined not to be cowed by his anger.

'That woman...' He swore in Yiddish.

'And are you?' She took a deep breath.

'I was.' He glanced away. 'Not now.'

A sense of relief lifted her, but still she wasn't clear. 'What do you mean?'

He began to pace the floor. She waited, something cold emerging now, in her heart.

'It was a long time ago. I was very young.'

'Dov, I don't understand.'

He swung round and walked slowly towards her, taking the chair and sitting straddled over the seat, the back acting as a flimsy barrier between them, she thought.

'You know they arrange a *shidduch* when children are very young? I told you about staying at my grandfather's when I was eleven or twelve, after I'd been ill for a year?' Sophia nodded soberly. 'While I was at my grandfather's court, he introduced me to a girl, who had come with her father to consult him. She was eleven, I think, timid, hiding her eyes from me, but very pretty, with long black hair and white skin. My grandfather asked me if I liked her and I said yes. And that was it. Girls and boys don't play together amongst the very orthodox. Men and women are always separated from the age of three.' Dov rolled another cigarette, his eyes dark.

'What happened?'

'I didn't know that an arrangement had been made between this man and my grandfather for me to marry his daughter, Yetta Fruma, when the time was right. How could I? No one consulted me, no one explained.'

'When did you find out?'

'In the nineties. When the Tsar began to incite antisemitism and pogroms. Papa lost patients, we had financial problems. I suppose I was fifteen when he told me. There had been money involved.' His face flushed red. '*Money.*'

'I don't understand. Do you mean a dowry?'

'Exactly. The girl's father was so keen to be connected with my grandfather's family – because he was learned, leader of his court – that he offered a large dowry to go with the girl. Disgusting, isn't it?'

Sophia shook her head.

'Did your father accept the money?'

'He needed it.' Dov shrugged. 'We were five children, remember, together with our parents. He wasn't earning enough.'

'Did you go ahead with the wedding?'

A look of shame filled Dov's eyes, and he dipped his head.

'I had a terrible row with my father. I felt so betrayed by my grandfather because I loved him. Still do, despite everything. But their joint betrayal...' He inhaled deeply. 'They *used* me. By then I had joined the revolutionaries. Besides, I hadn't seen the girl since I was twelve and had no idea what she was like. I wasn't allowed to see her until the wedding. My father said something about not necessarily staying with her afterwards, but I don't believe he meant that.'

'Did you tell your grandfather you wouldn't marry her?'

Dov sat back and explained how difficult it would be to alter these arrangements. Reluctantly, fearfully, just before he started university, he went to his grandfather's house and the wedding took place. In theory he was supposed to go and live with the girl's family, while he studied. Which he did. That was the tradition. But of course he wasn't studying in *a yeshiva,* a religious academy, but at a university, and after a few months he could bear it no longer. He came back to Petersburg, found a room with two other students and for a year did not go home, though sometimes he met his mother in the park. He refused to see his father.

'Underlying Papa's decision was his immense guilt at leaving his *Chasidic* background.'

Sophia asked why he hadn't divorced the girl. The strange thing was, Dov said, that Yetta Fruma refused to divorce, always believing he would go back to her. Besides, the community would see her as a tarnished woman. 'Married or divorced, it didn't matter to me. What mattered were my revolutionary ideals and activities.'

Sophia reflected, imagining the young woman sitting alone in her room waiting for her husband, and her face flushed with concern and even a touch of anger.

'But she's *tied* to you, Dov. You care so much about freedom, you don't think about her? She's an *agunah*, a chained woman. A woman can't divorce a man in Jewish law. You must free her.'

'You have a surprising knowledge of Jewish law.' He grinned.

'It's not a laughing matter.' She shot an angry look at him. He responded with a mocking smile. 'There was a situation in Archangelsk… So I read about it. Surely you should go back and free her?'

'What a woman you are, Sophia Krichevska.' He grinned.

'When *are* you going back to Saint Petersburg?' She shook her head, as though to dismiss his flippancy.

'I can't.' His face fell.

'What do you mean?'

'I can't just yet.' He stood up.

'Why?'

He placed his finger on her mouth.

'Enough already with the questions, my beautiful girl. I thought we were going to make love all day.'

CHAPTER 22

TWO WEEKS LATER, SOPHIA found the letter.

She had spent the morning at home, planning and writing an article about the American anarchist Emma Goldman for *Germinal*, and had come over to Dov's when the afternoon was merging with evening, or so it seemed from the darkening sky. As she stood in front of his desk, an oak table with drawers either side, stacking pamphlets for Poland and Ukraine, a few of them slid to the floor. Dov had gone to collect newly translated classics from Rudolf, to be sent honourably to Kletzkin in Vilna, the pamphlets hidden as usual at the bottom of the cases, and she was alone. Moving a chair to gather them up, she managed to tip over a wooden box she hadn't noticed before. A rather beautiful wooden box, its sides carved to imitate books, with a book-shaped lid. She'd seen it before on his mantelpiece and had remarked how original it was. Dov told her it was his grandmother's and very precious to him.

The box had fallen to the floor with a crash, its key skidding beneath the table, and three or four letters were scattered around. She frowned, angry with herself for being so careless. Pulling up her skirts she scrambled beneath the desk to retrieve it. On her knees, she examined the box.

Thank goodness there was neither a crack nor a piece of wood chipped off the side. Standing up, she put it on the table then bent again to gather up three or four letters that had slipped out when it fell. As she stood again, one drew her attention: it was folded with the writing uppermost and she noticed various comments down the margin, in a different writing: Dov's perhaps? She'd rarely seen him write and wasn't sure. The other letters were folded as usual, the script hidden. She wondered why this one was different. Curiosity made her pause. She was intrigued as to why Dov – if it was him – would comment on a letter when he could simply have replied.

Straightening up, she glanced around. The room was empty, and a little flutter of the heart told her she was doing something dishonest but she couldn't resist. She flattened the letter out on the table beside the untidy piles of pamphlets.

Dear comrade, it began. Well, nothing strange about that. But as she continued to scan the letter quickly, her eyes widened. When she came to the signature, she gasped: *Father Georgi Gapon*. After what Dov had said at Rudolf and Milly's about the priest and his betrayal, she couldn't imagine why his letter was here, in Dov's possession. She hesitated but felt compelled to read it properly.

> Dear Comrade,
>
> As you see, I have finally completed the arrangements.
> Mr Akashi, the wealthy Japanese businessman, is being most generous, funding all the munitions in the list below. The Japanese are winning the current

ridiculous Russo-Japanese war and this is his contribution. With his support, I have bought an American ship, the John Grafton, to transport the goods.

The John Grafton will await your arrival in the North Sea. I trust you have found a merchant seaman who will transport the above mentioned from London to the ship. The arrangement still stands with Konni Zilliacus, the exiled Finnish revolutionary. You will berth at Finland; he or his representative will take half the munitions, the other half will be transported to Petersburg, where they will be distributed among our comrades.

Your good friend,
Georgi Gapon

List of Munitions and details of transportation:
15,500 SwissVetterli rifles
2.5 million bullets
2,500 high-class English officers' revolvers
3 tons of explosives

An arsenal, Sophia thought. She lifted her head and stared around the room, as though she could find an answer nearby – on the bed, in the kitchen, through the window. *Your good friend, Georgi Gapon.* The priest. The priest the socialists had always suspected of being a traitor, in league with the secret police, yet portraying himself to the world as the leader of the Socialist Revolutionaries. After Bloody Sunday, when he'd joined the revolutionary cause and demanded arms to protect the workers, he'd become hugely famous in America and Europe. Politicians in the West approved of the revolutionaries' battle to rid of themselves of the Tsar and corrupt regime. But was this letter actually intended for Dov? It began with 'Dear comrade'. Who had written *Monsieur de Boissoudy, his stables in the woods, Streatham* in the margins? Words written in tiny, meticulous script. Then various names of Polish and Lithuanian men jotted on the back of the letter. Followed by the name *Robinson* together with the word *vans*.

Something about the John Grafton ship came to her. Maybe two months after she'd come to London. She recalled reading something in a Yiddish newspaper. It was July when the ship had run aground near the Finnish coast. There were gigantic headlines extolling the fact that some of the munitions had reached the Finnish rebels fighting Russia for independence, and others had gone to the revolutionaries in Russia.

Was Dov implicated? If he was, why was she so surprised? Surely with his belief in violence and the need to destroy the Tsar's regime, he would certainly do this. But so dangerous if he were caught.

She wanted to ask him about this at once. Never mind that she'd read his letter, she would gloss over that. She stood up trembling, but her desire to confront Dov gave her courage. Then came another more terrible thought and her eyes widened. Could he be in league with Georgi Gapon, working both sides? Going to the window where the low line of light left by the gathering darkness might clarify her confusion, and with her absent gaze on Stepney Green, her heart racing in her chest, she wondered what to do.

Put it back, she thought. She took a deep breath. Folding the sheet of paper, she walked over to the desk, flattened the letter down with her hand and pressed it to fit into the box, which she locked. Going to the fireplace, she returned it to the empty space on the mantelpiece, beside the clock, the box of matches, the spills in their purple cardboard tube.

Does anyone know? Rudolf, maybe. Rudolf hated violence, even as he recognised its necessity for the Revolution to eliminate the Tsar. She recalled her first day at the Soho club when Rosa had praised Dov for his activities. Did she know, and could she ask Rosa?

No, Sophia thought, she must ask Dov himself. I would say to him: *We should have no secrets from each other*. But would he tell her the truth? A little doubt surfaced – however much he *said* he loved her, would that override his dedication to the Revolution? Besides, she didn't want their relationship to be forced, they had to be free. She clutched her hands together, her head whirling. *And if I find out he's working with Georgi Gapon?* She took a deep breath. *Then, I shall face that too.*

Voices coming from the stairs, Dov's and Rudolf's, and Milly's beautiful contralto, told her she must collect herself. She forced herself to breathe slowly, to steady her fast-beating heart. When Dov opened the door, she was standing in front of the table, eyes down, but her mind in a whirl. She wanted to ask him at once. She couldn't ask him because she read someone's letter. But she needed to know if he was the gunrunner. Her face hot with emotion, she barely lifted her gaze to him, when he came in, placed some books on the table, and said,

'Sophia, get your coat. We're going to see the new club in Jubilee Street. Rudolf said it's nearly ready, then we can get something to eat. I'm starving.'

She kept her eyes fixed to the table and didn't look at him.

'Sophia, did you hear me? Do you want to stay here?'

'I haven't finished the pamphlets yet.' Heat rose in her cheeks again and she turned away.

'Never mind them. We'll finish them later.'

Sophia put on her coat, closed the door behind her, and followed them out of the building to the road, where a tram was just drawing up. They ran to catch it and she found herself sitting beside the window with Dov next to her, and Milly and Rudolf in the seat behind. She couldn't stop thinking about the gunpowder and the guns. Then she chided herself for being naive, for hadn't he always proclaimed, 'propaganda by the deed?'

He would shoot to kill and it sickened her somehow, yet she knew that in Russia it might be necessary. Then there was the danger to him, the possibility that if he were captured by the police there would be no reprieve, he would be shot or killed in some horrendous way by the Russian state. She sat, her body rigid, a frown in her eyes, almost unaware of where they were going.

They arrived at Jubilee Street.

Entering the former Methodist building the Anarcho-syndicalists had taken for a peppercorn rent, they were greeted by a surge of noise. Men and women worked in various parts of the huge room: carpenters sawing wood for chairs and tables, others building a stage, glaziers sealing windows, decorators putting finishing touches to walls, doors and window frames, and the combined smell of the paint and glue caught at their throats. People were talking and laughing, enthused by working together for the community, Sophia realised with a rush of surprise. For some moments, she forgot the letter.

'This downstairs hall with the gallery can take eight hundred people,' said Rudolf, a rare proud look in his eye, 'though insufficient to cater for all our followers. After all, we had five thousand at a meeting last year, but we've never had such a large building as a centre.'

'A club,' added Dov, wandering around, his shoes resounding on the bare boards. 'The Grafton Hall Club in Soho has a licence to sell alcohol. Are you contemplating that, Rudolf?'

'Not at the moment. I want it to be open to everybody, including children.'

Milly had walked to a window and was looking out. She turned.

'We'll need a few people to give English lessons, teach about English culture, art and politics. Have you any spare time, Sophia?' She touched Sophia's arm. 'I know you're so busy with *Germinal* and *Arbeter Fraint*, you work, and you help a midwife. I'm almost embarrassed to ask you.'

'I'd love to teach English. Mine is definitely improving and I know the grammar.'

'We'll add you to our list of volunteers,' said Milly with a laugh. 'Come, I'll show you the classrooms upstairs.

There's also a small hall, our library and a reading room,' she said echoing Rudolf's sense of pride.

Back downstairs, Rudolf and Milly were chatted to the people working, but Dov said, 'I'm starving, I need some food. Sophia, let's go to the Socialist People's Restaurant.'

She hesitated. If he came back to her room, she could ask him about the letter.

'No, let's eat at my place.'

Dov grasped Sophia by both shoulders. 'Your room is delightful for you but it's damp and cold. We need hot food and a warm room, and you can only get that today in Princelet Street.'

'All right. We'll go there.'

They left Rudolf and Milly talking to the workers and made their way down Brick Lane to the restaurant.

I'll have to ask him later, thought Sophia as they walked. *But if it really was him, if he transported all those guns and bullets, then he's in danger. I will persuade him.'*

'Come on, dreamer,' said Dov, 'we're there.'

They entered the restaurant, a room really, with posters and propaganda leaflets covering bare, peeling walls, rows of trestle tables with wooden benches on either side, and behind the tables that acted as a counter, Sophia read the prices chalked on a blackboard: Bowl of soup – 3d. Soup with meat – 6d. Bread – 1d. Potatoes– 2d.

'They're half the price of restaurants around here,' she said, smiling at Dov.

Already she was aware of people calling his name, asking him to come and sit with them, and gazing around, she recognised Sam Dreen at the furthest table, by the wall.

He rose. 'Dov, how good to see you! We'll come and chat when you've got something in your belly!'

'That smell of the food is like an aphrodisiac,' Dov exclaimed. 'Yes, do come over, Sam, I've loads to tell you.' He continued to wave and acknowledge people, but led Sophia to vacant seats near the counter.

The servers, a man and two women, knew their customers and almost slung the meat and potatoes onto their plates. There was scant conversation, except to ask for the salt. Sophia realised she was ravenous, having hardly eaten a proper meal since Wednesday, for although there was some tailoring work as they neared Christmas, and an abundance of new babies, she'd accompanied Ettie night and day to the confinements.

Twenty minutes later, wiping his bowl clean with chunks of bread, Dov called to Sam to join them, and he found a seat beside them on the bench, followed almost at once by half a dozen people, eager to know the latest news about the Revolution, to learn about Dov's role in the Petersburg Soviet of Workers' Deputies, to ask him to depict the strikes, the protests.

Having devoured his meal, he talked for over an hour about the first General Strike. Someone laughed. 'They wouldn't pay the printers for punctuation marks, it's pathetic.'

'Exactly. It is far more than that, as we know. It's not recognising human beings who work for you, who slave for you,' Dov said, 'and by the twelfth of October, when the railways and the telegraph workers joined the strike, Witte warned the Tsar that to save his country from revolution he must make great reforms, or impose a dictatorship. Did you know I was a member of the Petersburg Soviet of Workers' Deputies earlier this year? Comrade Nosar was its leader. We set it up again last month because the striking workers needed representation to the Tsar and his government. We worked as an alternative government. By the way, Trotsky managed somehow to escape from Siberia and join us. He's a clever devil.' He laughed. 'The Bolsheviks boycotted us at first, though of course individual Bolsheviks joined and Lenin soon persuaded the rest to participate.'

'The great thing is that similar soviets have been created in other cities.' Sam said.

'I agree.' Dov nodded. 'But it's impossible to get different factions to work together, which is essential. When Nicholas issued the October Manifesto, granting civil liberties and the Duma's consent before passing laws, he widened the electorate to include most citizens, but we, on the left, saw how ineffectual the Duma had become, how feeble. We wanted true revolution. We had pledged to get rid of a corrupt government, so we rejected it. To this effect, we printed our first newssheet, *Izvestia*.'

Listeners clapped, exchanged cheerful comments, beamed at him.

'Were you in Moscow when the Black Hundreds beat Bauman to death?' someone asked.

'No, in Petersburg, but I got there in time for his funeral, two days later. I've never seen anything like it. The demonstrations, the violence... The next day I was back in Petersburg, where we decided to end the General Strike because the increasing violence was bad for our cause.'

'What about the Black Hundreds?' asked Sam. 'They're extremely right-wing and funded by government officials. If we're talking about violence, surely they're instigating it?'

'Absolutely.' Dov stopped to light a cigarette. 'The Moscow branch of the Peasants' Union has just been arrested, which is bad news, but I know the Soviets still control the main cities. That's why I came back. I had important things to do here.'

His eyes met Sophia's and she blushed.

Listening, her hands folded in her lap, she remembered arriving alone in London and seeking him out at the Grafton Hall Club. Then her dismay at seeing Rosa with him as she waited by the door, the kiss Dov had given Rosa, and her own desire to run back to the Poor Immigrants' Shelter and hide. But Dov had seen her and drawn her into the group, calling her, *the Girl from Kyiv*. She recalled how Aaron had clarified the differences between the anarchist and socialist groups. Still true of socialism in London, she thought, while nothing could compare with the violent conflicts in the old country. English people could vote, some at least, and anyone could argue their political or religious beliefs at Hyde Park Corner without being thrown into prison or banished in chains, to die in the Siberian mines. Perhaps like Aaron's brother. She lifted her eyes to Dov – he was still talking.

'But comrades, we're winning! We're winning even though there may be setbacks.' Dov flung out his arms, gazing from face to face and they responded, laughing, smiling, thrilled with his view of the Revolution.

They surely longed to be over there, Sophia thought. But then, these brilliant images evoked what only a couple of hours before had shocked her. She shifted on the bench, a frown piercing her forehead. What should she do about the letter? When she was small, her mother used to say that asking too many questions made people cross.

'Why?' she would demand.

'You discover things if you're patient.' Mama would say, without responding to *why*.

I won't be patient, she thought. *Not today.*

Sophia rose, suggesting they leave, let the restaurant workers clean up the tables and go home. But walking back with Dov along the dark narrow street to her little room, she made a more measured decision: she would wait, say nothing about the letter. It would reveal itself in good time. Yet, despite herself, upon reaching the dark entryway to her building, she stopped.

'I have to ask you something. I'm not very proud of it, but today, Dov, I read one of your letters which fell out of your grandmother's beautiful box. It was an accident, falling from the chair where you must have left it. The letter shocked me. It concerned a list of munitions from Father Gapon. Was it addressed to you?' She stopped, seeing him narrow his eyes, his eyebrows drawn together in a frown, the curl of anger around his mouth, but then she carried on, 'Did you organise the transportation of those munitions?'

The words had burst out of her and she waited anxiously for his response.

He cracked his fingers, inhaled deeply, glared. Her fear of what he would think of her reading a private letter made her add, 'I'm really sorry. I've never done anything like that before and maybe I wouldn't have told you, but Dov, I'm so afraid for you.

He spoke. 'No need to be afraid. There are certain things I must do, and that's the sum of it.' He wasn't smiling.

Sophia shook her head. This was the wrong time to ask him, though she wasn't sure why.

'I guess,' he said, his tone light, mocking, 'your landlady will be there?'

How quickly he could change, she thought. 'Yes, she's there. Why?'

'I was thinking of coming in with you, but never mind. Work to do at home.'

'Shall we meet tomorrow?'

'Of course. I'll come for you in the morning and we can go over to Aaron's, tell him my news about the Petersburg Soviet. He didn't hear my talk at the Grafton Hall Club last week, and anyway, I want to see him.'

It was as though she had never said anything. Climbing slowly to her room, she hoped she could have a real conversation with him some other time, but she was coming to realise there would always be secrets about any human being – or at least a person like Dov – and one could never know them all.

CHAPTER 23

SUNDAY, THE FOLLOWING MORNING, they were taking the tram to the West End.

Descending the steps from her room, they walked into Wentworth Street through the milling crowds, turning into Petticoat Lane. Local people jostled elbows and backs to reach a certain stall or barrow, while sightseers from other parts of London came to stare at these strange Eastern European inhabitants.

'It's always the same. You'd think every inhabitant of London was packed into these two streets,' she said.

'Keep close to me and I'll forge a way.'

Sophia had been unsure of holding hands, she knew so many women who would be agog with interest and excitement. Who was this handsome young man? Were they going steady? Like Ettie, many of the older ones had arranged marriages and the possibility of choosing one's husband would fill them with curiosity and awe.

Sophia peered through the crowds. 'We'll pass Hannah Leah's stall. There. Just beside the man selling pens. I want you to meet her.'

She could see Hannah Leah reading a letter for a woman beside her who was weeping and clinging to Hannah Leah's arm. But the noise in the market obliterated their voices. They made their way, pushing and shoving, to the stall, and heard Hannah Leah saying, 'I'm deeply sorry that your mother has died, Mrs Sugarman, but we must always remember and accept, *Baruch dayan haemet*. Blessed is the true Judge.'

'I know, I know, but we're so far away.' The woman continued to sob. Wiping her face with a large handkerchief, she nodded slowly. 'Thank you, Hannah Leah.' She made her weeping way through the press of people. Hannah Leah gazed after her, then turning, smiled on seeing Sophia.

'Where are you off to this cold morning?'

'We're going to see your cousin Aaron, but first I want to introduce you to Dov Feldman.'

Hannah Leah, standing very straight, her blue eyes smiling, extended her hand across the stall to Dov.

'Delighted to meet you, Mrs Rivkin,' Dov said.

'Likewise. We've heard so much about you from our cousin.'

'Good things, I hope.'

'Of course.'

Sophia turned to gaze to where the woman had disappeared into the crowds, saying, 'Many of the women I meet with Ettie have told me how you read letters from home and write replies for them. It's a mitzvah. A good deed.'

'I'd rather they could read themselves,' Hannah Leah said dryly.

Dov was scrutinising the chipped cups and plates, King George the fifth mugs minus handles, the ashtrays, and a variety of bric-a-brac and junk on Hannah Leah's stall.

Reaching out for a little bowl holding rings, all with missing stones, he held one up. 'How much?'

'Three pence,' Hannah Leah said, a quizzical look in her eyes.

'I'll take this one. Don't give me a bag. I'll put it in my pocket.' He handed a threepenny piece to Hannah Leah.

'Why on earth do you need a ring?' Sophia gave him a puzzled look.

'Wait and see.' Dov grinned as he turned to Hannah Leah again, 'Will you be a witness?'

'A witness? What do you have in mind?'

Without answering, Dov approached the seller of wonky pens on the next stall, and asked him the same question. The man nodded, clearly bemused. Taking both of Sophia's hands in his, in a clear sure voice, Dov said, 'Sophia Krichevska, will you be my wife?'

Sophia gasped. 'I… I… what do you mean?'

Letting go of her right hand, he took the ring. Without waiting for her reply, he said in Hebrew: *Behold, you are consecrated to me with this ring according to the laws of Moses and Israel.*' He placed it on her index finger.

Hannah Leah and the pen salesman laughed and called *Mazal Tov*. As did several people who had stopped to watch. Within moments, thirty or forty people had gathered round to cry, 'Mazal Tov!' to Sophia's shock and embarrassment.

'You see,' laughed Dov, gesticulating to the smiling crowd of onlookers. 'They all approve.'

She flushed to the roots of her hair, didn't know where to look or what to say, her eyes still on the ring. This wasn't a real marriage was her first thought, even though they had two witnesses, although admittedly one was a woman. But several men were standing or passing behind Hannah Leah and they would have been witnesses, making this legally possible. Another thought, Dov *was* married, married already. Two wives. We are not in biblical times, he knows that. Frowning, she shook her head. She was about to speak when he bent and kissed her. 'Dov, not here!'

'Aren't you happy?' he said softly.

'It's a crazy joke. You don't believe in marriage,' she whispered.

'But you do,' he replied, 'and it's not a joke.'

'I suppose I do believe, for all my anarchist beliefs. But Dov, what about Yetta Fruma?' She tried to see if he was still joking, but he kissed the top of her head and called to Hannah Leah and the pen salesman, 'Thank you. That was a mitzvah. Come,' he continued, 'let's get the tram.'

Sophia raised her eyes to Hannah Leah. Powerless like a child. Although she'd never felt impotent as a little girl.

'Hannah Leah, I'm completely confused. I'd better talk this over with Dov on the way.' Her voice was high and shaky. 'Give my love to all the children, and see you soon.'

She removed the ring, putting it into an inside pocket of her handbag and looked up at him. 'We must talk on the tram.'

She began to push her away through the crowds towards the main road, comforting herself with the thought that it wasn't a proper marriage without a *Ketuba,* a marriage contract signed by Dov. And probably there were other formalities she wasn't aware of. A flush of anger rose in her cheeks and she walked ever more quickly.

They boarded a tram and once they were seated, she stared out of the window wondering what to say.

'I want to buy a newspaper,' Dov said, seemingly impervious to her feelings.

Turning abruptly to him she said, 'Why on earth did you do that?'

'Why are you angry? I thought you'd be pleased.'

'I just don't understand you. You reject all rules and restrictions, everything connected with religion, and you did that.' She looked up at him, her mouth in a thin line, a frown piercing her forehead. 'Well, I'm waiting.'

For some moments he stared ahead, then took out a cigarette and lit it. 'Sophia my darling, it's like this. There's the person I have to be as a leader of the Revolution – decisive, tough, positive. But with you I can be myself. We can laugh, we can play … games, be uncomplicated, without a mask. I want you to think of having this ring as—' He searched for a way to explain his thoughts and, smiling, said, 'Like a game we play together, can you do that? A game?' He paused, and his voice changed, 'It's also a token of how I feel about you.'

Sophia nodded, warmed by the look in his eyes. 'All right. I don't really understand. But yes, it's a game. I know there are other sides to you besides the revolutionary leader. Of course I do.' She moved closer to him on the bench, and he put his arm around her.

For the rest of the journey to Soho, they sat in silence, watching the lights in shops, the people hurrying down the street, parcels under their arms, ready, thought Sophia, for their Christmas.

It was a five-minute walk from Tottenham Court Road to 35 Howland Street where Aaron's first-floor flat was above a shop. As they walked, she asked Dov why he hadn't taken a room in Soho near his oldest friend, a stone's throw from the anarchist Grafton Hall Club, militant like him.

'Aaron's work is here. As a Menshevik, he'd already renounced violence, and since coming to England he's found inspiration in Rudolf's beliefs. He prefers to be close to his work, yet still be a revolutionary. That's why he's active with the Grafton Hall Club.'

'I understand that, but why do you live so far away?'

Mounting the stairs to Aaron's room, Dov explained that by living in Stepney his own activities would come under less scrutiny. On hearing this, Sophia's mind was drawn to what she'd found yesterday, and she wrinkled her brow, but having vowed to remain silent, she made herself continue listening.

'Being in the same building as Rudolf,' Dov said, 'is even a kind of protection. Almost in the countryside, away from the Jewish population, here or in the East End, is safer. Otherwise, nothing can be hidden; everyone knows the most intimate details of everyone else's life. And Stepney is peaceful. I can think.'

'That's true.' She stopped as they turned on the stairs. 'Is that music coming from Aaron's room?'

'Don't forget, Aaron is an opera maven,' Dov laughed.

At the door, the music surged sweetly, bitterly, over them, so that when he knocked several times there was no reply. In the end, he opened the door and Sophia followed him in. A large room, draughty even in summer, with a rectangular window looking out onto Howland Street, an elegant but shabby Adam fireplace, and the usual furniture, which took up little space on the threadbare blue floral carpet that came with the room. The low winter light from the window fell on the phonograph on the floor, where Aaron sat in an armchair, listening in shadow, his eyes closed.

Dov removed his hat, saying, 'Good morning, comrade. You have visitors.' His finger to his lips, he indicated chairs by the table to Sophia, and they went in.

'Two minutes. It's the final aria,' Aaron said, without opening his eyes.

So they sat silently, Aaron transported to ancient Egypt, Dov and Sophia waiting. The music ended, but the wooden needle continued to rotate, scratching against the record. Leaning forward, Aaron lifted it away, swinging it to the side, and carefully taking the record off the turntable.

'I'm so sorry. Why didn't you tell me Sophia was with you. Just one minute.' He slid the record into its buff-coloured cover, and stacked it next to others on the windowsill, all of which managed to stay upright, thanks to a pile of books acting as a bookend. Walking over to where Sophia was perched on a hard-backed chair, he kissed her on both cheeks.

'So pleased to see you. How are you, Sophia?'

'It's good to see you, Aaron. I hope we didn't disturb you.'

'Of course not. You were very polite allowing me to listen to the end of the aria.'

Suddenly, Dov grinned. 'Educate me, Aaron. I'm an ignoramus when it comes to opera, though my mother often played her beloved Tchaikovsky on the piano. What was that piece you were playing when I came in?'

'*Aida,* the story of a captured princess, beloved by a general. He must choose between the woman he loves and loyalty to his country.'

'And what does he do?'

'Come to the opera with me one day, and you'll find out.'

'I will. It may be important.' His face fell.

Listening quietly, Sophia took a breath. There it was, the very question she'd been pondering yesterday when she found the priest's letter.

Dov leaned back in his chair, stretching out his legs, saying, 'I have to tell you about the Petersburg Soviet and the progress we've made. You've probably heard from others, you've probably read about it, but since you're my dear friend, I wanted to tell you what I saw, what I did—'

'Have you seen the latest news?' Aaron interrupted, though sounding almost reluctant to mention anything.

Unsmiling now, his face intent, Dov pressed forward in the chair. 'No, what is it? After I left, they arrested the Peasants' Union. What else has happened?'

Aaron rose from his chair and handed him a folded newspaper. '*The Observer.* Look on page four, near the bottom.'

Dov opened the newspaper and swiftly turning the page, scanned it, then clenched his fist. His face suffused with anger, he stood up and swore.

'Let me see.'

He handed it to Sophia, who found the paragraph.

'All members of the Petersburg Soviet have been arrested and are in prison,' she read. 'Can it be true?' She looked from one to the other. 'Yesterday. Could the news have travelled so quickly?'

'They've journalists in Moscow and Petersburg who cable the news,' answered Aaron. 'There was nothing in the Yiddish newspapers today. Probably this week.'

'It could have been you, Dov.' Sophia's expression was full of anxiety.

'It should have been me.'

Averting his gaze, he rose and began to pace the room. Turning fiercely to face them, he spat out, 'I fear it's a serious blow for the Revolution. The Tsar introduced his provisional rules, removing some aspects of censorship, but they came down heavily on those who praised what he called 'criminal acts'. *Criminal acts* – we all know what they are.'

Sophia had listened, careful not to speak while Dov was so angry, but she addressed him now. 'It says they had arms and had turned to the army for support. Is that also true?'

Facing the window, his back to her, he didn't reply.

So, they did have armaments, she thought, and he knew – though it didn't mean he'd procured them. Dov sat back down and folded his arms, then jumped up again. 'I need a glass of vodka, Aaron. Don't you have a bottle in the cupboard?'

'You know I do. Help yourself. I'll have a small drink with you.' Turning to Sophia, he raised his eyebrows. 'Would you like some?'

She shook her head. 'No, thank you, but could I make some tea?'

'Stay there. I'll fill the kettle, and you can have all the tea you wish.'

Sophia found tea, sugar and milk on a shelf in a tiny alcove, Aaron's kitchen, like that of all the other anarchists she knew, and made tea in a large brown shiny earthenware teapot, hoping that Dov would have some, and stop drinking vodka. She carried the cups and saucers to the table and poured the tea. Dov was now talking to Aaron, his voice low, his eyes troubled. Aaron was shaking his head, trying to persuade Dov not to return to Petersburg.

'I know, I know they'll be searching for me. I feel like a coward not supporting them. Otherwise, I don't know what I can do.' Dov dropped his face into his hands and Sophia wanted to take him in her arms to comfort him.

'Dov,' she said, with her hand on his shoulder, 'every single one of us is fighting for the Revolution, one way or another. You mustn't despair. The revolutionary movement, here and over there, knows what you've done and what you continue to do. The Revolution will succeed, if not today, sometime soon. We shall triumph!'

Her gaze, full of concern and compassion, moved him; he took her hand as she leaned over the table.

'Thank you, my darling girl, you've given me heart. Maybe another glass of vodka?'

Swiftly Sophia poured the tea and handed it to Dov.

'Please drink some; better than vodka, it will clear your mind.' She wanted to add that it would comfort him, but knew it to be inappropriate, with Aaron sitting so close, nodding gently at her suggestion.

'You make excellent tea, Sophia,' Aaron said, as she poured him a cup. 'I still take it without milk but with plenty of sugar.' Taking two large lumps, he held them, one at a time, between his teeth and drank the tea. Dov was still sitting, shoulders hunched, head down, the cup of tea untouched in front of him.

Sophia raised her eyebrows, and in a motherly, slightly reproving tone, said, 'Come on, Dov, or it will get cold.'

'Yes, Mama, I'll drink it now.' Slowly, he reached out for it, glanced up, his gaze meeting hers, and smiled.

Sophia returned the smile, glad that she'd distracted him from his gloomy thoughts, and sat down again. She decided to change the subject, talk about happier things. 'The New Year's Eve Ball is only two weeks away. Will you be there, Aaron?'

'I plan to, but no fancy dress for me. I sew enough for my living, so I'll come in my usual clothes. But I'll certainly dance. You missed the last ball, at Yom Kippur, didn't you?' He shook his head, clearly remembering the cause of it all – Rosa and the militant comrades he saw so frequently at the club. 'You are fully restored now, and I'm glad.' Aaron lit a cigarette and handed one to Dov, who nodded his thanks and lit up.

'You certainly won't miss the New Year's Eve Ball,' Dov said to Sophia. 'The highlight of the year, a wonderful evening, and we'll dance until three in the morning.'

He grinned, and she saw with relief he'd regained his good spirits and was thinking ahead.

'I'm not sure about three o'clock in the morning, but we'll certainly dance, I'll dance with you and with Aaron.'

'Very generous of you,' Dov gave her a rakish look. 'How do you know he won't bring a lovely lady with him?'

'I really hope he does.'

CHAPTER 24

DOV BECAME ELUSIVE AGAIN. For a couple of weeks leading to New Year's Eve, Sophia would see him only at the Sugar Loaf pub. He was just as loving, but abstracted somehow, as though he were planning something, and she hoped he wouldn't disappear back to the Tsar's Domains. In the Sugar Loaf, he would sit beside her, his gaze elsewhere, and when she asked him if he was all right, he would say, 'You mustn't worry. I'm thinking.'

She wished he would share his concerns with her, although she wasn't surprised – the news concerning the progress of the Revolution had become increasingly dire, and activists and followers, which meant most of the East End, had become downcast. First the Moscow branch of the Peasants' Union had been arrested, then the Petersburg Soviet and finally, when rebels and militants tried to take Moscow through armed struggle, they were defeated by the vicious Black Hundreds. The police regime returned and the army swept across Russia, crushing all dissent. People were shot in the street, dragged out of their homes, thrown into prison. It felt as though the Revolution had failed. Black headlines and reports filled the press. To cap it all, East End workshops were idle, there was barely any work. Sophia was occasionally cheered seeing the Chanukah lights in the tenement windows, but naturally her mind turned to home, which didn't help.

To raise their spirits, Milly suggested they should wear fancy dress for the New Year's Eve Ball rather than the peasant dress they normally wore.

'A little more elaborate, but you can always wear a mask if that's proves too difficult,' she added.

The New Year Ball, one of their main money raisers, supported by anarchists and well-wishers from all over London, gave them something cheerful to think about. As Sophia attached flyers to gas lamps and the occasional telegraph pole, she hoped the prospect of the ball would cheer Dov up. He loved the socials and entertainments Rudolf and Milly organised and he would be sure to know many of the people coming to celebrate the New Year.

It will do him good.

What should she wear? While talking to Hannah Leah one morning, Sophia had an idea. Her friend had taken a narrow box from the back of her stall and, drawing out a white fan inlaid with tiny jewels, offered it to Sophia, who took it wonderingly.

'It's exquisite. Where did you get it?'

'A neighbour. I'd helped her out when her husband was ill. She cleans for a wealthy woman in Hampstead. After the woman moved, the box was left in the attic. My neighbour gave it to me.'

'How much?'

Hannah Leah waved her question away, but Sophia insisted on giving her what she thought it was worth. For at once she imagined herself as a Spanish dancer, and when she found two pieces of beautiful red silk material embossed with flowers, on a fent stall nearby, she knew they were perfect. She cut, pinned, basted and sewed the garment by hand, adding a frill to the hem and creating rose pom-poms for her hair, since who could find a mantilla in Petticoat Lane? Just before New Year's Eve, it was finished. Having climbed on the bed to check herself in the mottled mirror, she decided to ask Mrs Vine for her verdict.

'Beautiful. So you're going to the Ball with your young man?'

'You see everything, Mrs Vine.'

'Make sure you have a lovely time.'

The group of women anarchists who lived in Dunstan Houses or nearby – Mrs Linder, Mrs Sabelinsky, Mrs. Kerkelevitch, and Polly, Milly's sister, who lived on the floor below them – had been designated to organise the refreshments for the evening. Sophia had met them during her early days with the group and knew how energetic and dedicated they were. When she asked if she could help, Polly said, 'No. You do enough for the movement, writing articles, organising the flyers and pamphlets, and now I understand you're even selling the newspaper in the street. But you can take this bag of decorations to the Rhondda Grove church hall, where we'll have the ball. That will be your contribution.'

She arrived at the hall on Sunday morning, New Year's Eve, to find a dark damp building with an enormous snout-like black chimney pointing to the sky. The caretaker, who had been shovelling coal around the back, opened the building for her, pointing to a tiny kitchen across from the main entrance, and told her they should on *no account* touch the stove, it was unreliable and dangerous. Gazing around inside, after he'd gone back to the coal, she found it a dark and chilly place, the air fuggy, as though the windows hadn't been opened for months. How could this be the setting for an uplifting, exciting evening?

Returning to her room in Wentworth Buildings, she felt miserable, but in the early evening, her carefully folded fancy dress in a shopping bag, she went over to Dov's and her spirits lifted. She found him lying smoking on the bed.

'Let me see your costume.' He grinned.

'It's here.' She lifted the bag. 'It'll take me two ticks to get ready.'

Knowing there would be no transport after midnight, they'd arranged this beforehand. With her back to him, she slipped off her blouse and skirt, which she folded and placed on top of the portmanteau he kept at the bottom of his wardrobe. A flush of embarrassment warmed her cheeks, she couldn't think why. Giving herself a little shake, she drew on the Spanish dancer's outfit, which felt pleasantly smooth and soft to her skin, and turned to face him. 'You can open your eyes now.'

She watched him, a little self-conscious, wondering if he liked it, if it was suitable. She'd never been to such an occasion before and he had. For some moments, he looked her up and down, then rising from his bed, he held out his hands, saying, 'Hola, beautiful lady! You look wonderful.'

She let out a sigh of relief. 'You said you knew what to wear without any help from me. It's your turn now.'

'All right. Look the other way.' In a few moments, he called, 'Ready.'

She'd been gazing out of the window at the darkened Dunstan Gardens, where only the ghostly, stark shapes of bare trees were visible. She turned. He had on a white shirt with sleeves frilled at the wrist; a red cummerbund, and black trousers tucked into high boots. She couldn't believe how handsome he looked.

'How did you know?' she demanded.

'A little bird told me.'

'A cross between a toreador and a Cossack. That's you absolutely.' She let her shoulders drop as all tension fell from her.

'We only need Aaron's gramophone, a few records and we could dance here all night.'

'The cause! The cause!' She shook her finger at him.

He laughed, the dimple appeared in his cheek and she couldn't restrain herself from running to kiss him.

At half-past six, fancy dress hidden beneath their dark winter coats, they walked hand-in-hand to the church hall in Rhondda Grove. Sophia was glad to hear a more positive note in Dov's voice and smiled to herself. They were going to have a wonderful time, she was sure. Arriving, they found Sam sitting at a small table, counting out change in a purple tin, with the image of a milkmaid pouring cream into a jug, once a container for Cadbury's chocolate.

'Hello, Sam, ready to rake in the money?' Dov stopped to speak to him.

Sophia was amazed by the transformation in the room since her trip that morning. She gazed around at the soft light from the gas lamps pooling on the tables which were arranged in a semicircle around the hall. The blinds were down, there was a candle in a pot or jam jar, and the hall was warm and bright. And there was music, a little discordant it was true; on the stage, the band was arguing about what to play. An accordionist played one tune, the fiddles played something slow and melancholy, while the drummer, a squat, dark eyed man sat with his arms folded, staring into the hall. Then the flautist began a high, lilting folk tune and the musicians joined him. It had begun.

Across the room, before the kitchen, women were making sandwiches, and the smell of eggs and fish paste and pickled herring mingled with something of a smoky smell.

Sophia turned to Sam. 'Forgive me, I didn't say hello to you, I was overwhelmed by what you've achieved this afternoon. The room looks wonderful, like a ballroom in an elegant house.'

'Bit of an exaggeration, Sophia,' Dov raised his eyebrows.

'But it was dank and dark when I came with the decorations, and look at it now.' She pointed to the ceiling where streamers and bunting crisscrossed the roof, adding to the bright cheerful air. Then she sniffed. 'Is that smoky smell from the stove, Sam?'

'Like an icebox when we arrived early this afternoon. Ernst, Polly's husband, and I searched around and finding the coal hole at the back, we 'borrowed' a few shovels of coal and lit the stove.'

Sophia laughed. 'The caretaker warned me that on no account should anyone light the stove because it was unpredictable and only he knew how to handle it.' She gazed down the room at it, black and huge, like some crouching animal with its fat black pipe rising up to the ceiling. It reminded her of the stove at home. 'When it was really cold my little brother Alexei used to sleep on top of our stove.'

'We all did that,' grinned Dov. 'Well, I'll stay and help Sam for a while, Sophia, as we're early. Aren't there some raffle tickets somewhere?'

'I'll go and see if they need help with the sandwiches.'

Arriving at the two long tables where the women were working, she said, 'Hello everyone, what can I do?'

Milly, looking suspiciously like a nurse, with a white hat and apron, poked her head round the kitchen door. 'We're doing fine, Sophia. Almost finished, but if you like, you can take the plates of sandwiches round at the interval.'

Mrs Linder, fair and pretty, stopped buttering the edge of the sandwiches and said, 'Let's see your fancy dress, Sophia. I caught a glimpse of something red at your throat.'

'Yes, yes,' said Mrs Ruderman, doling out pickled herring on plates. 'You can hang your coat with ours in the kitchen and then show us your outfit.'

Sophia emerged from the kitchen.

'A Spanish lady. It's lovely, made it yourself?'

'Of course she did,' said Mrs Kerkelevitch. 'You'd be in the gutter here if you couldn't sew.'

'You aren't wearing fancy dress?' Sophia said.

'It's for you young ones. We'll wear masks later on.' Mrs Ruderman lifted her head to indicate Dov sitting by the door with Sam. 'Is he wearing fancy dress?'

He must have heard her voice, despite the noise in the hall because he rose and sauntered over. 'Of course I am. Want to see it?'

'How about a striptease?' one of the women called.

'Too cold for that.' Dov folded his coat over a bench.

'He won't say how he knew what I was wearing,' said Sophia, almost proudly.

'Milly has something for me in the kitchen.' Dov returned immediately, wearing a black three-cornered toreador-type hat. He stamped and shouted, 'Hola!'

'Marvellous. A pair of Spanish dancers,' said Mrs Linder. The women beamed at them, while Polly began covering the plates of sandwiches with tea towels.

'Sophia, these two long tables are for the Arbeter Frainters. They seat about twelve people each, so you and Dov can sit at one, and we'll join you when we're ready.'

Sam called, 'I'm opening up. There's a queue outside already.'

As he unlocked the door, they piled in, socialists and supporters from all over London, talking, shouting, and stopping to embrace somebody on both cheeks in typical fashion. The room filled with noise and laughter. Sophia felt her heart beat fast in her chest, for it had begun, The band responded to this, playing a lively folk tune, while people found places at tables and commented on the fancy dress – clowns, queens, fairies and witches like Baba Yaga from their folk tales, ugly and menacing. They carried bottles of vodka, whisky, and even sarsaparilla. Seeing people he knew from other socialist groups, Dov went to chat to them.

How wonderful to feel part of this group of people with such high ideals, and who wanted to change the world for the better, Sophia thought. She wished her parents could see her now, and resolved to describe every moment of the evening in her next letter home.

'The Rudermans are taking over from me and Sam,' said Dov, returning. With a great bow he added, 'Would you care to dance, señorita?'

But as she rose from her chair, she saw a contingent of West Enders pile in, Rosa leading them and making straight for their table. Did Rosa know she was most definitely with Dov now, and what comments would she throw at her?

Yet Sophia couldn't help but admire Rosa's outfit, a closefitting skirt in a golden hue with a matching long sleeved top, her hat laden with artificial apples, plums and cherries. She walked swiftly on high heels, a rarity among the anarchist women and, as she drew closer, she exclaimed, 'Quite a couple in your Spanish garb! And how are you, Dov? Haven't seen you in Soho for weeks.'

'I'm very well, Rosa,' Dov said. 'And what's with the fruit?' He pointed to her hat.

'She's the spirit of Summer or Autumn. Which is it, Rosa?' Sophia tried a light-hearted response.

'Autumn. Rich in abundance.' Rosa gave a flick of her head. 'I'm with Sebastien, that young Frenchman over there. Black hair, longest eyelashes.' Giving Dov a mocking look, she added, 'A new recruit to the cause…'

'I'll be delighted to meet him,' Dov said, 'but it's time to dance.'

Aaron had followed Rosa and now took a seat at the Arbeter table.

'Abandoning us, Aaron?' said Rosa.

'You're right. I'll have to divide my time between the two,' said Aaron with a laugh.

'Or join us, Rosa, with your friend. I'm sure there's room.'

'Thanks, Sophia. We'll see.'

She sashayed across the room, her shoes tip tapping on the hard floor.

The band played a Viennese waltz, Dov took Sophia's hand and they danced. Then followed a quadrille, but soon people were calling for folk dances – *der alter bulgar*, the *csárdás*, the *mazurka* – and they stamped and clapped and spun with the others, in the great circle dances. The band played faster and faster until breathless, Sophia collapsed on to a chair, laughing, and fanning herself until she cooled down. Dov went to speak to the West Enders, but returned as the band launched into a *freilach*, a wedding dance.

'This is for us,' he whispered, and she blushed.

'I've never been so happy.'

As the circle swung towards the entrance, she noticed those sitting nearest had stopped talking. Rudolf stood there. Instead of mounting the stage to speak in the interval as he always did, he appeared to be searching for someone, his gaze sombre. Sophia felt an uneasy jolt in her heart. As they passed the doorway, Rudolf beckoned to Dov and he broke away, but Sophia continued to be swept on by the momentum of the dance; she was nearing the stove at the far end before she could extricate herself, saying, 'Excuse me, Excuse me.'

She ran to the door, but Dov and Rudolf had disappeared.

'Mr Ruderman, do you know where Rudolf and Dov are?' Her voice was thin with anxiety.

'Gone out, I think.' He nodded towards the street.

The street was murky, dark, and she shivered. A few gas lamps cast a weak glow on the terraced houses. She made out two dark shapes further up the street, palely illuminated by one of the lights. There was something ominous in the way Rudolf talked with his head bent, a hand on Dov's shoulder. She heard a groan and caught her breath. Dov was reading a small square of yellow paper. *A telegram*. Gathering up her skirts, she ran towards them. Hearing her footsteps, Rudolf shook his head as though to warn her away, but she had to know, she had to be with him.

'What is it?' she cried, a horrible suspicion filling her mind. 'Is it...? She dared not utter the name. Dov's face was ashen, he seemed unaware of her. 'Dov?'

Seeing her, his voice shook and he croaked, 'It's Katya.'

She snatched the telegram from his hand and read: *Katya very ill. Come at once.*

'You can't go,' she cried.

Taking a deep breath, as though to control his feelings, and turning his gaze directly to meet hers, he said: 'I *must*.'

'But you can't,' she cried. 'The secret police will arrest you.' He shook his head, his gaze once more averted. 'Please Rudolf,' her eyes imploring as she turned to him, 'please tell him he mustn't go back to Saint Petersburg. For his own sake.'

'I know how much you care, Sophia – we all do – but there are occasions when we alone must make our decisions. And this is one of them.' His eyes warm through his glasses, he added, 'We support you in whatever you decide. Be aware of that, Dov.'

'Thank you, Rudolf.' A sudden red flush glazed his cheeks. 'Sophia, I'm leaving.'

CHAPTER 25

S HE RAN TO KEEP up with him.

Once in his room, she sat on the bed, her coat pulled tightly around her, the chill in the room like his anguish, seeping into her body. She watched, holding her breath as he flung open the desk drawer and began to throw papers onto the desk, the floor. At last, he found what he was seeking – his passport, evidently, and a sheet of paper whose contents were hidden from her gaze, since he stood with his back to her.

He shouted, 'No!' and groaned, then sank heavily onto a chair.

She waited, terror in her heart as, covering his face with his hands, he seemed to have forgotten her existence.

A pause.

She whispered, 'What is it?'

'The summer timetable for Finland,' he muttered. 'Thought I had the complete one.'

'Why not Petersburg?'

'The Port will be frozen.' Lifting his head, he cried, 'I can't bear it, Sophia. All because of me and that reptile Gapon. If only I'd never met him.'

He hit his head with his fists.

She rose from the bed and went over to him. 'Not because of you…' she couldn't continue, his shoulders shook as he began to weep. She held her arms around him and he rested his head against her, his sobs muffled by her body. Moments passed. He wiped his eyes with the back of his hands.

She straightened up. 'Katya will get better,' she said with as much authority as she could muster.

Ignoring her, his voice stronger, he said, 'I'll go down to the docks tomorrow. There's a public house where the sailors drink. They'll know about the times of departure to Finland. There's a captain of a trading ship I've taken before. If he's there, I can return with him.'

A little bell rang in her mind. He's been by ship to Finland before? That's what it said in the letter she'd read a few weeks ago. She was on the point of asking him but something more pressing told her to wait. Something that had come to her just now while he was searching for his passport. She was about to speak when he rose from his chair.

'Vodka! I need a drink.' Going to his cubby hole of a kitchen, he held up the bottle to Sophia. 'Want one?'

She shook her head, watching as he downed two full glasses one after the other. Coming back to the room, he seemed to sag.

'I'm exhausted. Let's go to bed.'

They lay, her arms around him.

Taking a deep breath, she said, 'I'm coming with you.' She faced him, her eyes intent on his.

'*No.*' He turned to her, resting on his elbow. 'No. You can't come with me. They're expecting pogroms in Petersburg. Never happened before. It's too dangerous.'

Sophia sat up and extended her left hand. The ring he'd given her, which she'd slipped on while sitting on the bed before, gleamed dully in the darkness.

'Dov, I'm your wife. That's why I'm coming with you. And this is my plan.' She raised her hand as he was about to interrupt. 'We dress as poor Jews in rags, and no one will notice us. We'll take tickets in the hold and you must stay there the entire journey. If anyone asks, I'll say we're going back to a shtetl near Petersburg.'

'They could still find us,' he muttered.

'I'll add I'm a nurse, looking after you – not so different from being a midwife and it will make it more official. There.'

'Quite something.'

She was glad to see that little mocking smile return to his face.

'I *am* coming with you, Dov. It will protect you from the police.'

'Maybe.' Her eyes were so passionate, he couldn't help but agree.

Her heart leapt. 'So get two tickets for the journey. I'll give you whatever money I have for mine.'

He laughed, pulled her to him and kissed her. 'That's why I love you, Sophia Krichevska.'

The following morning, Dov was already up and dressed when Sophia awoke.

'I'm going to the docks right away,' he said. 'There'll be a boat on Thursday, or Friday, at the latest.'

'I'll sort out the clothes.' Sophia smiled up at him. 'When will you tell me?'

'Give me a couple of days. I'll come as soon as I know.'

She returned to her room. New Year's Day was no different from any other to the stallholders in Wentworth Street and the Lane. On the second-hand stalls, clothes were piled in heaps.

'A skirt, lady?' said the round-faced Cockney woman. 'Look here. This come from a rich woman down on her luck. Poor thing,' she added with a mocking grin.

Sophia held up the long skirt, a kind of dun colour, though clean after so many washings. It smelt of mothballs and fustiness. There'd be no time to wash and dry it before the end of the week, but she took it. A shawl which her mother had crocheted in a rare spare moment lay in her trunk; Sophia trusted that no one would examine it closely. The image of a poor Jewish woman required a headscarf. She preferred to borrow one rather than buy, so when she complained to Mrs Vine how dank her hair had got in this foggy weather, (though hating to deceive her), Mrs Vine leant one to her. Her 'disguise' laid out on the bed, Sophia wondered about Dov, but he'd told her he'd borrow trousers from one of the Arbeter Frainters, for his clothes were always so good.

That was Monday morning.

Sophia spent the afternoon lying on the bed, dreaming of Saint Petersburg. Wonderful to be returning, but strange not to see her family. Could she go home for a few days? A journey of two days and two nights each way in the depths of winter? She pictured her mother's face on opening the door, how she'd fling her arms around her and embrace her over and over again. Questions. Exclamations. Surely an assessment of how thin she'd become, her mother pressing her to take second helpings of food, her favourite blintzes, desserts, soups. A wave of homesickness so acute broke over Sophia that she had to squeeze her eyes shut. *And supposing the train is locked in a snow drift seven feet deep?*

She saw the great wastes of fields covered with snow, the skeleton birch trees, the fir and pine, branches hanging deep, the lone peasant cottage miles from any town. The intense darkness.

Besides, she told herself, she was going in order to be with him. To support him, to comfort him if what she suspected – the bleak thought continued to leap into her mind – if Katya... *She will survive,* she said, rising to heat up the saucepan of thick barley soup she'd made on Saturday. Another reminder of home.

Dov didn't come on Monday, which was hardly surprising. On Tuesday, Sophia walked to the workshop to tell Mr Lazarus she'd be away for a while: *I don't know how long exactly.* The workshop was quiet, the sewing machines stood silent, like animals waiting for food, she thought. Mr Lazarus sat at one of them, idling the wheel with one hand. No cloth beneath the needle. He shook his head, his long face sallow and thin, bags beneath his eyes.

'There's no work, Sophia. Or I'd have sent for you.'

'How's Mrs Lazarus and the baby?'

His eyes lit up. 'Both well, thank God. They've gone to the market. So where are you going, Sophia?'

'To help a friend.' The simplest reply to the question she knew would come.

'There should be some work soon.'

In her room, she began to pace. Had Dov found anything yet? She told herself to be patient. She'd write to her brother Sasha in New York, and to her mother, without mentioning Petersburg of course. Letters finished, she posted them, then returned.

The afternoon sky was darkening, she sat by the window to get as much light as she could and thought about Dov's family. On Sunday night, as he calmed down lying in her arms, she'd said, 'Dov, tell me something about them. I'd like to know more.' She kept her arm tightly around his waist until the tension fell from his body.

'We are in the Podyachesky area now. Where most of the Jewish people live in Piter.'

'I stayed there one night, before leaving Petersburg. With Papa's friends,' she said. 'It's behind the Nevsky Boulevard, I think. A wide road with beautiful shops and hotels, but arriving at night, I barely saw it.'

'You're right.' He glanced down at her, nodding. 'Our building is on the southern edge of the area; we're on the ground floor where Papa also has his surgery. A squeeze when we're all there. But my sister Alicia's married and my brother Leon's studying medicine. There's only Ivan, who's twenty, and Katya…' his voice broke, and she moved closer to him. He took a deep breath. 'Only Katya, at home.'

'And your mother, does she still play the piano?'

'Of course, but she makes do with an upright. She sold her grand piano when we had to move.' He frowned as though the thought of this great loss pained him too. Then adding, his voice gentle, 'You'll like her. She's spiritual without being religious, loves nature and flowers, walking in the parks.'

A glow of joy burst into her heart. She would surely meet his mother.

'I bet you fought a lot when you were little.'

'Like little lion cubs, Mama would say.'

They continued talking until she said, 'It must be about one o'clock. Let's get some sleep.'

That evening she had another bowl of barley soup and went to bed early.

By Wednesday lunchtime, she hadn't heard from him and anxiety stalked her mind. He'd said he hoped to leave on Thursday and yet she knew nothing. Perhaps there was no boat going to Finland on Thursday or Friday, that's why he hadn't called round. *I need to know what's happening.*

In her long coat she walked down the stone stairs at Wentworth Buildings, the smell particularly sour and pungent that day, and took the tram to Dunstan Houses. Horses and carts, trams, automobiles and pedestrians crowded the road and she waited to cross, her fingers clenched, her eyebrows drawn together with anxiety. Up the steps, a left turn and down the corridor, she hastened to his room. She knocked, but there was no answer.

She opened the door which was never locked, calling, 'Hello, Dov.'

The door slammed against his wardrobe door, which

stood against the wall behind it. Why hadn't he shut it with the wedge of folded newspaper? In the room, she gazed around. A feeling of absence. The bed was tidily made; all pamphlets and papers had been cleared from his desk. There remained a lingering odour of his cigarettes but the ashtray was empty. Turning, her heart beating faster in her chest, she called his name again, then went into the cubby hole of a kitchen, only to see the teapot and kettle sitting on the two-ring burner, and the tiny table where Dov prepared his food quite bare.

A pulse throbbed in her neck; breathing fast, she went to close the wardrobe door and stopped. His portmanteau had gone. She was staring at an ominous, gaping hole. The room was gloomy with early twilight and she bent, feeling around with her hand at the bottom of the wardrobe. Dust, a couple of tram tickets, shoes.

Has he left without me? She glanced around again as though he might be hiding somewhere. *Don't jump to conclusions. I'll go up to Rudolf and see if he knows where Dov is.*

She was panting when she reached the fourth floor. A knock on the door, but no reply and she peered in. At the end of the room, Rudolf's table was littered with books and papers, as usual. She knew Milly would be at work if she had any, and though Rudolf was usually there, he could be at the club, supervising something, or visiting a comrade.

There was a hollow feeling in her stomach.

Closing the door, she walked with a heavy tread down the stairs. Outside, she drew her coat around her and shivered. Five o'clock and it was dark. Who else would know?

Aaron, Rosa? She couldn't stand the thought that Rosa might know while she didn't.

I can't stay here. I'll come back later, 8 o'clock maybe. He should have returned by then.

She waited in the dark at Wentworth Buildings, hoping against hope that Dov would come with the tickets and news of when they'd take the boat, but as it grew later, her breathing quickened. At eight o'clock, she put on her coat again, took her handbag and was about to leave, when there came a knock at her door.

Dov stood there.

'Dov, I was getting worried. Come in.'

'I don't know what you're worried about. I'm here with my travel bag. You can put your things in it. We don't need much.' He grinned.

Placing it on the floor in front of the fireplace, he put his hands on her shoulders. 'The boat leaves tomorrow at seven in the morning. I'll be here with you at six.'

She was shaking. A frown pierced Dov's forehead. 'What's the matter?'

Her head bent, she muttered, 'I thought you'd left without me. When I looked for you in your room and everything was tidy and you weren't there… I had the strangest of feelings.' She lifted her gaze to his, noting the change in his expression as he averted his eyes.

'Be ready tomorrow. We'll walk to the port. The captain's called Captain Contact, clearly not his real name, but I know him and he's happy for us to travel with him. In Finland, we'll take the train from Vyborg.'

CHAPTER 26

SOPHIA'S INTENTION TO PROTECT Dov, by persuading him to stay in the cabin while she took small walks around the deck, was immediately in disarray. A much smaller ship than the one they'd taken for England, and smelling of exported winter wheat, fish, oil and tar, there were no other passengers apart from themselves. But it was winter, and crossing the North Sea was a shock to her. The winds were bitterly cold, it was stormy, the boat rose and fell on the waves and, by the end of the first day, she was utterly overwhelmed by seasickness.

This didn't affect Dov at all; now he had a plan of action, he'd regained his positive spirit. While she spent hours lying on the bottom bunk of their tiny cabin, Dov would go for short walks, saying he wouldn't be long, but he would take his time chatting to sailors or the captain. It was Dov who brought her bowls in which to be sick and would remove them. When he also offered her food, soup or stew from the galley, she turned her head away trying not to see the constantly moving wall.

One morning the captain knocked at the cabin door and peered in. Dov was standing behind him. He'd introduced the captain to her on the first day, saying, 'Meet my old friend, Captain Contact.'

'Welcome aboard, Mrs Feldman. It's a pleasure to meet you.'

Sophia had blushed on being called *Mrs* but had shaken his warm, calloused hand and said, 'Thank you, Captain Contact.'

Wearing a thick navy jacket, heavy black trousers, his grey hair cut close to the scalp, his beard evidently freshly trimmed, he looked a veritable ship's master, solidly built and calm. His sharp blue eyes were startling in a face so tanned by wind and sun.

'We are hoping to have a grand journey to Finland.' He turned to Dov, 'Better than your last, I would wager, Mr Feldman.'

What were they talking about? This must be something to do with the letter she'd discovered in Dov's room. She'd told herself that there would be plenty of time to ask him about the armaments during this voyage. But seasickness had overtaken her – her mind was vacant.

Today, the captain said, 'Mrs Feldman, May I come in?'

Her eyes closed, she tried to shuffle up the bunk but felt too weak. She nodded.

'I hear from your husband that you're having a bad journey. Winter is not the best time to travel north.'

She blinked away the tears running down her cheeks and tried to focus.

'I might have the solution for you. The cook has baked a fruitcake, cut a slice and smeared it with jam. It's an old-fashioned cure.'

She shook her head, nausea rising in her gullet at the very idea of fruitcake with jam.

'Try, Sophia,' said Dov, from the door.

'You may be surprised.' The captain held the plate out to her.

'All right,' she croaked, her lips dry.

Dov came round and, putting his arm beneath her shoulders, helped her to sit. Holding a glass of water to her lips, he encouraged her to drink. Then taking the plate from the captain, he broke off the smallest morsel of cake and said, 'Just a tiny piece, Sophia. Please try.'

It will only come back, she thought, her stomach churning at the mingled smell of baked raisins and raspberry jam. But she put it into her mouth, forcing herself to chew. Then another, and another. To her surprise, they stayed down.

'Excellent. You'll soon be eating with me at my table.' Grinning, the captain shut the door behind him. Sophia continued to eat until she'd finished the cake.

'Wonderful!' exclaimed Dov. 'Colour's coming back into your cheeks. Now take it slowly. When you feel ready, try to stand.'

Fixed to the floor, their table was covered with a dark green velvety cloth; Dov took a chair and sat facing her.

After a while, she said, 'I think I can now.' Gingerly, she swung her legs around and stood up. 'I'm not sick,' she said in astonishment. 'The boat isn't rocking so much. What a miracle.'

From this day – there were passing through the narrow straits into the Baltic Sea – they dined every evening with the captain in his most comfortable cabin. Twice the size of theirs, his table stood on a richly patterned Axminster carpet. Sophia presumed that this was where he kept the ship's log and whatever paperwork might be necessary for a merchant ship. Family photographs adorned his carved oak sideboard, his bed was hidden by a long red baize curtain. While they had two small oil lamps fixed to the wall softly lighting their cabin, he had four, plus a large table lamp that he placed on the sideboard when they came in.

One evening he was regaling them with stories of his voyages around the world. He had been in the Black Sea, where the sailors, led by Matushenko on the Battleship Potemkin, had revolted against their officers. He and his crew had been stuck in the port of Odessa because of a widespread strike in the city; they couldn't load or unload, but they had an inside view of the revolt spreading on the Tsar's ships.

'They say it all started because the meat was riddled with vermin, but of course, the entire country was in revolt last year. We watched them burn their ships as revolution spread. But, tragically, they lost in the end.'

'It will continue,' said Dov gravely. 'Give us time.'

'Talking about ships burning,' continued the captain, pouring a glass of brandy for himself and Dov. 'Were you present when Captain Nylander blew up the *John Grafton*?'

Frowning, Dov gave the captain a brief shake of the head as if to say, 'Don't continue', but Captain Contact was focused on tamping his pipe with tobacco, and clearly didn't get the message.

'I think my wife is ready to retire, Captain Contact, aren't you, Sophia?' Dov pushed back his chair.

Curious, surprised by his tone, she shook her head, giving Dov a questioning glance, aware that he was hiding something from her, the very thing she longed to know.

'This is so interesting,' she murmured. 'I read about it in the newspaper, of course.'

Ignoring her comment, Dov insisted: 'I'm sure the captain has work to do. Perhaps we should go.'

The captain glanced from one to the other, sensing some conflict. He liked the couple and didn't want to exacerbate it. Still, he shook his head and indicated the glass of brandy just poured.

'Don't go without finishing this very good brandy.'

Dov was forced to sit back in his chair and accept a glass. 'I'm sure you read about it in the newspapers,' he said. 'I believe it was big news back in England.' He gave Sophia a warning look and she stared at the table.

The captain agreed. 'Of course it made the headlines. A ship carrying an arsenal of munitions. You know it took us two days to load it on here. Where you obtained them from I have no idea. I don't ask questions, you understand. But clearly, she delivered half the cargo at Kemi in the Gulf of Bothnia. I've been there many times – it was after the rocky Archipelago at Jakobstad that she went aground. Not that I'm blaming Nylander at all, ships run aground much too often.' He shook his head. 'Who financed it? A Jap?'

'Yes.' Dov said, in an undertone, his head down, a frown piercing his forehead. But as a guest, he was forced to elaborate. 'You know, in his wisdom, the Tsar had begun a war with Japan and was shocked when this tiny nation defeated him.' He laughed unexpectedly. 'It took the Tsar's fleet nine months to reach Japanese waters. Now Japan does everything to support the Revolution against the Tsar and his cronies.'

'So do we all,' said Captain Contact. Looking at his watch, he added, 'It's late, and travelling is tiring. Especially in this foul weather when one can barely keep one's balance on deck.'

Dov smiled. 'Thank you, we really appreciate sharing your table and hearing your wonderful stories. It's an honour.'

'Dov is right,' said Sophia rising from her chair. 'You have a wonderful cook and we benefit by him, but as Dov said before, I'm a little tired.' She smiled and the captain returned her smile.

'Tomorrow night, it's lamb with all the trimmings. Cook always exceeds expectations. Come at seven.'

He escorted them to the door, with old-fashioned courtesy.

In the cabin, Sophia said 'Why did you want him not to talk? Because of me?'

'Yes.'

Head down, Dov was removing his boots and she couldn't see his expression, but his voice was curt.

'But why? Surely we should share everything? Tell me about the John Grafton and the part you played.'

'In London, you were right.' Dov looked up. 'I was on the point of leaving without you.'

Sophia's eyes widened. 'Without telling me?'

'Yes. I wanted to keep you safe. Sophia, you have no idea about the Tsar's spies. They're everywhere, prowling every capital, reporting back to the secret police if they see anyone suspicious. I felt it was too dangerous for you to be with me. I still do.'

'Then why did you let me come?' Sophia sank onto her bunk.

'I wanted you with me. I want you to meet Katya, my family...' He lit a cigarette. 'I hope I've not made a mistake.'

'You remember I told you that I had read one of your letters?' Sophia said, after a pause. She hesitated but resolved to continue.

He raised his head. 'I don't want to talk about it.'

'But, Dov, we must.'

'I see no reason why.'

'From Father Georgi Gapon, enumerating an arsenal of weapons to be transported to the capital. Was it addressed to you? Surely these are the arms Captain Contact was talking about just now?' She stared up at him, determined to find out.

Dov glared at her. Finally, he said, 'It could be any revolutionary attending the Soho club or anyone recently arrived. Was the letter addressed to me?'

'No,' she admitted. 'It was headed only *Dear Comrade*.'

'Then forget it. I never want to speak of it again.'

Startled by his sudden fury, Sophia said no more, but once she'd undressed, she lay thinking about the Revolution, its ideals of making a better life for all. She thought about the Tsar and his government. Violence at its heart. Its fear and hatred of the people, its terror of change. Perhaps Dov was right to be a gunrunner, however much she loathed and feared the practice. Then she thought about Katya, wondering if they would arrive in time. She'd noticed during the days of the voyage, more than a week now, that Dov had said little about his sister. There were moments when he was silent, wandering around the cabin smoking, and she knew he was thinking of his family. But he'd never been angry with her like this before. She knew he would never tell her.

CHAPTER 27

O N REACHING VYBORG IN Finland, where Captain Contact had arranged to leave them, they
thanked him as they disembarked. He told them
he was looking forward to seeing them in two or three
weeks' time, on their return to London, and wished them
luck. From Vyborg they took a train to Saint Petersburg, a
short journey, then Dov hailed a horse-drawn cab waiting
outside the station, since it was too far to walk. Sophia
peered out expecting to see wide beautiful boulevards,
tall blocks of flats, and elegant shops, but it was just as
foggy as in London and she merely glimpsed them as they
followed the road.

They reached his apartment block on the outskirts of the
city, where Dov paid the driver. Sophia, watching, thought
he eyed them oddly, but forgot at once with the appre-
hension and excitement of actually meeting Dov's family.

An elegant four storey building, a little shabby. Dov's
apartment had a separate entrance beside the main doorway
leading to the majority of the flats. A flutter of excitement,
of nervousness, made her pause – for now she would meet
his family. She wondered what they would think of her,
arriving unannounced with their son.

He opened the door.

They entered a narrow hallway with doors on either side, one to the right was ajar, and Sophia glimpsed a large sitting room, with an upright piano at the far end. On the wall nearest the door, she caught sight of a mirror covered with a piece of linen signifying death, and her heart fell. Dov hadn't seen it and she wondered how he'd react when he realised they'd arrived too late. She hesitated, then made herself follow him, marching ahead and calling: 'Mama, we're here. Mama!'

Appearing at the end of the hall, his mother came towards them. A beautiful woman, Sophia saw, dressed in black, the ritual tear at her neck revealing a stark white triangle of skin. Her fair hair was swept up, and her eyes, like Dov's, were brown with amber tints.

'My darling boy, I'm so happy to see you.' Taking his hands in hers, she drew him to her and they embraced. Then lifting her eyes to his, she enveloped him in a sorrowful, compassionate gaze. 'I'm afraid, Dov … it is too late.'

He stepped back. '*No.*' His mother sighed. 'Oh Mama, I saw the *keriah*,' he pointed to her blouse, 'but it didn't register…' He dropped his head, his body sagging. 'I was sure if I could reach Katya, give her my energy, she would recover.'

'Come,' said his mother, 'and your companion. Come into the kitchen. You must be exhausted after such a journey. Hang your coats on the hall stand.'

Sophia was glad she'd changed on the ship, from her shabby skirt into her usual dark blue one. But she hung back. This was a private tragedy, a private grief. Why had she insisted on being with him? Taking off her coat, she followed them, finding herself in a spacious kitchen that ran the length of the far wall of the apartment. The warm, sweet aroma of freshly baked bread filling the kitchen gave her a modicum of reassurance. Two young men were sitting at the table. Dov's brothers, she guessed. Ivan, the medical student, a younger version of Dov, but with dark brown hair. Leo, tall, bespectacled, but with Dov's dimple, two years older, and undertaking research at the university. They rose to embrace him again and again, saying, 'You've come. We're so glad you're here.'

'But too late,' he said wearily, sinking onto a chair.

Uncertain, Sophia stayed by the door.

'Sophia,' he called, looking over his shoulder: 'Come, sit down by me.'

Leo rose, smiled, and drew back a chair for her. She thanked him. Their mother handed round glasses of tea, then stood behind Dov, her hands resting on his shoulders. They drank, and the clink of their spoons stirring the sugar sounded loud and oppressive.

Finally, Dov lifted his head. 'When?'

'Two days ago,' said his mother. 'The funeral was yesterday.'

'Oh God, if only I hadn't told you about Gapon's march last year…' He covered his eyes with his hands. Sophia longed to throw her arms around him but clutching her hands together, rigid in her chair, she was ever more conscious of being an outsider.

'Where is Papa?'

'In his surgery,' said Ivan. 'Just sitting. He wanted to be alone for a while.'

Dov nodded. 'Alicia?'

'She was here this morning,' said his mother, still standing. She pulled out a chair and sat beside him. 'She's gone to see to the children. She'll be at the *shiva*. But Dov, you haven't introduced us to your companion.' She glanced over at Sophia, who, feeling ever more uncomfortable, guessed what she was thinking – that she and Dov were together, or why else had she come? Yet Mrs Feldman showed no displeasure, for she smiled warmly at her.

'Sophia is a comrade. She comes from Kyiv.'

'I'm very pleased to be here,' Sophia said. 'Before taking the boat to England, I spent the night with my father's friends who live nearby. That's how I met Dov. On the ship.'

'So you're a revolutionary?' said Leo.

'I'm a follower of a great man who is an anarcho-syndicalist. He believes in peaceful measures to achieve better conditions for people.'

'That's excellent,' said his mother. 'Who is this man?'

They began to talk about the various divisions of socialist thought. Sophia was glad she'd given them something else to occupy their minds.

Sophia and Dov had arrived in the late afternoon. Before the evening prayers at eight o'clock, everyone gathered to eat. By now Sophia had met Doctor Feldman: a slim man in his fifties, his dark brown hair had touches of white at the temple, his blue eyes heavy. His gaze was distant, as though he was thinking of something or someone else. Katya, Sophia thought. He spoke little, whether this was his habit or the effect of his grief she could not tell. Nevertheless, he took her hand, greeting her warmly, before sending a quick glance over at Dov, who came to sit by him; they talked, their heads close together.

'People have brought so much food,' said Mrs Feldman. 'Please help yourselves, everyone.' They ate rye bread, herring, cheese and eggs, followed by slices of apple strudel, then made themselves ready for the evening. Dov's sister Alicia arrived with her husband. Dressed like her mother in a black blouse and skirt, she had something of Dov in her quick smile and strong voice. Having glanced quickly at Sophia and then at Dov, as though to assess their relationship, she kissed Sophia, saying how delighted she was to meet her. Soon they were chatting and Sophia felt a touch of relief.

'Let's go into the sitting room. I want to check that all is ready while the others are preparing themselves.'

Sophia followed her down the corridor into the red gold room she'd seen briefly, and now she appreciated how beautiful it was. There were two sofas and several chairs in dark red velvet, patterned with cloverleaf, many cushions, and rugs. The blue and gold tints of the carpet warmed her heart. On the wall, behind the piano, hung many black and white family photos. But in the centre, facing the stove, was a row of low chairs where the family, as mourners, would sit. Alicia straightened them, then sighed.

'I'd hoped it wouldn't come to this,' she said, looking up at Sophia. 'Papa worked so hard to save her.' She took a deep breath. 'He blames himself for not succeeding.'

'And Dov blames himself for telling you about the priest's march that day they call Bloody Sunday.'

'Blaming yourself achieves nothing,' Alicia said firmly. 'I believe we must accept. I have returned to our religion.'

She paused, frowned. 'You know Papa comes from a long line of distinguished *charedim*, but he abandoned everything to marry Mama?'

'Dov told me,' Sophia said.

'I wish he could find comfort in the thoughts of the great teachers, but I feel it's too late for him.' She swivelled round, saying abruptly. 'But where are you going to sleep?' Before Sophia could reply, Alicia continued, 'Whatever your relationship with Dov, you can't sleep in the same room with him here, even if we had the space. Come to my apartment, we live nearby, and that will please Mama.'

'Thank you. I didn't think of that when I persuaded Dov to let me come with him and neither did he. I thought,' she gave an embarrassed little laugh, 'dressed as poverty-stricken Jews, I'd protect him from discovery, and if we were, I'd say I was his nurse and he was my sick husband.'

Alicia smiled and touched Sophia's arm.

'People will be arriving any minute, let's join the others.' Walking back to the kitchen, she said, 'Crowds last night. Mama is so good with people, but Papa's a solitary man and only wants to escape to his surgery when the prayers have finished.'

Sophia heard the sounds of people scraping their snowy boots on a scraper, banging them against the outside wall. Someone knocked softly at the door, Doctor Feldman appeared and walked slowly to the sitting room while Alicia opened the door. They came in, women making for the kitchen and men for the living room, where the prayers would take place. The kitchen was crowded, women going to embrace Mrs Feldman and Alicia, nodding to Sophia, no doubt wondering who she was.

'My husband is leading the prayers,' Mrs Feldman said to Sophia. Speaking softly to the women, she said, 'This lady is a comrade of Dov's, Sophia Krichevska. I believe she's hoping to visit her family in Archangelsk, weather permitting.'

The women turned to her, speaking in whispers, saying little, as they heard the prayers being intoned in the other room.

'I want to hear my husband and sons saying Kaddish,' said Mrs Feldman after some minutes. She left, and Alicia and Sophia followed her.

Doctor Feldman, Dov, despite his beliefs, Leo and Ivan were facing the gathering of men as they said the Kaddish. Mrs Feldman took up a prayer book from the table and began to follow the service, while Sophia and Alicia shared a book between them. The ancient prayer, really words of praise to God, brought tears to Sophia's eyes. Then Mrs Feldman and Alicia joined the family, sitting on the low chairs while the women who'd been in the kitchen joined the men, to speak to the family, embrace them, to wish them 'long life and no more sorrow'.

The following day, Sophia felt more comfortable. She passed the morning talking to Mrs Feldman and Alicia about her family, her work in London as an assistant mid-wife and her deepest ambition – to become a doctor. Dov, meanwhile, had disappeared into the surgery with his father and brothers, and she didn't see him until lunch-time. Friends from the apartment building and nearby continued to bring covered dishes of stews and desserts, until the kitchen cabinets were crammed, and Mrs Feldman opened a door leading down to the basement, putting some of the dishes on the top steps. A rarity in the apartments, she told Sophia, with a convenient door from the basement to the yard. 'It keeps food cool.'

They prepared themselves for another evening of prayers. And again, the kitchen and living room were crowded. They had just finished saying the Kaddish, Sophia, Mrs Feldman and Alicia were standing by the sitting room door when they heard an imperious banging on the front door opening onto the street. Men and women stood frozen, women clutching the arms of their husbands, men straightening their backs. Everyone knew who it was.

'Open the door or we break it down!'

CHAPTER 28

DOV RAN TO SOPHIA and grabbed her hand. 'Come,' he shouted in English but she pulled away.

'Go, Dov. *Go*. You must escape. I'll be all right.'

He caught her in a brief kiss, raced down the corridor to the kitchen. Everyone, mourners and visitors alike, hoped he'd reach the basement before the police arrived.

Three men marched in: an inspector in a peaked cap and uniform, two others with badges on their heavy jackets, a long weapon strapped to their backs, a sword, wearing high boots which scattered lumps of grey snow along the corridor and onto the carpet. They pushed past Sophia who'd remained at the door the better to see Dov disappear and the police arrive.

The inspector thrust forward his chin, and stared all around. 'Which one of you is Dov Feldman? I have a warrant for his arrest.'

His face, Sophia saw, was strangely concave, with a jutting high forehead, long black moustache curling up towards his ears, his chin bare. He looked like a wolf.

There was the rustle of skirts, a movement of retreat and anxiety among the mourners when they heard his words, but after a moment of terror, Sophia felt her fear drain away in her resolve to do everything to protect Dov. She took a deep breath and walked into the room, standing close to Mrs Feldman who trembled slightly. No one spoke. Some stared at the inspector, others gazed at the floor. But then Doctor Feldman stepped forward.

'Good evening, Inspector, I'm Doctor Feldman but there's no one here named Dov Feldman. You are mistaken.'

Their backs straight, their eyes on the inspector, Ivan and Leo moved closer to their father.

'He was seen approaching this building yesterday,' barked the officer. 'I take it you are his father. You must know where he is.'

'I am his father. We haven't seen him for several years. He may be in America.'

'You are lying.' the man glared at Doctor Feldman; there was a gasp, a sense of shock, a flutter of unease at his words.

Sophia guessed that their neighbours and friends knew nothing of Dov's secret activities but saw him simply as one of the Feldman children. They wouldn't know that he came and went from Russia to England. Perhaps even his family knew little about his activities. But now she had to find a way to divert the inspector. She began to speak, just as the officer shouted, 'Present your papers to my men. All of you.' He turned briefly and stared intently at Sophia, making the skin on her neck tingle. What did he know?

Her heart pounded in her chest, a cold shiver ran down her back. Her papers lacked the requisite information allowing her to pass from place to place in Russia. She watched as the family went to gather theirs from various rooms in the house while others produced them from their pockets or their handbags. The police officers moved from person to person, demanding papers, reading them and thrusting them back at their owners.

The inspector stared at her. 'Where are yours?'

'In the kitchen.'

'Get them!'

Back in the sitting room, one of his men handed her papers to the inspector who took them while continuing to stare. 'She had permission to leave Russia in May 1905. Nothing for returning to Saint Petersburg.' His voice was deep, husky.

The inspector scanned them briefly, then gripping her arm, said, 'Feldman was seen at the railway station with a young woman. It must be you.'

'I'm here to visit my parents in Archangelsk.' Sophia took a breath, hoping her voice wouldn't break. 'The rail track is blocked with snow. I'm waiting for it to be cleared.'

'A fine tale.' He laughed, and his moustache dipped downwards, black insects crawling towards his neck, she thought.

Mrs Feldman stepped forward, her hands curled into fists. 'There's no Dov Feldman here, and Miss Krichevska is hoping to see her parents in Archangelsk. But this is a house of mourning, Inspector. Our youngest child died two days ago. Please respect our grief.'

There was a sigh from the people present, a breath of relief as they heard Mrs Feldman's brave approach. Others muttered *yes,* the family is in mourning.

The inspector stared at Mrs Feldman, his eyebrows raised, then barked: 'Dov Feldman is a known revolutionary, wanted for importing firearms and inciting revolution. You must know where he is.'

He moved closer, as though to threaten her, and Ivan shouted, 'My mother's speaking the truth. How can you doubt her?'

Mrs Feldman took a deep breath, perhaps to speak again, but the inspector shouted, 'Search the place.'

At once, the two men began opening drawers, pulling down books from bookcases, lifting the piano stool lid and throwing out sheet music and notes. From there, they could be heard in the bedrooms and marching along to the kitchen. The inspector followed them. Meanwhile people whispered or spoke in hushed murmurs. The family stayed silent.

Returning, one of the police demanded the keys for Doctor Feldman's surgery.

'Please. Not my patients' confidential notes.'

People watching muttered their disapproval but when the man returned empty – handed to the living room, the inspector bellowed, 'Go home, all except the family and this girl!'

The visitors departed, their expressions angry, puzzled, but also murmuring encouragement to the family. Finally, only the Feldmans and Sophia remained.

'The girl and Doctor Feldman will come with me to the station for questioning.'

Mrs Feldman's eyes widened; she was about to protest when her husband said, 'Don't be afraid. I have nothing to be ashamed of. Others will support me.'

At the police station, Doctor Feldman was led away while Sophia was taken to what was presumably the inspector's office. All the furniture: desk, chairs, cupboard were of yellow wood. There was also a settee against the wall. The inspector sat down at the desk while a subordinate stood by the door.

He repeated the questions from before – name, age, address – and then he leaned in, asking her about her political alliance. There were also questions about Dov, which she countered saying she hardly knew him, that she took the opportunity to travel in his company for her own security, that was all. For a moment she was afraid and swallowed, feeling her wrists chafe beneath the handcuffs. Determined not to weaken, she forced herself to observe him objectively, as though he were any middle-class man sitting in his office, somewhere in London's commercial district.

He must be in his forties, she thought, perhaps a little older. His narrow grey eyes were intense, demanding, a believer in violent action, she was sure, in violent punishment.

A Russian, after all. She would not weaken, she told herself. The longer she forced him to question her, the further away Dov would be.

'You have no political involvement, you claim,' he said disparagingly. 'Why did you return with a known criminal? Is he a friend, a political comrade? Maybe he's a lover and you do whatever he wants, however disgusting. Like any dirty Jew.' His thin lips curved into a jeer.

She breathed quickly, stung.

'Not a political comrade,' Sophia tried to control her anger, conscious she was trembling, 'Nor is he a lover. He's a friend, I told you before. I heard he was travelling to see his sick sister, so I asked to go with him. A woman travelling alone puts herself in danger.'

He leaned forward. 'Then what do you do?' Sitting back, a smirk on his face, he took up a pipe, tamped down tobacco and lit it.

'I am a midwife,' she said, lifting her gaze. 'I bring babies into the world.' She wrinkled her nose for the smell of the pipe was foul, then hoped he hadn't noticed.

He put down his pipe and stared. He leaned forward in his chair. 'A midwife? You know about women's bodies?'

She saw a change in his focus, he was staring at her with curious eyes.

'Yes,' she said. Why had he asked her such a thing? Was this something to do with prisoners, or some poor woman he'd impregnated?

He rose from his chair. 'Get them to bring my coach around,' he shouted at the man by the door. To Sophia, he said, 'Follow me.'

Was he was taking her to prison? Despite herself, she shuddered.

She followed him through a door in the wall she hadn't noticed, down another corridor to an exit leading into the yard, where several horse-drawn carriages were drawn up, their drivers seated beneath the awnings playing chess, despite the cold.

'Konstantin,' the inspector shouted. 'Get over here. I'm in a hurry.'

The driver, a portly man in uniform, ran heavily to a coach and drove it across to where the inspector was waiting, Sophia standing behind him. When it stopped the inspector told her to climb in. With handcuffs, it was difficult, and he pushed her from behind into the carriage, then climbed in and sat next to her. Her wrists hurt, her arms and shoulders ached; she wished he would loosen them as they chafed her wrists, but of course that wasn't his intention. She ventured to ask where they were going.

'To my home,' he said tersely.

His home? Was he going to seduce her, rape her? She thought of her little aunt and now she was afraid, knowing from experience the brutality of the Tsar's police, of Russian men. Could she jump out of the moving carriage, her hands still tied? She glanced up at the man beside her, biting his lip and frowning. She wondered why he was so anxious.

'Never speak to anyone about this,' he said suddenly, turning to look at her, 'or you'll end up in Siberia.'

She nodded. He was going to rape her. She vowed not to allow fear or horror to overwhelm her. She would survive. She looked to the windows, seeing the houses becoming fewer, noting they were in a suburb of Saint Petersburg, for there were no more apartment blocks nor shops; instead, individual houses with *banyas* in the gardens.

The driver now directed the horse to turn down a short path bounded by low fir trees and shrubs, to a small white brick stucco-fronted house, where they stopped.

Leaning over her, the inspector removed her handcuffs. Her heart pounded in her chest, she prepared herself for the worst. *I won't fight, I won't react. I pray I won't get pregnant.* Such a horrendous thought – pregnant by this man.

He led the way, unlocking a narrow pinewood door and they entered the hall. To her surprise she heard the sound of a woman's voice, moans, cries. Not rape, Sophia thought, in amazement, but a woman giving birth.

My wife,' he said. 'Go up those stairs.'

They climbed a narrow staircase where the sounds of crying and moaning increased as they reached the landing. The bedroom was at the end of a corridor, overlooking the rear of the house.

The inspector led the way into the room. Sophia stood behind him, gazing around.

'Here,' he shouted. 'I've brought you a new midwife.' To Sophia he said, 'Make sure she produces a live baby at the end of this. Or else…'

'Make sure? I can only do my best,' Sophia muttered.

It was dark. His lips curled as though in disgust, the man continued to stare across the room at his wife, a mound of body hidden in a heap of crumpled bedclothes, only her head and arms visible. Sophia saw she was lying with her arms stretched above her head, hands gripping the headboard, writhing. Beside her, an older woman with the brown wrinkled face of a peasant woman was sitting on a low stool, her head covered with a greyish white scarf. She was muttering, crossing herself. Was she the mother or the midwife? Sophia wrinkled her nose.

On the bed, black hair sticking to her contorted face, the woman screamed in agony. The sour smell of sweat and rank bed sheets was almost overpowering.

The inspector glared once again at Sophia, turned and ran down the stairs, banging the front door behind him. Sophia inhaled deeply. At least this wasn't a foreign land. She knew the terrain.

'Hello,' she said putting as much positivity into her voice as she could. 'I'm a midwife. I've come here to help you.'

She walked round to the old woman twisting her hands in her apron. 'You are the…?'

'I'm her mother. She hates midwives and doctors after she's lost three.'

Sophia asked if she could examine the woman.

'She won't let you,' the mother said.

'All right,' Sophia said, 'I'll talk to her. Tell me her name.'

'Mariana Nikolaievna.'

Kneeling by the bed while she talked, Sophia straightened the bedclothes.

'Good evening, Mariana Nikolaievna,' she said softly, 'I've come here from England to help you. I've been working as a midwife in London for a very long time and brought many babies into the world.' For a brief moment, Mariana stopped screaming and loosened her hands from the bedhead. 'Yes, Mariana, I'm sure I can help you. Tell me how long you've been in labour.' Carefully, she touched the woman's arm. 'I *can* help you.'

Sophia knew that if the knowledge of her coming from London got back to the inspector, her chances of freedom were slim, but she had to gain the woman's trust. If she actually managed to bring a live baby into the world, she would ask the women not to betray her. If the child was stillborn, it wouldn't matter anyway.

'London?' she whispered. The woman opened her eyes.

'Yes, London,' Sophia said firmly.

'All right, stay.'

Sophia examined her; the baby was nearly there. She proceeded to carry out all she'd learned with Ettie, calm the woman, tell her how to breathe, make her listen to her instructions. The woman had been in labour for twenty hours, so the birth could be imminent. Sophia made the grandmother wash her hands, bring hot water, towels, a sheet if necessary, and newspaper. They managed to roll the mother sideways, slip the paper under her, followed by the sheet. None of these artifacts created a problem; this was a comfortable, middle-class home.

At around eleven o'clock, the baby finally emerged. A boy. He lay motionless between the mother's legs. Sophia lifted him up, aghast to see he was white, soft, not breathing. She slapped him. There was no response. The grandmother crept to the bedside and began to keen, swaying backwards and forwards, uttering little sharp cries like some kind of bird, and crossing herself. The mother lay white and exhausted. Sophia groaned inwardly. Now she must find the courage to bring the baby back to life with Ettie's particular procedure, so successful with Mrs Lazarus's child.

She shouted to the old woman, 'Mother, bring me bowls of hot and cold water. And all the towels you can find. At once.'

The old woman stared but evidently used to obeying orders, pattered round the bed out of the room, returning shortly with a bowl of hot water and then the cold. She searched in a chest of drawers against the wall and brought out various towels.

Sophia worked, dipping the flaccid body into cold water, then into hot, again and again, for hours it seemed to her. Eyes wide, the grandmother cried: 'It's a stillborn. The baby is dead.'

The mother had come to her senses. She watched Sophia, crying out in a desperate voice, 'Not again, no. I want to die.' She began to cry weak tears.

Sophia massaged the tiny chest. Still the baby did not respond and Sophia bent over him, her brows drawn together, heart racing, willing him to breathe. 'Come on,' she whispered. 'You must live or I won't.' Tears gathered at the corner of her eyes. She was sharing the mother's desperation and for a second, was astonished at this thought. But she had to persevere. One more dip in the hot water, once more in the cold. She massaged the tiny chest again, almost giving up as he lay drenched and floppy on the towel.

Then the miracle happened.

A tiny cry, a little clot of mucus in the nose, colour in the ashen cheeks. 'He's alive!' Sophia found herself thanking the universe for its support. Grabbing a shawl hanging over a chair, she wrapped the baby tightly in it. 'Open your eyes, Mariana,' she called. 'You have a baby boy.'

'Show me, show me!' The mother gasped, as though she too had been submerged in water, and held out her arms.

Sophia placed the baby swaddled in the white shawl into the woman's arms and gave a great sigh of relief.

'A miracle. You've worked a miracle, midwife!' the grandmother cried.

While the mother nursed the baby, her eyes wide in wonder, a tiny smile playing around her mouth, the grandmother came and kissed Sophia's hands. 'Lord Jesus and all the saints pour blessings on you.'

'Let's finish this.' Sophia smiled. 'Mariana, please give your baby to your mother.' She pressed down on the woman's uterus to release the afterbirth. Within half an hour she had cleaned up the mother and it was done.

The door opened. The inspector walked in. He took in the three smiling women, then saw the child in his wife's arms.

'A boy,' said his wife proudly, smiling up at him.

'*A boy*? Let me see.' He was incredulous. In two strides he was by the bed, taking the baby from his wife.

'He has my eyes, my nose.' He allowed himself to smile. Turning to Sophia, he said, 'All right, midwife. Now return with me.'

They travelled back to the police station, but this time Sophia had no handcuffs to restrict her. In the inspector's room, she waited as he walked to his seat behind his desk.

'Whether you are going to see your family in Archangelsk or are really a revolutionary come to stir up the people against the state, I don't know. I suspect the latter. You should be in prison. Allowing you into my house… If it gets out, I'm in serious trouble. Therefore, you must return to London. You will stay in one of the police cells until I find a suitable ship. You have a ticket?'

'Yes.'

'When is it for?'

'I understand the merchant ship returns once every two weeks to London, so a week on Thursday.'

'Too late. One of my men will make enquiries. When it's time, a policeman will accompany you. You get on that ship and you will *never* return to Russia, to your family.'

'Never?' Her heart jolted in her chest. 'Exiled?'

He did not reply. Going to the door, he called to one of the officers who led Sophia to a police cell down another gloomy corridor at the end of the building. They passed men and women in cells waiting to be tried, some bawling, some cursing, one or two lying curled on the ground. Sophia shivered, wondering how many were political prisoners. The man unlocked the door. A tiny dark room, a window with bars high in the wall, a bunk for a bed. Over the three days of her incarceration, a jailor brought gruel, slops, suspicious looking soups. She had the indignity of using a primitive lavatory, a bowl on a stand.

Lying on the brick of a bunk, she shivered constantly. The cold had turned her hands white, for she'd left her gloves and shawl at the Feldmans' home, but that was nothing to the stink of urine and sour odours that permeated the place. She kept wondering about Doctor Feldman. Was he in prison? She worried for him and his family. Worst of all she lay agonising about Dov, imagining how they'd torture him if he was caught.

Finally, one morning, a guard unlocked the cell door and handed her the new documents. She was led to the yard, where a policeman waited. She had wondered if indeed she'd ever get out now she'd been imprisoned, and with a sudden clarity of thought, realised this procedure was to save the inspector from any accusation of wrongdoing. Yes, her passport was marked with details of her imprisonment, stamped by him: *Revolutionary*, *political prisoner*. *Exiled* in red, and stamped on each document and her heart fell. She was a criminal in the eyes of the state, but the inspector would have to silence his poor wife to make sure the name of the London midwife who saved their child would never be revealed. Sophia was sure that wouldn't be difficult for him.

CHAPTER 29

TEN DAYS LATER, SHE trudged up the steps of Wentworth Buildings, walked along the corridor until she reached Mrs Vine's flat. Relieved to see her landlady was out, Sophia opened the door to her room and uttered a sigh. Dropping Dov's travelling bag on the floor, she took off her coat and hung it on the hook they'd hammered into the door. Then kicking off her boots, she flopped onto the bed, a great heaviness in her heart.

She gazed around the room. Empty, cold, even though the temperature in London was far higher than in Petersburg. Her head down, hands clutched together, she let out another sigh.

Never to see Mama and Papa again, never to see my laughing brother Alexei? She closed her eyes. *I so wish this hadn't happened. Even though I really love Dov and would go with him to the ends of the earth, I never thought it would be at the cost of seeing my family. And Dov, where is he? What's happened to him? Has he been caught?*

Getting up from the bed, she went to the window and stared out. The journey back in the merchant ship, with a different captain who said not a word to her, was just as awful, with constant seasickness and horrible food from the galley, brought to her by one of the sailors. She had lain on the bunk, day after day, praying the journey would end.

She walked down the gangplank at Millwall Docks, so weak she could barely carry her bag. Seeing her stumble, a sailor had shown a little kindness by carrying it for her. Then there was the twenty-minute walk to Wentworth Buildings.

She inhaled deeply and turned to empty the bag. Somehow Alicia had been allowed to bring it to the police station and even to exchange a few words with Sophia through the bars of the holding cell.

'They let Papa return home next morning,' she whispered. 'We don't know why, and thank God, he's all right. We feared he would be imprisoned or exiled.'

Sophia wondered if it was because of her saving the baby, but she kept her own counsel. When she asked softly about Dov, Alicia held her finger to her lips and shook her head. Clearly, they had heard nothing.

She wept. Eventually, though it was only six o'clock in the evening, she undressed and climbed into bed. The following morning, having slept for hours, she wanted to escape into sleep again, knowing her thoughts would plague her. Taking a shaky breath, she covered her face with her hands.

I am alone with the beating of my heart.

She breathed slowly. Trails of mist floated around the room. Were they her tears transposed into vapour? At last, slipping out of bed, she put on her dressing gown – a tiny comfort – and drew back the sagging brown curtains, only to find yellowish fog pressing against the window, leaching through cracks between the frame and the outer wall. The air smelled stale. She crept back to bed and sat huddled up.

What if they catch him? It'll be Siberia, like Aaron's brother, or incarcerated in some filthy prison and I'll never see him again.

She pulled the covers over her head, but it was too cold to spend hours in her night clothes. She dressed, leaving the room only to walk to the end of the corridor, to the communal WC. The stink of urine, bleach, faeces blasted her, but she ignored it. Nor did she notice the wooden seat slither lopsidedly across the toilet bowl or how she had to pull the chain four or five times to flush.

She couldn't eat but made cups of tea when she knew Mrs Vine had gone out. In the evening she ate a crust of stale bread chewing it absentmindedly, her thoughts muddled, again and again turning to Dov. Then she sat with the shawl Mama had crocheted swathed over her back and shoulders. As though her mother were here in person, holding her in loving arms.

'Mama, if only I could see you now. Speak to you.'

The few tears creeping down her cheeks weren't worth noticing.

At some point Mrs Vine called through the door: 'Sophia, the midwife has sent for you. This boy is waiting to hear your answer.'

Sophia sat unmoving. Eventually, she said, 'Tell her I'm ill, that I can't come tonight.' Her voice faded away. She coughed to clear her throat. 'I'll go and see her soon.'

Never had she refused Ettie, but she could not think of going. Ettie would worm it all out of her. She'd known

Dov from the ship all those months ago and had warned Sophia against him. She couldn't bear Ettie's shrivelling disapproval.

The following afternoon, Friday, she heard women's voices: Mrs Vine's, and, Sophia took a shocked breath, Ettie's. Talking about her, a few feet away, on the other side of the wall. Ettie hadn't let it go after her refusal yesterday and was sure to have come by to see how she was. Sophia waited for the knock on the door. The conversation went on for some moments then came the knock.

'Sophia, are you all right?'

'Yes.'

'Come and have dinner with us tonight. I have a very stringy hen but there must be some meat on it.'

Sophia opened the door.

Ettie's gaze was searching. 'You aren't ill?'

'Not exactly.' Sophia took a breath.

Ettie frowned. 'Then wash your face. Get your coat and come back with me.'

Sophia obeyed. Ettie walked swiftly with Sophia. The fog and damp outside made her shiver but in minutes, they reached Ettie's home. All was ready, the white cloth on the table, the candles in the brilliant candlesticks, her husband in his black yarmulke sitting at the head, perusing the prayer book.

'My son is with friends tonight, so it's just the three of us. Take that seat at the end, Sophia.'

She sank into the chair until it was time for Ettie to light the candles, for her husband to make the blessing over the bread, for them all to take a sip of Kiddush wine.

Ettie served the chicken soup with noodles, and Sophia felt herself grow warm inside, her heart less constricted. They ate the 'stringy' chicken, potatoes and carrots. Ettie said nothing about her illness, and Sophia was grateful for her reticence.

Following the Grace after Meals, she smiled. 'Thank you, Ettie, you've saved me.'

'I don't know about that but there's nothing that a bowl of chicken soup can't cure.' In an undertone she added, 'Whatever it is, it's not the end of the world, Sophia.'

She then insisted that her husband accompany Sophia back to Wentworth Buildings. On the way Sophia found herself asking how he'd become a scribe. He told her he followed in his father's footsteps, how awe-inspiring it was to write the holy books without making a single mistake, though he feared such close work might eventually affect his eyes. He offered to check the scroll in the mezuzah on the outer door of the flat. Sophia said it was not hers, but her landlady's and she couldn't speak for her.

Days passed. She had no work to occupy her, no money. She'd spent what she had on the Spanish dancer's dress and the dun-coloured skirt, both bundled in newspaper at the bottom of her trunk. Babies continued to arrive; she would assist Ettie, who gave her some of the remuneration received from the families, however little. Those babies, Sophia thought, they don't know what a dreadful world they're entering.

She had no news of Dov and the longing to be with him surged so fiercely in her throat, she wanted to cry out. There were days when she would stand shivering outside the post office, wondering if the postmaster, Mr Feldman, had received, what? A telegram? A letter? She was deceiving herself but couldn't help it, knew he wouldn't write … too dangerous … the censor… Why did he have to be involved with such violent politics? *Why?* His need for violence evoked a thin line of anger within her but for now, she swallowed it.

One morning, she searched in her purse and found only a few coppers. Not enough to buy a loaf of bread, let alone meat or vegetables.

I'm not proud. I'll go to the soup kitchen. I won't let my friends feed me, they need their food.

At midday she went to The Board of Guardians, a forbidding place in Middlesex Street. She remembered coming here a few weeks after her arrival to help poor Betsy. Now it was she who was standing in front of those men with their high starched collars and disapproving jowls. They cross-examined her about her circumstances and having answered their embarrassing questions, she received a chit allowing her to join the queue of families waiting for the door of the soup kitchen to open.

She gazed up at the imposing red brick building with its faux Greek pillars around the door and saw above the lintel, *SOUP KITCHEN FOR THE JEWISH POOR (5662 – 1902).* In the triangle beneath it, was a sculpted bowl of soup.

I never noticed this before.

There were women queuing who recognised her; they thanked her for help with the birth of the latest child and showed the baby off to Sophia with pride. Wrapped tightly in their mother's shawl, their faces were barely visible, yet Sophia told the mothers how beautiful their baby was, and their mothers gave a beaten smile.

Today, she looked further up the line, nearest the door, and recognised Betsy queuing with her youngest children.

'Betsy, 'Sophia called softly.

Betsy turned.

'Goodness, Sophia, how wonderful to see you again.' A frown pierced her pale forehead. 'But I'm sorry that...'

She stopped as the queue moved forward and a surly looking man with thick black eyebrows meeting across his forehead appeared at the door.

'I'll come and sit with you,' called Sophia. 'Can you save me a seat?'

Having collected a bowl of stew and a loaf of bread from the counter, they took their places on benches at long tables. Sitting beside Betsy with her children, Sophia leaned forward to inhale the aroma of the stew. Delicious. Their heads down, silent, everyone consumed the rich stew until they'd scraped every vestige from the bowl. Betsy made sure her children finished every scrap of the meat and potatoes, then breaking pieces of bread off the loaf, she told the children to wipe their dishes clean.

She smiled at Sophia.

'I'm not really surprised to see you here for I know there's so little work at the moment. But I thought you were joining your brother in America?'

'You're right. When I have the money, I will. Meanwhile, I've been working with the midwife Mrs Gutenberg, and the anarchist movement, and—' she stopped, no point in mentioning Dov. 'I'll probably see you here over the next few days,' she added.

They left the building, carrying their loaves of bread. Non-Jewish people stood near the door, their hands out, waiting. Sophia broke the bread in half, a half into two, and gave a piece to two of these men.

Days later, a leaflet fluttered to the pavement, as she walked down Brick Lane.

GRAND OPENING
The Workers' Friend Club
Jubilee Street
Saturday 3 February 1906

But that's tomorrow. I was supposed to help them. I've been so immersed in my own misery, I have forgotten about everything.

She hurried down Commercial Street, along Whitechapel Road, passing the London Hospital and on to Sidney Street, then turned into Jubilee Street. She opened the door of the new club and went in.

'Sophia, we thought you were ill. Are you better now?' Mrs Linder was sweeping fragments of sawdust across the stage while other comrades were setting out rows of chairs. Walls and door frames were brilliant with new paint and the air smelled powerfully of wood and varnish. Sophia straightened her back.

A beam of light had pierced the darkness consuming her mind for the past weeks. Moved by the buoyant enthusiasm of the Arbeter Frainters putting the finishing touches to this huge enterprise, she began to feel clear, focused again.

A kind of illness, she realised.

'Yes, thank you, I do feel better. But bad about not contributing to this.' She approached the stage, waving the leaflet in the air. 'So many illustrious speakers tomorrow night.'

Mrs Linder leaned on the brush handle. 'It will be the most wonderful affair. Even the *Jewish Chronicle* might write a good word for once.'

Sophia laughed. What an odd sensation. She lifted her eyebrows thinking she hadn't laughed since New Year's Eve. 'We can't count on them. They think we're undermining the state, that we're dangerous revolutionaries!'

'Even dangerous revolutionaries must sweep floors,' said Mrs Linder, taking up her task again. 'I'll tell Milly I've seen you. Arrive early tomorrow night, Sophia, or you might not find a seat. I understand that hundreds intend to come.'

Hundreds came. Sophia stood by the entrance counting, along with Mr Kerkelevitch, until they saw the hall and gallery were packed.

'Sorry, friends, no more!' shouted Mr Kerkelevitch and locked the doors.

The first row of chairs was allocated to speakers and dignitaries. Once again, Aaron sat beside Sophia and she had the fleeting, uncomfortable thought that there was more than friendship in his eyes, when she saw how his face lit up on seeing her.

As Rudolf read out messages of congratulation from every trade union, from Malatesta and the mathematics professor, Tarrida del Mármol, there was a storm of cheering and clapping, but he stopped mid speech. He frowned and ran down the steps to the front of the hall. The great Peter Kropotkin stood there, leaning on his cane, a smile on his benevolent face.

Sophia could just make out Rudolf's whispered words: 'Please don't address them, Peter. I fear for your heart. Your doctor has warned against it, I know.'

'He will speak despite Rudolf,' Aaron said in an undertone. 'He'll think this is an occasion at which he must be present.'

With Sam and Rudolf supporting him, Peter Kropotkin walked up the steps and onto the stage. His voice low but confident, he spoke for half an hour.

'This is the start of our golden years,' he said, describing all the setbacks and small successes that had led to this great achievement. At the finish, he sank white and exhausted onto a chair, his head back, eyes closed; Sophia wanted to run up and support him.

'He looks very ill,' she whispered to Polly, seated to her left.

'He's a man of utter dedication, but this was unnecessary. I hope no harm has been done.' Polly clucked her tongue. Later they would learn that Prince Kropotkin had had a heart attack on return to his home and they felt very guilty about it.

Meanwhile, the audience continued to cheer and clap. Sophia had a momentary thought about Dov and how she wished he were here to see his idol, Prince Kropotkin. She took a long, sad breath, then recalled the concert at Crown Hall in the summer, when she'd first seen the great man, but it came accompanied by the bitter memory of

Dov entering the hall with Rosa, his hand at the nape of her neck.

Where was he now? Had he been caught by the Okhrana? A shiver crawled down her back and she stared at the floor. She mustn't allow such a miserable thought to spoil this marvellous evening, the pinnacle of their work.

Teaching English, attending Rudolf's lectures on literature and history, and taking her turn at the Sunday school with the children occupied Sophia's mind over the following weeks. But her heart was heavy, almost like a painful stone, and she could not relieve it. A month passed and still no news of Dov. His escape from the Okhrana no longer a secret amongst the anarchist circles, they debated about the young woman said to have accompanied him. Sophia walked away to hide her sadness. She continued going to the soup kitchen, depending on the loaf of bread for breakfast and supper. There had been a small portion of butter left on the windowsill while she was with Dov. It was rancid but better than eating dry bread. Soon that was gone.

Still, she held onto the hope there would be work in March. There usually was, Mr Lazarus told her. But a letter arrived one afternoon, and she crumpled.

CHAPTER 30

S HE HAD WRITTEN TO her mother and father about the club's opening, forcing herself not to mention her abortive visit to Dov's family, for what good would that do? It would only worry her parents, and might even endanger them, since letters were frequently opened by the censor's lackeys.

A few days after she'd posted hers, one arrived from her mother, too soon to be a reply. Trying to avoid the break in her heart when she visualised them at home, she raced through the pages until her eyes widened and her heart thudded against her chest. Rigid, barely breathing, she reread these lines by weak gaslight until she clung to the table for fear she might fall.

Darling, another thing, her mother had written.

Do you remember our friends from Petersburg whom you stayed with overnight when you made the journey to England? They wrote about a most strange happening at a shiva house they attended. It seemed a young girl had died after a year's illness despite her father's dedicated care. A doctor, a revered and generous man, they said. That a young girl dies is a tragedy but not uncommon. They mentioned that she was talented and beautiful, only about sixteen. I believe she was named Katya.

One of her brothers who'd been working abroad had returned when the family had alerted him to how ill his younger sister was. The second night of the shiva, when the rooms were crowded, the secret police broke in, searching for this young man. Through the uproar and consternation, he disappeared. No one saw him leave, nobody knew how he escaped. The police demanded to know where he was, but everyone stayed silent. They searched the apartment, overturning tables, dragging open and searching drawers, emptying the doctor's private files over the floor. Nobody could leave until they'd been questioned. The police ignored pleas to refrain out of respect for the bereaved family. This was a house of mourning, after all. A young woman who'd accompanied the brother was taken into custody, along with the doctor. Fortunately, he was released the following morning, but no one knew what happened to the girl. Such a strange and upsetting thing to hear, our friends said.

I'm glad you are safe in England, my darling, not having to face the turbulence that is erupting all over this country. But it's late, now and I shall stop, as I have lessons to prepare for the girls tomorrow. We hope you're in the best of health and that we'll all be together very soon. Your loving Mama and Papa

(Not to mention Alexei who is creating a beautiful object for you from wood, but he won't tell me what it is!)

Pushing it away, she pressed her hands to her heart. Shudders ran up and down her back. Oh Mama, Mama, she thought, if only you knew I was that young woman. I was even planning to visit you for a few days, leaving Dov with his family. If it hadn't been for the skills I'd learned with Ettie, I could be in prison or exiled to Siberia. I ought to be grateful. But I'll never see you, Mama, Papa and Alexei, unless you come to England, or we manage to go to America. What can I do? I've barely enough money to buy an onion for barley soup.

During the dreadful journey back, she'd been haunted by the question: who was it that betrayed Dov? The coach driver who'd ferried them from the railway station to Dov's home? Someone in the street? Dov had been right, she thought bitterly, there were spies everywhere.

And who did she know in London, who'd understand her anguish at never seeing her family again? At being in exile? She longed to share her heartache with someone. Not Milly, who was so brave, and who encountered all difficulties with resolve. Hannah Leah? They hadn't met since Dov had bought the ring from her stall. Ages ago, it seemed. She couldn't reveal to Hannah Leah she'd travelled to Petersburg with Dov, like a married woman. Sophia thought of one person – Aaron.

On Sunday, she walked from Wentworth Buildings to Howland Street, in Soho. Over an hour, but she had no money for the fare. If he wasn't at home, she would leave him a note. Mounting the stairs, she heard something sweet and restful playing on his gramophone. In the draughty hallway, she took a deep breath. *How calming that is. How beautiful, I could listen to it forever.* At last, gathering her courage, she knocked on the door and heard footsteps. Aaron was there, a bemused smile on his face.

'Sophia, come in. What a surprise.'

She stepped into his room and gestured towards the gramophone. 'What is that beautiful music, Aaron?'

'It's Schubert…' He looked at her closely. 'You look exhausted. Please, sit down.'

'I walked here.' She gave him an embarrassed smile.

'Come, take this comfortable chair. It's the only one.' He laughed. 'I'll make some tea.'

Soon, with the inevitable cup of black tea in her hands, Sophia settled, but concerns and uncertainties soon clouded her face. Trying to ward them off, she said, 'How are you, Aaron? Have you got work?'

'Yes, I'm fortunate. Conditions are slightly better in the West End. And you?'

He must have known she wasn't working, but she said, 'I hope to, in a couple of weeks.'

Aaron lit a cigarette and waited. Sophia continued to stare at the floor. His eyes concerned he said, 'What is it? Can I help?'

Sophia bit her lip, raising her gaze to his. 'You know about Dov?'

'Of course.'

'Did you know I was with him in Saint Petersburg?'

'I knew that too.'

'How?' Her eyes widened.

'Dov told me before he left. Actually,' Aaron gave her a worried look, 'he wanted to leave without you. He feared for your safety.'

'And you persuaded him…'

'Not an easy man to persuade.' He gave a rueful laugh.

'That's true'. Her gaze faltered. 'Have you heard from him?'

'No. But he'll lie low, then he'll be back.'

'I do hope so.' She dipped her head.

'You look troubled.' Aaron leaned forward.

'Something serious happened when I was in Petersburg. I haven't told anyone.'

'It's safe with me.'

'It's not that.' Confused, the words wouldn't come to her. Finally, she muttered, 'Certain people wouldn't care. They'd be proud. Believing it was all for the cause. I'm ashamed I don't feel like that.' He smiled to encourage her. 'Aaron,' her voice breaking, she whispered: 'I've been exiled.'

'Ah.' He rolled a cigarette and lit it, leaning back in his chair. 'Can you tell me about it?'

His voice was so warm, so uncritical, she told him everything.

'My greatest fear is never seeing see my family again. It breaks my heart.' She covered her face with her hands, then looked up. 'I went believing I could protect Dov. Dressed like peasants. What a fool I was.'

Ignoring this, Aaron said, 'But you don't know that you'll never return there.'

'How? I couldn't go by some secret way, like Dov or the others. I fear the effect on my parents. I know exile in London is nothing, nothing compared with Siberia, yet I'm full of worry and sadness. Your music – I heard it in the hallway – was like a balm to my troubled mind. But I haven't got a gramophone. Maybe, when I'm working, I'll save up. I can see how it's a great comfort to you.'

She stopped, fearing she'd said too much; she hardly knew Aaron and thought it presumptuous to suggest he needed comfort. Yet wondering if he'd left the Pale of Settlement for other reasons than his political beliefs, she was about to ask, when he said, 'I don't miss my father; I miss my mother and sister, and naturally, my brother whom I'll never see again. That is painful.'

'It's dreadful.'

'But in addition, I was married, had a little boy aged two. They were both killed by the first motor car that drove through our village. I left those memories behind when I left Visokaye.' Aaron inhaled deeply.

Shocked, wanting to reach out, touch his hand, she thought better of it. 'I am so sorry.'

They sat with their thoughts until Aaron looked up.

'You're fairly safe from pogroms in Archangelsk. Why did you leave?'

'Simple. I was rejected by Moscow Medical School for being a woman and Jewish. I followed my brother to London en route for America. The agent swindled us, only one ticket was valid. I planned to work here until I could buy tickets for myself and my family, but instead, I got involved with Rudolf's movement.'

'Ganufs. Such thieves. But maybe you can study medicine in London? I believe there's a college for women in Bloomsbury.'

'You know of it? The London School of Medicine for Women?'

'That's the name. Why don't you apply?'

'I haven't enough money for the omnibus from the East End to Soho, let alone fees.' She shrugged.

'Perhaps they have funds for poor students. You should enquire.'

'I never thought of that. You know where it is?'

'Not far from the British Museum.'

'If I could become a doctor, however long it would take, I could bring my family here.' Her eyes lit up. 'How do I get there?'

'Take the Underground from Mile End to Kings Cross, then ask the way.'

'Thank you, thank you. Aaron, you're a wonderful friend.'

CHAPTER 31

S HE BORROWED MONEY FROM Mrs Vine for the ticket, promising to repay her when she had work. When she told her landlady the reason, she beamed her approval.

'I wish you luck, Sophia,' she said. 'It wouldn't do for you to arrive dishevelled and dusty.'

'Exactly. I can walk back.'

The journey by the Underground was new and exciting. She'd once or twice been with Rudolf and the others to the British Museum, but this was her first trip travelling alone. Something about going down the escalator into the bowels of the earth, the roar and swish of the Tube train stopping, even the blackness of the tunnels fired her imagination. More comfortable than the tram, she observed the other passengers to see how they behaved, when they got up from their seats, when to hang onto the leather strap if the coach was crowded, or, as the train approached the station, the doors opening on wheels.

Going out at Kings Cross station and walking towards the medical school – a man in a bowler hat had directed her – she felt elated. Even the air was cleaner, clearer, and she stopped to take a deep breath. Trees in their tiny plots of earth along the pavements were sending out green buds, a forerunner of the spring. There were far fewer pedestrians, but they walked with purpose, dressed smartly, looking prosperous. Well fed, she thought, with a wry smile.

Reaching the medical school, she stood on the opposite corner and gazed in astonishment. It was a smart modern building of red brick stretching along Hunter Street and round the corner into Wakefield Street. She'd expected something ancient, forbidding, and had steeled herself beforehand not to be afraid. This was a beautiful building on three floors, with slim, elegant windows, their shape echoed in the tall, narrow chimneys on the roof. Slender Grecian-style pillars stood either side of the entrance, and she watched several young women, carrying bags under their arms or pressed against their chests, walk into the building in ones and twos. She noted their plain skirts, long coats and sensible shoes, similar to those worn by Milly or Polly. A relief, considering her meagre wardrobe. Once they had all disappeared, she crossed the road, straightened her shoulders and, taking a deep breath, walked in.

All the doors were closed but she discovered one on the right with a plaque saying: Miss Douie MA MB – Secretary. Taking another deep breath, she knocked.

'Come in,' called a voice.

Sophia opened the door, finding herself in a high-ceilinged room, light from the tall window illuminating an oak desk, on which stood a large typewriter. A youngish woman with brown hair neatly parted in the centre was sitting behind it. She looked up at Sophia, pen in hand. No more than thirty, thought Sophia, the secretary had a round face but something of a stern look in her eye.

'Oh,' the woman said, 'I was expecting someone else. Won't be a jiffy.' She put down the pen and began to type.

Sophia waited, noting the glass-fronted cabinets crammed with books, the files on the secretary's desk, the faint scent of 4711 fragrance, and thinking how different, how lovely this was.

At last Miss Douie stopped. 'Sorry about that. Something I had to finish. Now, what can I do for you?'

'I come to find out about studying here,' Sophia said, painfully conscious of how foreign she must sound. 'I want to become doctor,' she added, as though to cover up her mistakes.

'Yes, Miss. . .?' The secretary leaned forward.

'Krichevska. Sophia Krichevska.'

'Ah yes, Miss Krichevska. What exactly do you want to know?'

'How to have a place here. Cost of study. That kind of thing.'

'Here's a brochure describing the school.' She handed Sophia a folded brochure. 'But forgive my asking, it may be important. You aren't English?'

'I'm from Ukraine, originally.'

Miss Douie cocked her head to one side. 'How interesting. I, personally,' she glanced around as though she thought someone was listening, 'I have followed events of the Revolution with the utmost interest.'

'Yes?' Sophia was nonplussed.

Miss Douie took a breath. 'Well, in order to study medicine here, you need to be qualified in several subjects. Have you any scientific knowledge – biology, chemistry. . .?'

There was a gentle tap at the door. A woman dressed in black and wearing a locket around her neck came into the room. Looking from Sophia to Miss Douie, she stopped.

'So sorry to interrupt, but I've come for the account I left you to type up, Miss Douie.' her voice took on a questioning tone.

'I've only just finished it, Mrs Thorne. At long last, I hasten to add, but there you are.' Rising from her chair, Miss Douie passed a thick folder over to Mrs Thorne who, with a quick smile, crossed in front of Sophia to take it. 'Actually,' continued the secretary, 'if you have a moment to spare, I'd like you to meet Miss Krichevska. She's enquiring about coming to study with us. Miss Krichevska, this is Mrs Thorne. One of the famous Edinburgh Seven, who fought a long battle to enable women to become doctors.'

'The Edinburgh...?' began Sophia, flummoxed by this torrent of words, but Mrs Thorne took a chair and sat down. Elderly, Sophia saw, with white hair, lovely blue eyes and a sweet expression.

Taking Sophia's hand, she said, 'So you want to be a doctor?'

'All my life,' replied Sophia, happy at last to understand what they had said.

'Miss Krichevska is from Ukraine,' broke in the secretary. 'I'd just begun to fill her in on what is required but I'm sure you can do that far better than I.'

'Willingly. Miss Krichevska, as with all medical schools, you require a certain standard of education in order to matriculate. Then you start your medical studies.'

'Matriculate?' Sophia took a breath.

'A proof of having passed the examinations before you apply to university and if they deem your level is high enough, you are ready to undertake a degree. Sometimes, students must take examinations at the London University before they come here. Do you have any evidence of your qualifications, Miss Krichevska?'

'I do,' Sophia said, opening her handbag and taking out a sheet of paper. 'I studied science, biology, physics and chemistry at home in Archangelsk.' She remembered to pronounce it in the English way. 'And my results were sufficient for me to be accepted by the Moscow Medical School. But unfortunately, they didn't take me.'

'Why is that?'

'Only a certain number of women are accepted. And...' She hesitated, then decided she would lose nothing by being honest. 'Because I'm Jewish.'

Mrs Thorne and the secretary shook their heads.

'Dreadful,' said Mrs Thorne, 'but the same the world over. At least, about refusing women their place in society. We've fought for forty years for women to be treated like men in this sphere, and slowly, we see progress.' She bent her head several times as though to emphasise the pace.

'Did you, by any chance, notice the plaque above the front door?' The secretary leaned forward proudly.

'I'm afraid I didn't.' Sophia laughed. 'I was so nervous about coming here, I didn't look up.'

The women laughed, and Mrs Thorne said, 'The London (Royal Free Hospital) School of Medicine for Women. That is what you'll see above the door. The last seven years, our women have been able to work in the hospital alongside the men, carrying out their medical practice. Now, Miss Krichevska tell me something about yourself. Why do you want to become a doctor.'

Sophia told them of their flight from Kyiv when the secret police threatened her father with Siberia for false dealing, although these very charges were lies. She mentioned the pogroms all around the South of Russia and the women looked grave. How she'd left the school she loved and the family had travelled to Archangelsk, where she helped her mother teach young girls, and assisted when a woman gave birth. That she'd met a midwife on the journey to London and had been practising midwifery with her for over a year now. Mrs Thorne and Miss Douie exchanged glances when Sophia described some of her midwifery experiences.

'Excellent,' exclaimed Mrs Thorne, her eyes alight with interest. 'That is most valuable, and unusual for a prospective student. Most of our ladies learn theory only by attending lectures.'

'Since living in the East End of London among the Jewish immigrants, I'm even more determined to be a woman's doctor. So many die in childbirth, so many babies die too.' Wondering again if she should mention contraception, she decided to do so. 'I've heard about Doctor Aletta Jacobs in Amsterdam, who is teaching her patients about contraception. I would like to do this even though it goes against Jewish religious precepts.'

'A woman after my own heart,' said Mrs Thorne. 'But we don't encourage our doctors to advocate contraception. Not yet.' She continued by telling Sophia about her early married days in India when she had need of doctors for herself and her children, and came to the decision that a doctor for women would be imperative. 'So many women, because of their religious customs, refused to see a male doctor, with disastrous results. I've advocated this for many years, and I'm delighted that you have the same opinion, Miss Krichevska.'

'But how do you live now? How do you earn your keep?' said Miss Douie.

'I work in a sweatshop, as a seamstress. Living in the East End of London I've discovered conditions I never knew existed when I lived with my family. These must change too.' Sophia flushed red, surprised by the determination in her voice.

'We have a fighter here,' said Miss Douie. 'Mrs Thorne knows much about fighting battles. As I said before, she is one of the seven women doctors who set up the school, when one of them was expelled from Edinburgh University simply for being a woman. And look what they've achieved.'

'The battle is ongoing,' said Mrs Thorne, 'but we will succeed. I see, Miss Krichevska, you demonstrate some of the qualities I've written about in this account of the history of the school.' She pointed to the folder she held on her knee. 'I was secretary of the school for many years, I wanted so much for it to succeed. At the end of this account, I listed some of the qualities a doctor needs and I think you have them. Empathy, conscientiousness, a high moral standard. Strength of character and body. And there are many more that I won't bore you with. It's very hard being a doctor. Now, Miss Krichevska, we come to the most difficult subject – there are fees to be paid.'

'Of course, I would like to know more.'

When they told her the cost of the academic fees for each year, Sophia swallowed but said nothing. Mrs Thorne passed Sophia's examination results to the secretary, asking her if she could find a translator to verify Sophia's ability to start medical studies.

'In the meantime, I suggest you go to London University and make enquiries about matriculation. They may advise you to re-sit some science exams, I don't know.'

'If you do, the cost is five pounds,' said the secretary. 'As soon as I have found a translator, and we know what this means, I'll post it back to you, together with a letter.'

Mrs Thorne rose from her chair. 'It's been a pleasure to meet you. Mary will fill you in on anything else you might want to know. Thank you for typing up my document, Mary. It's been a wonderful help.'

After her departure, the secretary told Sophia about the medical school, the laboratories, the library and class-rooms, the cafeteria and even a place for the bicycles in the basement. 'I see you look crestfallen. There may be solutions for the fees. There are bursaries and funds, but first of all, you must qualify.'

'It's very wonderful, Miss Douie. I do hope to study here sometime. Thank you for your help.'

Feeling both elated and disappointed, Sophia trudged back across London, her mind swirling with new ideas and possibilities. The medical school was like a dream. Classrooms, laboratories, even a place for bicycles! And working in a hospital with patients. The women were so welcoming, so interested and encouraging. But she wondered sadly, *where on earth will I find the money?*

CHAPTER 32

'SLEEVES!' SAID MR LAZARUS, when Sophia walked into the workshop, a week later.

It was truly the spring, warm and wet, with the occasional stark tree along the streets attempting to produce buds, though with little success.

The meeting at the School of Medicine had filled her with hope, until she learned of the cost of tuition. Mrs Thorne had told her it was less expensive in Edinburgh or Paris, but that was out of the question. Sophia wondered how many sleeves she would have to sew to cover the fees. Thousands upon thousands. She sighed as she worked the treadle with her feet. There was a low buzz of conversation; people were relieved to be working again despite the long hours.

She placed a sleeve beneath the sewing foot and began. Sewing was soothing. She let her thoughts wander but always came back to Dov. Three months since she'd seen him and she'd heard nothing. As though he'd disappeared into the snow or the forests. Surely he wasn't still in Petersburg, or one of Rudolf's contacts would have alerted them? Her pain at never seeing her parents again was not so fierce, coming back sporadically, but her concern about Dov was growing. Not a word, not a dickybird, as one of the men had said in the workshop, and she'd asked him what it meant.

'Cockney rhyming slang. It's how the English speak round here. A language unto itself.' Mr Myerson had laughed as he explained it to her.

They worked at most three days a week. She didn't hesitate to take meals at the soup kitchen in an effort to save money. Especially now, since there was much talk of strikes, and some had already taken place – the stick workers had become militant. Men who made walking sticks, sticks with fold up seats for wealthy men at the races, even sticks for umbrellas, they were out on strike, as were the cabinet makers in London and in Liverpool.

At the new club, Rudolf quoted with satisfaction from the *Jewish Labour News*:

> The Jewish labour movement appears to have entered a new era in its glory. The hitherto submissive Jewish workman has been roused to a consciousness of his power resulting from combination with his fellows. Apathy in the masses is evidently destined to become a thing of the past, giving place to independence of character and determination to secure freedom and human treatment in the proper sense of the term.

This has to come soon, thought Sophia, looking around the workshop. Moshe, in particular, looked drawn and pale, stopping frequently to grasp his chest as though in pain. She was sure he was ill.

One morning, a sudden clatter caused everyone to stop work. They saw Moshe fall towards the pressing table. Catching his head as he fell, blood spurted from his forehead onto a pair of sleeves of navy worsted. Sophia leapt up, followed by the others.

Crouching down, she saw his eyes were half closed while there was a great pallor in his face. She cradled his head in her arms; Mr Michelson and Mr Lazarus lifted him, carrying him awkwardly into the kitchen to the worn settee. Moshe lay, barely conscious, blood blackening his waistcoat and hands where he'd tried to protect his head.

'He must go to hospital,' Sophia said, glancing up at the men.

'I'm not going to hospital,' muttered Moshe. 'You die there.'

They called the doctor, who, taking Moshe's pulse and feeling his neck, agreed with Sophia. Between them, they helped him walk to the tram stop and onto the tram. They held him up as he sagged forward. On reaching the London Hospital, Sophia called a passing nurse who found a chair and wheeled him into an inner room while the others waited. When a doctor arrived, Mr Lazarus sprang up to ask if he could go in with Moshe, but the doctor shook his head, telling them to wait until he'd seen the patient.

Fifteen minutes later, the doctor emerged and addressed Sophia. 'Are you his wife?'

'No, I'm a friend of the family; we work together in Mr Lazarus's workshop.'

'I need to speak to his wife. All I can tell you is that Mr Rifkin has agreed to be admitted for observation.'

Mr Myerson returned to work while Sophia ran through the market until she found Hannah Leah behind her stall. The moment she saw Sophia's face, Hannah Leah cried, 'It's Moshe!'

'Yes.' Sophia was about to speak when Hannah Leah, face contorted, cried again, 'Where is he?'

'The London. He fell at work and cracked his head against the table, but I don't think it's just that.'

'For weeks, he's been sending one of the boys for dyspepsia tablets because of the pain in his chest. He refused to see the doctor. I fear this is something worse.' Turning to a fent stall next to hers, Hannah Leah asked the woman if she'd keep an eye on her stall until she returned. 'I'll be as quick as I can.'

'Would you like me to come with you to the hospital?'

'No. I'll go there alone. Thank you, Sophia.'

At the workshop they talked in low tones about Moshe and his family, some of them expressing anger at the conditions they worked under, even though Mr Lazarus was a reasonable master.

'It's the sweating system,' Sophia said. 'We must fight to change it. Something must happen soon.'

A few evenings later, to her consternation, one of the children was at Mrs Vine's door asking to see Sophia. In the corridor, the older boy said, 'Mama said can you come at once?'

Sophia found Hannah Leah rocking backwards and forwards, her eyes closed, while her mother stood silently beside her, and her father was deep in prayer. Blindly, Hannah Leah reached out for Sophia and grasped her hand.

'It was his heart. He's *gone*.'

The funeral was the following day. Hannah Leah ran along behind the hearse, windowless in accordance with Jewish law, clinging to a railing at the back, screaming and tearing her long blonde hair until Sophia managed to drag her away.

'You know it's not permitted for women to attend the funeral. Let's go home,' urged Sophia, leading a sobbing Hannah Leah back to her apartment.

Another injustice, thought Sophia, her eyes blazing.

As Mrs Levi never left the house, Sophia had prepared the ritual meal of hardboiled eggs, bagels and herring. She waited with Hannah Leah until Mr Levi returned from the cemetery.

'Hannah Leah, you've eaten nothing since yesterday afternoon.'

'Who can eat when Moshe lies in the cold earth?'

'You must eat,' stated her father, pointing to the white cloth, the food, the stubby memorial candle. 'It's a mitzvah.'

Sophia slipped away when she saw Hannah Leah take her seat with her parents and children, their gaze uncertain and sad. Walking back to her room, her heart filled with concern for the Rifkins and how they would manage without Moshe's earnings, however small, she reflected once again on the horrors of the sweating system. Moshe had studied architecture in Poland, coming to this country with high expectations, plans of buildings in his case, but ending his life as a presser, one of the most onerous roles in a sweatshop. He was thirty-eight. As for herself, despite hearing nothing from Mrs Thorne about her documents, she would never abandon her dream of becoming a doctor, but for now, she would throw herself into anarchist work and the forthcoming strike that the anarchists knew was imminent.

One Sunday morning she was sitting in the Jubilee Street Club, taking advantage of the warmth while writing an article for the *Arbeter Fraint,* when Sam Dreen burst in.

'Sophia, have you seen this?'

'Holding up a newspaper he pointed to a hazy black and white photo on the front page.

Sophia stared and recoiled. 'Horrible! Who is that?'

Others gathered around, pointing at the gruesome image of a man hanging from a hook on a wall. No doubt about it – in huge black letters, the headlines proclaimed the death of Father Georgi Gapon, the world-famous priest who claimed to be the revolutionary leader of the masses but was really a police spy. Other members arrived, carrying different newspapers, all with the same horrific news.

Sophia took a sharp breath and covered her mouth with her hands. A feeling of dread overwhelmed her – was Dov involved? When she read that four unnamed members of the Socialist Revolutionary party were implicated, but who vehemently denied any connection with the assassination, she was certain.

Taking the newspaper from Sam, she scanned the article.

> When he heard about the publication of the Octo-
> ber Manifesto, it stated, the priest returned from
> exile to Saint Petersburg and begged Sergio Witte,

the statesman acting as first or 'prime' minister to let him reopen the Assembly of Russian Workers. Witte refused unless the priest agreed to support the Tsarist government, and himself, Sergei Witte, in particular, otherwise Gapon would remain in permanent exile.

This was at the very time in December when the Petersburg Soviet was arrested and thrown into prison.

A handsome charismatic man, famous in Western Europe and America, he was however unable to follow any party rules, acting only in his own best interest. Some called him a madman. He agreed to Witte's demands and kept his side of the bargain, praising the Tsar, calling for moderation. Witte, on the contrary, was determined to pacify the country by force. Even before his exile after Bloody Sunday, Gapon had been a police informer and he continued in this role.

The priest's reputation crumbling, there was another blow when the New York Tribune printed a photograph of him at the Casino in Monte Carlo, with the grand Duke Vladimir. Father Gapon's love of gambling and drinking was famous, but this happened while the Moscow revolutionaries were facing the Cossacks across the barricades.

Pausing, Sophia lifted her head and asked the people around, deep in discussion, whether this man's sins were sufficient for him to be murdered in this awful way. She was shouted down.

'It is suspected that Evno Azef, head of the Socialist Revolutionary Assassination Section had ordered the killing. But at present, the names of the perpetrators are unknown.'

She swallowed as she came to the final paragraph describing how the priest had arranged to meet his friend, socialist Pinchas Rutenburg, in Ozerki, a small village north of Petersburg. Here the deed took place.

He was attached to a hook on the wall and weighted down by their bodies until he suffocated. His body has just been found, apparently a month after his fateful ending.

Sophia shuddered. Handing the newspaper back, she told the others she was meeting a friend on Brick Lane. Of course, there was no meeting – she needed to absorb this dreadful news. The ache at the pit of her stomach, the memory of Dov's eyes when he heard Katya had died, his fury at everything connected with Father Georgi Gapon. Though not a member of the regular assassination section, she was sure he was involved.

For some moments, she stood outside the Jubilee Street Club, her eyes closed, her head pressed against the wall and asked herself why? Why did Dov need such violence to express his revolutionary beliefs? Anyway, this was something else; she was sure he participated out of revenge. *Revenge.* Suddenly she was angry. A whisper of doubt about their relationship had been troubling her since she returned but had now become a roar. She couldn't ignore this. A rare bird sitting on a rooftop chirped, people traipsed past, a mother scolded a child. Unseeing, unhearing, Sophia folded her lips and walked heavily away.

CHAPTER 33

HOT SUN BEAT DOWN on dusty East End streets, women removed their shawls, men wore jackets and people looked up to the misty blue sky above the chimney pots, marvelling that London could experience such a heatwave. Making her way through the crowds to the workshop, Sophia smiled to herself. *Today, we strike. Today, we transform people's lives. I wish Dov were here to see there's a better way for change than 'propaganda by the deed'.*

Climbing the stairs to the workshop, she recalled the title of her *Arbeter* article, earlier that week: *A Spontaneous Walk Out. On Friday the 8th of June, we strike. All through the spring, many strikes have erupted and been quelled by the masters, but this Friday will be the start of something different. Last week a group of workers were locked out of their workplace for demanding an increase of wages from 3d an hour to 4d hour. This is the springboard for this strike.*

She opened the workroom door, greeted the others, some of whom nodded to her, their eyebrows lifted as though to indicate they were ready. Settling at her sewing machine, conveniently near the door, she nodded to Mr Michelson who'd taken over the work of presser since Moshe had died.

Watching him wield the heavy irons, she wished so much that Moshe could be here to see their action. He would certainly have joined them. She recalled going to the house of mourning the day after the funeral and greeting Aaron sitting with the others in the crowded living room. Later, after he'd left, Hannah Leah said, 'You know Aaron is very fond of you.'

She had brushed this off with an embarrassed laugh, wishing he felt differently. She liked him so much as a friend, but that was all. Gathering up the sleeves, the everlasting sleeves, she basted them, then glanced around. People were working: Mr Lazarus, his measure around his shoulders, assessing the cloth; Mrs Lazarus making buttonholes, her little girl, now twenty months, sitting on the floor near her mother's feet, playing with empty bobbins and cotton reels. What will they do, Sophia wondered, when we hear the call and walk out?

She knew soon enough. Even on the fifth floor, men's voices could be heard roaring through fog horns: *All out! All out. Join the strike!*

The door swung open. Sam Dreen peered round; seeing Sophia, he gave her the thumbs up sign and withdrew. He clattered down the stairs, his boots like horseshoes, clip-clopping along the way. Startled, everyone lifted their heads. Their gaze fell on Sophia, and Mr Michelson gave her a questioning look.

She rose from her stool.

'Comrades, the strike has begun. We must stop working. Please follow me.'

'What? Are you going to strike?' Mr Lazarus' face contorted into disbelief and anger.

'We are.'

'You can't,' screamed Mrs Lazarus, catching up her daughter as though they had threatened the child. 'If you go, you will never work here again.'

'Mrs Lazarus, you and your husband are good employers but you're victims of this system as much as we are. Think how your husband has to crawl to the West End masters to give him decent work for us. All for a pittance. Join us.'

Mrs Lazarus gasped, silenced for once, and shot her husband a questioning look. 'Are we victims?'

'I suppose so,' he muttered. 'But we can't join them.'

He wiped his forehead with his handkerchief as if to eliminate his doubt, though it was also piping hot at the top of the house. He had engaged two women at the beginning of the year. Mrs Ellenbogen and Mrs Finkelstein, both middle-aged, whose children had grown up but who needed money for their grandchildren. They sat at the bench, staring around in confusion.

'Do we go? I don't know what my husband will think.' Mrs Finkelstein looked alarmed.

'Please join us,' Sophia said. 'All for one, and one for all. If we all strike, the masters will listen. Look how little you earn each day for the long hours you work.'

The women rose slowly and followed the others out of the room, leaving the door ajar.

In the street, crowds of workers stood chatting and jostling outside every workshop entry, at every corner. Sam Dreen appeared at the top of the street shouting, 'Meeting at the

Wonderland Theatre this Sunday afternoon, to decide on tactics. We are doing this because of the men who were locked out only two weeks ago. We do this for a better life for you all. Remember, the Wonderland.'

Between Friday and Sunday, Sophia and Milly handed out dozens of leaflets, pinning them to lamp posts and onto walls announcing the Wonderland meeting. On Sunday afternoon two thousand people crammed into the seats and gallery in the Wonderland Theatre. Rudolf walked to the front of the stage and welcomed the huge crowd, then asked Sam Dreen to speak.

'It's wonderful to see all of you here today. Please offer suggestions to us about how we will conduct this strike,' Sam said.

Many jumped up to speak. When one of the strikers suggested they should be cautious, he was shouted down. Within half an hour, a series of decisions had been made and the tailors agreed unanimously not to return to work until the masters agreed to their stipulations. Sophia jotted them down in her notebook, preparatory to writing an article for the *Workers' Friend*.

> *All workshops to employ union members.*
> *All shops have a chairman other than the master.*
> *Day work to replace piece work.*
> *The working day to be from 8 am to 8 pm with one*
> *hour for dinner and half an hour for tea.*
> *Work to be equally divided amongst workers.*
> *The master must give a week's notice and will give*
> *an acceptable explanation to the workshop chairman.*

There must be humane treatment in the workshop.

Rudolf rose from his chair.

'This time, we must succeed. These are almost identical to those drawn up in 1889 at the last great strike. Regrettably, they were never upheld by the employers. Now they must be.'

As she listened, Sophia asked herself what she'd tell other women who were afraid to strike. She would describe her growing despair at their dreadful conditions; remark on the little she earned and her longing to become a doctor but that she was unable to afford the fees; the hunger; seeing Moshe die; Betsy's dreadful situation when her husband died; the poverty of women who became widows; or the dangers for young women alone, leaving their simple homes and falling into penury or worse. She stood up.

'May I say something, Rudolf?'

'Of course. Please come onto the stage. We will hear you better.'

Holding up her skirts, Sophia climbed the stairs and walked to the front.

'Comrades, it is marvellous to see you all here this afternoon, but I want to address the women amongst you, and your wives, mothers, sisters and daughters who may be at home. There are women working in the sweatshops terrified of losing their place if the master chooses to lock them out. Afraid of joining the strike. I say to them: Please do not fear. Right is on our side.

We should not be working fourteen hours a day, going home exhausted, barely able to look after our children and families. We are human beings; we need respect and care, just as we respect and care for our family and friends. Be not afraid, ladies. We will help and support you. We are setting up strike funds and, when you go to the shops, you can take a credit slip with you.' She held one up. 'You can't see this but almost all the shopkeepers in the area will accept it. We've arranged this with them. They will give you products – eggs or cheese or tea, or whatever you need – in exchange for one of these. This credit note is a promise that you will pay them when the strike's over. There will be funds. House-to-house collections. So ladies, support the strike and have no fear. And gentlemen, I know you will tell your wives and daughters what I've said today.'

Sophia's speech was greeted with huge applause. She smiled, gave a quick nod, and walked swiftly down to her seat.

'Our own Emma Goldman,' someone shouted from the gallery.

'Revolution,' Sophia called up to the man, 'but never with violence.'

People in rows behind patted her on the shoulder. 'Well done, we shall certainly tell the women.'

Sophia let her gaze fall to the floor, remembering the first great occasion, the concert she'd attended with Aaron. What a greener she was then and how confident now, in her role as an anarchist.

'I enjoy speaking,' she whispered to Aaron. 'I'm surrounded by this group of idealistic, loving people who instil me with confidence, wonderful friends, giving up everything to make life better for others.'

'Absolutely right. You must continue to speak in public, Sophia. I think you have a gift for it.'

As they talked softly, the meeting was coming to its conclusion. People were co-opted onto the committee to deal with overseeing funds, collecting contributions from house to house, organising donations of food.

'What about pickets?' someone shouted.

'Give me your name if you wish to be on the picket group,' Sam called.

Many hands shot up.

Rudolf concluded the meeting saying their headquarters would be at the corner of Old Montague Street, where they would gather daily.

Aaron rose and turning to face the crowds behind him and up in the gallery, began to sing, '*Allons enfants de la patrie…*'

They stood and sang with him, two thousand people on strike.

A week later, in the Jubilee Street Club, Sam Dreen marched in and threw a sheet of paper onto a table, where Sophia and Milly were discussing their progress.

'The masters have thrown down the gauntlet,' he exclaimed. 'They've locked us out. So we must negotiate on their terms, not ours.'

'Have you just returned from their meeting?' asked Milly, frowning.

'They let us in only at the end. They're at the Jewish Working Men's Club, in Great Alie Street. Their headquarters.'

'What did they say?'

'Six conditions, counterproposals to ours, which we must accept before they let us return to work.' Other members gathered round, their gaze serious. 'The worst, and well they know it, is that they won't negotiate with any employees in a body unless they're represented by an English Trade union and, I quote, "authorised with sufficient authority to enforce any decision arrived at." Ganufs, the lot of them. They were in our position once.'

Milly groaned. 'We're stymied because they know we're not members of English unions. Rudolf has been trying for years to persuade our members to join them.'

'But the English unions refuse to have us,' put in Mr Sabelinsky, looking grave.

'They'll depend on blackleg labour,' said Sam, sinking into a chair.

'We'll use all our arts of persuasion, ' Sophia said, 'to cajole, persuade and encourage those who won't join us.'

Having found her voice, Sophia continued to use it. Daily she spoke to striking workers at street corners, and especially at Buck's Row.

'Comrades, keep up the good work. You're striking for better conditions. You will help your families; mothers, you should never go hungry in order to feed your children; fathers, you will feel pride when you bring home more money. Too long have you slaved and toiled in these awful conditions. They must cease. We didn't come to this tolerant land to be slaves in Egypt once again!'

People laughed and clapped. Her heart swelled with joy when she saw them walking away with greater resolve.

Finally she was making her world a better place for all. There were many acts of kindness during the strike – women brought plates of bagels, with chopped and fried fish covered by a tea towel, to the strike headquarters. 'For the workers.'

One night, an explosion of screams, shouts and curses awoke her. Mrs Vine put a terrified face round the door. 'Something awful is happening. Come with me, Sophia. I'm afraid to go alone.'

In their nightclothes, they crept onto the corridor. Sophia recognised two members of the Arbeter Fraint group dragging a man along the corridor. She laughed softly.

'It's not serious, Mrs Vine. I know them.' She led her landlady back into the room. 'The man they're dragging is a blackleg. He's been seen working several nights and refuses to strike.'

'What will they do to him?' Mrs Vine's face was unnaturally white in the gaslight.

'They'll shut him in a room until his family pays the money he's earned while working.'

'I thought you said this was a peaceful movement.' She frowned.

'It is. We don't beat him or attack him. His earnings will be added to the strike fund, then he can leave.'

Sophia had wondered about the legitimacy of this procedure, but nobody had involved the police, who were, she knew, great friends with Rudolf, so she'd thought no more about it.

But the masters were winning. They transferred their work to Liverpool, Manchester and Leeds, so that a group of East Enders travelled north to encourage the tailoring workers in those cities to join the strike, but without success. The employers also had funds in reserve. They could eat.

Two weeks later, the strike committee met to discuss the worsening situation. There was no reprieve. People were hungry, little by little they were going back to the sweatshops. On Sunday 24th June there was another mass meeting to discuss the masters' offers. Strikers and employers agreed certain principles; abolition of piece work; a twelve-hour day, with one and a half hours for meals, a union representative in each workplace. So much was lacking and many left the tailoring unions.

What was worse, significant members of the Arbeter group were bitterly disappointed, some even deciding to emigrate to America.

'I've worked so hard for the cause and gained very little.' Sam, usually so cheerful, sat slumped in a chair when the meeting was over. Sophia had never seen him downcast.

'Oh Sam,' she said, 'I'm so sad you're leaving .I hope you find more success in New York. And Mr and Mrs Sabelinsky, what will we do without you?'

'We'll give America a try,' said Mrs Sabelinsky. 'We might well come back if we change our mind.'

That evening Sophia walked home through the stifling streets, sweat pooling on her forehead and trickling down her back.

Should I go to America? Is it really better there? I'm caught in a web of contacts and obligations here. I hate the thought of leaving the Arbeter Frainters, who've been so kind to me. They have made me what I am. And there's Ettie, but I guess she could find other assistants. Dov, I don't know what to think about you. So passionate, and I believed you. But I'm certain you've forgotten me. Almost six months since we were together.

She climbed the dirty steps to her walkway and opened the door to the flat.

Will you ever come back? Her heart gave a little leap when she thought about him, a downward swoop that she might never see him again. *Then I've heard nothing from the London School of Medicine for Women. Perhaps writing to my brother, and I've barely heard from him this year, would help me decide. I'll ask him to enquire about medical schools in America.*

What stupid thoughts. What about money?

In her room, she opened the window as wide as possible. Dov might be right after all, she thought, wiping her hot face with a cold, squeezed-out flannel. Maybe violence is the only way, but I won't believe it.

CHAPTER 34

S HE AWOKE WITH A feeling of dread. A new word she'd learned that week, a single letter transforming its meaning. A dream that had woken her, a nightmare really, had been about Dov.

He was riding a black horse. Riding away from her. The darkest of nights, without moon or stars. She was running after him, calling his name, but he never looked back and as she ran, she fell. Scrambling up, she could see he was heading into a sky of red, gold and purple flames, a brilliant fiery sunset. A dreadful blaze.

'Turn back. Don't go there, Dov,' she heard herself scream but he carried on. Then she heard the inspector's silent voice, his mouth gaping words without any sound. 'You killed him. You killed my boy.'

'No, I gave him life.'

Sobbing, she fell to the ground.

She awoke slick with sweat, hair sticking to her forehead, her hands hot, latched together. Before sleep, she'd rolled the sheet down to her feet, but the room was stifling. The heatwave had continued to burn and parch the citizens of London, especially the inhabitants of these close-set tenement rooms.

She sat up. Dov galloping away on a black horse filled her vision and she took a few deep breaths to steady herself. What did this mean? She wished she could ask the psychologist Freud, who'd written so extensively about dreams and the unconscious, but she hadn't yet read his work. The words 'dread' and 'dead' invaded her mind, but she thrust them away, as she padded barefoot across the room. Soaking a flannel in the bowl of scummy water she'd left on her trunk the previous evening, she wiped her face and arms. No need for a towel, her skin dried at once.

What now? It was Sunday, the first of July, and she had nothing arranged. There would be no trip to the British Museum today as Rudolf intended to visit Mr Kropotkin in Surrey. The failure of the strike had left a hollow emptiness in her heart. Dead or dread? Stop it, she told herself, but as though guided by hidden strings, she went to the drawer where she kept Dov's ring. Took it out and stared at it. Walking to the fireplace, she gazed for a few seconds at the empty blackened grate then dropped the ring in. It gave a brief tinkle as it disappeared through one of the metal slats and into the dark area beneath.

The end of a so-called marriage, a marriage that never was, she thought.

With a sigh, she went to the window and looked out. Already men were sitting on steps and orange boxes, wearing only their vests, their trouser braces evident on their skinny chests; children ran around in underwear, played with enamel bowls of water, splashing each other, screaming.

Relieved she had no obligations or duties at the Jubilee Street Club that day, a thought occurred to her. Maybe this week she would make enquiries at the University of

London, though she wondered if it would be open now it was July. Surely there were administration people around? A letter, together with her sheet of examination results, had arrived a few weeks after her visit to the School of Medicine. Miss Douie had written saying that her results were excellent but she would need to matriculate before starting her medical course. With preparations for the strike, there'd been no time to investigate and then there were her concerns about Dov and the Orthodox priest.

'Mrs Vine, are you up?' She knocked on the inner door.

'Yes, Sophia, I'm decent.' Mrs Vine was sitting in her nightdress at the table, a cup in her hands.

'Cold tea is good in this weather, Sophia.' As Sophia said nothing, she continued, 'Are you going for water, by any chance? Could you please take my jug and get some for me?'

'Of course. Tell you what, I'll go twice.'

Sophia filled Mrs Vine's bucket from the tap at the end of the corridor and then made a second journey for herself. Back in her room, she washed herself all over in the welcome cold water and then, taking a hint from her landlady, was drinking cool tea, when she heard voices coming from next door. At this hour? She saw it was already past nine o'clock and settled to eat some stale challah she'd bought on Friday, when a knock on her door surprised her. Rising quickly, she opened the door to find Rudolf and Milly waiting.

'Come in, please,' Sophia said, her heartbeat racing. They had never once visited her. Why were they here so early, on a Sunday?

'Please, sit down.' She indicated the rattan chairs she'd bought for a few coppers at the market.

'No,' Milly said, her eyes serious, her voice low. 'I think *you* should sit down, Sophia. We have some news for you.'

Rudolf's gaze was sombre. Their manner disturbed her.

'What is it? Please tell me.' She faced them.

Rudolf's height and bulk seemed to fill the room. He took a breath, 'We've heard what may well be simply a rumour, but we believe you should know before it becomes common knowledge.'

'Dov?' The dream surged in her mind. 'Tell me, I must know.'

'He's been caught by the Okhrana,' said Milly. 'Imprisoned. We don't know for sure, but we heard he was to be executed.'

Sophia gasped and pressed her hands to her heart.

'The night before the execution, he poured oil from the prison lamp over himself. I'm afraid Sophia, he set fire to himself.' Rudolf's voice dropped to a lower key as he spoke.

'He's dead?' She fell back against the bed. 'No,' she cried. 'Dov would never do that. I don't believe it.' But a small voice in her head said: *It is Dov. He would not give the Tsar the pleasure of killing him.* She had a fleeting thought. 'Couldn't they save him?'

'The guards were too late.'

'Sit down, Sophia, you're white. I'll get some water.' Milly led her to a chair.

Unable to move a limb, as in a dream, Sophia watched Milly pour water and hand the glass to her. She saw Rudolf's face, his brows drawn together, his eyes full of concern, but now they were strangers … distant … puppets in a play.

She found herself saying aloud, 'Dead? Dead or Dread?'

She saw Milly give Rudolf a sharp look.

'It may be true, or it may not. But you're strong, Sophia. You can deal with this.'

'I can't believe it, Milly. If it's true, how horrible.' She cried out then, picturing Dov burning, in flames. 'No. No.' She fell forwards, her head in her hands. 'I can't bear it,' she cried, 'the flames, the agony, the pain. No, Dov stop. Don't do that.'

A strong arm lifted her up and led her, blinded by tears, to the bed. Someone helped her lie down. She heard a woman speaking. 'You go. I'll stay with her.'

Time passed.

The images were horrifying. She twisted and turned on the bed, crying out, her hands covering her eyes as though to block out the terrible scenes, but they continued to haunt her.

She heard another voice. Someone she recognised. Someone she trusted. The doctor.

'Sophia, I'm giving you an injection to calm you. Then you'll sleep.' His voice became a mumble. She heard: 'I'll be back tonight. Call me if you need me. Keep her cool.'

She heard someone saying: 'I'll sponge her with cool water.'

'Not too much.'

She slept.

Another woman was sitting in the armchair by the bed. This time it was Ettie, who rose from the chair. 'Sophia, you've slept for twenty-four hours. How do you feel now?'

A strange mumbling in her head told her something bad had happened, but she couldn't remember what it was.

'Yes,' she said. 'Yes.' She lay silent.

'Are you cold? Hot?' Ettie eyes were worried as she peered at her. She took Sophia's hand.

'No. no.' Sophia shook her head.

'Doctor Feldstein will be here soon,' Ettie sat back in her chair, took up some knitting. 'Rest a while, Sophia' Something blue, Sophia thought. For a boy? Ettie spoke firmly. 'You need it. Sleep.'

Later still that day, the doctor looked in. 'How are you now?'

Sophia opened he eyes. 'Yes,' she said. He repeated the question. She drifted off as he was talking. Then, in the evening, she woke up. All was normal – the doctor smiling by the bed, Ettie calmly knitting.

Ettie said she must leave. 'I'll see if anyone else can sit with her.'

'She has lots of friends,' said the doctor.

Sophia fell asleep to the murmur of voices, waking, next time, to find Rosa sitting in the chair and the memory clicked in her mind.

'No.' She cried out and began to sob.

'Be strong, Sophia. I know you're strong.' Rosa's voice was low but bracing. 'We've had awful news about Dov, but we can't be sure.' Rosa straightened her shoulders. 'We must believe he's alive. He's always escaped.'

Sophia sat up. 'He's dead. Rosa, I can't bear it.'

'We must bear dreadful things in life.'

Sophia lay back against the pillow, her limp arms resting on the sheet.

'I saw something in my dream that night, before Rudolf and Milly came. I know what happened. But he wouldn't give the Okhrana the satisfaction of taking his life. I'm broken, Rosa. Broken.' Her voice oddly calm, she took Rosa's hand.

They sat together in silence.

Eventually Sophia said, 'I'm better now. Not better exactly, but you don't need to stay any longer. Thank you, Rosa.'

'Only if you're sure.'

'Please go home. I shall survive.' Sophia climbed out onto the cold floor.

Rosa clasped her in her arms for some moments, kissed her and left. Sophia sat for hours thinking about Dov, her spirit empty.

CHAPTER 35

S HE WAS DEAF TO the jostling, shouting crowds as she walked to the workshop. Usually so receptive to others, so willing to empathise, now she was a column of silence, sitting rigidly as she sewed. A machine tending a machine. But no one noticed, for the weather was even hotter, if that were possible. Passing the newsagents, she noticed the word, 'Scorcher' heading an English newspaper, proclaiming the hottest August in living memory. Searching for it in her little dictionary, she shuddered when she read the meaning. *Burning*. She was burning too.

There were moments of clarity, when the horrifying images subsided from her mind and she could think rationally about Dov, his life and hers, and she found to her surprise that she was angry. Why did he need violence to carry out his aims? She argued with him. He could have been a Menshevik like Aaron, prepared to use parliamentary methods to affect change. She could hear his voice: *Sophia, don't you understand? Tsars, the people, they only understand violence.* She would reply to him in her head: *We have become civilised people. It's only the Tsar and his close circle.* The argument would fade away and she'd see him burning in the cell. In Hell.

It was easier not to think at all. The only way to continue, or she would go mad again.

One evening, she lay on her bed in her undergarments the better to cool her weary overheated body. Her eyes closed, her mind empty, she heard the hum of voices from Mrs Vine's room. She opened her eyes. Could it be? She turned over, facing the window, telling herself she was imagining things again, that her mind had become unbalanced. Then came a knock at the door, Mrs Vine's voice calling, 'Sophia, a visitor for you.'

'I don't want to see anyone.'

'This is someone special you will definitely want to see.'

She sat up, her heart racing, and pulled on her blouse and skirt which were lying at the end of the bed, then padded in bare feet to the door. She opened it. In that instant, she saw him, and behind him a jubilant Mrs Vine, shaking the pink knitted garment on her needles like a flag.

'No,' Sophia cried. 'It can't be. No, I don't want to see you. It's too much.'

'Sophia?' Dov stood, his eyes wide, disbelieving. 'Why, what's the matter?'

Close behind him, Mrs Vine was whispering, 'I tried to explain it to you just now.' Turning back, holding out his arms, he said, 'Sophia my darling, I've longed for this moment for months. I wanted so much to see you, hold you close to me.

'*Go away, I can't take any more.*'

Again, Dov cast a confused look at the landlady, and she nodded as though to say, 'Go in. Go in.'

'Sophia, my darling girl, Mrs Vine said you'd been unwell but you're better now.'

'That's why I don't want to see you.' Tears streaming down her cheeks, she closed the door against him, but he held it open.

'Please, let's talk so that I can understand.'

His gaze, so troubled, so earnest, wrenched at her heart. She weakened.

'All right, five minutes.'

They sat, one each side of her little table in front of the window. Dov lit a cigarette, Sophia avoided his gaze.

'Tell me,' he said softly, 'I hate to see you upset like this. Mrs Vine didn't know the details.' Reaching out, he took Sophia's hands in his and despite herself, she welcomed the warmth of his touch.

Taking a deep breath, she began to speak. 'We thought you were ... dead.' She pulled her hands away but kept her agonised gaze on him.

'But why?'

'They came here, Rudolf and Milly.' A deep cleft in her forehead, closing her eyes for a moment, her words halting and uncertain, she said, 'They'd never been before. I knew something was dreadfully wrong. They wanted me to know first. Before anyone else.'

'What was it?' He frowned, leaned in.

'You'd been arrested and sentenced to death for gun-running.' Her voice barely above a whisper. 'The night before the execution you'd...' She turned her head. 'You'd doused yourself with oil from the prison lamp ... and the guards were too late.'

He swore.

'Oh, Sophia, that was Moshe Tokar. A brave comrade, often confused for me. What a terrible thing for you to hear. It breaks my heart.'

He tried to take her hand again but she snatched it away.

For some moments they sat in silence. But unexpectedly relieved of that terrible vision, knowing it was some other poor revolutionary, Sophia felt herself become stronger. When he asked how she'd been after she received this news, for her landlady didn't know the facts, she looked straight at him. Anger fuelled her words.

'I collapsed. The doctor gave me a sedative.'

Dov groaned. 'Were you alone while this happened?'

Sophia shook her head. 'I couldn't speak, only saying yes or no, but as the drug wore off, I came to myself, though I stayed in bed for two or three days. But they came: Ettie, Milly, and even Rosa, sitting with me until I regained my senses.' Suddenly she cried out, 'It's you, Dov. You and violence.'

'I know.' He stubbed out the cigarette, dropped his head into his hands.

'Why do you need it? Violence, I mean. There are other ways to affect change...'

'They only—'

'Don't give me that, Dov. What about Aaron? And Rudolf? He might use violence in self-protection. I know he has. But I mean the violence you undertake to achieve the Revolution. It affects *everything* you do, everything you think.'

Dov stared, astonished by her vehemence. 'Not everything...'

'I've been thinking about it. About you and me. We can't be together. You were right last year when you kept your feelings to yourself.'

'Don't say that. I adore you. I've waited in hiding for this day, longing to see you, to hold you.'

'Not always in hiding. What about Georgi Gapon?' Dov stood up and turned away. 'You were one of them, weren't you? You did it out of *revenge*—'

'No. Not revenge. I did it for Katya.'

'The same thing.'

'Maybe. But he was one of the madmen the country produces regularly who'd have betrayed the cause.'

Assured of the strength of her anger, yet unable to control it, she continued, 'Did he deserve to be hanged on a door hook? Weighted down by your bodies so he was throttled? How despicable. It was in all the British newspapers.

'He gained the publicity he always sought,' Dov muttered. Seeing her widened eyes, her flushed face, he muttered, 'I admit, it was a bad business.'

She rose from her chair.

'It can't go on. We can't go on. I love you, Dov,' she cried suddenly, 'with all my heart, but I can't live like this. So, go!'

'No. What must I do to change your mind?'

Strong, her voice level for the first time since hearing the terrible news, she said, 'Give up violence.'

'Give up violence?'

'Yes, or leave.'

'I have to think about this.' He began to walk towards the door.

Watching him, she wondered if he could change, if anyone could. Could she shoot to kill? If the inspector had raped her and she'd had a gun, she would probably have killed him. Relieved she'd been spared that decision, she said, 'I know how hard it is to change, Dov. I've discovered that living here in London. So think carefully.'

His hand on the doorknob, he stopped. 'What am I doing? Of course I can change. I will. I will do anything you want.' He passed a hand across his eyes. 'Violence has caused me indescribable grief – losing Katya, and thinking I'd lost you to the Okhrana after I fled. I was nearly out of my mind with worry about you.' Turning back into the room, he held out his hands. 'I can, and I will.'

Feeling the glow of hope in her heart, she cried: 'Dov, Dov, I love you...'

He held her in his arms, they embraced, laughing and weeping together.

Later, Dov said, 'It's stifling in here. Let's go to the river. It will be cooler there.' She was about to walk to the door when he said, 'Where's your ring?'

With a blush of embarrassment, she said, 'I threw it away. In the grate. Because I was so angry with you.'

'We can't have that.'

In two strides, he was kneeling in front of the pale yellow tiles surrounding the grate and lifting it up with both hands. Searching around among the blackened clinkers, he came upon the ring and held it in the air. He blew on it and dust flew everywhere.

'What's a little coal dust when you're in love?' Standing, he went to her and placed it on her finger. 'Married again.' His voice was full of satisfaction.

'Really?' she said.

'I've something to tell you, but let's get out of here.'

'I've something to tell you,' she said, thinking of her visit to the medical school.

Passing into Mrs Vine's domain, Sophia saw her roll up the knitting and wrap it in a rather grimy piece of muslin.

'Roses in your cheeks again.' Mrs Vine almost preened, as though all had been her work. 'I knew you would want to see your gentleman friend.'

'Thank you, Mrs Vine, we're going for a walk to get some air,' Sophia said quickly.

'Good idea. It's like a bathhouse in here, I don't know how we stand it.'

'Thank you very much, Mrs Vine,' Dov grinned.

They walked through the ever-crowded streets, people jostling and shouting wherever they were until they came to the River Thames. They leaned over the parapet and watched large and little ships moving and berthed, the Tower of London in the background.

'How did you know I was back here?'

'I didn't. I hoped against hope that you were, but I had no certainty. Nobody, neither my family nor my contacts, knew what had happened to you. Alicia visited you once in the cell, yet the following days when she called, they told her you had gone.'

'I was there for a week.'

'Really, they refused to let her visit you again. But Sophia, how did you get back here?'

She told him about the police inspector, going, she thought, illegally, to his house. How his wife had been in labour and had refused to see a doctor.

'It's clear that everywhere, Petersburg or London, women hate consulting a male doctor,' she said lightly. She hesitated, wondering whether to tell him her news. No, she would tell him first what happened. 'The baby was stillborn, but I'd watched Ettie use a special technique to revive him. It almost didn't work, and if it hadn't, he would have imprisoned me or sent me to Siberia. That's what he threatened. In repayment,' she gave a hollow laugh, 'he said I could go free, but could never see my family again. On my passport he's stamped the word *Exiled.*' Turning her head away from him, she gave a deep sigh.

'My darling, what vermin the Russian police are.'

Lifting her gaze, she said, 'Back here, I felt cut off forever from my family. As though something had been torn from my heart. I told nobody, in case it would affect you. One day, I felt so alone I had to speak to someone. I knew Aaron would understand. And he did.'

'I love that man. He's a *mensch*.' He drew her closer to him. 'What did he say?'

'We talked for some time. Then he asked me why I had come to this country, leaving my family in Archangelsk, a relatively safe place.' Now's the time to tell him everything, she thought. 'When I told him I wanted to be a doctor, he asked me why I didn't make enquiries at the London School of Medicine for Women—'

'Is there such a place?'

'Dov, I went there. It's near the British Museum, in Bloomsbury.'

'Wonderful, I'm sure they liked you.'

'They told me about the battles women had here to study like men, and yes, they were very encouraging. I left feeling more hopeful.' Her voice dropped.

'But?'

'Money, mostly.'

After hearing the details, he said, 'I've a great idea. Come and live with me at Dunstan Houses. I want you to be with me, and you'll save from renting your room, and with my work—'

'What are you going to do?'

'Bookbinding. I'm a skilled bookbinder. You'll see in due course.'

'Boastful, as usual. Is that all you're going to do?' She shook her head.

'The man I most admire, Peter Kropotkin, is exiled to England yet he carries on with his revolutionary work and so will I. There's plenty to do, my darling.'

'I'll think about coming to your room,' she smiled to herself. 'What else were you going to tell me when we left Wentworth Buildings?'

'Shall we walk a little?'

Once again, they climbed Tower Hill, where they saw an extraordinary sunset – purple, yellow, red and gold streaking across the sky. Sophia lifted her gaze, realising that in all these weeks of heat, for the first time she could welcome this glory without thinking only of fire, of burning. 'What then?' She turned to him.

'I'm no longer a married man.' He grinned, the dimple in his cheek seeming to echo his delight.

'How come?'

'In hiding, I had time to think. Once I'd made up my mind, I made a secret trip to speak to my grandfather.'

'Weren't you afraid of the Okhrana?'

'Your idea. Disguise. A false beard and the black garments of the very orthodox, and no one could distinguish me from any man in my grandfather's court.'

'Wonderful.'

'I'd already written to Yetta Fruma and she answered saying she couldn't stand it any longer. Her family was pressing her to accept the divorce; they already had a suitable man lined up. And though she was very sad, she wanted children. Grandfather collected one or two rabbis to act as judges. I made my way there in secret, and in half an hour, it was done.'

'Dov, you're already a changed man. I'm so glad, I felt badly for her.'

They were sitting on the grass, now Dov stood and helped her up. 'Let's amble back,' he said.

A few days before the Jewish New Year, in September, Sophia received two letters, one from her mother, the other from the London School of Medicine for Women. She opened the latter first.

Dear Miss Krichevska,

We've made enquiries and are delighted to tell you that, if you matriculate at London University, we have obtained a bursary which will cover most of the cost of your first year of study, then we'll see. Please let me know what you think.

Kind regards,
Miss Douie

She clapped her hands, thrilled to read this. She put the letter from her parents in her handbag, and took the tram to Dunstan Buildings.

'Dov, Dov,' she cried, as soon as he opened the door to her. 'I have a place at the London School of Medicine for Women.'

'Doctor Krichevska, if ever I'm ill, l shall consult you first!'

It was only that evening she remembered the letter from her mother. She read it with tears streaming from her eyes. They were coming to London. Sasha had bought the tickets, and before going to America, they'd spend some time with her. Sophia waltzed around the room, kissing the letter, and thanking whatever destiny had led her to this happy place.

At once, she sat down and wrote:

Dearest Mama,

Wonderful news, and I have marvellous news for you too...

The End

ABOUT THE AUTHOR

SUE WAS BORN IN London but grew up in Manchester, England where she still lives.

She has always written but in her fifties, and on discovering Womanswrite, (a writing group for women, based in Manchester), began to write seriously.

She has published poems, short fiction and novels in England and America. Previously, she taught French to children and adults, English as a foreign language and worked with people with learning disabilities and mental health problems, but writing is what she always considered her 'real job.'

Now she spends her days dreaming up historical novels set in exciting places. Babyday, a novel about a woman who 'has' seven babies, and must find out who they are and why they've come to her, will be published later in 2023.

You can find out more about Sue and her writing at
https://www.facebook.com/suesternwriter
and www.suestern-writer.co.uk

REFLECTIONS AND ACKNOWLEDGMENTS

THE GIRL FROM KYIV was inspired by the brief, tragic life of my grandmother Sophia Krichevsky, who arrived in London in around 1905 and died in 1913, in Friern Barnet Mental hospital, following the birth of my mother, her third little daughter. Sophia was 29. My mother and her sisters knew only that she had died of 'milk fever' and never knew where. Probably a good thing. I was named after Sophia and always felt a kinship with her, a closeness. It took me several years to research a few details about her, together with the anarchist movement which she joined. She met my grandfather, Adolf Lotting, in the anarchist meeting house in Soho.

I've written this novel for her, the kind of life she should have led, for we know she wanted to be a doctor, that she was intelligent and educated, and from the one photograph we have of her, beautiful.

To understand the Anarcho-syndicalist movement in London, I read widely, including Rudolf Rocker's book, with his description of his partner, Millie Witcop and his followers in London, at this time. They were real people while others – Sophia, Dov, Aaron and Ettie came to me in the course of writing, some based on people I'd known, all very real characters in the story.

If you want to know more about this fascinating but little known period, here are several books I consulted:

Rudolf Rocker, *The London Years,* Five Leaves Press
Fermin Rocker, *The East End Years,* Freedom Press
William Fishman, *East End Jewish Radicals 1875 – 1914,* Duckworth
Ralph Finn, *Time Remembered, The Tale of an East End Boyhood,* MacDonald
Voline, *The Unknown Revolution, 1917-1921,* Black Rose Books

Deepest thanks to the Manchester Novel Writers' Group, to Cath Staincliffe, Mary Sharratt, Anjum Malik, Livi Michael and Sophie Claire, for their warm and insightful feedback.

An especial thank you to my niece, Jenny Taylor, Czech translator and proof reader, who corrected my erratic punctuation and showed me how to spell Csárdás.

Praise for *The Child Who Spoke With Her Eyes*

'A moving and finely written account of motherhood, the challenges of caring for a disabled child and the quest for identity.'

CATH STAINCLIFFE, award winning novelist and radio playwright

'Truly compelling'

MARNIE RICHES, award winning author of mystery fiction

I truly loved this book!
It was an incredible account of maternal strength to overcome insurmountable difficulties, prejudice and gain an understanding of her daughter's needs. Sue is a lioness of a mother both protecting and fighting for her daughter to be the best she could be whilst also making the ultimate sacrifice for her little boys when she needed to make the hardest of decisions.

TRACY KINGSLEY

Praise for *Rafi Brown and the Candy Floss Kid*

I stayed up till stupid o'clock reading this book!
This was a fantastic read and once I had started it I could not put it down. I had to finish it in one go because it was such an awesome book. Mrs hegarty the evil school

teacher reminded me of a teacher in my school. I hope she writes another one soon because this one was epic.

WOODY

The book is written fluently and well, in language that neither insults the intelligence of adults nor makes it impossible for its target audience to understand. In other words, it's simply but not stupidly written and in the convincing voice of a young boy. The dialogue sounds fresh and believable, the characters leap off the page and you feel that by the end of the book you really know them and moreover, that you like them with all their faults…

ADELE GERAS, Widely acclaimed writer